RUTHLESS

GENA SHOWALTER

RUTHLESS

HQN

Recycling programs
for this product may
not exist in your area.

ISBN-13: 978-1-335-42754-0

Ruthless

Copyright © 2022 by Gena Showalter

For questions and comments about the quality of this book, please contact us
at CustomerService@Harlequin.com.

HQN
22 Adelaide St. West, 41st Floor
Toronto, Ontario M5H 4E3, Canada
www.Harlequin.com

Printed in U.S.A.

To the usual suspects: Jill Monroe and Naomi Lane,
who went above and beyond, reading and offering feedback
even though their own lives were at maximum business.
You are both heaven-sent!

A huge thank you, thank you, thank you to editor Michele Bidelspach,
who rallied the troops and kept us all on track after I broke my foot
and underwent surgery in the midst of this book's production.

And to the members of Gena Showalter's Legions. What a blessing
you are! Supportive, kind, caring, hilarious, all-around wonderful
human beings. May love fill your hearts, laughter abound, peace reign
and your admiration for me never fade. (What?)

RUTHLESS

PROLOGUE

Astaria, the fae realm

Five-year-old Viori de Aoibheall raced to her parents' bedchamber, frantic. A thick, overpowering odor infused the air, stinging her nostrils. *Death comes…*

Tears welled as she placed a bowl of fresh water on the nightstand, next to her beautiful doll, Drendall. Viori's most beloved possession. There was no lovelier sight than Lady Drendall, with her colorful porcelain face and lacy pink gown. A treasured birthday gift from her favorite person in all the realm, her older brother, Kaysar.

Fighting for calm, Viori grabbed a clean rag from the nightstand's top drawer. She dipped the shabby fabric into the cool liquid, uncaring when droplets splashed her dress. For weeks, her parents had suffered with "the crimson sickness." A plague that had decimated half their village.

As pixiepetal harvesters who worked public land, Momma and Papa made little money. But that little kept their family of four fed. No money, no food. Already supplies ran low, with only a few potatoes left.

To make up for the loss, twelve-year-old Kaysar now spent the whole of his days slaving in the fields. A backbreaking job too difficult for one person. And yet, he never complained.

Agonized moans whisked her back to the present. Momma and Papa lay side by side, a sheet tangling as they thrashed. Unnatural heat radiated from them, cooking both from the inside out.

Viori swallowed a barbed lump, pasted on a smile and hurried to her father. She wrung water into his mouth, telling him, "Don't worry, Papa. Everything will be all right." Kaysar had promised, and he never lied.

The frail man coughed up blood.

More tears welled as she hastened to her mother. Trembling, she squeezed the rag directly over Momma's chapped lips.

Before this, anyone who'd met Viori and her mother had called them twins. They sported the same auburn hair and green eyes. Same delicate features and golden skin. No longer. Momma's face had become a travesty of sunken sockets and hollowed cheeks, framed by a sallow complexion.

Do not sob. Viori tenderly cleaned the blood from the woman's nose, then returned to her father. An ox-strong charmer too beautiful for words, admired by too many ladies in town, according to Momma. With thick black hair, darker, dusky complexion and rich brown eyes, he resembled an older version of Kaysar. Or he *used* to. Like his wife, he looked ready for a grave.

As gently as possible, Viori wiped his brow. He cringed from her touch, the slightest pressure seeming to bring him incomparable suffering.

Do. Not. Sob.

"Heal…us," he rasped, his voice wretched. "Please. Must… try."

Distress choked her. She gave her head a violent shake. "I… I can't." Every day Kaysar had warned her: *Do not even consider it, love. Not yet.*

He believed her glamara—a fae's strongest supernatural ability—mirrored his. That she must only speak a command to force others to obey. And maybe he was right. But she had rarely practiced. With good reason!

Fear, sadness and anger delivered a bad outcome for Kaysar. The listeners might obey him, but they did it...wrong.

Her brother had explained it this way: *Words are vessels containing everything we feel. Our secret and not so secret intents. When we speak, we unleash a creative force no one can outrun. A gift, if we use it right.*

Before she dare attempt to control a fae, she must first harness her emotions.

"Please, darling," her mother echoed, barely audible. "Can't make it worse. Dying, anyway."

"No! You aren't allowed to die." To stop herself from agreeing to sing, Viori mashed her lips together. *Do not even consider it.* Except, she *had* brought birds, cats and deer back to life.

What if she could do this?

What if she couldn't? She'd helped the animals only *after* she'd calmed. A process that had taken days.

Momma issued a louder moan, almost a scream, and Viori sniffled. Did she have time to calm? *Could* she calm? Whenever she tried, she ended up hiding under her covers. But...

What if she could save her parents and didn't? Could she live with the guilt? Could Kaysar?

What if he grew to hate her? What if she grew to hate *herself*?

If she succeeded, all became right, exactly as he'd promised. Momma would smile again. Papa would ruffle her hair and tell her she wasn't allowed to marry until she reached the age of two hundred and fifty—at least! Kaysar could finally return to his studies. How he must long to do so. No one enjoyed books and learning more.

And if she *didn't* succeed?

Did it really matter if emotion warped her commands at a

time like this? If she was her parents' only chance, shouldn't she offer one?

Indecision gnawed at her. She wrung her fingers and glanced out the window, where a dirt path led to the pixiepetal fields. Should she speak with Kaysar first? A ten-minute sprint to the closest field meant another ten-minute sprint home. And if he labored in the second field, twenty minutes away? Neither of them possessed the ability to flitter—moving from one location to another with only a thought. Not yet, anyway.

If he refused to help?

"Please, darling," Momma beseeched. "Never hurt so bad."

Tremors starting up again, Viori pressed clammy palms against her belly. What use was her gift if she couldn't help the people she adored? "V-very well. I will try."

She trudged to the foot of the bed and drew a deep breath in, out. Like Kaysar, her glamara strengthened when she sang. Unwilling to hesitate, she closed her eyes and released the first note.

A soft melody floated over the chamber. Her parents went quiet. She freed the second note and peeked through a slit in her lashes. Peace fell over the pair, their thrashing easing.

I'm doing it? Relief poured through her. She increased her volume, commanding the couple to feel no pain.

Neither moved, yet ripples disturbed the bedsheet. Odd, but not jarring. With the animals, she'd felt a wind that wasn't there.

Viori sang even louder, utilizing the full power of her glamara. And oh, wow. Black dots wove through her vision. Threads of weakness invaded her limbs, nearly toppling her. But she refused to stop until the last vestiges of the sickness faded from her parents.

Had the pair healed at all? She focused on their expressions— and gasped, stumbling back as horror torched her relief. Momma screamed in silent agony, blood leaking from her eyes, nose and ears. Papa gritted crimson-smeared teeth. The sheet had somehow risen, taken the shape of a fae and sat with crossed legs between them. The creature had a hand wrapped around the throat of each patient.

Viori smashed her lips together, ending her song.

What is…? How can…? Impossible! And yet, she felt a connection to the sheet, as if it were somehow a member of her family. Her child, like Drendall. She even knew its name—Fifibelle.

"What are you doing?" she cried. Bit by bit, life drained from Momma's and Papa's eyes. "Stop that!"

The sheet held on, seemingly proud of a task well done.

"S-stop this, Fifibelle. Please."

Too late. One parent expelled a final breath within seconds of the other, both peering into an afterworld Viori couldn't see.

Weakness intensifying, she tumbled to her backside. At the same time, Fifibelle lost substance and whooshed into a puddle, reverting to a simple mound of cotton.

Trapped sobs escaped. Momma and Papa were…dead? She'd killed them?

Must know. Legs quaking, she lumbered to her feet and approached the bed. Slowly, she stretched out her arm to flatten a palm against her mother's chest. The spot Viori loved to rest her head when they told bedtime stories to Drendall. No heartbeat. Ice-cold skin.

The moisture in her mouth dried. Vision blurring, she stumbled over to check her father for signs of life. Finding none.

Realization heralded shock. Yes, they were dead. And it was *her* fault. She'd killed her parents with a song. Had viciously *murdered* the pair.

"I'm so sorry. So sorry. So—" Another sob cut her off. Tears rained freely, scalding her cheeks. Over and over Kaysar's warning replayed in her head. Like Fifibelle, Viori had refused to listen. Now she must suffer the consequences.

And so must her brother.

He would hate her now. If he didn't, he should. Her voice wasn't a gift, but a curse.

Overcome by grief, she snatched Drendall from the night-stand and sank to the floor. With her friend clutched tight to her chest, she curled into a ball and rocked back and forth. Why had she done this? Why, why, why?

What if she did it again? She buried her face in Drendall's soft hair. Was Kaysar to be her next victim? What if Viori harmed him when she tried to explain? What if Fifibelle awoke? What if she created something *worse*?

Panic collided with desperation, both exploding inside her. *Can't harm Kaysar. Not him. Anyone but him.*

But what if she did it? Soon, he would return to the cottage…

She squeezed Drendall tighter. *Must be quiet. Mustn't say anything else.*

Ever.

Eight months later

"Why don't I sing to you, hmm?" Kaysar led Viori through the Forest of Many Names. He kept a firm hold on her hand, as if he feared she might dash away.

Viori clung to Drendall, refusing to speak. *Won't harm my brother. Not now, not ever.*

Morning sunlight filtered through a canopy of gemstone-colored leaves. A narrow brook rushed over moss-covered rocks. Wind blustered, whirling specks of dirt into tiny funnels.

"I'll sing anything you wish," he added with a twinge of regret. "Something about a princess and her prince, perhaps? Or what if I sing to Drendall instead? Would she like a song all her own, do you think?"

Insides compressing, she looked anywhere but in his direction. His ragged condition would only wither the pieces of her broken heart. Thanks to Viori, he had no family or home. No job. No way to earn money. He was forced to shuffle her from village to village, stealing food and clothing whenever possible, bunking in any halfway stable shelter.

Yet, not once had he blamed her. Though he should. She *de-served* blame.

When her chin trembled, she retreated to a deep, hidden chamber of her mind. The safest place for her. A dreamland without thoughts or memories, words no longer needed.

As they marched on, she lost track of time. At some point, Kaysar drew her out of seclusion, beseeching, "Tell me how I can help you."

His anguished desperation pulled a response to the edge of her tongue. Or had he used his glamara? Either way, she resisted the urge to speak and won. *Say nothing.*

A group of pixies flew past, snagging Kaysar's attention.

Dread prickled her nape. *There are no better troublemakers than pixies,* her mother once said. *They're thieves, the lot of them. You see one, you go in the opposite direction.*

Homesickness assaulted every cell in her body. *Miss you so much, Momma.*

"One second, love." Her brother halted and released her to study the map he'd drawn on his forearm using a metal claw and blood-ink. A necessity. No one survived the winding maze of gnarled trees, invisible interrealm doorways, fae-hungry trolls, organ-starved centaurs and poisonous foliage without aid.

He sucked in a breath, strain emanating from him. The tips of his pointed ears twitched. Did he hear something?

He dropped into a crouch, pulling Viori down with him. When seconds ticked by without incident, he straightened enough to pull her to her feet, and swept her in the opposite direction.

Her stomach's growl stopped him. Looking wrecked, he shifted his gaze between Viori and the path they'd abandoned. With a curse, he reversed course, steering her toward the brook. Specifically, a knotted patch of poisonvine with a hollow center.

The sweetest scent coated her airways, courtesy of the foliage. Her brother encouraged her to sit amid the mess without brushing against it, then settled Drendall in her lap.

"You know I'll always protect you, yes?" Bleak eyes searched hers. "Stay here and remain unmoving." He whispered the command as he placed the satchel filled with their meager belongings at her feet. "I'll find out what's going on. While I'm gone, I want you to remember how much I love you. All right? I'll return shortly."

The admission of love heaped buckets of coal upon her guilt.

Cupping her cheeks, he kissed her brow. Then he kissed Drendall's brow and darted off, never looking back.

Viori yearned to shout for his immediate return. As much as she hated being a drain on Kaysar's life, she hated being without him. He and Drendall were her everything.

Say. Nothing.

Hours ticked by, sunlight waning. Finally, full darkness arrived, cloaking the forest in writhing shadows and bringing bone-numbing cold. Tremors plagued her. Her teeth chattered, her thin dress no match for the weather. Howls and growls reached her ears, and her gaze darted. But she didn't stray from her spot.

Where was Kaysar? Why hadn't he come back yet? When would he return?

Would he ever return?

By morning, everything inside her screamed, *Find him! Help him!* But still she stayed put. *Won't go against his orders. Not again. Never, never, never.* She would rather rot.

She didn't move the next day or night, either. Nor the next. Her empty stomach seemed to eat itself. Fear came and went. During daylight hours, she overheated. At night, she froze. But Kaysar did not return.

Dizzy and weak, eyelids heavy, so heavy, she teetered in place and smacked a swollen tongue. Wait. Was that...? Clutching Drendall tight, she squinted into the distance. Though her vision proved blurry, she thought she spied a hazy glow. Her breath caught. Had Kaysar returned— Excitement died in an instant. Two burly centaurs trotted closer.

A full armory of weapons draped them. From the swords strapped to their backs, the bow and quiver of arrows hanging at their sides and the spears gripped in hand. Bear fur draped muscular torsos. One had dark fur, while the other was white with spots.

Wizened features brightened when the pair spotted her. They stopped mere feet away, and her heart thudded. Too terrified to move, she forgot to inhale. Centaurs were far worse than pixies. To gain immortality, they ate fae alive, both young and old.

"My, my, my," the tallest said. "Look what we have here." He nudged his speckled friend. "Told you I smelled something tasty."

"That you did," Spots replied with a grin.

Acting on instinct, she shrank back. A mistake. Her elbow grazed a stalk of poisonvine, and agonizing pain ripped through her. Muscles spasmed, paralyzing her limbs. A temporary condition supposed to last two endless minutes, but she needed to hide now, now, now.

Too late. Laughing, Tallest latched onto her ankle and yanked her from the tangle. As frail as she was, she dropped Drendall, the last link to her family. No!

The centaur withdrew a long, stained blade and slashed her dress. Her skin. A jolt of pain freed her vocal cords from their unused state. A high-pitched scream tore from her, the cadence unpleasant and raspy.

Her attacker dropped the blade. Both males covered their ears. But just as soon as she quieted, they recovered.

Spots withdrew a sharper dagger from a side sheath. "You're gonna pay for that, girl."

Shaking off the last of the toxin, Viori scrambled back and prepared to run. The next thing she knew, something whizzed past her, snatched up the fallen weapon, and stabbed Spots repeatedly in the face. The groin. His hindquarters. No part of his body was safe.

That something was... Drendall. Viori could only gape.

Before Tallest realized what had transpired, the blood-soaked doll stabbed him too. Rivers of crimson flowed from a wealth of wounds, forming a macabre pool around their corpses.

Sweet Drendall dropped the blade and smiled at her. "I did it, Momma! I did it! Did you see me? Huh? Huh?" She hurried over and nuzzled her wet cheek into Viori's throat. "Are you so happy now?"

"H-happy. Such a g-good girl," she stammered, clutching the doll close as shock engulfed her from head to toe. Her doll had come to life with a scream—a song of fear?

Her glamara didn't mirror her brother's, did it? Kaysar had been wrong. But he'd also been right: her voice was a container. A seed loaded with everything necessary for life. Like a farmer, she could grow whatsoever she planted. And she could do it in a matter of seconds.

Viori glided her gaze over the males who'd thought to harm her.

Perhaps speaking wasn't such a bad thing, after all.

CHAPTER ONE

Not quite present day

Fifteen-year-old Micah spun slowly, his jaw slack. *What is this place?* Spears of lightning forked across a dark sky heavy with darker clouds. Glowing silvery orbs hung from tree branches, illuminating a forest clearing he wished he hadn't discovered. The eeriness of it all boggled the mind.

From the outside, thick white fog had enveloped the interlocking trees set in a wide circle. From the inside, however, he had an unobstructed view of the dried blood that stained the bark—and the faces carved within. Fierce expressions projected everything from dread to malice, and he shuddered.

Someone had gone to great trouble to make the gnarled giants resemble *belua*. Monsters of unimaginable strength, somehow birthed from the elements themselves. Able to live and breathe and walk among fae.

Micah tightened his grip on a makeshift dagger—a twig he'd sharpened with his teeth and what remained of his nails.

Beady eyes seemed to track his every movement as he trod

deeper into the clearing. A large, moss-covered stone with a wide base and a flat top occupied the center of the ring. An altar?

A chilled breeze blustered past, rousing goose bumps on his skin. Scanning... The vibrant moss provided the only foliage here. There were no animals or insects. No other life whatsoever.

Death reigned here.

A crack of thunder boomed, punctuating his thought, and he almost jumped out of his skin. The next lightning bolt charged the atmosphere; electric currents pricked his spine. Micah dragged in the scent of ash and... What *was* that? Sweetness itself? A unique fragrance brimming with all the glories of the Summer Court. Sunshine, flowers and citrus.

His mouth watered, and his empty stomach protested. When had he last eaten?

Twig at the ready, he approached the stone and gathered a fistful of moss. The first bite proved bitter, the second more so. But as the greenery settled in his stomach, some of his pains faded; he only desired more.

He shoveled another fistful into his mouth, then another and another, unable to slow himself. For over a year, he'd wandered the wastelands of Astaria alone. Originally, he'd traveled with his guardian. A great warrior named Erwen. A great man, period. He'd found baby Micah inside a basket, and saved him from being eaten by trolls.

He bit his tongue, tasting blood. Erwen had died in battle with a *belua*. A massive snow beast in the Winterlands.

Micah had expected to perish alongside his guardian. A part of him had *hoped* to die. How he'd loved Erwen, his sole companion—the only person willing to be near him.

Like his guardian, Micah was a chimera. A rare fae born with dual glamaras that were constantly at odds. The clash created a negative force field around them. Unwanted by fae and humans alike. Feared by everyone. Known for scarring—outward evidence of weakness and a badge of shame.

Chilly wind rattled branches. Lightning peppered the sky, spotlighting— Micah froze, his breath hitched. Were their limbs untangling? Had the one to his left narrowed its eyes?

An illusion?

Genuine belua? Had he stumbled into a nest?

He dropped the newest handful of moss, preparing to bolt. But, from the corner of his eye, he perceived an array of color. Smooth gold. Vivid pink. Gleaming scarlet. He meant to glance, nothing more. A quick peek to ensure no one sneaked up on him. Instead, he stared and reared back, his eyes going wide.

Was he seeing what he thought he was seeing? Surely not. And yet...

Maybe.

Heart jumping, he lurched closer to the stone. Sucked in a breath. A girl. A fae. *Exquisite.* She slept upon the slab, seemingly growing from the surface. Or from the forest itself.

Lightning flashed, there and gone, showcasing a smattering of freckles, pink cheeks and cherry lips that were bowed in the center. Other details hit him, throwing him for loop after loop. They might be the same age. Flawless skin the color of sunlight, vibrant with life. Delicate features usually only found on royalty. A plain gown too short and tight to cover the abundance of shapely curves.

Who was she? Why was she here? What color were her eyes?

Excitement arced through Micah. Would she mind being friends with a chimera?

A rolling rumble precipitated the first splatter of rain. Cold droplets splashed his cheeks, and he grinned. Let the liquid soak him. What did he care? He'd uncovered a treasure of unsurpassed value.

The rain deluged her, too, her gown becoming transparent. Trembling suddenly more pronounced, he reached out to brush droplets from her cheek.

A rustle sounded behind him, and he wheeled around, ready

to defend his prize. Too late. A tree loomed before him, and the truth hit, hard.

"*Belua!*" Hiding in plain sight.

A fat branch slammed into his head. He flew across the clearing, dropping his makeshift weapon when he crashed into another tree.

His lungs emptied. *So dizzy.* No time to recover. Another branch flung him in the opposite direction.

Ribs broke on impact, and agony seared him. Before he could rise, roots coiled around his ankle and attempted to eject him from the clearing. He clawed at the ground, determined to hold his position and shield the girl. Dirt and blood coated his tongue.

Bark scraped his spine. Limbs stabbed into different bones. Wheezing, fighting the urge to vomit, Micah rolled out of the way.

A limb pierced a vital organ, and an agonized scream burst from him. The pain! Then, suddenly, he was airborne, soaring across the expanse. When he landed, a world of darkness crackled open its jaw and swallowed him whole.

As Micah healed, he realized a startling truth. The monsters safeguarded the girl. They hadn't attacked until he uncovered her. More than that, they hadn't struck to kill him. Otherwise, he would be dead.

Why they guarded her—why they had shown him mercy—he didn't know. But he wondered. Was little Red on that stone slab of her own volition or a captive?

There was one way to find out…

Micah returned to the clearing—to her—with a firm goal in mind. Befriend these *belua*. If he could join them, protect the girl until she awoke…

Was this a betrayal to Erwen and everything he'd stood for? Surely not. His guardian had lived by four rules.

Do no harm to the innocent. Protect what's yours. Always do what's right. Never be without a backup plan.

The sleeping beauty was vulnerable and in need of another fae. Just in case the trees held her against her will.

What better path to travel than keeping her safe?

Micah advanced on the creatures cautiously, both hands lifted. "You had every right to eject me," he told them. In their minds, he'd committed a terrible offense. Touching a female without her willing consent. Or theirs. Now, he hoped to prove the innocence of his intentions. "I did your fair lady wrong. Allow me to present her with a gift of apology. And respect." He revealed a red crystal he'd dug from the earth bright and early this morning. "So much respect."

A prolonged hesitation followed his words, anticipation stealing his breath. Finally, the trees opened a doorway for him.

Giddy but remaining vigilant, he entered slowly, placed the present on a step leading to the altar and backed away. Rather than exit, he faced the largest of the bunch. "I mean her no harm, and I won't touch her again. If you'll let me, I'll help you with her protection."

He wasn't immediately impaled, a good sign. Micah set up camp. As one week blended into another, the trees relaxed around him. As their tension faded, bright leaves budded, creating a vibrant paradise.

For the first time in Micah's life, provision without price abounded. Various species of flowers, fruits and nuts flourished without cease, dropping from overburdened limbs. Nourishment rained all hours. In offering or apology, he didn't know which.

Morning and evening, he thanked his companions for the bounty. Never had Micah enjoyed such delicious meals. But... *when will she awaken?*

Fresh moss covered the girl, protecting her from sun, wind and rain. Her sweet scent magnified daily, coating the air; he considered every inhalation a precious gift.

How did she sleep so deeply? And why? For how long? Why did *belua* continue to protect her, no matter how much time passed?

Did she crave a friend? If the beautiful fae with freckles sought a fellow fae companion, shouldn't he oblige her?

Longing gripped Micah. *But you aren't a fae, are you? Not exactly.* He shifted in the bed he'd constructed with twigs and fallen hanks of moss. He just…he wanted to belong to someone. To be welcomed. Maybe even admired.

What did such affection even feel like? And what was the beauty's name? Would she like his offerings? There were many.

Anytime a troll or centaur neared the clearing, Micah departed the ring to end the threat. He collected supplies left by the dead, amassing a treasure trove of weapons, dried meats, clothing, maps, coins and jewels. All for her. Well, mostly for her. He'd kept some of the clothing for himself, exchanging a filthy, tattered tunic and ripped leathers for higher quality garments. Even a cloak to help him hide the scars left by the tree attack.

Would she like *him*?

As he gathered an array of fruit for breakfast, he stole glances at her. For the first time, much of the moss withered, baring her fully. Morning sunlight lent her golden skin an otherworldly glow. Silken locks of auburn hair gleamed. Curling black lashes cast spiky shadows over pinkened cheeks. Plump red lips with a bowed center and a stubborn chin added to her captivating allure.

The girl— Wait. Had that cherry mouth parted? Micah froze, every cell buzzing. Even the trees stilled, as if time suspended. Then…

A soft moan left her. The first sound she'd made since his arrival. Then she stretched her arms over her head.

He dropped the bundle in his arms, pink-and-red fruit thudding to the ground, rolling away. Startled by the noise, the girl jolted upright, auburn locks tumbling around her delicate shoulders. She blinked to orient herself.

His mind raced with a thousand thought fragments. *Even more beautiful… jade eyes, brighter than the leaves…gown soon to tear apart at the seams…friend… Mine?*

She turned, maneuvering her legs over the side of the bed. Standing. Stretching. As graceful as a swan he'd once spied in the Summer Court.

Micah stood in awe, utterly transfixed.

As if sensing him at last, she looked his way and gasped. Her mouth floundered open and closed, fright overtaking her expression.

He hurried to offer a reassurance. "I mean you no—"

A high-pierced scream burst from her. The most horrifying sound he'd ever heard. Sharp pains stabbed his brain, hot blood dripping from his ears. He slapped his palms over the blood-soaked shells, but it didn't help.

The trees snapped to attention. In an instant, leaves wilted. Fruit dried up. The *belua* army lunged at him, and this time, they attacked to kill, stabbing and pummeling full force. Pain wracked him, each injury teaching him a new lesson in agony.

Deserve this. He'd foolishly shown favor to an enemy. Had thought to become friends with vessels of evil.

But the girl…

Will come back for her. The trees wouldn't harm her. Even now, they kept her out of harm's way. If she required freedom, Micah would free her. But first, he must survive.

He escaped the clearing, crawling out of range before collapsing in a beam of sunlight, eating dirt. Then the darkness came…

CHAPTER TWO

Fifty-three years closer to the present

From the shadowed alley between two mud huts, Micah the Unwilling observed the eligible males lining up in the street to stand shoulder to shoulder. Most had cleaned their teeth and combed their hair. Some wore a freshly pressed tunic and their cleanest leathers. Others had come straight from hunting or tending a *cibus* garden. A tasteless but nutritious bulb that flourished underground, even in the worst of climates.

Marriage season had officially begun.

From the confines of his hooded cloak, he scanned the rest of the Forgotten Village. Home to roughly two hundred fae who had abandoned the oppressive regime of Astaria's four courts to live freely in the Dusklands. A dangerous territory teeming with more and more *belua*. Hunting kept Micah busy.

Sunlight suffused the abysmal terrain, highlighting bits of ash carried on a mild wind. Two charred mountains loomed in the background. The village itself rested in a valley between rocky tundra and the wooded but dead Grimm Forest, with dwellings of various sizes scattered throughout.

Home.

Once, Micah had stood among the marriage hopefuls. After several decades of tracking and killing *belua*, he'd longed to experience the good life—family life. A wife to enjoy. Children to pamper. But the females of this settlement had preferred weak and cowardly mates over a chimera.

He didn't have to wonder why; he'd heard how his mere presence made those around him wish to peel the flesh from their bodies. The force field, thanks to his dueling glamaras: an ability to madden beasts versus an ability to subdue them. But even still, he'd rallied from the rejection. A year to prove his worth? *Challenge accepted.*

He'd used the time to build an impenetrable shelter, convinced he was destined to be the first chimera in Astarian history to happily coexist with other fae. As big and strong as he was, he had believed *some* female could come to see value in him, despite his wealth of scars. Marks he'd earned at the hands of countless *belua*. Most especially the ones delivered by the trees that guarded little Red.

His ribs clenched around vital organs. Whether she—they—realized it or not, he *did* have value. He never took what life threw at him; he fought for better. He defended those in his care and worked tirelessly to grow a paradise like the one he'd lost. Trees heavy with fruit. Lush foliage. Fragrant flowers. A dream he refused to relinquish, no matter how many hindrances he faced.

And yet, no one had chosen Micah during round two, either. He'd left disappointed and yes, humiliated. The females had made it clear—they held no desire for the chimera. Their males had made it much clearer—he wasn't a welcome addition to the town.

But leave? No. More and more *belua* entered the area each year, and few fae possessed the skill to emerge victorious.

Giggling abounded as eligible women congregated under a

tattered cloth canopy, adjacent to the males. Farther back, tables provided an array of food, flavored with herbs and spices Micah had donated. Tantalizing scents wafted, urging him closer. His mouth watered. He was so tired of eating *cibus* stew, the quickest and easiest meal for a busy fae without a family. But he wouldn't be sampling any of the dishes. He'd made the mistake of attending a festival only once.

A light patter of footsteps sounded behind him. He tensed, but didn't turn. A soft fragrance accompanied the noise, the approacher's identity registering. Elena Adelina. The top contender every male hoped to claim today.

She paused at Micah's side, drawing his gaze. For a beat, he took in her fall of pale hair, white skin and fragile-as-a-doll features. An ivory gown clung to slender curves.

She was the gentle, meek fae he'd once imagined wedding. Someone he could have made happy, if only she'd given him a chance.

"Are you not joining the hopefuls this year?" she asked with a soft, hesitant tone, looking anywhere but at him.

"No." He pursed his lips, admitting nothing else. Why was she talking to him? Why had she approached him at all? She never had before. She must want something. An enemy slain? A bigger tent built? Riches?

"How I envy you." She heaved a mournful sigh. "No one is forcing you to wed before you're ready."

"Because I do not *let* others force me to do anything." The longtime viceroy—the settlement's leader—had issued a mandate earlier this week. Women of a certain age must agree to wed this year or find a new home. "Say what you have to say," he demanded, his tone flat.

She chewed on her bottom lip. Wringing her hands, she rasped, "My brother—Norok. He says he'll accept a wife to prove the new law is just. He's going to ruin his life because mine is being ruined." She stomped her foot and hissed. "That wench Lavina will do anything to snag him."

Lavina Atwater, the viceroy's daughter. Pretty on the outside, a terror on the inside. Nearly as bad as *belua*. The whole species had only grown more aggressive over the years. "Yes, and her father will do anything to snag you." No longer did the viceroy hide his leer when she neared. "What do you want from me?"

"Help," she blurted out, still unwilling to meet his gaze. "I seek help. An equal exchange. We both know the viceroy avoids you. He's unwilling to listen to your ideas about crop production, expansion and defensive measures. If you end the marriage line before it starts, I'll speak to him on your behalf."

"Where's Elena?" the viceroy called before Micah could fully absorb her offer. "We won't commence without her."

The crowd shouted suppositions, some even glancing her way while doing so—without spotting her. Elena possessed a unique *glamara*. An ability to blend into her surroundings. Something only Micah seemed to have noticed.

"Please, Micah," she croaked.

A muscle jumped beneath his eye. No need to consider his answer. She expected him to drive everyone away, earning more hatred and distrust, all because she was a coward. "Norok's choices are his own. So are yours. If you have no wish to wed, don't."

Could she survive on her own? The Dusklands were not kind to anyone, much less delicate beauties like this…not without *belua* protectors.

His chest tightened again. *Stop thinking of little Red.*

"I'll be exiled," Elena said, blanching.

"And I wouldn't?"

Her shoulders rolled in, and she hung her head. "You're right. I'm sorry." She kicked a pebble with the toe of a too-soft slipper. "Where could I go? And do *not* say one of the courts."

"Why?" Resources were plentiful in each of the four. "I'm

willing to escort you wherever you decide." An offer he immediately regretted.

To what end would he do this? Yes, the Summerlands provided lush fields forever in bloom, with honeycombs appearing to drip from every tree. The Winterlands offered bountiful game with tender, succulent meat. The Autumnlands boasted great bodies of fresh water. And the Springlands cultivated herbs and the sweetest fruits. But...

A merciless dread plagued the courts—a male known as Kaysar the Unhinged One. He possessed a voice unlike any other. When he sang, a terrible madness gripped your mind and gut-wrenching pain ripped through your body. You felt as if you were being torn asunder—you wanted to be, just to make it end.

Micah had crossed paths with the male twice, but only at a distance. Close enough to glimpse dark hair, brown skin, and eyes like amber—and to sense a kinship. Was this Kaysar a fellow chimera, though he evinced no hint of scarring?

"Well?" he demanded. "Do you wish to take a husband or a trip?"

"I choose..." She looked from her brother to Micah, hurriedly darting her gaze back to the male with white hair, black eyes and skin as white as his sister's, before squaring her shoulders. No one ever peered at Micah for long. "I'll stay. My family is here."

Family. Something he would never have. He curled his hands into fists, telling her, "Joy to you and yours then." Ready to be alone, he nodded a goodbye, pivoted on his heel and stalked off.

As he snaked around a corner, a roar sounded in the distance. A second roar erupted on its heels, followed by a third.

Belua.

Micah gripped a serrated dagger, irritation instantly superseded by determination. A horde rarely ventured this close to a village, but when they did, they hungered for bloodshed...

"The beasts come!" The frantic warning echoed across the streets. "Run! Run!"

Panicked shouts filled the village. Micah returned to Elena. She'd paled, her navy blues wide as a stampede of footsteps joined the chorus, fae splitting in various directions up ahead. Only a handful of males stuck around and withdrew swords.

Micah told her, "Protect who you wish to protect or hide. But do *something*."

Another roar. Louder. Elena swallowed and nodded.

He jogged past the males who'd stayed behind, calling, "Guard the females." He could subdue multiple beasts at once, but not quickly and not easily. Better to head them off before they arrived.

Micah's hood flew from his head as he raced through the wooded terrain, tracking spikes of aggression in the air. Behind him, a twig snapped. He spun, ready to toss a dagger, but caught sight of Norok the Insatiable, Elena's brother, and spun again, sprinting on, shouting, "What are you doing?"

"Aiding you," Norok responded, giving chase.

"Are you sure? You are glamaraless." If rumors were to be believed. "Can you do battle?"

A derisive snort hinted at the retort to come. "You aren't the only *special boy* in the village, chimera. Prepare to be impressed."

"If you survive, I'll be impressed. How's that?"

"Fair enough."

The ground shook, tripping Micah. He regained his balance and slowed. Stopped. They'd reached a clearing filled with massive black stones piled as high as the trees. Stones with faces expressing pure malice.

Inner barbs flared. *Found you.* The entities emitted the sweetest scent as they stood at attention. A familiar fragrance. *All the glories of summer.*

A growl percolated at the back of his tongue. Was little Red nearby? When he'd awoken after his second filleting, she'd been absent, never to be seen again. He'd searched to no avail before finally giving up.

Micah still didn't know if the species served her or enslaved her. Not that he needed to. Nothing would change the outcome of the coming battle.

He counted a dozen stonemen. More than usual. Not enough to make a difference.

A pallid Norok gaped. "Are they…? Do they…?"

Had the male never beheld a living *belua*? "Yes, they are, and they do." Micah dropped his dagger and balled his hands into fists. Thin, sharp metal would do little good today.

His companion mimicked the actions. "I hope you excel in battle the way everyone claims."

"Try to keep up." He never lost. Not anymore.

The first stoneman charged forward, swinging. Micah was ready. He ducked, yanking Norok out of range. A rocky fist whizzed over their heads. Micah leaped up, pulling back his elbow. Striking…

Impact! Knuckles to rock. Bones cracked, searing pains rocketing up his arm, but he swung twice more in quick succession. Bones *shattered*, fragments cutting through his flesh.

Worth it. The stone cracked, too, branching across that impossible face.

Satisfaction glimmered within reach as his opponent crumbled and he healed. Of course, the other stonemen wasted no time, attacking in unison, seeming to forget Norok's presence altogether. Both of Micah's glamaras blazed. He fought to maintain balance. If his emotions took over, he would empower one ability more than the other.

The whole world should quake at the thought.

Grunting and hissing, *belua* struck at him with punishing drive. Micah ducked and dived as needed, avoiding contact. Mostly. He punched, kicked and elbowed, his skin burning as the war between his glamaras continued to boil in his veins. Sweat trickled from his nape, dripped down his back and soaked his tunic. He— Shock stopped him in his tracks. Was that…?

He rapid-blinked. It *was*. Little Red was laughing and twirling between stonemen. Only, she wasn't so little. She was here, and she was beautiful. A woman fully grown, those freckles still evident.

Ensnared by the sight, he moved closer. Couldn't halt himself. So a *belua* did it for him, plowing through Red as if she were mist, slamming a hard fist into Micah's sternum. He flew backward, crashing into a tree. Impact rattled his brain but failed to erase his thoughts. She'd been a figment of his imagination?

Jumping to his feet, scanning. No other sign of her. Fury threatened to rise. "Did you see the redhead?" he demanded of Norok.

"What redhead?" the warrior demanded as he ducked, avoiding a cuff to the temple.

Other giants homed in on Micah, ending the conversation there. He threw himself back into the fray, thoughts whirling. Why had he beheld her now? Had he seen reality or a figment of imagination? Where was she? When could he see her again?

After taking repeated blows, he forced the female out of his mind and threw a punch. Another. He...would...not...quit. To his surprise, Norok lunged in front of him a time or twelve, absorbing blows meant for him. Whatever the warrior's injuries, he rejoined the skirmish as soon as he healed. More and more creatures became piles of dust and debris at their feet.

Micah whaled on his next target, unleashing the worst of his disappointment in today's outcome. A figment. Only a figment. Not that it mattered. What would he have done with the real Red, anyway?

No, it mattered not at all.

In the end, his ability to subdue the beasts won, and the final three stonemen surrendered. One after the other, they sank to their knees, the ground shaking with every hit.

Norok wiped blood from his nose. He struggled to catch his breath. "They bow to you?"

"They do. Always." Micah ended the trio exactly as he'd ended their brethren: savagely. No mercy. Not with *belua*.

With the last foe vanquished, he faced his companion. Double blink. Elena and other villagers had trailed them and observed the battle from a short distance. The viceroy included. The group gaped at Micah.

One of the males gulped, lowered his gaze and slowly sank to his knees. Others noticed the action and followed suit until the viceroy stood alone.

"But...he's a chimera," the male groused.

The citizens didn't rise. Instead, they bowed their heads.

What was happening right now? Micah floundered for words. He took a step forward, intending to...what?

The viceroy dropped like a brick in water, babbling, "All hail the new viceroy." There was a noticeable tremor in his voice.

Others echoed the statement. "All hail the new viceroy."

The *citizens* submitted to Micah? To his rule? Willingly?

Viceroy? Me? He could never... Oh, but he could. And he would. The glimmer of satisfaction resurfaced as the weight of responsibility settled on his shoulders. "I accept command of the village."

Finally, the people could implement his planting ideas. Under his authority, the valley should thrive as never before. And the citizens... they would be his family.

May he always strive to provide for and protect those in his care.

CHAPTER THREE

Present day

Viori de Aoibheall awoke with a gasp as lights switched on inside her head. She jolted upright, her heart pummeling her ribs. Blood rushed, catching fire and spreading. The cold evaporated from her limbs.

Where…what…? Bits of greenery tumbled from her hair, and her stomach sank. Moss? How long had she slumbered this go round, dead to anyone who stumbled upon her? Decades? Centuries? How much of the world had changed? Had she remained in the mortal world or returned to the fae realm? The two were similar in many ways, but different in so many others.

She surveyed the surrounding terrain— Fae! But nowhere she recognized. Shallow pools of murky water encircled her, weaving through a dense cluster of bald cypress and black gum shrubs, minus their leaves. A dank, dismal swamp. Her fault? Had she done this, draining the land of resources as she'd seemed to do to so many others?

Cursed to ruin everything I touch.

But Viori pasted on a bright smile. Eighteen towering oaks

stood nearby—her creations. Her children. Creatures she'd sung to life now watched her with eager anticipation.

She gave an encouraging wave. "Hello, my darlings." The roughness of her voice proved disconcerting, but her happy facade never wavered. "Did you miss me?"

The group hurried over to nuzzle against her. A cacophony of happy sounds rang out, and her smile turned genuine. Those breathy sighs and low clicks soothed her ragged soul. There was no sweeter music.

No, that wasn't true. Words—conversation—would have been nicer, but Drendall alone possessed the skill, and she'd vanished ages ago.

Well. Goodbye soothing, hello sorrow. The loss of her precious doll still cut.

The trees noticed her darkened mood this time and twittered their concern. Exactly what she'd hoped to avoid.

"I'm fine. Truly." Inhale. Exhale. In—oh! The air smelled unexpectedly pleasant. Extremely so. Hints of orchid and jasmine coated each of her inhalations. Perhaps a trace of orange and lemon.

Embers of excitement sparked. Were her children soon to bloom for the second time since their conception?

She clapped, uncaring that she must look like an idiot. The first time she'd encountered this intoxicating blend of fruits and flowers occurred when a handsome stranger waited nearby. A boy she'd dreamed about for months beforehand. Reveries of a tall, lanky fae who'd begun to show promises of incredible strength. She'd never forgotten his cap of spiky, jet-black hair and glittering ebony eyes. Or the fact that he'd sneaked in and out of her territory, presenting her with a sea of jewels.

She'd dreamed of him many nights since, watching him grow into a fierce and battle-hardened alpha who conquered villages throughout the Dusklands. Unbeatable. *Gorgeous*.

She'd seen him recently, too. Hadn't she? *Yes, that's right.*

Memories inundated her. He and an elder had materialized in a swamp—uh, *this* swamp?—insulted each other and clashed violently. Before vanishing in retreat, the loser had called her dream hottie Micah. Was that his name? Had he ventured here, searching for Viori? Where was he now? Nearby?

She began to finger-comb her hair, stopped herself and scowled. Early on, she'd nearly died learning life's most valuable lesson: trust no one. Even the nicest of beings brewed secret plots of evil in the cauldrons of their hearts.

Though she *was* curious. What had happened to this maybe–maybe-not Micah? Were the dreams real or merely products of an overactive imagination?

Why had he given her jewels she couldn't bring herself to part with, anyway? How had he caused barren branches to bear fruit? Why hadn't her protectors attacked him *before* she'd screamed? Whether born in the land of humans or fae, her babies always preferred to strike first and care never.

Had Micah survived his wounds, all those years ago? Or had he died, his bones dust?

Guilt flared. But only slightly. The teensiest tiniest bit, really. Hardly worth mentioning. He bore the brunt of blame, after all, for daring to trespass on her property. He deserved what he'd gotten, just like everyone else.

And that settles that. Done with the topic, Viori kicked her legs over the side of the stone she'd used as a bed. Several trees lowered their branches, offering help. She gripped the two closest to her and rose. Unused muscles shook and burned, her knees knocking. She wobbled but managed to hold her ground.

"Thanks, guys." Viori bestowed a smile and caress upon each child, like a boss of a Disney princess. Beings worth any cost. And there was always a cost. Singing inanimate objects to life weakened her terribly. Especially when she raised giants—the dearlings responsible for her prolonged dozes. The times she'd fallen through a mystical doorway, leaving the fae world to enter the mortal one. Or vice versa.

New clicks, drenched with happiness. Happy sighs.

"Oh, dear. Look at me. Such a mess." Though she'd fallen asleep in a T-shirt and shorts, she wore a gown. Courtesy of her family? The threadbare fabric pulled taut over an ample bust. A free-flowing skirt with its frayed hem reached her ankles, revealing her bare feet.

Krunk, the firstborn of her treemen, nudged his siblings aside to scoop her into his limbs and carry her to dry ground, where he gently released her.

What a gentleman. "Gather the rest of our family." She stroked his lovely face, exalting as bark prickled her palm. "Everyone is to come here as soon as possible. We'll celebrate my awakening." She'd sing. They'd dance. Laughter would echo through the night.

He discharged a string of mournful clicks, and she knew. Not all her babies had survived without her.

Anguish clogged her throat. While her children guarded her and her territories with unwavering determination, they weren't infallible to attacks. Throughout the centuries, she'd gleaned an assortment of whispers involving the two warriors responsible for the slaying of her *belua*. A term meaning "monstrous."

The first, a fae she knew only as the Unwilling. The second… Kaysar.

Despite his raids and butcheries—whether unwitting or not—she loved, adored and missed her brother with every fiber of her being. How she longed for their reunion. An impossibility until she found a way to make up for the tragedies she'd caused him.

Yes. Tragedies, plural. So much more than the death of their parents. Because of Viori, he had suffered untold agonies. Horrors she'd gleaned from those whispers. If he thought to punish her for his pain…

Deserved.

Krunk brushed a limb against her cheek, a gesture of comfort.

"Your brothers and sisters will be avenged, I promise," she told him. While she accepted Kaysar's treatment as her due, she showed the Unwilling no such courtesy. He would be found and stopped. He must be.

Her stomach rumbled, hunger suddenly clawing at her insides. A common occurrence after an awakening. She sighed. "I must leave you for a bit to visit a village." There, she could steal a decent meal, bathe and pilfer a clean garment or two. She would listen for more whispers about the Unwilling.

Worry radiated from Krunk, so she stroked his face. In many ways, they'd grown up together. He'd seen her chased by centaurs eager to eat her organs to extend their lives. Hunted by fae intent on using her in some despicable way. Tracked by ogres seeking to enslave her. Pursued by trolls determined to breed. Used and discarded by the only male she'd ever (thought) she loved.

"I'll be safe," she promised. She was *always* safe nowadays. *Strike first. And last. No exceptions.*

Krunk clicked to the others. Linda—another favorite, because they were all favorites—scrambled to hand over a strip of brown cloth.

Love lapped at Viori's heart as she draped the material over her head, hiding her mass of auburn hair. "So thoughtful," she praised, and Linda's trunk seemed to swell with pride.

Stomach protesting with increased vigor, she blew kisses to her adored ones. "I love you all. I'll return as soon as I can, I swear it. Just…wait for me here, and all will be well."

Viori ignored the clench in her chest and flittered to a town she'd looted once before. Hmm. Huts reduced to rubble. No one about. What had happened here?

To another town she went… Hmm. It, too, lay in shambles. So was the next. And the next.

A sole location remained. The worst of the bunch, located in the farthest part of the kingdom, past a stretch of gnarled trees and toxic plants, at the edge of Grimm Forest. A dangerous land teeming with ogres, trolls and centaurs.

Or a formerly dangerous land. She found no sign of life here, either.

She flittered to the border of a mountainous terrain—nope. She most certainly did not. Brow furrowed, she tried again. But again, the ability failed her. What—why—*what*?

Testing her capabilities, she returned to Grimm Forest, beside a tangle of crooked trees. Okay. All right. Her ability still worked. When she aimed for a spot past this one, closer to her desired destination, however, she met with another failure. So. There must be a dividing line between flitterable and nonflitterable zones. Why? How?

With no other choice, Viori walked past the tangle of limbs, only to draw up short when she exited. Her jaw plummeted. A bustling campsite loomed ahead.

A small, impoverished village used to exist here, complete with mud huts, laundry lines and a lone well. Now tents and structures built from wood and stone lined cobbled streets. Males and females of every age and color bustled and hustled as far as the eye could see. Cooks chopped what looked to be black potatoes near blazing fire pits. Beyond them, soldiers sharpened weapons and trained in groups.

An incredible aroma drew her focus to the firepits. *Stews and porridge and breads, oh my...* Throughout the centuries, Viori had stolen delicacies, rummaged through garbage cans and scavenged for morsels in the earth. Nothing beat the home-cooked meals parents prepared for their families.

Smacking dry lips, she tripped forward. Multiple conversations infiltrated her ears, the words and tones merging. So much noise. Too loud for her untrained ears. Tremors invaded her limbs, her steps slowing. But did she stop? No. *So hungry.*

If anyone presumed to approach her, she would go on the

defensive and make them sorry. For her, any being she encountered fell into one of two categories: foe or potential foe. All foes responded solely to aggression. Viori's specialty.

As she closed in on an abandoned cauldron, someone bumped her. She tripped forward, nearly crashing. "My apologies!" that someone called. A lovely blonde who continued on, the hem of a well-made blue dress swishing at her ankles.

Hissing, Viori swiped out with sprouting claws. Unfortunately, she scratched the air.

Any other day, she might've given chase to teach the girl a lesson. *Mess with me and suffer.* But a throng rounded a corner, others bumping into her. She spun this way and that, gasping. Thoughts jumbled. Too many people! Too close! Panic threatened to constrict her airways.

Viori shrank into herself, making her body a smaller target as she hurried onward. Up ahead, an assemblage of soldiers escorted two huge, hulking beasts in chains. Trolls. Once the most dangerous beings in the realm. With good reason! Horns with razor-sharp tips flared from their scalps. Long, thick fangs extended over their lips. Six-inch claws curled from their nail beds.

Hatred and hunger glittered in their eyes and crackled in their roars, tempting her to both attack and run. Forget food. Forget clean clothing. She would flitter home—argh! The ability failed her.

Rerouting… Okay. She would walk to Grimm Forest, then flitter to the swamp from there. She— A strong hand clamped on her upper arm, wrenching her to a halt. The owner of that hand stood at least a foot taller than Viori. He was shirtless and stacked with sweat-glistened muscles. A head of curly white hair matched the thick beard covering his jaw. The finest of lines bracketed his eyes. He was a father, then.

Immortal fae parents aged ten to twenty years after they sired children. They would age another ten to twenty years if their children sired children.

This dad glared as if Viori had committed some unforgivable crime. Had she?

Whatever. *Threat!* Hiss. Swipe. Four gashes appeared on his face, blood welling from torn skin.

He revealed no reaction to the injury. "I've never seen you in camp, and I've seen everyone." His lids slitted, his grip becoming bruising. "Who are you?"

Waste time explaining she was his doom? No need. She preferred to respond with an example.

Viori yanked free, slammed her palm into his nose, snapping the cartilage, and dashed off. A move she'd learned among mortals on the mean streets of New York—during her first trip—where she had been considered nothing but a gutter rat. This time, Pops reacted with a howl of pain and anger. Sadly, her weakness cost her. He caught up with her in seconds, snatching her wrist and nearly crushing the bone.

"I asked you a question, girl," he spit, any hint of tolerance eradicated. "Who are you? Why are you here?"

As she struggled, hissing and clawing with renewed energy, he latched onto her other wrist. After that, there was nothing she could do to stop him. He tied both arms behind her back, then clasped her shoulders, attempting to pin her in place. And failing! She would struggle against him forever if necessary!

With his mouth at her ear, he snarled, "The oracle said I'd find a spy today. Is it you? Did Kaysar send you?"

Her brother's name reverberated in the corridors of her mind, and she went still. "What?" Warmth evaporated from her body. A bombardment of emotions hit, longing at the forefront. "K-Kaysar?" she echoed hollowly. Had he returned to the Dusklands? Had she stumbled upon his land? "Wh-where is he? Where is Kaysar?"

Can't let myself see him. Not yet. Did he hate her? He must. If he didn't, he should. He had deserved a far better fate than he'd gotten.

My fault. She owed him, and she *would* repay. But how? How did you make up for the ruination of a loved one's life? Nothing struck her as good enough.

With great shame and regret, she recalled how he'd returned to their cottage from the pixiepetal fields to discover the death of their parents. How he'd cried while attempting to alleviate her distress. How he'd vanished from her life only eight months later.

To halt a sob, she pressed her lips together. For more than two years, she had believed him to be dead. Then the whispers had surfaced. After leaving her in the poisonvine tangle, he'd sought supplies…and gotten nabbed by Winterland royals—the same royals he'd spent most of his existence torturing. Many citizens now referred to him as the Unhinged One. All feared him.

"Red," her captor gasped, combing his fingers through her hair.

The scarf had fallen, she realized, wrenching free, severing contact. Without the use of her arms, she struggled to maintain her balance as she spun to face him. "You do *not* touch me." He dared to manhandle her? *As good as dead.*

The moment she gained her freedom, she would strike. She knew the rules. Retaliate quickly or suffer afresh. Another lesson she'd established early on. *No mercy!*

Lids slitted again, he stalked closer in pursuit. "You're coming with me, girl. You can tell the king why you're here."

King…as in Kaysar? Or someone else?

Shock warred with aggression, plans for revenge momentarily sidelined. She allowed Pops to grip her biceps and roughly haul her through the growing crowd. If she spotted her brother… One glance. Only one. What could it hurt?

Her captor stopped when they reached a battlefield. No sign of Kaysar but… Viori gawked. An army stretched before her, countless warriors brandishing swords, spears and daggers. Metal clanged against metal. Each combatant wore a wrist cuff adorned with stones of varying shades, leather pants and boots—and nothing else.

So many muscles.

No, no. Look away. Muscles had only ever caused serious trouble for her. In her experience, those slabs of beefcake had been wielded by males determined to take what she hadn't offered. Fae and human. No matter the world or state or country. And she'd traveled to many. New York on three occasions. Oklahoma. West Virginia. Scotland. Some forest, somewhere.

The only man she'd loved had used his muscles to cause her the *most* trouble. Laken, a mortal in New York who'd won her over with months of wooing…and destroyed an already fragile ability to trust, turning romantic bliss into a lifetime of memories she wished to torch.

Another lesson learned.

"Micah," her captor shouted over the sea of grunts, groans and barked instructions. "You'll want to see what I found."

Her eyes widened. *Micah.* Was he—this Micah, *her* Micah— the king?

Individual battles ended in an instant, combatants splitting apart, forging a path. She traced the expanding breach with her gaze—and gasped. Him. The boy who'd given her jewels. The man she'd observed in her dreams. She would recognize that magnificent face anywhere. The same dark eyes framed by a fan of curling lashes. The same proud nose and stubborn chin. The same pale skin and spiky jet-black hair.

He stared right at her, and she gulped. He was taller than she'd realized and the most muscled of all, judging by the straining tunic that covered his chest. A bigger cuff than most with double the stones adorned his wrist. Scuffed leathers hugged powerful thighs.

Did he remember her?

"You," he breathed.

Her heart pounded, her feet suddenly as heavy as boulders. Oh, yeah. He remembered.

CHAPTER FOUR

Little Red. *She's here. Another hallucination?* A likely possibility. Micah had spied her dozens of times throughout the centuries, but only when he'd battled *belua*. Never any other occasion. Until now. For once, he was seeing her outside of combat. Could this version of her be…real?

He stood transfixed, awed. She'd grown more beautiful than ever. Too beautiful to be true?

Elena lingered at his side, droning on and on about Lavina, her sister-in-law. The two were forever at odds over something. Anything. Everything.

"How terrible for you," he muttered when she paused for breath. His concentration remained on Red.

Long auburn hair gleamed in the afternoon sunlight. Smooth golden skin glowed with vitality. Features somehow as delicate as they were bold provided a delightful contradiction, inviting further—endless—study.

No, this perfect creature wasn't real. Such a flawless masterpiece of carnality could only be a figment of his imagination.

How many nights had he dreamed of those jade eyes? That

straight nose with its adorable smattering of freckles? Those plush
cherry lips? The plumper bottom with its center dip taunted him.

Exquisite.

"I'm a valued member of your army while she's a drain on
society," Elena continued, unaware of his disregard. "Norok
never should have wed her. And to do so a year after you ter-
minated the marriage line? How could he be so foolish? He's
usually smart."

"Intelligence doesn't guarantee wisdom." Red's dirty, frayed
gown revealed a wealth of curves lusher than he remembered,
and his mouth dried.

"I mean, I guess I understand. Being without a glamara makes
him feel less than the rest of us. But to settle for Lavina because
he was afraid he'd be unable to win anyone better…" She shuddered. "She got pregnant on purpose. Did you know that? Norok
probably felt forced to accept a permanent connection with her.
But did that permanent connection have to be forever?"

"Forever," Micah parroted. Between one blink and the next,
memories replaced his present and he lost sight of imaginary
Red. Norok's son, Warren, used to trail Micah's every step.
Unlike everyone else, the boy hadn't minded being near the
chimera.

Warren had grown into an amazing man. Strong. Loyal.
Fierce but kind. A dedicated soldier who never left an injured
fae behind. Now dead, killed on the battlefield. Not that there
had been any kind of battle. The enemy ravaged his contingent
of soldiers.

The tendons in Micah's neck distended as muscles bunched.
Acid waves of grief and sorrow washed over him. Fury and
guilt. The once-jovial Norok had changed since the lad's death,
becoming hardened and somber. They'd all changed since the
devastating loss.

Voice thicker, Elena asked, "Do you think he'll ever recover
from the loss?"

Will I? "I honestly don't know." Many others had lost sons that fateful day. Fathers, brothers, uncles and friends, too. *And the blame is mine.*

If only Micah had slain the couple responsible when he'd had the chance. Kaysar the Unhinged One and Cookie the Uncrumbled, a female more demented than her deranged husband. Instead, Micah had stayed his hand.

At the time, he'd still wondered if Kaysar were a chimera. Chimera sensed each other, after all. The very reason Erwen had found baby Micah in the middle of a forest. Micah had never forgotten his pull to Kaysar. Had hoped to save one of his own. Now he suspected the opposite. The male was pure fae and nothing like him. *Showed mercy for nothing.*

The worst part? He'd known better. Both before and after Micah's crowning, the other royal had often ventured in the Dusklands to hunt *belua*. The only other warrior in Astaria able to overcome such unfavorable odds without the aid of another. Even Norok, Micah's most dedicated and decorated warrior, required a partner.

"Kaysar's execution will help." Oh yes. Micah planned to rectify his error. Soon.

Mollified by the assurance, Elena returned to her original topic. He listened...for half a second. He'd caught sight of Red again.

He let his gaze drift over her body, savoring certain swells and dips.

Appearing shocked to her core, Red reared back. At least, she tried to. Something kept her tethered.

"...listening to me?" Elena asked.

"No." He searched for the block—a familiar hand that led to a masculine arm. Broad shoulder. White beard. Norok. Micah stiffened. *She's real.* She must be. Contact could not be made with a figment of his imagination.

His heart beat fast. Faster. *She's real.* Excitement overtook him. Then confusion. Why was she here? *How* was she here? Why now?

Did she recognize him as the boy who'd given her jewels so long ago?

He stepped forward, his feet moving of their own accord. Paling, she shrank into herself. He jolted and stopped, annoyance and resolve overshadowing everything else. Did she fear him, like so many others?

To his surprise, she quickly blanked her expression and assumed a come-at-me pose. Hmm. She might be afraid, but she was also brave and determined. An improvement, considering she hadn't screamed.

As Elena protested, he stalked toward Red. Anyone in his vicinity bowed as he passed. A lot of anyones. With might and cunning, he'd assembled a vast army. Together, they had destroyed monsters and conquered hordes of trolls and centaurs. They had eradicated goblins. He and his people had eventually swallowed up every village in the Dusklands until Micah was the last viceroy standing. At that point, there'd been no reason *not* to crown himself king and forge his own fae court. The Forgotten. A homage to his first home.

The people didn't care for him—never had, never would—and most had no desire to be his family, but they served him willingly. He ensured they prospered at every opportunity. Had built an indestructible palace and constructed villages that fed into a central marketplace. He'd given the citizens what no one else had been able to: peace of mind and safety.

Until Kaysar and Cookie invaded.

Micah waggled his jaw left and right, loosening taut muscles. When he caught a whiff of Red's scent, the sweetest fog filled his head. Sunshine, florals and citrus. His greatest weakness.

"Bow," his second-in-command told her. "Show respect to our king. He may be a chimera, but he's the best male in the land."

"I bow to no one." She raised her nose and glared at Micah. "What's a chimera?"

Her voice. Soft and raspy when she wasn't screaming. A caress to his ears, its unique tenor reminding him of music.

He ground his teeth as he halted in front of the pair. "Let her go, Norok." An undeniable order, even as his focus remained steady on Red.

The warrior hesitated only a moment before complying. "Is she the one you've searched for?"

"You searched for me?" she asked, arching a brow with a frustrating combination of smugness and pleasure. "Is there a reward for my capture? Because I might turn myself in willingly to collect."

He ignored each question and asked his own. "Do you know who I am?"

"Yep. I heard your soldier." She squared her shoulders. "You're the king head honcho of this village. King Micah."

He double-blinked at "head honcho" but affirmed the information with a clipped nod.

A sugary sweet smile bloomed on her too-beautiful face. "Well. You'll want to be a good royal and offer me food and a willing farewell. Your kingdom won't survive what happens otherwise."

A threat? Tensing, he scanned the area. Had *belua* accompanied her?

Though he noted no sign of them, he barked an order to Norok. "Gather our fiercest units and surround the camp. If a single *belua* nears, attack, provocation or not." He *hoped* the trees neared. Many nights, he'd dreamed of torching every leaf and branch.

Again, Norok hesitated before he obeyed, stalking off and barking directives at others.

Many kept their attention on their king. Micah scowled and clasped Red's arm, tugging her forward, only then realizing her wrists were bound behind her back. Without a hitch in his step, he unsheathed a dagger, sliced the rope and stored the weapon. As she rolled her shoulders, he readjusted his hold to her hand.

His breath hitched. *The softness of her palm…*

"I won't thank you," she snapped.

"Don't want your thanks." As he marched her through the heart of camp, he forced her to keep pace or be dragged behind.

Red snorted. "Liar! Everyone seeks praise."

They shouldn't. "Those who require praise for doing what's right lack character."

"Yes. Well. What's a chimera? You never said. And where are you taking me?"

His brow furrowed. How did she not know the meaning of *chimera*? Those like him were rare, but parents often used his kind to frighten their children. *Do what I say, or the chimera will come while you sleep…*

He pressed his tongue to the roof of his mouth. "We're headed to my tent, where I'll ask questions and you'll provide answers." How he wished he had retained ownership of the palace. Instead, Kaysar and Cookie had moved in. *Another crime they'll answer for.* "In case you're curious, I'll start the interrogation with this. Why did *belua* protect you?" The others never guarded anyone but themselves.

"Because they wanted to. Why else?"

A glib response that told him nothing. He ran his tongue over his teeth.

Anyone who spotted him—meaning everyone—bowed in acknowledgment of his title if nothing else. To this day, those he neared wished to peel the flesh from their bones, inch by inch. According to Elena, the sensation had only worsened over the years. Red probably suffered with the sensation now. Not that he cared.

Micah kept his head high and his gaze fixed straight ahead.

More bowing ensued. Lots of pursing lips. He wasn't the most highly esteemed sovereign nowadays.

Families had beseeched him repeatedly. Kill the usurper king and his queen and scatter their pieces around the camp's perimeter. He had declined. Eleven months ago, he'd agreed to a one-year truce with the couple, and he wouldn't break his word. He'd needed time to recover. To plan. To wait…

Cookie possessed the rare glamara to grow plants, trees and vegetation in the Dusklands. Flowers. Herbs. Fruits. Nuts. Medicines. Things he'd longed—and failed—to produce on his own. Amid the wait, she had transformed certain parts of the kingdom into a veritable paradise. True oases.

When he took everything back, he and his people could enjoy the bounty.

Few acknowledged the method to his supposed madness, too impatient for vengeance to endure. Many had already cut ties with him. Their mistake, their consequences.

Two guards flanked the door of his tent. They kept their attention off him, yet he sensed their astonishment at his approach. Never had Micah escorted a female inside his private quarters. Not when he'd lived in the palace, and certainly not in the campground. If ever he desired companionship, he visited his mistress, Diane.

"You are so fortunate I have a curious nature," Red muttered as he led her through the entrance. The flap settled behind her, sealing them inside.

Alone.

Convinced herself curiosity glued her to his side rather than his iron grip, had she? Would she run as soon as he released her?

Micah freed her and prepared to give chase, even as he continued forward. To his surprise, she stayed put, examining her new surroundings, and exuding increasingly sharp disappointment. His cheeks scalded.

He scanned the dwelling with a critical eye. The spacious

enclosure provided a pallet of the softest furs, an antique desk, an empty copper tub, an armory, multiple trunks and two tables. The shortest displayed a basin of fresh, cool water. Maps littered the longer one. Poverty compared to his palace; luxury compared to his childhood.

At the basin, he splashed his face and wiped away the grime. Then, he crossed his arms over his chest and fixed his attention on Red, acutely aware of the sweat and dirt marring his clothing.

She stared right back. Of course, any moment now, she would look away. Everyone always looked away. Even Norok.

Yes, any moment.

Surely within the next five seconds.

The next thirty?

"What's your name?" he barked.

She huffed with irritation. "You may call me... Vee."

"Where have you been since our parting?"

"Here and there."

Did she not know the answer? Had she slept? "Why do you slumber as if dead to the world?"

"Why do you trespass where you don't belong?" Rocking back on her heels, she pivoted away from him, breaking eye contact at last.

"Were you a prisoner of the *belua*—or their master?"

She padded through the tent, tracing a fingertip over sundry items, saying, "Do you hope to punish me if I command your attackers?"

Yes! No. "You are safe with me. They are not."

A hitch in her step—born of concern for the monsters? Or eagerness? What if she'd been a prisoner, and he'd failed to find and help her?

"Do you think to kill the trees?" she asked, and he...sensed nothing. Meaning, what? That she expertly hid her emotions or that she evinced an undercurrent of indifference?

"Think? No. I will do so." In fact, the hunt was set to begin the day after Kaysar died.

"No, Majesty. You'll do nothing of the sort." She offered him a toothy smile over her shoulder. "They're already gone."

That smile...wild and calculating, as if she knew a secret he did not. Already he yearned to see it again. "You wish me to believe you killed them?" Why?

"Do you think me incapable of such a feat?" Another toothy smile, only wider.

Muscles jumped in reflex. Scrambling, he drew in a deep breath. Slowly released it. Better. And worse. No one smelled sweeter than Red. The citrus. The florals. The utter rightness.

"Perhaps I'd have an easier time believing you if I knew why they kept you," he rasped.

"Because I'm keepable?"

Though she continued her inspection of the tent, as if she hadn't a care, the barest bit of color drained from her cheeks. Suspicions flared. Did she know King Kaysar, as Norok believed? Had the royal freed her and sent her to kill Micah at long last?

"This inquisition grows tiresome. You should feed me and send me on my way." She dipped a finger in the basin and swirled the water. "You'll be oh, so glad you did or desperately regret that you didn't. Your choice."

A declaration of war. Not that he cared. Prisoners often made such overconfident statements. "The inquisition ends when I decide, not a moment before."

"Are you sure?" How smug she sounded. "Ask me another question, and let's find out together."

All right. She might win this argument. Unused to a refusal or loss in this camp, Micah grated, "You will answer me, Vee."

"Nah. I'd rather be beaten." She blew him a kiss. "So do it. Beat me. Do your worst. Then prepare yourself. Because I'll do *my* worst."

Oh yes. She'd won. Micah deflated, unwilling to harm her to get what he wanted. "Tell me *something* at least!"

With haughty disdain, she flicked her scarlet mane over a shoulder. "You could try answering one of *my* questions and see if it helps your cause."

What could she possibly wish to know? He gave a clipped nod. "Ask."

"Why did you give me those jewels?"

He frowned. Of everything she could have asked, why address such a trivial matter? And admit the truth and listen to the flawless beauty laugh at the scarred beast tamer? Tone flat, he told her, "Because I was a teenage boy, and you were the only female in the vicinity." Nothing false about that statement. "Why else?"

The way she blanched…

He wished to snatch the words from her ears. Suddenly weary, he asked, "Why are you here, Red?" Why now? Had she searched for him the way he'd once searched for her?

She hiked her shoulders in a negligent shrug. "The answer doesn't concern you. I won't be staying long."

Doesn't concern me? He ground his teeth. So. She hadn't been searching for him and might not know Kaysar. Not if she planned to leave. Two queries answered, at least. What if she *had* killed the trees?

"I'm king here," he snapped, "my word is law. You'll stay as long as I desire."

He didn't have to worry she'd do any flittering. Though he'd lost his palace, he'd retained his stockpile of *tollo*. The campground itself. The special dirt covered the ground, nullifying certain fae abilities. Unless, of course, you wore an *amplio* stone. Or power restorer. Which he did. In his wrist cuff. So did every commander in his army. On their turf, they had the advantage—foes had nothing.

"Do you have a family?" he asked. People who anticipated her return?

She made a huffing noise. "Why do you want to know? So you can torture them in front of me?"

He blinked. What had those trees done to her? "Your family is safe with me. I inquire about the members merely to discover whether or not they require saving."

"Saving? Are you kidding?" She offered a humorless laugh. "Look, if you value your people and your lands, you'll release me. I'm serious about that. Been super-up-front with you, too. So let me go. With food. Lots and lots of food."

No, she hadn't killed the trees. "You fear they'll find you." A statement, not a question.

The tent's entrance swished open, Norok striding inside without awaiting permission. A privilege only he and Elena enjoyed. Warren, too. Once. "I come bearing news."

A glower darkened the warrior's sunburned features. Red shrank back, realized what she'd done, then bristled, as if the invader had no right to occupy *her* space or breathe *her* air.

Mmm. That shrinking… The same reaction she'd exhibited with Micah. What had this girl endured throughout her life?

"Pops here took a little too much pleasure in bruising this perfect little peach." She pointed a clawtip at Norok. "Punish him. You are king, as you like to assure me, and I am your honored guest, apparently."

That claw. Some fae grew them, most didn't. They usually only developed when a glamara dealt with animals or nature. So what could this girl do?

Norok raised his white brows at Micah. "A wee bit bloodthirsty for your tastes, eh?"

"Seems so." Micah pressed his tongue to the roof of his mouth. His tastes. During his years as king, he'd enjoyed a grand total of three lovers. The only fae willing to pretend to care for him—for a price.

"Tell me your news," Micah grated, earning another scowl from Red.

"Fayette has alerted me to an upcoming meeting with Kaysar. He arrives in but a few hours." Norok leveled his most menacing glare upon Red. "The fact that the false king is visiting the same day the oracle informed me I'd find a spy proves my suspicions. Your little Red is here to aid our enemy."

"So beat me already," she bellowed.

Micah pinched the bridge of his nose. Demanding a beating was her answer to fear. Noted. But what did she fear now? For the life of Kaysar, as Norok suspected? What if her threats to leave the camp had been empty?

"Sound the alarm and prepare for battle," Micah commanded. "I'll join you shortly."

Norok opened his mouth to protest, no doubt, but quickly thought better of it. He nodded, as was his custom, and exited.

Silence stretched for several minutes as Micah and Red peered at one another. She had blanked her expression. An irritating turn. Part of him wished to force a reaction. To glimpse her true thoughts by any means necessary.

A swift internal debate raged, ending when he decided to test her. Would she attempt to escape—or to spy?

"You war with the Unhinged One?" she asked, wielding her don't-care tone. Except, a slight tremor accompanied her words.

"I do. Or I will." *And what of you, little beauty? Do you align with him? We'll find out soon enough.* "Kaysar is a killer without mercy. He uses a voice of compulsion to drive those around him mad."

Micah and his soldiers were not immune. For any meeting, they must consume a concoction to temporarily deafen themselves.

Red licked her lips, and Micah stifled a groan. "He sounds dangerous," she said. "Will you strike at this scourge?"

He opted for honesty. "Not unless he strikes first. My truce with him lasts another five weeks." Then... Oh, then. The things he planned for Kaysar and his queen... Micah grinned, and it must have been a terrifying sight.

His companion jolted and eased back, fluttering a hand over her throat. "I should wait here while you prepare for your meet and greet, yes? We can finish our interrogation upon your return."

Suddenly so willing. "Agreed. You'll stay in my tent." If she exited the dwelling for any reason, his most capable spy would know it.

"Well? What are you waiting for?" She shooed him off. "Go, go! Don't let the tent flap hit you on your way out."

Before he'd taken a step, her stomach growled, loudly. His cheeks reddened. Thrice she'd mentioned food, and thrice he'd ignored her.

Do no harm to the innocent. Protect what's yours. Always do what's right. Never be without a backup plan.

"I'll have food brought to you immediately." Cursing himself, Micah stalked to his armory. He sheathed two short swords at his back and a handful of daggers at his side, then drew on his hooded cloak. He headed for the door. "Vee, I'll share an unshakable truth with you, in case you haven't realized it yet. I can be a powerful ally...or a terrible enemy. As you are fond of telling me, the choice is yours."

CHAPTER FIVE

Viori bustled through the tent, searching every nook and cranny for weapons. Frustration whipped her. She pried one of the chests open, revealing tunics and leather pants, but failed to open the others. A song would awake the stubborn locks, but why use up precious energy? Or risk being observed at such a crucial time?

Micah and Kaysar. At war. For reasons. A fraying truce. What to do, what to do? *Think!*

Summon her children to destroy the campground and everyone in it? A gift to Kaysar and her act of apology. But what if her brother wished to spare certain individuals? And why put her darlings in harm's way? For the time being, Micah assumed they were dead.

If Kaysar suffered harm because she didn't act?

She paced at a clipped speed, wringing her hands. Soon, her brother would arrive in this camp. The only fae she longed to see and hold with every fiber of her being. But she hadn't yet earned the right. She should leave, yes? At least for a little while. He was strong. Beyond strong. No one could harm him, not even Micah. After she figured out a plan of action, she could return if needed. Better not to stay and tempt fate. But…

Would Kaysar even recognize her?

What if he didn't?

Perhaps she *should* stay, just in case he required backup. She just… She…didn't know. According to Micah, the ceasefire expired in five weeks. And, judging by the ruthless smile he displayed when he'd spoken of the end, he expected violence and relished the thought.

He must be stopped.

Pops had called her a spy. Why not oblige him? Stick around, listen and learn, then sabotage Micah's schemes against Kaysar.

Her brother mattered to her. The people here did not. They were pre-enemies. Those who hadn't yet had an opportunity to turn on her. But they would, if she let them. *Only a matter of time.*

Why hadn't she listened to her brother's warning?

The tent flap lifted, and she shrank back, startled. An array of fae and humans swept inside. Servants. Each carried something. Food. Buckets. Clothes. Tension eased from Viori as the most amazing aromas wafted to her nose. Succulent spices. Tender meats. Hunger pangs nearly doubled her over.

Garments were draped over the pallet of furs. A pink gown. A gold gown. Matching scarves. Oh wow. A nightgown and delicate underthings.

Her breath caught. Did Micah expect to see her in the scantier apparel?

No one glanced her way or spoke. They ignored her so completely, she wondered if she were invisible. Micah's orders? Someone tidied the table, moving the maps, while others arranged the meal. An assortment of breads, cheeses, meats and fruits. Things not typically found in the Dusklands.

Do not elbow the staff and shovel in the buffet!

Liquid splashed, pulling her attention from the feast. Oh, wow. The buckets overflowed with clear, steaming water—water the servants were transferring into the tub. Buckets and buckets and buckets. Of water. *Hot* water. For bathing. In the

Dusklands. Here, water was so rare. So precious. And warm water? Unfathomable!

Outside of the mortal world, she'd only ever bathed in a shallow basin, small ponds or whatever she'd drawn from a village well. Although, in New York, pre-Laken, she'd been forced to use mostly bathroom sinks—after she'd learned how to work a faucet. In Scotland, she'd gotten to splash around in a frigid lake. In Oklahoma, she'd stayed in an abandoned cottage and had a bathroom all to herself. By far her favorite location, second only to home.

Why had Micah arranged a bath for her? Did she smell? Viori sniffed herself and wrinkled her nose. Maybe? She didn't know!

As speedily as the servants arrived, they departed, leaving her alone. With water. And food. Stomach close to upending itself, she careened to the table and dived into the meal. As the first deluge of flavors registered, her eyes rolled into her head.

This is mine. She shoveled apple slices into her mouth. *Mine.* As she chewed, she eyed the creamy cheese spread over a sphere of bread. *Also mine.* She ate and ate and ate, strength infiltrating her limbs and easing her tremors.

Hands overflowing with morsels, she let her feet carry her to the tub. How divine the water looked. Clean and clear, with ribbons of steam curling up. So inviting. She hadn't soaked in a tub since—a long time ago.

No childhood memories allowed. Not now. Perhaps not ever. Should she risk a bath? Here? If Micah returned…

No, there'd be no risking it.

A plan finally formed. *Escape. Observe the meeting with Kaysar. Decide what to do.* Yes! Viori draped the yellow scarf around her head, hiding her hair, and circled the edges of the tent, toeing the fabric. There must be a vulnerability *somewhere*. Guards stood outside the exit, but they didn't patrol the perimeter. Did they?

Here! She expelled a relieved sigh. The material wasn't anchored properly.

Heart drumming, she dipped to her belly to peek through the slit between tent and dirt. No guards patrolled the area. Any booted or sandaled feet she spotted moved away from the dwelling.

Here goes. She scrambled through the opening and popped to her feet, acting as if she'd always been there. A quick scan. Males and females, again a mix of fae and humans, dashed in the same direction. Armed guards directed the throng from the fringe, issuing commands over the frantic voices creating a cacophony of noise, her brother's name at the fore.

The drumming accelerated as Viori motored forward, blending into the masses. She attempted to flitter at every opportunity to no avail. Gah! She needed to veer off course at some point. No way she should follow the crowd to their destination. Not if she hoped to witness the meeting. But the moment she eased out of line, someone would spot her. Alarms might rise. She'd have to create a distraction.

Easy enough. Without hesitation, Viori tripped the fae in front of her—one of the larger males in the group. He stumbled into the human before him, who shoved into someone else. Gasps were drowned out amid cries of panic as bodies piled up. She jumped out of the way at the beginning, avoiding the collision, at the same time ensuring the person behind her slammed into the one she'd tripped.

Zero guilt. These people had watched as their king dragged her away. They deserved what they got.

Guards hurried over to help, and she jolted into action. Running. The right direction? She didn't know. Wait! Did she detect a soft pitter-patter of footsteps behind her? Swift glance. No one seemed to give chase. The area appeared deserted.

Relieved but wary, Viori pumped her arms and increased her pace. Sunlight seemed to follow her, brighter than before. A spotlight she couldn't shake. Breath sawed in and out of her mouth as she zigged and zagged.

Oh, thank goodness! The border of the camp loomed ahead, near the section where she'd first landed. If she could get there, she should be able to flitter to a different area to— Argh! She lurched to a halt and spun behind a tent.

Though she'd stilled, her eyes darted and her heart raced faster. Icy blood drained from her head, leaving her dizzy for a moment. A high-pitched ring erupted in her ears. Some awful, wondrous emotion reached up and gripped her throat, choking her.

Her mind replayed what she'd just seen. *Two powerful fae, arriving in the camp. Royals. A male and a female, both covered in expensive velvets, casually stepping from a mystical doorway. Behind the couple, a veritable paradise of lush flowers and lapping waters stretched. The door closing, the paradise vanishing, the pair remaining.*

That doorway reminded Viori of the ones she'd inadvertently opened the times she'd used so much energy to create her children, she'd burned a hole through the atmosphere. She'd fallen asleep in one world and awakened in another.

Forget the doorway. It wasn't the headline but the buffer to her utter devastation. The male possessed black hair, dark eyes and dusky skin several shades darker than Viori's own. Tall and built like a mountain. The image of Papa.

Kaysar.

Her brother stood a shout away. He'd arrived early. With a woman. An employee? A paramour? A friend or ally? A wife?

Did he have a new family to love and cherish?

Tears welling, limbs quaking, Viori pressed as flat as possible against the tent, without upending the entire structure. Her brother had come through a mystical doorway. Opened by the pink-haired female? Was she a rare fae able to conjure portals between worlds and within realms at will?

"I do so enjoy when our Eye outsees other eyes," he said, amused.

That oh, so beloved voice hit her awareness, a battering ram to her veneer of calm. She fought a sob. Once, that voice had promised all would be well. But nothing had ended well. Not for her brother. Not for her.

Viori shut her eyes to block horrifying memories of starvation, isolation and fear. Of fleeing danger. Never belonging. Always wishing.

"Ah. Micah," Kaysar said, and she jolted. The king had arrived? "So good of you to greet us personally. Belated courtesy that it is. If you think to defeat me, you should slay your current oracle and imprison yourself a better one."

"Kaysar. Cookie," Micah said, ignoring the taunt. "Feel free to serenade us with your favorite song. We won't mind."

Viori's brow wrinkled. While Kaysar's voice had only deepened during the passage of centuries, Micah's had altered in multiple ways in a matter of minutes. Flatter. Zero emotion. Each syllable overenunciated.

A chill skittered along her spine, and she stole a quick look around the tent. Oh, wow. This male wasn't the boy who'd given her jewels or the leader who'd provided her with a feast. Here stood a warrior without mercy. The type of fae she'd always avoided—or killed at first opportunity. Tall, muscled and hooded.

"You expected an attack, so you deafened yourself again," the woman said. The doormaker must be this Cookie. But what did she mean, Micah had deafened himself *again*? "I'm offended. As if I would kill you today. You know I prefer to toy with my victims first." A scolding tinged her words. And her accent... Southern? Did that mean she was human and hailed from the mortal world? How did she have power then?

Viori stole another quick peek at the group, concentrating on Cookie. A short, curvy beauty with pale skin and eyes of green and silver. Fine boned, like a doll. Definitely fae, not human. Kaysar remained beside her, with a strong arm draped around her waist. Metal claws tipped his fingers and gently tapped her hip bone. A romantic hold.

Viori wracked her brain. Last she'd heard, her brother eschewed matters of the heart.

He chuckled, a sound she'd missed more than anything, everything, and a hoarse croak leaked from her. She slapped a hand over her mouth and held her breath, lest she utter another sound. Had anyone heard?

Heartbeat. Heartbeat. Heartbeat.

In the stillness, longing she'd never been able to shed sharpened. She *must* prove herself worthy of this male. Must help him in some way. Then she could see him. Might be able to hug him. Finally!

Inhale. Exhale. No shouts of alarm. No footsteps.

"Why are you here?" Micah asked.

"You're right," Cookie replied with a cheerful tone. "Business first. Fun and games after." A pause, clothing rustling. "Go ahead, baby. Tell him."

Kaysar—baby—didn't hesitate. "It seems our beloved Pearl Jean hasn't gotten over her— What's the term you used, pet?"

"Crush," Cookie told him.

"Ah, yes. That. Her crush." Kaysar's words seemed to contain a smile. "I remember hearing a mention of *buns of steel* and *abs of iron*. After numerous temper tantrums and bouts of pleading, she has convinced me to grant her request and offer you an erotic time-out. Her words, not mine."

Phrases Viori understood. Was this Pearl Jean human?

Kaysar continued, "Here are my terms. You'll surrender, swear your eternal fealty to my family and agree to do whatever Pearl Jean asks of you. In return, I won't make you watch as I destroy everything you hold dear the moment our truce ends."

The more he spoke, the harsher he sounded, until even Viori quaked with fear.

"I look forward to your attempts," Micah said.

She thought she heard a smile in his voice as well. He truly believed he could emerge the victor.

Could he?

Foreboding prickled Viori's nape. Air hitched in her lungs, a decision solidifying in her mind. She would remain in camp. Study Micah up close and personal. Discover his strengths and weaknesses and sabotage any schemes he crafted. Meanwhile, she would play either the part of furious captive, or besotted vixen. The latter attacked first and often. The former flirted and charmed.

Only female in the vicinity, Majesty?

Her nails sharpened into claws. They'd find out. *If* she decided to venture that route. Thanks to Laken, she'd learned how to flirt from a master.

As soon as Micah returned to the tent, she would decide the direction to travel based on his treatment of her. Afterward, she'd find a way to send a message to her babies. Should be easy to do, considering only three words were needed.

Prepare for war.

CHAPTER SIX

Micah and Norok occupied one side of a long, rectangular table, while Kaysar and Cookie perched on the other. So far, the impromptu assembly had facilitated nothing more than uncomfortable staring and an intermittent exchange of insults and threats.

Had his ears worked and his emotions not been numbed courtesy of the *surdi* root tea, he would have boiled with hatred. Warren's killers. Here in the flesh. Vulnerable. How easy it would be to strike. But even now, he couldn't bring himself to break a vow—or erase Red from his thoughts. What was she doing? What path had she chosen? When could he see her again?

"When I deign to visit, I should be worthy of a better hovel," Kaysar commented, his features pinched with distaste as he scanned the setting.

Beyond easy. "You are worthy only of death."

They occupied a small mud hut at the farthest edge of the campground, built exclusively with *tollo*, preventing flittering.

"Yes, but no refreshments." Cookie pouted. "No amenities of any kind."

He allowed no servants to enter this area, ever. Why endanger innocents? "Tell me why you are really here or leave. I won't allow you to waste more of my valuable time."

Kaysar winced, as if embarrassed for him. "How sad. You haven't yet realized you're already a dead man walking."

Micah watched the royal's lips to identify the words. "You're wrong. I've known it for quite some time." It was the reason he made such a great king. He had no needs of his own, only those of his people.

Like the indomitable Red, his "guest" held his stare without wavering. "You *do* realize I could declare an end to our truce right now, yes? We know your men sneak onto our land to steal food and water. A clear violation of our terms."

"Once again, you're wrong. I agreed to lend you the use of my palace for one year. *Only* my palace. The lands around it are *mine*. I steal nothing. I merely take what belongs to me."

"Is that so?" Kaysar steepled his hands and drummed his metal claws together.

Cookie peered at Micah while petting her husband's chest, as if she sought to calm him from a hulking rage. "I am better for the citizens of the Dusklands. You comprehend this. And anyone who'd prefer to join my team is welcome to do so at any time," she added with a smile at Norok. "But spies best beware. I bite."

Steady. The queen's time is coming. "The same is true of *your* spies."

To Norok's credit, he simply glared at her, obeying Micah's order to silence his retorts. No doubt he plotted a thousand ways to murder the royals.

The couple deserved whatever death they were dealt. How they had laughed as they'd wreaked destruction upon a legion of soldiers. Cookie had used her glamara to sprout poisoned vines from her fingertips and squeeze the life out of good fae. Throughout the massacre, Kaysar had sung a lethal song, increasing her power.

"What I know," Micah stated, "is that you are a sovereign

who insists on granting your every whim at the expense of the people. You are nothing more than a tyrant, unworthy of a crown."

"Take it from me." Challenge crackling in her eyes, she blew him a kiss. "I dare you to try."

"Soon," he vowed. Oh yes. Soon indeed.

Kaysar slapped a hand against the table, gaining Micah's attention. "You do not wish to become a true foe of mine," the other male told him, seeming serious for the first time. "I'll stop at nothing to deliver pain like you've never known."

His coldest smile bloomed. "You will stop—when I make you."

Kaysar smiled right back, a sinister contortion of his lips. "So be it. Five weeks then." He stood and drew his wife to her feet. "Come, love. I'm eager to acquire new jars for the tongues I plan to add to my collection. I'll call them Micah's Regret."

"Oh, I love it!" Cookie praised his brilliance while opening a doorway. The two vanished from view.

Micah wasted no time. He had a prisoner to check on. Jumping up, he claimed his cloak. As he donned the material, he caught Norok's gaze and demanded, "Bring me the oracle." He hated to admit this, but…the Unhinged One was right. Fayette should have foreseen the early arrival of his foes. Something she used to do with ease.

For decades, the oracle had predicted the most minute details of his life weeks, months and sometimes years in advance. As the most powerful seer in the entire realm, she had helped him win villages in a matter of hours. Yet today she failed to predict the exact moment his most despised opponent arrived? No. Something was off, and only one explanation made sense. She had purposely impaired Micah.

The more he pondered the prospect, the more he smoldered with resentment. Early this morning, Fayette had warned Norok to be on the lookout for a spy. Now Micah wondered…had she lied to distract them? Planning, hoping to blame her actions on another, such as a newcomer like Red?

Had Fayette and Kaysar arranged this together?

Expression as sharp as a blade, Norok unfolded from his chair. "Do you want her here, your tent or the dungeon?"

The warrior suspected something was off, too? "I'll be on foot. Find me."

A nod. Then his friend flittered off.

Walking, hoping to level his mood, Micah stomped from the hut. He motioned to two guards posted nearby. Two of many, but the only ones visible. They understood. They were to return the most vulnerable citizens to their homes. Those who'd sought shelter in common areas Micah designated for occasions such as this.

He headed for his tent. For Red. He would put his eyes on her, then deal with his oracle. Dirt flung from the toes of his boots. Anyone in his way moved as hastily as possible. The sun was setting in the distance, turning the sky into a blanket of plum streaked with lavender.

A sullen Norok appeared at his side, keeping pace. *She's not where I left her, and clothes are missing from her tent,* he signed. Hands were simpler to read than lips when they trekked.

Micah's resentment heated, melting into rage. Had Kaysar sneaked out the oracle? He must have. Why else pretend to desire an extended, lifelong truce? Not for a moment did Micah believe the other king wished to placate that crone Pearl Jean, a former human who'd eaten a royal fae heart to gain immortality.

Had Fayette willingly left with Kaysar? She despised the Unhinged One and his bride, yes. Like Norok, she'd lost someone in the battle. A husband. Did she seek revenge? Or had she foreseen Micah's loss in the war, and she thought to abandon him to serve the victor...

Denial roared inside his head. Lose his home? His lands? His future? Lead his people to the ultimate defeat? No! He had yet to unleash the full scope of his ability upon his rivals. They knew nothing of the troll armies waiting on the sidelines, his to command.

Only five weeks to go. Thirty-five days. Vapor, there and gone.

Find her. Bring her to me, Micah signed. He required a new oracle as soon as possible. In times of calamity, foresight often proved necessary. But who could he trust? And where could he find a new seer? Among their kind, the ability to peer into the future remained rare.

It will be so. You have my word. Norok vanished.

Seconds later, Elena approached from the opposite direction. No longer did she wear the blue ensemble. Instead, she'd donned a black tunic and leathers, her preferred attire when utilizing her glamara, merging into any background, undetectable. The reason she'd earned the exalted role of royal spy. Or mole, as she sometimes called herself. In their first year together, she'd proved herself to be a valuable member of his inner circle.

"Well?" he demanded. The *surdi* root was wearing off, his ears switching on, picking up noises. More than that, his curiosity was as bothersome as a rusty nail stuck in his heel. Was Red friend or foe?

"Your prisoner did indeed attempt to escape," Elena informed him.

Relief hit. Finally, a bit of good news. Kaysar's spy would not endanger herself to flee the one she hoped to probe for information.

His companion huffed. "Why do you look so happy about this? If you'll stop thinking with your dangle bits, you'll do the right thing and kill her. She's pure trouble."

Kill Red? No. "Her treatment isn't up for discussion. And what do you know of a man's…dangle bits?" If ever his spy had entertained a lover, he didn't know it.

His first act as viceroy, he'd ended the annual marriage line.

At any time, Elena could have chosen a temporary companion; however, she'd had no interest in being "tied to misery." A sentiment Micah understood. Never mind that secret part of him had never quit craving a family of his own. To finally experience the sense of belonging so many of his soldiers took for granted.

"My knowledge isn't up for discussion," she replied with a humph.

"Why would I kill Red, anyway?" he grumbled. Despite any lingering effects of the tea, irritation seeped from him. "She isn't a spy."

"Don't be so sure of that," Elena snapped. "She knows Kaysar. Or knows *of* him. I'm sure of it."

And? "*Everyone* knows of him."

"Does everyone hide when he crosses their path?"

"Yes." Everyone but Micah.

"I'm telling you, she recognized him as more than a legend of mass destruction," Elena continued. "Distress etched her features. Tears welled. Though she had ample opportunity to vacate the area to circumvent him—and you!—she opted to return to your tent."

Red had returned of her own free will? Because she feared contact with Kaysar? Did she think to use Micah as her shield? *With pleasure, little beauty.* He *burned* to eliminate Kaysar and Cookie. "She's there now?"

"She is. I stationed guards around the perimeter. She's well and truly trapped now," his spy said. "So? What will you do with her?"

"Recall my earlier words—her treatment isn't up for discussion." But…what *was* he going to do with the girl? He knew he should avoid her until morning, when the *surdi* root tea fully left his system. But he had questions and she had answers. Stay away? He couldn't.

"Micah," Norok said, materializing nearby and jogging over.

"That was fast." They'd only been apart a few minutes.

The warrior nudged his sister aside and said, "A citizen spotted Fayette. She's heading east."

East. Toward the palace—toward Kaysar. Micah flicked his tongue over an incisor as multiple muscles turned to stone. Fayette *was* the spy, and she *did* expect him to lose.

"One more thing." Norok pulled at his collar, meeting his gaze for a moment before looking away. "She isn't alone. With her are four of your elite and a female. They were seen speaking with a stranger before the meeting. I'm sorry to tell you this, but the female was…is…Diane."

Diane, his current mistress? She'd betrayed him to an enemy?

Fury and humiliation seared him. He had paid the female well. Had never abused or harmed her in any way. Had provided for her every need. Yet she'd thought so little of him, she'd helped arrange his defeat? "Go. Find them and bring them to me. Alive."

"This shall be done. You have my vow." Norok dashed off without another word.

"Go," Micah commanded Elena as well. "Enjoy your night. Tomorrow I have a special assignment for you." He might not employ an oracle anymore, but he did have his self-proclaimed mole. Not even Kaysar or Cookie wielded enough power to sense Elena when she activated her glamara—a fact she'd already proved.

He would send her to the palace. She would learn their plans and hear the suggestions of their oracle, Amber, keeping Micah informed.

Though Elena looked as if she had a thousand other things to say, she nodded and branched away from him. He quickened his gait, soon coming to his tent. As promised, guards circled the entire structure.

The wall of men parted, allowing him to stride inside without a hitch in his step. He braced, unsure of what he'd find…

Red sat at his desk. Spotting him, she bolted to her feet. His frown returned, but quickly morphed into a scowl. Dirt streaked her from head to toe, both old and new. She hadn't bathed.

He stared at her as he removed and tossed the cloak, waiting for a blurted explanation, expecting her to avert her gaze any moment. Again, she held his gaze, shocking him—forcing *him* to look away.

Micah focused on his anger. Did she have any idea how many of his men had risked their lives to siphon water from palace lands? How generous her new king had been, to offer her his own daily portion?

His hands curled into fists. Unlike his foes, he didn't ally with Jareth Frostline, ruler of the Winterlands, whose glamara created ice, which in turn created great lakes. As a wedding present to the Unhinged One and his new bride, King Jareth had gifted them with massive blocks of ice, which had already melted into great bodies of water.

My water. In thirty-five days.

He stalked to the long table, where he'd instructed servants to arrange a meal for two. Only crumbs remained. Vee had eaten everything? How hungry she must have been, to consume his portion.

His gaze returned to her. Healthy color bloomed in her cheeks. Those jade irises were brighter than before. In the endless span of his life, he'd gone to bed hungry on multiple occasions. For the first time, he experienced satisfaction, too.

I provided for her needs. Me.

"What?" she demanded.

"I'm curious. What did you do during my absence?" Would she give a truthful answer?

She jutted her chin, telling him, "You'll have to beat the answer out of me."

Back to the beatings? Fear? He heaved a sigh. At least she hadn't offered a lie. "In other words, you escaped and returned."

She bristled. "You had me followed. Well. Try to interrogate me about my decisions. I dare you."

Micah scoured a hand over his face as fatigue infiltrated his limbs. A bone-deep weariness that seeped from his innermost being. Perhaps their next argument could wait?

As he strode to the tub, he began to lift his shirt, only to remember his scars and release the hem. Allow this perfect creature to behold the scars her army of tree guards had wrought? No.

There'd be no bathing for him tonight, either. But waste the water? Again, no.

Micah flittered inches from her, earning another gasp. He swept her into his arms, flittered again and dropped her into the tub. Cold water splashed over her and soaked his boots.

She leaped to a stand, sputtering and hurling insults at him. When she realized the fabric of her gown had become transparent, revealing generous curves that slackened his jaw, she plummeted of her own accord, drew her knees up to her chest and wrapped her arms around her legs.

"How dare you," she spit up at him, her freckles stark. Water droplets clung to her lashes. How adorably bedraggled.

"Do not blame me for this, Red. It's your fault. Had you bathed earlier, this wouldn't be necessary." Let her suffer a bit. Perhaps she'd do as he expected next time. "Now," he said, pulling the desk chair to the side of the tub and sitting. "We will talk."

"You're right. We will." She met his gaze without reservation. "Tell me how you can flitter, but I cannot."

"So you've tried and failed." A statement, not a question. Now, at least, he knew she possessed the ability; not every fae did.

"Of course I have. Many times."

Her honesty snuffed out any lingering flames of anger. "As you can venture only where I allow you, you don't need the ability to flitter. No," he said when she opened her mouth to respond. "No more questions from you. Only answers."

"Try to pry them out of me. Be my guest." Her teeth chattered. "Believe me, I can be silent far longer than most."

"How did you kill the trees?" he asked. He hadn't changed his mind: she'd lied. She must have.

She humphed at him. "This again?"

This always. "Why did they safeguard you?"

Silence reigned as she rested her cheek against her knees and batted her lashes at him.

Unwilling to capitulate, he forged ahead. "Before, you mentioned the reason you arrived in my camp doesn't concern me. If not me, who?"

More silence. Terser.

"Did a human raise you?" Sometimes her speech patterns threw him.

Nothing.

A muscle jumped in his jaw. Since his crowning, few beings had defied him. Only *belua* and trolls, really. Usually, the skinpeeling was enough to ensure cooperation. He wasn't sure how to proceed with Red.

Perhaps she would be willing to negotiate for protection. "Are you Kaysar's enemy? Did you do something to earn his wrath?" No one else took exception to innocuous actions more than Kaysar the Unhinged One.

The color—the vitality—drained from her cheeks. For once, she averted her gaze. "What makes you think that?"

"Did you?" he insisted.

A sheen of tears glassed her irises, and her bottom lip trembled. She nodded. "I did. Very much so."

As he'd suspected. He disregarded the tightening in his chest. "Tell me what you did to him, and I might be inclined to aid you."

With an angry swipe of her eyes, she snapped, "Why don't you come in here and make me?"

Okay. Commands and coercion were getting him nowhere. He was ashamed to admit it, but he wasn't opposed to bribery. "Tell me, and I *will* protect you. From Kaysar, and from any *belua*."

Her mouth opened. Closed. She gulped. "You can defend me from beings as powerful as Kaysar the Unhinged One and... *belua*?"

"I can," he boasted, confident. The trees *must* have held her prisoner.

Another lick of her lips. "How?"

No need to mention his ability to tame beasts. Few knew. Oh, they witnessed the results of his glamara, but they didn't understand the how or why of it, and he preferred it that way. He had a single weakness—something beasts could use to subdue *him*, if ever they discovered it. Therefore, he planned to take his secret to the grave.

"I can," he repeated. "There's nothing more you need to know."

She traced a fingertip over the surface of the water. "You *say* you can, but why should I believe you?"

"Shall I hunt a *belua* now, and bring you its head?"

"No need to go to such extremes," she told him with a brittle smile. "A simple battle plan will suffice."

"First, it's no extreme. *Belua* are monsters who terrorize my people, and the death of one would cause great celebration. Second, you'll get my assurance, nothing more. I have fought—and will always fight—to the death to protect anyone under my care."

She stiffened, saying, "Good to know." Gradually, she relaxed in the tub. No, *relaxed* wasn't the right word. She brooded, all sharp edges and cold calculation. "If I do it, if I tell you what you wish to know, you'll vow to defend me and my family, always and forever, from *every* threat, no matter what?"

He wasn't the only one willing to give bribery a try. But "always and forever" was a long time. Too long. And yet...

It wasn't dread he experienced at the idea. "I will vow to defend you and you alone from any threat until Kaysar and his bride are dead. After that, we'll have to renegotiate as necessary."

She gulped with more force. A reaction he couldn't interpret. "Does that mean you'll keep me by your side every minute of every day, no matter what you're doing? You must. If we part, you can't guard me as promised."

A thrum of eagerness almost swayed him to her cause. But agree to such unrelenting terms? He could not. "I will assign others to act as your shield whenever I'm otherwise occupied."

"No." A violent shake of her head. "I'll only accept you, and only with limitations. I don't trust new people."

That, he understood. Still. "There will be times I cannot be with you. However, I *can* assure you those times will be few and quick. So. Do you agree or not? You'll share with me everything I wish to know, when I wish to know it, and in return I'll oversee your safety and security."

Again, she brooded in silence. But it wasn't long before she sagged, a position of defeat. "Very well, Majesty. You win. I'll tell you what you wish to know."

He'd won? Micah nearly belted out a victory shout. By some miracle, he contained himself. "Do it. Tell me."

She steeled herself, as if expecting a blow. "I've spent time with humans between my sleeps. And the...*belua*. They feed off my energy. That's how they stay alive. Sometimes they require so much energy, I'm forced to sleep to recover." Her voice wobbled with shame.

So. A captive, after all, exactly as he'd suspected. Everything inside him softened. "Why not tell me the truth from the beginning?"

"Uh, did you hear the part where I said I do not trust new people?"

Her snippy tone drew the barest smile to the surface. "How did you escape the trees?"

"I awoke this morning, dealt with them, and flittered. Okay?" She scrubbed the dirt from her arms, and even her movements were snippy. "How else would I do it?"

"How did you deal with them? If you did. Spell it out for me."

She didn't miss a beat. Just scrubbed more dirt. "Now you demand an accounting of death and destruction? Why not let me freeze in peace?"

This girl had an answer for everything. "You awoke before this day. I know this. *Saw* this." Sometimes, when he slept, he still heard her scream. "Yet you didn't flitter off then. Why?"

Scrub, scrub, scrub. "I *have* flittered from them. Many times. They've always found me."

Guilt pierced him. Yes, he should have searched harder for her. Longer. Never should've given up. Maybe she'd fought her way free and assumed she'd killed them. "You're safe now. But why did you come to my camp? Did you seek me?" Dare he hope?

"No." She hooked a lock of damp hair behind her ear, graceful and feminine. A spark of anticipation scorched him, and he gritted his teeth. There was no reason to feel such a thing. "I planned to acquire food and clothing, nothing more." Cupping water in her hands, she splashed her face. "Can we end the interrogation already? I've shared more with you than anyone else—ever."

The admission did something strange to his insides. How lonely she must have been throughout the centuries. A sentiment he understood all too well. "Tell me what you did to Kaysar the Unhinged One, and yes, we can end it. For now."

"Very well." Red peeked at him through her lashes as a hoarse, agonized whisper left her. "I murdered his parents."

CHAPTER SEVEN

Viori huddled in the frigid water, relatively clean, shaken to her core, and frozen to the bone. But stand, revealing the shape of her body to Micah, whose hawk eye tracked her movements? No. Already he held her at a massive disadvantage. He knew more about her than her brother!

To allay the king's suspicions, she'd been forced to share some truths about her children, as well as her deepest shame. As perceptive as he was, he would've ferreted out a lie. Not that she would have told a lie, regardless. As a child, Kaysar had despised liars. The rumors and whispers she'd collected throughout the years suggested his hatred had only flourished as he'd aged.

Homesickness choked her. To be with him again…she would do anything.

Before childhood memories and unfulfilled dreams invaded, Viori focused on Micah. Kaysar's enemy—*her* enemy.

The overconfident sovereign owned everything she required. Dry clothes that weren't transparent. A store of food. Information.

He had an army at his beck and call. Incredible strength, even without the use of his glamara. For that matter, what glamara did he wield? And who was the real Micah? The boy who'd given her jewels? The warrior who'd fed her a feast and promised not to harm her? Or this one, the hardened king who pressed and pressed and pressed?

Whatever the answer, her strategy had become oh, so clear amid their conversation. Let him think he must protect her from Kaysar and "*belua*," ensuring he remained as close to her as possible for as long as possible. Track his movements. Listen to gossip around the camp. Guarantee he never struck at Kaysar—not successfully, anyway. No need to flirt.

Part of her wished to kill Micah now, now, now. End the threat he presented while she had the chance. He would never see her coming...

But his demise would do her no good. Another tyrant would surely rise in his place, resuming the war against Kaysar. Probably Pops. Norok. The awful male would demand Viori's immediate harm.

Micah sat straighter, no doubt preparing to probe for details about the death of Kaysar's parents.

Viori rushed to shut him down. "Don't forget your agreement. The interrogation ended the moment I answered your most important questions, remember?"

"*This* interrogation ended." His eyelids slitted. Considering another negotiation to kick off a second interrogation? Well, too bad. The more she shared with him, the more precarious her circumstances. If he lost faith in her and expelled her from his camp...

Unacceptable! Time to unsheathe the biggest sword in her arsenal. Sadness. "I've endured enough for one day, yes? Awakening. Gaining my freedom. Capture by a pitiless king with either a poor memory or a dishonest tongue."

Despite the insult lobbed his way, his features softened. "Very well," he said and sighed. "We'll stop. For now. I won't launch the *next* interrogation immediately after the last."

Tricky king. *Must remain on guard.*

He stood and crossed to the other side of the dwelling, where he gathered a towel and a nightgown. To her bafflement, he returned to drop the items beside the tub.

She frowned. "You tend to me?" Bitterness prompted her to add, "What, are there no other females nearby?"

"I could have another if I wanted one." He said no more, instead turning his back—but not before she witnessed the return of his tension. Wait. He had turned his *back*. Had willingly put himself in a position of vulnerability. With her, a stranger. Not a common practice for any soldier of war, especially a royal.

Confusion swamped her, the bitterness retreating. Why treat her as a trusted ally? Even a childhood pet could bite its owner when cornered. "I don't understand," she admitted softly.

"You've soaked long enough," he rasped. "Dry and dress."

Ahhhh. The crux of the situation crystallized, and her hackles rose all over again. Once she donned the scanty gown, he planned to toss her into bed. Or perhaps he merely used the garment as bait, thinking to strike *before* she dressed. "If you think to have me without a fight, you're a fool. You'll have to beat me first!"

He gave another sigh. "You are clean. The water is freezing. I do not wish you to suffer needlessly."

Did she detect a hint of exasperation in his tone? Better question: Did she dare believe his claim? "How magnanimous of you," she muttered.

Viori sprang to her feet, ready to claw if he made a single move in her direction. He didn't budge as water sloshed over the sides of the copper tub, pooling on the hard, packed earth. Keeping her eyes on him, she stripped from her sodden clothing and grabbed the towel, clutching the material to her damp body. Though she stood still, her heart raced. If he rotated the slightest degree...

But he didn't. Could he be trusted?

Who was she kidding? Trust someone only if you desired betrayal.

"Use me to balance if you must," he said, his voice little more than a growl.

He was angry now? Why?

As hastily as possible, she stepped from the water, wiped the moisture from her skin, and tugged the nightgown overhead—without using him for balance, thank you. A moan slipped out as the material settled in place. Good gracious! By far the softest thing she'd ever had the privilege of wearing…and as transparent as her soaked gown.

Despite her noises, Micah maintained his position. She announced, "All done."

Still, he didn't turn. Instead, he removed and stored his weapons, then strode to the furs, kicked off his boots, and stretched out, getting comfortable. Never saying another word. He closed his eyes, making himself vulnerable to her yet again. But…

"You're going to rest?" she gasped. "Now?"

"Not if you continue shrieking like that," he murmured, never cracking open his eyes.

Shrieking? She sputtered. "*Are* you a fool? Be honest. I mean, what if I came here to cut out your internal organs while you sleep?"

"I'll grow new ones," he told her, as confident as he was commanding. "Like you, I've endured enough for one day. Settle in and hush."

Settle in? Settle in! Hush? "I'll do nothing of the sort." As if such a thing were even possible.

"You will. Because your king commands it. And I *am* your king, Vee. By your own agreement—no, by your own *insistence*—you fall under my protection. You need me, but I do not need you."

Her king? Hardly. And oh, how the crack about their needs—or lack thereof—burned. But she had a role to play, did she not?

Viori grumbled, "I'm not tired." Of course, at that precise moment, a yawn nearly cracked her jaw.

So, she might be a little tired. But only a little! Thanks to her centuries-long slumber, she lacked stamina.

"Settle. In. And. Rest," he grated.

His voice. A cascade of shivers started at her nape and ended in her toes, leaving tingling heat in its wake. A heaviness followed, infiltrating forgotten muscles, as if preparing her body to obey. As if...no. No way he could compel the actions of others with his words, the way Kaysar did.

Right?

Right! Though like abilities often called to each other, drawing two people together. For war. Or romance. Look at her parents.

No! No reason to fear his voice either way. She had the strength to resist this king. Viori did *not* settle in. She paced at the foot of the pallet. "You expect me to share a bed with you?" she snapped. The outrage! "We're total strangers."

He huffed with irritation. "Pick a chair. The floor. I care not. The decision is yours. But be quick about it. You do not wish to provoke my ire, Red."

Oh! He chose his comfort over hers? The honored guest? A worse outrage! "I will *not* spend the night in a chair or on the floor. Give me the pallet. *You* take the floor."

"Stand there if you wish." That said, he rolled to his side, effectively ending the conversation. Because, only seconds later, his breathing leveled out.

He'd...he'd...fallen asleep. The worst outrage of all.

Why, she should slay him to prove she could—yes, perfect plan. Why not save her brother the trouble? So Norok would take Micah's place? So what? She'd kill him, too. So she would be harming a defenseless man? So. What? She'd done worse to others.

Except, she kind of sort of only wished to deal with *this*

male. The one who'd given her jewels, provided a sumptuous meal and kept his hands to himself when a naked captive stood within reach.

"Moron," she muttered, stomping to his side of the bed. If he handled the rest of his kingdom business this way, he was destined to fail against far weaker foes than Kaysar.

Did Micah truly slumber? In front of an enemy, no less? He wasn't pretending?

The absurdity of such an action! The absolute folly! Yet there he lay, unmoving. He *must* be dozing.

"You need to learn a valuable lesson—the same lesson I was forced to learn far too early in life," she muttered, testing him. "Prepare to hurt."

He didn't stir.

"I'll strike. See if I won't."

Nothing.

Well. For Viori, a threat was a promise. As she prepared to punt him in the gut, she remembered, *He promised to keep me safe.* And so far he had—even from himself. How could she do this to him?

She balled her hands into fists. She believed in like for like. Tit for tat. Most people earned their tat in a matter of minutes. He hadn't. Not yet. But he would. Wouldn't he?

Argh! She rocked to her heels, curiosity replacing irritation. When he was awake, he exuded the most piercing—and sublime—intensity, and she had trouble looking away. But even as she stared, she'd failed to take in his individual features, too firmly snared by the total package.

Shouldn't she seize this opportunity to examine his smaller details?

Canting her head, she studied him without interference for the first time. His features were softer than usual. Almost boyish. Long, black lashes curled at the ends. He possessed skin so perfectly pale, every inch seemed painted over muscle. High, sharp cheekbones. Full lips. Black scruff covered his jaw and throat and—hmm. What was this? Peeking from the neckline of his tunic was a spot of thick, raised tissue. As if he possessed a... What was the word? A scar? Yes, that was it. Scar. She'd seen them on humans. Did Micah have one? But how? He was fae. Fae didn't scar...unless they were chimeras, like Micah? Whatever chimeras were. She still didn't know.

Curious to see if the scar extended, Viori knelt and reached out to pinch a section of Micah's tunic. Slowly, so slowly, she drew the material aside. Her heart thudded with anticipation and nerves; her fingers shook.

Had he just tensed?

Jolting to her senses, she froze. *What are you doing?* If he awoke, discovered her hands on him and demanded to return the contact...

She shuddered. Yes, shuddered. Tremors of distaste and *nothing else.* Definitely not excitement.

Scowling, she dashed from him. Obviously, she required time to regroup, her sanity teetering. But she wasn't as moronic as Micah. She wouldn't be sleeping. However, she *would* find a place to close her eyes and think, welcoming peace and common sense back into her mind.

Yes. Excellent plan. Zero flaws. She plopped into the chair—as good a spot as any—and spent far too long contorting this way and that, attempting to get comfy. No luck. With a flare of temper, she flung herself to the ground. Grumbles escaped as she tried again to find a cozy position. Gah! The dirt was too rigid. Too cold.

Only one alternative...

She peeked at Micah under her lashes. The unwise king snoozed on, undisturbed by her torture. And it was beyond irritating. He deserved whatever pain Kaysar visited upon him; he truly did.

A sharpening mood drove her to her feet again. Micah rolled

to his back, moving for the first time, flinging an arm over the side of his face. A tendril of his warmth wafted from him, enveloping her...urging her closer. And closer.

She hesitated a split second before easing onto the pallet. Which wasn't as dumb as it seemed. No, no, it wasn't dumb at all. Unlike Micah, she did the intelligent thing. She stayed aware and as far away from him as possible while remaining on the furs.

Ohhhh. As she settled more deeply into the softness, she gasped at the decadence. This was nice. Extremely nice. Bordering on divine. In mere seconds, he radiated more warmth than Laken during the totality of their relationship.

A pang of regret blossomed, fertilized by endless fury. She'd made so many mistakes in her life, but Laken might be the worst. Trusting someone, putting her heart in his palm, only led to squashing. Yet, knowing this, she couldn't stop herself from inching closer to the mighty king of the Dusklands. Merely the tiniest bit, though, and oh, so careful not to wake him. Very much worth the risk. Hmm. Much better.

She burrowed in place, ready to do her thinking...except, being nearer to him first might not be such a terrible idea. Stealing a bit more of his warmth could only aid her coming thought processes.

Viori scooted closer. And closer. Yes, yes. She'd made the right decision. She could literally *feel* herself getting smarter. When her arm grazed Micah's, she stiffened in horror and groaned in pleasure. In unison. Too close! Not close enough! His skin had the same effect as a branding iron, singeing her. And he smelled like citrus and flowers. The bouquet she'd scented too long ago.

Even as her mind warred over distance and desire, she curled into his side and moaned, content. Defenses toppled without warning. Before she kicked off reconstruction, a wild flurry of thoughts registered.

This man. He was, without a doubt, her enemy. And yet, she might kill to remain in this bed. His bed. With him. Not for pleasure but comfort. Only comfort. And conversation. Though gruff, he had been nothing but kind.

No, no. He simply played the part of innocent better than most. That was all. A facade he couldn't keep up for long. The truth of his nature lay in his desire to end her brother and her children. In his heart of hearts, Micah was a killer.

Well. Consider the rebuilding of her defenses completed. She didn't need conversation *or* comfort. She had her family and her purpose. Proving her worth and reconnecting with Kaysar. Micah stood in her way, so Micah was getting axed. End of story.

On instinct, she curled her fingers, preparing her nails for battle. Today, the king had encountered his downfall. He just didn't know it. He was... He...

Heavy eyelids drifted closed, and her mind faded to black.

"Up, up." A slight shaking accompanied a firm voice.

Viori nestled against the warmest, most amazing blanket in history, snug and at peace for the first time in...ever. But that blanket moved, attempting to squirm free of her weight.

"Mine," she muttered, sinking her claws into the fabric. Hmm. Since when did cotton develop so many muscles?

A hissing sound preceded the fan of breath on her ear. The sleepy haze encasing Viori's mind thinned, and she blinked open burning eyes. So bright!

Memories of a freezing bath and hot embrace flashed, and she scrambled upright. She'd fallen asleep, leaving herself unprotected? Wait. A familiar tunic caught her attention. She wasn't lying on the realm's sexiest blanket? No, oh no, no, no. She'd fallen asleep on top of *Micah*, hadn't she?

Radiating impatience, he dumped her and rose, keeping his back to her. "Get dressed. After we eat breakfast, we're taking a trip to my dungeon." He gathered a bundle of clean clothes and strode toward the exit.

Wait. "Dungeon?" she echoed, jerking upright. Had Micah discovered her true identity?

Cold, hard reality settled in, the tail end of the dream haze waning. A trip to a torture chamber? A prison cell? Allow herself to be abused and confined? Never. "You'll have to beat me to death first!"

He paused with one foot out of the tent, the muscles in his shoulder bunching. "What is it with you and beatings? No, you know what? Don't tell me. Next time, do us both a favor and remember my vow when you doubt my intentions instead of assuming the worst of me." That said, he was gone, taking his furnace of a body with him.

As if his vow had anything to do with anything! He would break his word the moment he learned of her connection to Kaysar. He— Wait. If he knew she and Kaysar were siblings, he would have grabbed the nearest set of chains, not left her to her own devices. No, he wasn't planning to incarcerate her.

Relief deflated the bubble of panic. She hadn't been found out. Her plan rolled on, making her a fae on a mission, with a specific purpose. Learn and sabotage.

On her feet, she marched to the desk, where a bowl of fresh water had been placed next to an array of toiletries. But, to her left, she noticed an extensive selection of pastries and jams waiting on the maps table. Her tongue thickened. *Food. Hungry.*

Viori stumbled over and dived in, gobbling up the treats. Even the crumbs. No more? She searched for even the smallest morsel. Alas. Far from appeased, she returned to the water, washed her face, cleaned her teeth and combed her hair, then donned the pink gown left by the servants. Not a color she'd ever worn before. Had Micah selected it for her, or chosen blindly?

Silly question. What did the answer matter? She'd made her decision and chosen her course. She had no interest in garnering his admiration. She wanted his war plans, not his heart.

Although, winning his heart might be a wise move. Beyond

wise, actually. Possibly brilliant. Win his heart and earn his trust. A valuable commodity indeed. A male who trusted her would *willingly* share his war plans.

Yes, yes. She could do this. Perhaps the quickest path to victory, after all. Though she wasn't the only female in the vicinity—she gnashed her molars—she had wiles. So many wiles! She'd learned from the best. Honestly, she had only to follow Laken's example. Use her outward appearance to make her target stupid. Charm and flirt. Dangle the carrot and pretend to care. Boom. Micah would happily share his deepest secrets. Then she could destroy him the way Laken had destroyed her. Simple. Easy.

That series of internal twinges means nothing.

As if her musing had summoned him, Micah whooshed through the canvas flap, entering the shelter. "Are you—" he scanned the tent "—ready?" His voice broke when he spotted her. His eyes widened, and his jaw dropped.

Oh yes. She could win him.

Instantly drunk on feminine power, Viori scanned him from head to toe. Slowly. She lingered on his hardest parts. "I'm definitely ready."

He swallowed, his throat bobbing. When she held his gaze, shock registered on his expression, then a reluctant, grudging admiration. The same transformation he'd undergone *every* time they'd locked eyes. It never failed to thrill her, and she suspected she might be a wee bit addicted.

"I should have offered you a proper greeting when I first awoke, Majesty. Allow me to remedy my mistake." She wet her lips, and he groaned, the sound reverberating deep in her core. Using her sultriest voice, she said, "Good morning, Micah. I'm *very* glad to see you…"

Micah was taken aback. *The way she looks at me.*

The woman nigh devoured him with her glittering gaze, as

if he were merely a slab of roasting meat but...he didn't hate it. Or the changes in her scent. Mmm. Did he detect peaches now? And what of her smile? How did a simple twisting of cherry red lips ever appear so diabolical?

The freckled beauty before him would do anything to get what she wanted.

Sweat popped up on his brow, and he tugged at the neckline of his tunic. "Good, um, morning, Vee." He forced himself to look anywhere but at his beautiful captive. To ignore the desire suddenly clawing at his insides.

"Enter," he called when shadows crossed the door flap.

Servants pushed inside, one after the other, each carrying a tray of food to replace the pastries his new charge had consumed. More fruits, breads, meats and cheeses, pilfered from Kaysar and Cookie. After placing those trays on the table, the group swiftly exited.

Red bounded over as if she hadn't eaten in weeks and dived into the meal before Micah had a chance to offer her a chair, much less the choicest pieces. A reverenced custom in the Dusklands. A show of honor between a warrior and his woman. Something he'd never experienced. Though Red wasn't his woman—

The clawing worsened, blanking his thoughts.

"Mine," Vee growled when he inadvertently shifted in her direction. She threw out her arms, protecting the food.

"Half the meal is for—" Oh, why bother? Appeasing her appetite would bring him more satisfaction than appeasing his own. Of that, he had no doubt. "Enjoy," he said.

By the time she finished the last crumb half an hour later, he wanted to pat himself on the back—and punch himself in the face. Had he ever witnessed a more titillating or heartbreaking display? She licked and savored her favorite foods. Twittered and chirped at him, at ease and yet also on edge, as if on the lookout for trouble—but only as long as he sat statue still. Any sudden movements led to a spike of tension and all ease fled. To have such highly developed defenses, she must have endured worse treatment than he'd imagined.

"All right," he croaked. "Time to visit the dungeon."

She tensed up again. "Why?"

"Norok captured two traitors, and we're going to check on them." Micah received words mere minutes before he'd forced himself to awaken Vee. Before then, he'd foolishly, ashamedly basked in her softness. "I must touch you in order to flitter with you. May I?" he asked, shaking off a sense of dread and striding forward, extending his hand in her direction.

She leaned toward him, as if welcoming the connection. Just before contact, she hissed and clawed his face before jumping back.

He paused and wiped blood from already healed wounds, certain the superficial cuts hadn't left marks. "A simple yes or no would have sufficed."

She lifted her chin. "I'd rather walk, thanks."

Walk, simply to avoid touching him? She rejected his handling *now*, after snuggling against him throughout the night? After calling *him* "mine," sinking those little white claws into his pectorals to keep him pinned beneath her? Actions that *still* set his cells on fire. Earlier, he almost hadn't rallied the strength to leave her without kissing those cherry lips first.

Anger and resentment sparked. "I am king, and I say we will flitter."

Her diabolical smile made another appearance. "My apologies. I was wrong to attack you. And snap commands. After all, you are His Almighty Highness, aren't you? Yes, you are. Had I not been...affected by your nearness, I might have mentioned a stroll will allow us to spend more time together. Doesn't a stroll sound nice? We can get to know each other better."

From shrewish to acquiescent, to facilitate his capitulation? How desperate did she consider him? "No walking," he grated.

His preferred tone with her, he realized. "We'll flitter. Besides, you know everything you need to know about me."

Walking her to the dungeon would cause too many problems. Namely, revealing an entrance to the underground maze only Micah and the Adelina siblings comprehended how to navigate. Not even the trolls remembered, though Micah had forced them to dig the myriad of corridors and chambers while mining the plethora of unique stones and metals he used to this day; they'd forgotten the moment he'd issued the command to do so.

"Very well." Fire all but crackled in Red's eyes as she offered her hand to him, choosing to remain acquiescent. "By the way," she offered sweetly. "Appreciate the heads-up that you aren't worth learning more about. I'd wondered."

He worked his jaw. If only he could leave her behind. But she was to be his constant companion today. She had insisted, and he had agreed.

Motions jerkier than intended, he linked their fingers. With only a thought, Micah teleported his charge to the cell that contained his captives. Fayette and Diane. Iron chains bound their arms above lolling heads. Sweat soaked their skin and drenched their garments.

Diane's grim expression brightened when she spotted him. "Micah, Micah," the exquisite strawberry blonde cried, hope dripping from the undertone. Her bedraggled appearance, so different from her usual flawlessness, struck him as oh, so wrong. "Please! I didn't mean... I was confused... I'm so sorry."

He clung to his calm as if it were a sword required for battle.

"Micah. Please. I'll never do this again, I swear it. I'll be so good, do anything you desire." Her attention slid to his companion, and she whimpered. Tears trickled down her cheeks. "Y-you found my replacement."

Vee stiffened, and Micah inwardly cursed.

He looked to Norok, barking, "Explain."

The warrior stood between the detainees, his chin lifted high, his shoulders squared and his arms anchored behind his back. A stance of pride. He peered somewhere over Micah's shoulder, not even sparing Red a glance. "Minutes to midnight, the pair dived into a lake near the palace. Once I saved them from drowning, I transported them here and followed protocol, chaining them and administering a dose of our strongest venom."

The venom. Extracted from a rare triple-headed snake. It did more than cause unending agony; it prevented its victims from using their glamaras, no matter the stones strapped to their bodies. The punishment for conspiring with an enemy and betraying their king. Until an antidote was given, their pain would continue to increase. Soon, both women would beg for death.

Micah disregarded a twinge of unease. "Excellent job."

"Don't you wish to know how I won Diane to my cause?" Fayette asked. The pretty brunette slurred her words, thanks to hours of agony.

"I do not." He understood how. She had convinced his mistress he would lose the war. Had probably pushed pictures of his defeat into the other woman's mind. An ability wielded by most oracles, and Fayette's area of specialization, her talents surpassing any other he'd come across. No one else took clips from various visions, fused them together, then twisted them to present a lie. A painful process for her, especially if the recipient resisted, but he had paid her well to do it.

"She tricked me, Micah," Diane burst out, able to stay quiet no longer. "Confused me."

"You *let* yourself be confused." If she had trusted him over a vision, she would be tucked safely in her bed. "You'll get no mercy from me."

Fayette laughed, blood on her teeth. "Would you like to see what's coming for you, Majesty?"

"Keep your visions." For years, he'd depended on her talents, permitting her to push images into his head. He smiled.

"Or try to force one." His mental barricades were more layered than most.

"Your loss." Like the mistress, the oracle slid her red-rimmed eyes to Vee. Another laugh bubbled up as she returned her attention to Micah. "But be warned. Such nice packaging cannot hide the condition of a rotted heart for long. She'll betray you, and you'll suffer for it. You'll deserve every second of your misery."

She dared to paint *him* as evil? As if Micah hadn't treated her like a cherished member of the royal house since the day he'd discovered her in a village, beaten, starved and chained, at the command of a malicious viceroy.

Had he treated her *too* well? Had she tricked herself into believing he would never retaliate against a former ally? That he possessed no real malice? No taste for follow-through when a lady delivered the blow of treachery?

Did Red believe the same? *Would* she betray him in some way?

What did he really know about his seductress? Other than she was temperamental, combative and rebellious at every turn. But also brave, resilient and amusing. Mysterious and unpredictable. Never not hungry. Not exactly honest. Bewildering. Another word for confusing.

His words came back to haunt him. *You* let *yourself be confused.*

Not knowing what else to do, he tugged Vee in front of him and gripped her shoulders, putting her face-to-face with the prisoners. "Red, I'd like you to meet my former oracle and my former mistress."

"Okay. So, I've met them." Pique saturated her tone. "Help me out. What point are you trying to make here?"

He'd started this, and he would finish it. "I thought my new captive should see what happens to someone who plots against me."

CHAPTER EIGHT

There was no reason to ponder the king's warning; Viori had no intention of being found out. By the time he unraveled the depths of her duplicity, she would be far away. And he would probably be dying.

Micah returned her to the tent, released her and strode to his desk, where he sat, scouring his maps. "Tea," he called, and it wasn't long before a servant entered with a steaming cup of an odorless liquid. The king drained it, and out went the servant.

"You aren't the only thirsty fae in town, you know," she muttered, but he never glanced up. No, he ignored her completely.

The oracle had inferred Viori would betray him. An accurate prediction. But she hadn't worried because *the oracle* was a traitor in Micah's estimation, and he shouldn't believe anything she said—in theory. But what if he did?

As the rest of the day progressed, she observed him amid a cocoon of silence, unsure how to proceed. Her attempt at subservience had led to a veiled threat and possibly an accusation of duplicity. Flirting had earned her a couple scowls. This was day two in camp, and she was learning nothing about the leader or his war with Kaysar.

The king remained at the desk, oblivious to the world unless he summoned a specific soldier. Those soldiers brought stacks of paper. Documents she wished she could read. Alas, she'd never had an opportunity to learn.

At some point, Viori moved to the bed, where she lounged, thinking to work up a new plan of action. An hour passed, and she decided nothing. So, she paced. Moved trunks for no reason other than boredom. Devoured any meal brought in by servants, leaving nothing for the king.

She hoped to elicit a complaint from him, at the very least. When that failed, she asked questions.

"What are you doing?"

"Are you done yet?"

"Why are you treating me as though I'm guilty, when I've done nothing wrong?" Yet.

He disregarded her existence, only pausing from his studies to drink more tea. He stayed as removed from his emotions as yesterday when he'd met with Kaysar.

"Fine. Be that way," she snipped when frustration got the better of her. Did he look up? No. "Your loss. I'm great company." At least, her army of adoring children thought so.

Would Kaysar believe the same when he got to know her? Not that it mattered. Nope. Not even a little.

Still no response from Micah. No *Thank you for understanding, Red*. No *Do you need anything, Vee?*

"You are such a troll." The worst insult she could dish. "I mean that from the bottom of my heart, and I hope you know that."

What seemed to be a thousand hours later, her host rose from the desk and stalked to a new porcelain basin filled with fresh water. Must have been delivered while they were visiting the dungeon. After scrubbing his face, he removed and stored his weapons, then kicked off his boots. His bedtime routine, apparently.

"I'm ready for bed," he said, climbing into the furs and clos-ing his eyes without bothering to glance in her direction.

This again? *Such* an annoying male. "Is this how it's going to be while we're together? You work and I occupy myself? Be-cause I've honestly had a better time being sized up for a spit by a horde of centaurs." Or being chased down an alley by a meth dealer.

More silence. Buzzing with irritation, Viori settled onto the furs as far away from Micah as possible. Her eyelids grew heavy too quickly. Tonight, she would *not* cuddle up to him. No matter how deliciously warm he was. Not again. It was her last thought before drifting off…

"Rise, Red. Now."

At the sound of Micah's rough voice, Viori jolted to aware-ness and discovered she had indeed draped herself over him a second time. Cheeks burning, she scrambled to her knees, sev-ering contact. "Really, Your Highness. You've got to stop bur-rowing your way underneath me. It's unseemly. Whatever will your people think?"

From his position on the pallet, he scoured a hand from the top of his brow to the thicker-than-usual stubble on his jaw, erasing his expression—or trying to. He couldn't mask the tight-ness around his eyes or douse the flames inside them. Couldn't hide the soft lips he'd compressed into a thin line, or the stub-born slant of his chin.

Tremors invaded her limbs. Was she making progress with her flirtation—without flirting? Did he desire her, as she'd pre-viously suspected? Did he crave her specifically? Or was she merely a receptacle right now? The female currently available?

Viori buried her claws in the sheet rather than his face. "Let's try this again. Good morning, Micah," she said as cheerily as she was able. "Please assuage my curiosity. Am I worthy of con-versation today?"

"When I have orders for you, I suppose you are." He rose from the pallet, his dark hair a mess and his clothing wrinkled.

"We're going to be spending a lot of time together. Shouldn't we *try* to be friends?" A friend. Not something she'd ever had. Not something she could ever afford. She ignored the tide of longing. "Well?"

"No." He splashed water on his face. Cleaned his teeth. Gathered clean clothes. Finally, he glanced at her over his shoulder, his eyes narrowed. But it wasn't anger or upset he projected.

Oh yes. This male desired her specifically. Exactly what she'd hoped. A delightful turn. For her mission. *Breathe. Just breathe.*

"Wh-what?" she stuttered when his stare persisted.

"You are an enigma."

Though her cheeks burned, she pretended she knew the meaning of the word. "How dare you. I am no such thing."

Blink. The semblance of a smile. "You think you are easy to understand?"

"Easy to— Oh. Um. Yes?" She gulped, hot shivers pricking her skin. Flutters ignited in her belly. Suddenly she didn't know what else to say.

"Hmm." He stepped behind a privacy screen.

Whoa. Hold up. A privacy screen? *That's new.* Relief warred with disappointment. She hadn't intended to dress in front of him, but she'd kind of looked forward to watching him dress in front of her. The muscles hidden beneath his tunic...

As garments rustled, her breath jammed in her throat. How should she handle Micah today? Flirting more and encouraging stronger desire now struck her as...risky. But oh, how she coveted his secrets. And only his secrets. The fizz of excitement sprang from thoughts of success—of reuniting with Kaysar— and no other reason.

"Micah," she purred. "I'm happy to draw you a map of my needs and wants to aid your understanding." Or perhaps a bit more flirting couldn't hurt. "I know how much you love to study your maps."

Her bottomless pit of a stomach growled before he responded.

"Eat," he commanded, his tone giving nothing away.

"Well. If you insist." She scanned the area— Yes! A feast was already spread over the table. What a glorious sight. But also annoying. How many servants had entered the dwelling without her knowledge, while she dozed atop their exalted king?

A worry for later. Viori hurried over and devoured the meal, lest anyone arrive and think to steal a morsel for themselves.

When Micah walked over and snagged the last delicacy from her death grip, she almost stabbed him with a fork. Then an ember of guilt singed her. Shouldn't she share *something* with her host? He'd eaten so little. And she *was* in the process of charming him.

"Clean up," he commanded, then tossed the small croquette into his mouth.

"Why?" she asked with a pout she couldn't contain. "So you can spend another day showing off your dungeon and ignoring me? Pass."

"We'll be venturing somewhere new today."

Really? A chance to further her cause! Bubbling with triumph, Viori hurried to wash and change into the yellow gown.

When she abandoned the screen, Micah looked her over and gulped before giving a clipped shake of his head.

"Shoes," he announced.

Don't waste time arguing. Shouldn't give him a chance or reason to change his mind about our adventure. "Whatever His Majesty desires, of course." *Most importantly, don't cringe.* Too late.

Grumbling under her breath, she padded back to the screen. She'd noticed the footwear, but she'd hoped *he* wouldn't notice the lack.

Viori tugged on the boots. Such heavy soles. Ugh. She wrinkled her nose. How uncomfortable. If she considered anything but her cramped toes, she would be shocked.

"Come." Micah wrapped an arm around her waist and ushered her outside, past the guards, then released her. He didn't take her hand to ensure she stayed close. Nope, he marched through camp, expecting her to follow or be left behind.

She couldn't bring herself to care—much—about his disregard as a cool, crisp morning breeze caressed her face. *Like coming home.* Boots and toes faded to the background of her thoughts, and she shed the remaining vestiges of her bad mood fast. "How long have you lived here?" she asked, all but running to keep up with him.

"Almost a year. The entirety of my truce with King Kaysar."

"Not long then." Barely a blip when you lived centuries. "Why does your tone suggest *forever*?"

"A single day at this site proved too long."

Oh, oh. Did she detect a wealth of bitterness? "Is that because you're a chimera?" A girl had to try.

He might have rolled his eyes. "A chimera is someone with two glamaras."

Are you kidding? "What a blessing!" Twice the power? Talk about amazing. Except, he planned to use those two glamaras against Kaysar. Not good. Not good at all.

"Blessing? The abilities constantly clash, neither working correctly until one supersedes the other. And only for a short time."

"What abilities—"

"No more questions," he interjected.

Fine. "Subtle hint taken." Lapsing into silence and hating that he was so interesting, she scanned her surroundings. A part of the camp she hadn't seen before. Busy, bustling fae went about their day. The morning sun bathed the stretch of flatland, turning what should have been a dismal site into a beautiful fantasy. The dirt-covered ground gleamed like dark, molten gold, reminding her of Micah's eyes. Tents of varying colors rippled in a soft breeze. Nothing like the towering buildings in New York, with metal cars zooming between them. Thankfully, she hadn't spent much time there.

Now, curious people glanced at Micah, only to jerk their attention elsewhere. Anyone who noticed Viori inspected her at their leisure. And clearly found her lacking.

She bristled, ready to lash out, until she caught a whiff of the roasting spices and simmering stews coating the air. Despite her recent meal, her mouth watered.

"When do we eat lunch?" Had she slurred her words? Was she drooling? "And will we get to sample everything made by everyone? Because we should. You *are* the king."

"We?" He cocked his head at her, one brow lifted in amusement. "The cooks aren't working on lunch. A hunting party raided palace lands and only returned an hour ago. The catch exceeded expectations, but it must tenderize. What you smell is dinner."

Dinner. "Eight to twelve hours from now. Basically, the equivalent of *almost a year* in your world." A whimper escaped.

"I will satisfy you before then," he offered gruffly.

Her heart skipped a beat, her thoughts swerving straight to the bedroom. Parts of her tingled as if to say, *Yes. Do it.*

Goodness gracious. Viori steered her mind to her mission. Gaining information. Like…palace lands. Had her captor violated the truce with his raiding party?

"Do the hunters venture out often?" To the left, another party gathered, warriors congregating together, each loaded with weapons.

Micah grunted. No more, no less. Which meant…what?

Frustrating male. Did anyone's mood plummet faster?

Another sight snagged her as they marched on. Norok, holding an ebony beauty by the waist. The pair stood between two tents, enveloped by thin shadows unable to conceal them. He grinned as he bent his head and whispered something in her ear. By the time he finished, she was grinning, too, and wrapping her arms around his neck.

So, he didn't spend every waking minute nabbing redheads for his king.

Throughout the rest of the camp, more fae bustled, washing or corralling children. Up ahead, soldiers trained with swords, spears, whips and daggers. Preparing for the coming war with Kaysar?

Well. That just wouldn't do.

Micah bounded off without warning, startling a scheme right out of her head. He approached a grandmotherly fae who struggled under the burden of an overlarge wicker basket overflowing with laundry. "Allow me," he said, redistributing the basket's weight.

The elder paled and tendered a brittle smile, keeping her gaze on the ground. "Thank you, Your Majesty, but I have no need of assistance." Hiding her face behind hanks of frizzy silver, she hurried off.

Micah stood in place, unmistakable pride stamped into every inch of him. *Injured* pride. Viori wasn't sure what sensation sparked within; she was only certain something did, in fact, singe her chest.

She glared at the woman's back. *If I sing the laundry to life, she'll accept whatever help she can get.*

Whoa. Anger? Here, now? On Micah's behalf? Ridiculous! Besides, his gesture of kindness was nothing but a show. An endeavor meant to impress—or trick—his captive into relaxing her guard.

He jerked his fingers, waving Viori closer. She hesitated, then trudged the distance, rejoining her mysterious host.

Host? No. Enemy. Yes. Best she remember that fact.

When she stood at his side, he didn't immediately stalk off, as she expected. Instead, he searched her eyes. She searched his, too, wishing he wasn't quite so beautiful. His features... Did she perceive a hint of vulnerability? The barest softening?

Whispers roses around them. "Look at that scarlet mane."

"She slept in his tent, you know?"

"Is she the new paramour?"

"The king would never choose someone so unrefined."

"Are you certain? He's a chimera."

Her cheeks burned. Unrefined? Unrefined! *Viori?* She was plenty refined! Not that she cared what anyone believed. Micah's citizens meant less than nothing to her. But why had the speaker used such a disgusted tone when mentioning Micah's dual glamaras?

More annoyed by the second, she whipped her focus to the crowd and hissed. Most jumped, alarmed, before scurrying off. Stragglers glared daggers at her.

"Go. Now." Micah's harsh command sent the others branching off in various directions at top speed.

Viori almost followed as hotter shivers threatened to melt her bones. She heaped coals on her determination instead. Physically reacting to her captor? Unacceptable.

Remember the mission.

"Come," he repeated. He kicked into motion.

With a huff, she gave chase. When an oncoming group created a path for them, she glued herself to Micah's side to avoid the touch of a stranger.

"You never told me why you hate Kaysar," she remarked, getting back on track.

"I have *many* reasons to despise the male." Of course, he offered no more.

"Let's hear the top three." They had to start somewhere, right?

"Very well. *After* you answer a question for me." He spun in a blink, catching her by the waist. "Deal?"

Breathing became an activity of the past, the air too thick to pull into her lungs. Like honey on a melting comb. They stood frozen, staring at each other yet again. An enchantment she couldn't break. His warmth enveloped her, and his incredible scent... The power he exuded. A tide he must have banked. What glamara did he wield?

Golden sunlight played over his features, and for a moment, he projected an otherworldly aura. A hardness no being could ever have the strength to penetrate. He looked as if he'd been created for total domination. In fact, his lips were the only soft thing about him.

Her legs shook. "What is it you wish to know?"

A beat of silence. Then, "Where is your family?"

To respond or not? "I... They..."

His expression gentled. "Do they live? Or are you alone in this world?"

Why did he wish to know this? Was he, perhaps, concerned for her well-being? No, no. *A trick, remember?* "Hardly. I might be forgotten by some—" unforgivable, unwarranted bitterness and defensiveness crept into her tone as she wondered whether Kaysar ever spared her a thought "—but I'm missed by others." How worried her children must be.

Bile seared the back of her throat. She had ordered the darlings to stay in the swamp, so stay in the swamp they would unless and until she summoned them. Which she refused to do—for *their* protection.

Micah absorbed her words with a thoughtful nod. "I showed King Kaysar and his atrocious wife mercy, and they showed me treachery, murdering an entire contingent of my army in a matter of minutes. While I doctored my injured and burned my dead, the couple claimed my palace."

"Oh." The moisture in her mouth dried. His reasons for despising her brother...well. They were good. But allow him to end Kaysar's life? Always and forever no.

"Come. There's much to do." Micah swiped her hand and resumed their journey. Silence crackled between them, somehow worse than ever before. The next time he stopped was at the edge of the training field filled with shirtless, sweaty bodies. "I must train my men, so you must join me on the field. I can teach you to protect yourself."

Enter the masses? "No, thanks. I'll stay here," she replied with a shudder. Better to observe and absorb. "No need to teach me anything. I'm quite capable of defending myself. I've never lost a fight." Truth.

He turned his head, again scrutinizing her with one brow arched. "Do tell."

She wasn't offended by his reaction. Let him consider her as weak. In fact, why not throw fuel on the fires of that amusement with more truth he most certainly wouldn't believe? "I unleash rage."

His amusement brightened. "You mean your protectors jumped in and fought for you."

Her protectors. The supposed *belua*.

"No, King Beyond Wrong. Not thanks to my protectors." Not always. Yes, she did summon her children or create others at times, but only when rage failed her. The times she stood among a sizable throng of potential attackers.

"Please," Micah said, clearly amused. "Enlighten me. How do you unleash rage?"

She humphed. "I do it like everyone else. With my fists of fury."

The corners of his mouth twitched, the sight unexpectedly sensual. "I'm sure you are quite...ferocious."

She gave another humph, ignoring the flutters in her belly. He had no idea. "Since you'll be leaving my side, you should probably give me one of your daggers."

"Very well," he replied without hesitation.

What? So not the answer she'd expected.

He unsheathed a blade and laid the hilt upon her open palm.

"You trust me with this?" she asked, hanging the weapon at her waist. Or did he test her? Or both?

"I'll keep you in my line of sight and flitter to your side for the slightest need," he said, bypassing her question. "There'll be no reason for you to...unleash rage."

She nibbled on her bottom lip and batted her lashes at him, upping today's flirt. Or finally starting it. "I'll be safer if I can flitter myself, don't you think? Tell me how."

His throat bobbed. Then he shook his head and motioned to someone over her shoulder. "Vee, this is Sabot. A former viceroy, now a royal guard. He will see to your safety while I'm otherwise occupied." That said, Micah stalked off without another word.

Someone approached her from behind. She sensed him before she heard him and turned. Well. A fae with dark skin and maybe–maybe-not kind eyes. A warrior who was more than a protector, obviously. He was a monitor, meant to ensure she kept her word and stayed put. Micah might trust her with a dagger, but he didn't trust her with freedom.

What secrets could she glean from this male? "Hello," she said with a forced grin.

His muteness persisted as he kept his attention fixed somewhere over her head. She tightened her grip on the dagger. Could he ignore her if he were bleeding to death?

No, no. Reconnaissance first. She returned her focus to Micah, who never left her view as he instructed his men. When he demonstrated certain moves, muscles and sinew rippling in golden sunlight, the flutters in her belly reignited. Her pulse galloped. His pale skin flushed from exertion. Sweat beaded here and there, resembling diamonds. He never removed his shirt, like the others, but she didn't mind. The fabric strained against his bulging muscles.

Every so often, he glanced her way. His irises smoldered, and *she* flushed. *Did* he desire her?

"Not like that, unless you hope to die," he told a soldier, a split second before he swung the longest, sharpest, most lethal-looking sword she'd ever beheld. "Do you *want* to die?"

The recipient of his attack barely blocked the weapon with his own sword. "No, sir."

"Then defend yourself with purpose, not panic."

Purpose, yes. In that, they agreed. *Must maintain my course.*

New whispers snagged her, galvanizing her hackles. A collection of onlookers amassed nearby, observing the men. Well, some watched the men. Others studied Viori. The blonde who'd first bumped into her stood among them. All wore clothing as well-made as hers.

Must be ladies of the court.

"He treats the little beastie like a queen," one of them said.

A heavy weight settled over her shoulders. Little beastie?

"He never let Diane spend the night in his tent," another added. "Or any mistress, for that matter."

Diane. The lover in chains? Viori hadn't forgotten the exquisite strawberry blonde. Who'd been quite similar to Blue Dress, in fact.

Curiosity seized her. Did Micah have a type? And why hadn't he spent an entire night with a woman?

She must know. For her endgame. Only her endgame. And she could find out. These gossips had information. Why not use them to acquire it? She could be nice...for a few minutes.

Viori pasted on her best *I'm harmless* smile. "Hello." She eased forward, closing in.

Most gasped, as if fearing for their lives, and broke apart, sprinting away. Only two hung back—Blue Dress and a pretty brunette.

Irritation rose, rousing an urge to create a dozen dirt children. Then the runners could go nowhere without her express permission. And she could actually do it. Small creatures required the least amount of power. Only when she created armies of giants did she weaken.

"Do you not fear me?" she asked the pair.

The question received a snort from both, nothing more.

"I'm Elena," Blue Dress said. "Micah's…friend. I'm currently working on an assignment, so you'll see me only when I return. If I'm lucky, I won't see you at all."

Viori went on instant alert. That hesitation…what did it mean? And what was her "assignment"? Was *she* the replacement paramour? The fact that she had used her king's name rather than his title spoke volumes.

"How…interesting to meet you." Oh yes. This Elena *must* be the new paramour. Or perhaps Micah enjoyed a stable of lovers, and the betrayer had been one of hundreds.

Viori swallowed a growl. Today Elena wore a gown with roses stitched into the pale pink bodice and stems riding the length of the flowing skirt. Another sign of her exalted status.

No wonder Micah had ignored Viori's presence yesterday. The growl escaped as quiet as a whisper, but as sharp as a dagger.

"I'm Lavina." Though the other woman was inches shorter than Viori, she somehow excelled at looking down upon her. "Do you prefer to be called Red, Vee or Spy Worthy Only of Execution? Norok—my dear husband—has referred to you as each."

Norok belonged to this poor woman? Norok. As in Pops? The flirt who'd cozied up to a servant in the middle of camp? Wow. Disgust nearly choked Viori. A husband willing to betray his wife, a confidante he had vowed to love and cherish above all others, could be trusted by no one. Deceive one, deceive all. A traitor was a traitor, no exceptions.

Did Lavina know? If not, she should. "You may call me anything you like," she replied with an airy tone. "Allow me to offer my humblest apologies for not recognizing you as Norok's beloved spouse." Viori smiled sweetly. "Considering I spotted him in the arms of someone else only minutes ago."

Hurt contorted the other woman's face before fury took over. With a huff, she spun on her heel and marched off.

New sparks of guilt flared, rousing a more conspicuous surge of irritation. *Kaysar's enemies are my enemies.*

"I love my brother," Elena said, "but there's no denying he's a whore. Feel sorry for Lavina, however? No. She understood the consequences when she trapped him into their sham of a marriage."

Norok was this beauty's sibling? "The wife isn't wholly to blame." The words emerged sharper than she'd intended. "Your brother had only to stay away from her to avoid a wedding."

Elena glowered at her, but grunts and groans from the field grew louder, ending the conversation.

Viori's gaze shot to Micah of its own accord. He was staring at her again. Her, not Elena. A hand fluttered to her racing heart, and he took a single step toward her. Norok rammed into him, tossing him to the ground.

Viori's first instinct? To laugh. Her second wasn't so innocent. Pops *dared*? Why, she would tear his heart from his chest and feed the organ to the birds! She—

The other woman cleared her throat, now that the noise had died down, drawing Viori's attention anew.

As if sensing her intentions to cause harm, Elena leveled her with an expression of pure malice. "Micah is the most honorable male I've ever had the privilege of knowing. Loyal to the extreme. Honest. Hardworking and kind. I know he radiates a terrible ferocity, his presence making you wish to peel your skin from your body. But he deserves only the best."

Terrible ferocity? Peeling skin? *What?*

"He's a good man," she persisted, more intense by the moment. "The best. I love him, and I take great pleasure in eliminating any threats against him. Just as he takes great pleasure in eliminating any threats against me. Against his people."

A definite warning. But so what? Invisible armor buffed and shined, Viori puffed up her chest. Squared her shoulders. And not because of the implied insult—as if she wasn't the best. Not even because she cared that the blonde might have a romantic relationship with Micah. She didn't. Not the slightest bit. *Pleasure each other with my highest compliments.* No, threats against her and those she considered hers were not to be borne. Not now, not ever. The speaker must suffer. Always. And yet, her hands were currently tied. Harming the blonde would merely paint her in a bad light.

Cage the rage. For now.

For Kaysar.

Before any retorts spilled from Viori's tongue without permission, she sealed her lips shut and offered her choicest nontoothy smile. And yes, it felt brittle. "What Micah is or isn't has no bearing on the situation." Except it…might. To earn this kind of unwavering loyalty from another…

What if he *was* honorable? The first of his kind—a noble fae? Someone maybe, perhaps, possibly worth…keeping. A companion to lean and rely on. A friend. Something she'd secretly desired the whole of her existence. The reason she'd fallen for Laken.

For so long, she had believed such a mythical creature extinct. However, evidence to the contrary *was* stacking up. Micah hadn't harmed her. Hadn't touched her during her weakest moments. Instead, he'd fed her without complaint. Given her shelter, clothing and comfort. Guarded her. Helped her, as well as the older fae, a mere servant.

Could Viori truly destroy such a being, much less part with him? For Kaysar, yes. But what if she didn't need to?

She returned her gaze to Micah. Air lodged in her nostrils. He was staring at her again.

A flush infiltrated her cheeks, and her heart stuttered in her chest. A strange pliability spread. If he *was* honorable…what would she do then?

CHAPTER NINE

The week rolled on with startling speed, yet Viori was no closer to discerning the truth about Micah's honor. Or lack thereof. Her nerves were frayed at best.

As promised, he never strayed from her side. On the other hand, he avoided any place of importance, refusing to give her a tour of the most innocent of places, like the centaur stables. Refusing to touch her. Why, why, why?

She was no closer to locking in his affections, making her suspect his previous desire had nothing to do with her. For that matter, she had yet to discover a single detail about his war plans. Honestly, she was no closer to anything.

No, not true. She'd learned how he flittered. A small but powerful pebble. Micah wore one on a wrist cuff and often carried a spare in his pocket. What would she have to do to snag a stone for herself?

She'd tried to filch the extra one multiple times without success.

Each morning, she awoke and yes, okay, she'd had to scramble away from him in bed while pretending she hadn't unwittingly draped herself over him during the night and luxuriated in his cocoon of strength and warmth. He'd then provided her with a bath and a new gown.

Though she'd opened the door to multiple topics, he hadn't engaged in any kind of serious conversation with her. She'd smiled often, hoping to put him at ease. Ghosted her fingertips over the seam of her lips to draw attention there. Uttered suggestive phrases. He'd only grown more aloof.

Except during the suspended moments he stared at her, and she stared back. Sometimes she swore satisfaction glimmered in the depths of his eyes. Other times, aggravation. But more and more, he'd stopped glancing her way.

Viori loathed losing a battle. Any battle. Why couldn't she win this male over? What would it take? And why did she continue to play with the notion of ending the war with his surrender rather than his betrayal and…staying with him? Him. At least for a little while. No way he would ever accept her children.

So, sabotage him she would. Decision made. No more backtracking. Maybe. Probably.

"…the ambush the second the truce ends."

Uh-oh. What was this? He sat at the maps table, Norok standing at his side. They muttered back and forth before the second-in-command exited, tossing a glare in her direction.

Viori perched at a desk, pretending to read the book he'd given her. Where was this ambush to take place? What weapons did he plan to use?

"Are you hungry?" he asked. "Shall I summon a meal for you?"

Was it mealtime already? The brightest, darkest portion of her days. "No, thank you." Whenever they dined, they chatted about nothing while Micah ensured she received the tenderest of meats, the juiciest of fruits, the creamiest of cheeses and the softest of breads. As she dined, he exuded so much satisfaction *she* became light-headed—satisfaction without aggravation; she only craved more. Which made her stomach hurt! A terrible cycle.

"Not hungry? You? Are you ill?" Concern contorted his features. He dropped his papers and looked her over. "I'll summon a healer *immediately*."

"I'm fine, probably," she assured him, but he was already shouting for the camp's best physician.

A fae who tried to examine her and got clawed in the face for his efforts.

"I believe I sense that she is healthy, Majesty," the male said, swiping blood from his cheek.

"Go," a wary Micah replied, dismissing him.

Again, she caught herself wondering if he was worth keeping. If she could possibly, somehow facilitate a lifelong truce between kings, saving Micah the anguish of defeat, paying her debt to Kaysar *and* giving him more time with his wife. His new family. If she could find a way to make him love the "monsters" he hunted.

A sharp inhalation lodged in the center of Viori's chest. Her brother. Happy. Content. *As he* should *be. As he deserves.* And yet...

Her lungs deflated in a gush. For the first time, a part of her might...resent him. He'd moved on and found joy without Viori. His cup of contentment brimmed just when she had found a way to pay her debt to him. What if he had no room in his life for her?

And what if she decided to keep Micah, but he didn't want her, either?

No. No! If she wanted Micah, she could have him. Today, she would prove it. Whatever it took.

Micah's ears twitched as water splashed. An innocent sound. Unless his captive was involved.

He scrubbed his face with the palm of his hand. Red currently bathed behind the screen he'd acquired, preparing for bed. She moaned in delight, and he did his best to ignore the blistering arousal rampaging his veins. She'd been like this for hours. Not bathing—that had started endless minutes ago—but *softer*. Almost needy.

How many times had she grazed her nails against his skin or ensnared his gaze, making his heart race? How often had she traced her lips with the tip of her little pink tongue? He was never not rock-hard and throbbing. Whether in her presence or away from her. Circumstances no longer mattered.

Again and again, he mentally chanted Erwen's rules. *Do no harm to the innocent. Protect what's yours. Always do what's right. Never be without a backup plan.*

A lesson he'd learned well. Without a backup, you might not live long enough to regret its lack. The very reason he'd enslaved the trolls. With Red, however, the backup—ignoring her presence—failed him at every turn. He remained aware of her minutest action, some hidden part of him weaving long-lost dreams with new found desires. A danger in a variety of ways.

He knew better than to crave a bed partner of his own. Especially an unpaid one. Especially *this* unpaid one. Already he'd begun to anticipate—or fear—her loss. Fear was an enemy more treacherous than Cookie, more devious than Kaysar. Fear was the downfall of Micah's ability to subdue and control beasts.

"Mmm." With a throaty voice, Vee told him, "The water feels so good against my bare skin, Micah. Want to feel it?"

The water or her golden skin?

No. No! He needed to get out of here before he acted how he shouldn't. "There's something I must do. I've stationed men outside. You're safe here."

"Wait. What? You can't be serious."

Micah drew in a deep breath, but he couldn't escape Red's incredible scent. "I'll return shortly."

"You can't leave—"

He flittered to the underground tunnels. The cavern filled with his trolls. His path to victory against the Unhinged Ones.

Torches lined the walls, casting golden light over the endless sea of motionless prisoners chained by his will. They stood shoulder to shoulder. Packed inside like chattel. They did not age. They did not doze. They did nothing but think.

Today, they were not alone. Norok stood upon an overhead platform, peering down upon the masses.

"What are you doing here?" Micah asked after transporting to his side.

His friend shrugged. "The end of the truce looms. I think I came to remind myself that we will win our war with Kaysar. With the trolls, we cannot lose."

Micah rested a hand on his friend's shoulder. "There's no need to worry. The clock counts down, the ambush planned."

Norok patted his hand in solidarity. "That, I know. I fear Kaysar and Cookie finding and killing our trolls before we can use them."

"The royals could send hundreds of spies, oracles and troops and they would not solve the tunnel mazes."

The underground world—and that was exactly what it was, a whole other world hidden beneath Astaria—was created long ago and wound through court after court. But no fae could flitter where they hadn't visited previously, so no one was able to materialize here.

"We will win," Norok said, confidence making his voice as hard as granite. "We've worked so hard, come so far. We'll stop at nothing." He paused. "The girl—"

"Is still not up for discussion." A statement and command, rolled into one.

Still, Norok persisted. "Will she alter your plans for the future?"

That, he could happily share. "She will not." Nothing would.

"Are you certain? I know the opposite sex better than I know my own. Trust me when I say your little Red is pure trouble."

Oh, she was trouble indeed, and Micah needed to deal with

her. Hissing at those who angered her. Issuing insults to others left and right. Eating other people's food. Only with Micah did she ever seem to relax.

Suddenly, he longed to see her as she'd been in his hallucinations. Smiling. Dancing. Carefree. Perhaps he could.

He massaged the back of his neck, unable to halt his next words. "Spread the word. Tomorrow I declare a Feast of Remembering." A time Dusklanders wiped any obstacles from their minds and reminded themselves that they were fae, and they could do anything. "A reprieve is overdue."

This particular festival occurred only at the king's command. Meaning any moment, for whatever reason he decided. In the past, Micah had declared a Feast of Remembering when he'd hoped to encourage his people. This time, his people were far from his mind. He wasn't sure what prompted his actions.

Liar! His own conscience issued the accusation and a verdict of guilty.

Desire for Red had raged in his blood, and there was no denying it. To strip her when she rolled on top of him in bed. To touch and to taste. To hear her cries of passion in his ears. An impossibility.

Despite the cost to his sanity, he treated her with the respect and honor due to a guest under his personal protection. No unrequested contact. No—or rather, few—lingering glances. No suggestive or leading comments.

In the beginning, she had reminded him of a feral cat. Distrustful, jumpy and highly defensive. When perceived insults or threats were delivered, her claws came out. Strain emanated from her most days. Most hours, really. But there were minutes when he could almost believe she desired him, too. And today's softening...

He had to turn away from his second-in-command to adjust himself. What had changed for Red? Did it matter right now?

It happened. Without obstacles…what would he want from her? What would he do?

He would act the fool, that was what, trusting her not to betray him. In this dream world without tribulations, she wouldn't be disgusted by his scarred skin—proof of a weakness he despised. He would be able to envision a future with the female he had dreamed of most of his life. A sleeping beauty who sought his strength and warmth with eager delight each night. They could be friends. Hadn't she suggested such an outcome? Perhaps they could be…more.

No perhaps. They could. This was a dream world, after all. One day, he could have a family, a home, as he still craved with the whole of his being. Something his kingdom had never been for him, though he'd wished otherwise.

The admission cut deep but with no falsehoods to impede him; he had no defenses against such an astounding truth.

"Micah," Norok began.

Did he sense Micah's own softening? "We'll talk later. Do not forget the order." He relocated to another room in the tunnels, a place Norok had not visited, guaranteeing the male couldn't talk him out of the celebration.

Only Micah had entered this hallowed space. His treasure room, filled with things he'd hoped to gift to his wife, if ever he married. Special things. Gold coins and bars. Trinkets. Goblets. Gowns. Shoes. Weapons. Enchanted objects. Books.

He selected a garment for Red and returned to the tent… where he discovered her draped in a silken nightgown, lounging across the pallet of furs, a vision—a fantasy come to life.

"There you are." She smiled as he fought to breathe, then patted the spot beside her. "I missed you. Come to bed."

She'd missed him? Him.

He stepped toward her. Stopped. Curled his hands into fists. Did she know what she asked of him? If he neared her, he might lose control. "Sleep," he said, placing the gown behind the screen.

"With you, yes?" The high-pitched question signified...what?

"No." Even the idea of settling into bed and doing nothing but holding her acted as an arrow to his gut. *Don't look at her. Don't*— He looked and almost roared. She exuded disappointment.

Disappointment. Because she wanted to be in his arms.

"I'll be nearby," he croaked.

"But—"

As his resistance to her teetered on the brink of collapse, he flittered outside and dismissed the guards.

He stood there for hours, without relief. He yearned to return, but didn't give in to the urge until a series of pained groans registered.

Micah palmed a dagger as he flittered to the bed. He geared to strike whoever dared to harm— *She is alone?* For the first time, Vee wasn't resting calmly. Mumbling pleas for help, she thrashed atop the furs. His chest clenched, and he dropped the weapon. Resistance? He had none. He tucked himself under the covers and drew her close. She sagged against him as he murmured assurances.

"I'm here," he cooed at her. Strangely, his lusts didn't overtake him. They were no match for his protective instincts. "Everything will be all right. I'll keep you safe tonight." *Every night.*

He clutched her tight, never allowing himself to drift off. She didn't stir until morning light filled the dwelling.

"Micah?" she asked drowsily, as tempting as she was vulnerable. "Couldn't stay away, hmm?"

The protective instincts slipped into the background, his deepest lusts attacking with a vengeance. *Make her scream your name.*

He rapid-blinked dry, tired eyes, then climbed from the bed. Sweat beaded on his brow, the calm exterior he strove to preserve beginning to crack. How much longer could he stop himself from seizing what he craved more than breath?

"We have somewhere to be. Dress. Behind the screen," he added as she reached to remove the nightgown in front of him. How much longer would he have the strength to avert his attention?

"Have you always been such a prude?" Red claimed the dagger he'd given her, yanking it from beneath a pillow. She went nowhere without that weapon. "You can look at me, you know."

"My sensibilities aren't the reason you should obey me right now," he grumbled.

A hint of intrigue glittered in her eyes, nearly felling him. "Well. Isn't that interesting?" Grinning as if she knew her effect on him, she tromped behind the screen to don the new gown he'd provided for her.

As fabric rustled and beads clinked, she oohed and aahed over the garment. His anticipation to see her magnified.

He hurried to wash up and change into the clothes he'd selected for himself. A tailored black tunic, slightly worn black leathers and freshly polished boots. Lastly, he brushed his teeth and combed his hair. Still, she did not emerge. Did she purposely make him wait to torment him?

"You should be nice to me today, Red."

"Aren't I always nice to you, Majesty?"

"Only when compared with your treatment of everyone else." Still as much a shock as her frequent stare.

"So, despite the great honor I pay you, you waste precious seconds complaining?" She tsk-tsked. "What's so special about today, anyway?"

"I'll tell you once you finish."

"Please. You'll be too tongue-tied to speak." Head high, she glided from behind the screen.

Tongue-tied? Yes. Wonder snatched the air from his lungs. Light adored every inch of her, highlighting the perfection of her golden skin. Those jade eyes were softer, too, while her freckles were more pronounced. Her dark red hair hung in glistening waves, framing a curvy body now draped in vivid blue studded with sapphire and diamond chips. The blade hung at her waist.

Say something. Anything. "Beautiful," he blurted out, and his cheeks flushed.

Her cheeks flushed, too, but not in embarrassment. No, she evinced delight as she held out the flowing skirt and issued a proper bow. "You really think so? You aren't pretending?"

He fought an unexpected grin. "I'm not pretending." Must she always be so adorable? But oh, this softer side…*devastating.*

Dangerous.

As if struck by sudden vulnerability of her own, she shifted from side to side and patted the fabric of her gown. "To bestow upon me a garment such as this means one of two things. You value me…or you enjoy dressing me up."

"It cannot be both?"

An almost smile tugged at the corners of her lips. "Are you often gruff and dismissive with those you value?"

"Now who's complaining about special treatment?" He pulled at the neckline of his tunic, then held out his arm. "Shall we?"

For the first time, she accepted his touch. "Don't forget you promised to explain what's so special about today. Then I get to inspect you the way you inspected me. Actually, let's switch the order and start with the examination." Her eyes slid over him. Voice thickening, she told him, "You are…delicious."

His eyes practically popped out. *He* was delicious? Him? Hot blood deserted his head, flowing south fast.

Leaving him reeling, she glided past and stopped at the table, where they usually ate their morning meal together. Or rather, where she usually ate the morning meal and he devoured her with his eyes.

"No breakfast?" she asked with a pout, making his blood burn hotter.

"Not here. This is a special occasion. The Feast of Remembering. We'll eat each of our meals with the people." Dusklanders prized their traditions. "There will be no training, only celebrating."

"A feast. Of remembering?" Her brow wrinkled. "Never heard of it."

"It is a sacred time when we wipe any obstacles from our minds, reminding ourselves that we are fae, and we can do anything."

"Okay, but obstacles to what?"

He leveled his shoulders. "To the things we want most."

"So…you celebrate your victories before you actually achieve your victories?"

"Exactly right." Long ago, during his first year as king, he had learned a hard but valuable lesson. Excuses were merely fears dressed up in a pretty package. When you looked beyond them, the answers to your questions became oh, so clear. What you desired most. The life and future you craved. "We look back and see what fear has stolen from us, then do our best to return to our destined course."

"I see."

Why did she project such sadness? What had she lost? The family she still refused to discuss?

"No obstacles. Destined course," she echoed. "Hmm." Growing pensive, she scanned the dwelling, as if seeing it for the first time. Or searching for answers she'd lost forever ago.

"What do you long for most?" he asked.

Panic bloomed over her expression. "Oh, I…"

Music and cheers sounded in the distance. Deciding to take pity on her, he extended his arm once again. "Never mind. Forget I asked. Let's go have our breakfast with the people."

"Yes. Let's." A half smile teased the corner of her mouth as she reached for him. Then she frowned and drew back. "Um, I think I'd rather stay here. You may bring me food, however."

He'd noticed her aversion to assemblies greater than two. But in this, he declined to relent. No excuses, no fears. Rather than tug her along while she dragged her feet, Micah bent, pressed his shoulder against her middle and lifted. Her body draped over his.

"You dare to haul me like a sack of potatoes?" she demanded with shock and...amusement? "The indignity!"

He entered the cool of the bright morning, a deserted campsite greeting him. Everyone congregated in the common area, feasting. He expected protests to follow Vee's question. A giggle escaped her instead. A giggle that reminded him of a purr. The most enchanting sound he'd ever heard.

Micah nearly tripped over his own feet. Then his chest puffed with pride, feeling as if he'd conquered a *thousand* enemies. He, the king who made others yearn to peel the skin from their bones, had made a beautiful feral kitten purr.

"It was either this or I flittered you," he teased, "and we both know you prefer to walk."

"You are *so* lucky I love my gown too much to unleash my rage."

Merry, fast-paced music spilled from the seams of an overcrowded area. People clustered around the perimeter of the largest tent, drinking, talking, laughing. Enjoying life, as they should.

Everyone who spotted him with the "little beastie," as they'd begun to call her, gaped. To his complete bafflement, many of those people smiled at him, as if forgetting his awfulness.

Red noticed the attention and stiffened. "What are the peasants gawking at?" she asked Micah. "Shouldn't they go about their business?"

Before she could demand someone beat her, he entered the shelter, keeping her draped over his shoulder. Legions seemed to throng the space. No humans or centaurs present, only fae. Some occupied long tables that were set in rows, each piled high with an assortment of treats and meats. Only one table defied the rows—the royal one. Positioned perpendicular to the other tables, it allowed the occupants to face the entire assembly.

Contrasting scents hit his awareness. The array of foods. Dirt. Soap. Sweat. Sweet wine. Yet nothing overshadowed Red's fragrance. The citrus he'd missed for longer than he cared to admit.

He made his way toward the only empty seat in the area—a chair reserved for him, placed between Norok and Elena. Lavina occupied the seat at Norok's other side.

The moment Micah reached the chair, Elena leaped up. So far, her spying had resulted in few nuggets of information. Kaysar and Cookie holed up in the palace with oracle Amber and nuisance Pearl Jean. Occasionally, King Jareth stayed for a week or two. The group rarely spoke of war. They played games and laughed. It was maddening.

She glared at Red's backside before nodding a greeting at her king. "If you'll excuse me, Majesty."

Without waiting for his permission, she stomped off, disappearing in the crowd. He frowned, ready to call her back. In the end, he let her go. If she picked a fight with Red, his captive might revert to her hissing ways. He'd rather hear her purr again.

Micah set her on her feet, and she immediately pressed against him, as if seeking a safe shelter. His chest tightened as he helped her into her seat, then claimed the one next to her. She kept her chin high and her defenses up, challenging anyone to approach.

"Don't mind my sister," Norok told him, patting him on the shoulder without peering up at him. "She's certain your little Red is nothing but destruction." He didn't attempt to filter his volume, his voice booming. "I, on the other hand, have decided to embrace the celebration and tolerate her presence. Anyone who distracts you enough to allow me to topple you—twice—can't be too bad."

Micah slung an arm around the back of Red's chair, delightfully surprised when she leaned into him.

"One day I'm going to flay the skin from your second-in-command, just for the fun of it. See if I don't," she said conversationally. With an innocent smile, she popped a grape into her mouth. "The male rubs my nerves the wrong way."

He fought another grin. "He rubs *everyone's* nerves the wrong way," he announced, causing Norok to snort. "Would you agree to let me teach you how to use a bow and arrow if we use him as the target?"

"I'll *demand* you teach me," she responded promptly. "Oh, will you, Micah? Pretty please?"

The grin broke free. "I'll consider it."

"As if a few arrows will stop this bird from soaring." Smiling wide for the first time since Warren's death, Norok patted Micah's shoulder. "I'm undefeatable."

The change in his second pleased him greatly. What a great day this was turning out to be. He should have enacted a feast days ago.

"By the way, there's something changed about you." The smile faded as Norok pursed his lips. "Did you cut your hair? No. Trim your scruff? No. Oh, what does it matter? Now that you've arrived, the real fun can begin." He raised a goblet to the entire tent. "Where are my pleasure seekers? Line up, line up!"

New cheers rang out. The multitude shifted, unmated males hurrying to line up before Micah's table, unpaired women scrambling to line up *beside* it. Old and young. Rich and poor. Quiet descended fast.

"Oh! Is this the execution queue?" Red asked, clapping with excitement. Her voice rang out, drawing horrified gazes her way. "If so, I'd like to offer a suggestion for its head. And its tail."

Micah believed she meant the words in jest as much as a threat, and he had to battle another grin.

Norok snorted. "You'll not ruin my good mood. For your information, I'm expressly forbidden from joining the fun. Apparently only unattached males may participate."

"Unattached, you say?" She gazed at Micah with astounding curiosity. "You, the king, take no part, either?"

A burn traveled the length of his spine, radiating to his limbs. "I do not." Hopefully she would allow the subject to drop.

"Have you ever?"

He rubbed a constricted spot on his chest. "I have."

"Not since becoming king," Norok piped up. He inclined against Micah's side and popped a large grape into his mouth, mimicking Red. "Our Micah chooses not to participate any-more. Not since the eligible ladies of our village left him standing for two years in a row. Although, those lines were for marriage, rather than a single night."

A growl brewed in Micah. Norok had a big mouth when he imbibed.

"I see," Red repeated, pensive.

As the festivities continued, one female coming forward at a time to select her companion, Micah stared straight ahead, his eyes slitted. Red watched him. He sensed it—gloried in her awareness in the marrow of his bones.

To his amazement, she edged closer and rasped in his ear, "If there were truly no obstacles today, I would pick you for the night."

His head whipped in her direction. Then he recalled her pro-pensity for snuggling. "This, I know. You like to use me for warmth."

"Yes, that's true. But tonight I would demand so much more."

He swallowed hard. Would she now? "Tell me the obstacles I must overcome." What would he do to have her, if only for a few short hours?

He thought he might do anything.

She leaned forward and brushed the tip of her nose against his. "End your war with Kaysar before it begins. Offer your sur-render, and I'm yours."

CHAPTER TEN

Stiffness invaded Micah's limbs, his deepest suspicions flaring. He glared at Red, who continued to hold his stare, unwavering. Kaysar was the type of male who punished anyone for any perceived crime. If he knew this female had killed his parents, he would not stop pursuing her until her head decorated his mantel—or Micah removed his head.

He easily imagined what had happened with Red and the depraved king's sires. No doubt *belua* had murdered the couple in defense of their sleeping beauty, and now Vee carried the blame. But why request *this*?

"You wish to spare the sadistic king who swore revenge against you?"

"No, you big dummy." She cupped his cheek, keeping his face angled toward hers. A willing touch, offered of her own free will. Soft and gentle, yet also demanding, with her sharp nails ready to pierce his skin at the slightest provocation. "I wish to spare *you*."

Oh. Ohhhh. Air burst past his lips, a sun seeming to dawn inside his chest. She sought to protect his life. *His*. Because she considered him delicious and hoped to…be with him? An out-come beyond his wildest imaginations.

Intoxicated by the notion, he nuzzled into her palm. *Not enough. Want more.* He turned in his chair and bracketed her legs with his own, caging her in. "You have nothing to fear from Kaysar. Not for yourself, and not for me. I'll win the war against him, I assure you."

As he spoke, she ogled his mouth as if she craved a taste. "Should you be indulging your confidence, Your Majesty? I be-lieve your former oracle tried to advise you otherwise."

Did she crave his kiss? Without payment? Every cell in his body became hyperfocused on fulfilling such a desire. He must make her understand his viewpoint *immediately.* "Free will af-fects an oracle's visions. Meaning, those visions are constantly subject to change." Gripping the flare of her hips, he urged her closer. Closer. "Ask anything else of me, and I'll do it."

Bending into him, she brushed her nose against his. A show of affection he relished—the first he'd ever received. "Why don't I explain your reward first, if you decide to indulge me?"

He nuzzled his stubbled cheek against her smooth skin. "Are you attempting to bribe a king?"

"Yes," she whispered, unrepentant. Jade eyes sparkling, she toyed with the ends of his hair. Perhaps the greatest sensation of all. "Is it working?"

It must be. His mind fogged. Red…*rewarding* him…kissing him. More? "What do you offer? Exactly?" Best to be clear.

She grazed her lips against his. "Anything you desire."

He sucked air between his teeth, one word rolling through his mind again and again. *Anything…*

Accept! His next inhalation scraped his lungs. No, no. He must think of more than his own yearnings. How to make this female understand? "Trust me, sweet Red." *Please.* "There are legions of trolls awaiting my command. Their numbers are in-calculable, their ability to destroy unfathomable. When the truce with Kaysar ends, there won't be a war. There will be an anni-hilation." He combed his fingers through her silken hair. "The moment I accepted responsibility for your well-being, the Un-hinged One ceased being a threat to you. He has no defenses against me—he just doesn't know it yet."

Micah's threat echoed in Viori's head. Her first instinct? To strike out and stop him now, now, now. Let him harm her brother? Never! But. This was the Feast of Remembering. She was a mighty fae, and nothing was impossible for her. And, if nothing was impossible, she had no reason to cave to anger. Anger wasn't the best path to take, anyway. Especially on a day without obstacles.

No obstacles, no fears to shield her deepest desires. In a per-fect world, she would...what?

Easy. Forge a lasting relationship with Kaysar. Save her chil-dren. Promote peace with the male she suspected she might... like. Micah wouldn't loathe her when he discovered her con-nection to Kaysar and the "monsters" he wished to slay. No, her delectable host would want only to make her happy. She could belong to him, and he could belong to her.

Was such a life even possible? Maybe? If she fought for it?

So why not fight? No one had a better chance at victory than Viori. Despite the odds stacked against her! Perseverance had kept her alive as an orphaned child, and perseverance could see her through this.

"Do I receive my reward? Because of my strength and cun-ning?" Micah asked, needy and hopeful. Leaning in... "With-out surrender?"

Her chest constricted, the eager king eliciting the same need-iness and hope inside her. She should resist, yes? At least until he agreed to her terms?

"Vee," he breathed against her lips. He was so big he blocked out the rest of the world.

Shivers rocked her against him. "Perhaps you *should* get a reward." For one night... No obstacles, no thoughts. Only pleasure. The pulse in her throat jumped. Oh, how she missed pleasure. "Not everything, but something."

Peering at her through the thick shield of his lashes, he rasped, "What will you give me?"

She scooted closer, all but climbing into his lap. "What if I offer you one night to do your best to convince me to see things your way—while I do my best to convince you to see things *my* way?"

His pupils expanded, reminding her of ink spilling over parchment covered in erotic artwork. "I might refuse."

When she flinched—ouch!—he added, "I'd want more."

Ohhhh. A slow smile bloomed, anticipation burning through her. "Since I intend to win, I would definitely consider giving you more."

"May I speak with you, Micah?" A familiar voice shattered the illusion of seclusion.

Irritation flared, hot and sharp. Viori stiffened and eased into her seat. Elena had returned just as events had taken a titillating turn. Micah desired her *greatly. Her.* Not Blue Dress. But, um, why was everyone now watching the king with varying degrees of shock and awe, as if seeing him for the first time? Some even smiled at him. With fondness. Before this, everyone only glowered at him.

To his credit, Micah appeared as annoyed by the interruption as Viori. "Unless someone is dying—"

"They might be," the other female stated with a flat tone. "The prisoners are missing."

"What!" He sprang to his feet, his hands fisting. Everyone around him quieted, smiles erased. Norok paled.

Viori's mind whirled. Missing? How unfortunate. She'd hoped to question both the oracle and the mistress at some point to uncover their secrets. As much time as she'd spent with Micah, there'd been no opportunity.

Disappointed, she drained her goblet. Oh, wow, what an amazing flavor. Smooth, sweet and rich, settling in her stomach as if created to be there.

Lavina rubbed Norok's shoulder. A gesture of comfort, but he shrugged her off, telling Micah, "I locked the two up securely. They couldn't have gotten free on their own—that I swear to you." Of course, his gaze strayed to Viori and slitted in accusation. So much for deciding to tolerate her.

"You caught me," she snapped. "I sneaked away without Micah or Sabot's knowledge." Speaking of, where was her guard dog? She hadn't spotted him all morning.

When Norok opened his mouth to respond, the king gave a clipped shake of his head. The second-in-command maintained his silence.

"Go to the cell and await me." Micah's hard tone allowed no argument.

Norok hesitated, then stood and flittered, vanishing.

"My brother isn't wrong. Someone had to commit this crime," Elena piped up with a pointed glance at Viori. "None of our people would dare. None of our people *can*. They've never visited the dungeon. But who knows where your little pet has been? She could've sneaked out of bed last night and—"

"Red isn't responsible for this," he interjected harshly. A statement, but also another command. The most fervent of all. Say nothing else against Viori. "She never left the shelter of my arms. This, I can guarantee."

"Never left his arms," Viori punctuated with a smirk. "All. Night." Where she'd be spending this night, too. Maybe?

Micah's shoulders rolled in. He faced her, his expression almost sad. "I must leave you, Red."

"What? Why?" She jumped to her feet, confronting him head-on. "I can help you find and catch the traitor responsible." And question them. But, um, wow. The ceiling and the floor were in the process of trading places. A giggle erupted. "Thanks to my glamara, I can unearth secrets." Oops. Why had she admitted to such a special skill? Especially when she hadn't yet employed her "special skill" against Micah.

A crease formed between his brows. A sign of confusion? Then he slid his gaze to her empty goblet. The corners of his mouth twitched. "Enjoy your party. You'll have a wonderful time without me. I'm certain of it." He snapped his fingers, and a servant hastened to refill the chalice. "Sabot will keep you safe."

Her party? A slip of the tongue or truth? Was it possible he'd done this to…impress her? Wonder suffused her. "Fine," she said. "Go if you must. You've scrambled my thoughts enough." She waved Micah off and lifted her brimming cup. Time away from the sumptuous king might do her some good. Allow her to think more clearly and make higher-quality decisions.

Down the hatch! Mmm. The second batch of wine tasted even better than the first.

A husky, sexually charged chuckle left Micah. At least he wasn't upset anymore. He motioned to someone across the room, his muscles flexing.

Viori couldn't help herself. She squeezed his biceps and twittered with delight. "So big."

Micah gaped at her, and even that proved to be a delight.

Oh! Sabot. There he was. He took a post beside Elena.

After barking a brusque "Continue celebrating" to the crowd, Micah met Viori's gaze. "Miss me," he said, his tone all gentleness and hope.

I might. "We have a negotiation to complete," she replied. "Hurry back to me."

"To you. *Only* you." Eyes as fierce as a sword, he gently traced a finger along her nose, right over her freckles, before he flittered away.

Viori stood in place, staring at the spot he'd vacated, already longing for his return. When a strange ache sprouted in her chest, she snapped her fingers at a servant. The second she had more wine, she drained every drop. Wow! Even better the third time around. More potent than anything she'd ever sampled. Head spinning, she swayed into the table with an outright laugh.

Half of the congregation watched her with open curiosity, while the other half tried to hide it. For once, she didn't mind having eyes on her. But she wouldn't tolerate it, either.

"You heard your king," she called, giving her arm an imperial wave. "Celebrate! Or else."

In a blink, conversations restarted and music played. The servant returned and refilled her cup. Viori sat and reclined, scanning the masses.

A young girl with long, dark hair and beautiful brown skin hovered nearby, clutching a ragged doll to her chest. She wore a plain, dirt-streaked tunic and pants.

After glancing right, then left, the little girl broke from the crowd and eased closer. A small smile bloomed when she stood before the royal table, revealing a missing front tooth.

For some reason, the sight of her affected Viori. Her eyes burned, tears threatening to well.

"Are you our queen?" her visitor asked. "Or an evil seductress?"

Queen. What a novel idea.

"She isn't our queen," Elena snapped from behind her. Had she inched closer to Sabot? While he stared straight ahead, the blonde glared at Viori.

"Go away." Viori humphed at her, then smiled at the gap-toothed girl. "You are the first to accuse me of being a seductress. Thank you. It's a title I'll forever wear with pride."

The child beamed at her.

No doubt the girl had heard the insult from gossiping adults. What did she care if they considered her an unrefined temptress? Not. One. Bit. So she tasted blood on her tongue. So what?

"But," she added with a tight voice, "the pitiful embarrassment of a fae behind me is right. I'm not your queen. But I could be, if I so desired." A prideful boast without substance. Though Micah *did* desire her. And, really, becoming queen wasn't a terrible idea. Definitely not her worst.

As Micah's wife, she could sway his decisions in ways a lover could not. In fact, she would gain equal command of their armies, helping control who those armies slaughtered. She could also decide which blondes resided in camp and which faced immediate exile. And if her new husband died at her brother's hand? Or her new husband killed her brother? What then?

A shudder almost pitched her out of the seat. A silly reaction, considering she could and would take measures to prevent such outcomes. Obviously.

So. Why not snap up Micah before that Pearl Jean person sank her claws into him?

Viori tightened her grip on the goblet. Why, this Pearl Jean might be a *true* seductress, plotting ways to win Micah's eternal devotion even now.

Well, too bad. The king of this campground had brought *Viori* jewels as a teenager and elaborate gowns as an adult. Vowed to protect *Viori*. Requested *Viori* miss him. Held her through the night and ensured she ate proper meals.

What are you doing? Getting possessive? More silliness. She'd never considered accepting a husband before; that was all. Well, not openly, anyway. Only ever in secret. And only when she remembered the joy her parents had brought each other and forgot the pain Laken had caused. But marriage was serious business. An unbreakable tie between two people.

She and Micah would be forever bonded. If she was mistaken about him...if he (rightfully) accused her of betrayal when he discovered her connection to Kaysar, rather than forgiving her... And he would find out. There'd be no hiding the secret forever.

Again, her mind offered a negation. She wouldn't be betraying

Micah per se—she would be protecting his wife and brother-in-law. A feat due a reward. He might even thank her for keeping herself—his cherished queen—alive and happy.

Or should she admit the truth before anything permanent happened between them? *If* something permanent happened between them. Should she get him to agree to the truce with Kaysar, *then* admit the truth? *I am a spy!* Not that she had done anything wrong. Yet. She'd merely reacted to circumstances as they'd arisen, changing course as warranted. Surely he would understand.

What she comprehended beyond a shadow of doubt: she and Micah desired more from each other. But a forever union?

Did she enjoy the nights she spent in his arms and dread the day they ended? Yes. Had she shaken off the shackles of loneliness for the first time since childhood? Also yes. Mostly. Could she remember where she was going with this? Not even a little.

"What's your name?" she asked the girl.

"Cakara."

"I was speaking to your companion," Viori told her primly, earning a delighted giggle. How she missed her sweet Drendall.

"Her name is Nema." Cakara propped herself over the table to softly admit, "She's afraid of the king."

"Is she now?" Viori whispered her words, too, acid beginning to churn inside her stomach. "Has he been cruel to her, then?" To any child? If so, Viori's decision was made. No union.

A shrug of the girl's delicate shoulders. "No, but he makes my skin feel funny and *belua* always hunt him. My friend Tiberius says that's because he's a monster too." Head tilt. "The headmistress says my manners are as bad as yours."

Did she now? Viori snuffed out her irritation and hummed a quiet tune while focusing on Nema. The doll blinked and flashed a bright smile at her.

"Would you enjoy hearing Nema tell you how much she loves you?" Viori asked.

Cakara nuzzled her cheek against the doll's face. "Oh yes. More than anything."

"Put your ear to her mouth, then, and listen." She nodded to the doll. "Go on. Tell her."

Cakara obeyed, willing to play along. But Nema obeyed as well, whispering her love to the little girl. Only Cakara heard; she sucked in a breath, her eyes growing wide with wonder.

"Well?" Viori prompted.

"Nema loves me more than anything else in the whole world!"

"You must be special then." She winked, even as she chided herself for being a fool and risking the revealing of her powers for something as trivial as this.

"Cakara. There you are." A harried centaur with brown hair and spotted fur fought her way through the crowd, making a beeline for the girl. "You know better than to leave your assigned seat."

The headmistress to the rescue. Did she secretly dream of dining on her charges to extend the years of her life?

Viori's nail beds heated, claws sprouting. "Is your headmistress cruel to you? Shall I rip her beating heart from her chest?"

Cakara wrinkled her face and straightened. "No, she's not too bad. She takes care of us."

"Cakara is an orphan," Elena explained, eager to share her unwanted opinion as usual. A problem a queen could address. "Her parents died in battle last year."

Cakara hugged her doll close. "They were wonderfully brave."

A year ago. Viori's stomach sank. The girl's momma and papa had died during the battle between Micah and Kaysar, most likely. "I'm sure they were." Despite her unease, she shifted in her seat with the grace of the queen she might or might not decide to be and peered at the headmistress. "If any harm comes to this girl, I'll hold you personally responsible. I'm sure you can guess the punishment. I'm an evil seductress, after all, and Micah will agree to my verdict."

The centaur's eyes flared before she clipped her chin in acknowledgment and lowered her gaze. "My apologies for the disruption, ladies. Come, child."

The centaur urged the orphan away. Cakara glanced over her shoulder and waved, and Viori nearly commanded her return. Goodness gracious. What in all the realm was wrong with her today? As shaky as a leaf, she emptied her goblet. Oh, look. A servant had already filled her up. Or maybe she'd snagged Norok's cup. Who could remember anymore?

"I'm surprised," Elena said, easing into Micah's chair. "You didn't hiss at the child."

"I save my hisses for the deserving." That said, she swung around to hiss at the blonde, who jumped, startled.

Elena narrowed her eyelids. "Must you be so defensive?"

"Yes, thank you. I must." Who else would oversee her safety?

But after a while, she forgot the other woman's presence and sipped her newest wine. The room continued to spin, her spirits rising and crashing as her thoughts whirred. What to do, what to do? Become queen or not?

Spotting a servant with a tray of desserts, Viori belted out a command without thought. "You. Come here." The fae dashed over and bent low, offering the assortment. She selected the best one…then used her arm to slide the rest onto her plate. *Mine.*

Elena snarled as the servant hurried away, "Micah gives you his daily ration of food and water, denying himself his favorite luxuries. What do you give him in return, besides grief?"

He did what? An ember sparked in the center of Viori's chest, forking out. She loathed the thought of Micah going without while she maybe, perhaps, occasionally glutted herself. Still, she said, "What I provide for him is his business, not yours. What I'll offer you is a piece of advice. Stop lusting for him. It's only going to bring you pain."

The blonde reared back, a hand fluttering to her heart. "I

don't lust for him. I could *never*. He's like a brother to me." She shuddered, as if truly horrified by the notion.

But…she must be lying. Who *wouldn't* crave a male like Micah?

"Who are you really?" Elena demanded, angry again. "Why are you here? The timing of your arrival is questionable at best."

Ugh. She sounded like her brother. "As a potential queen, I'll do the asking. As my inferior, you'll do the answering." As the other woman glowered, she demanded, "Why hasn't some buxom beauty already married the king? There must be a reason."

The fae rolled her eyes. "Stop pretending you don't feel it. It only makes you seem guiltier."

This was the second time Miss Blue Dress had implied people experienced a skin-peeling sensation in Micah's presence. A lie meant to scare Viori away? But even Cakara had mentioned it.

No, it *must* be a lie. One perpetrated by the entire campground. Elena *must* desire him for her own. Who wouldn't want to snatch up such a prize?

A good man. Honorable. Was he?

Longing consumed her. Oh, to be the one to snare such a rare creature. A possible friend, worthy of trust. Except, foreboding tickled her nape. A familiar sensation. The herald to loss.

She'd felt this only three times before. The day her parents died. The day Kaysar vanished from the forest. And the day she discovered Laken had a wife, and he'd merely dabbled with Viori for fun.

She gulped. *Going to lose Micah sooner rather than later…*

No. No! This was the Feast of Remembering. What if there were no obstacles between them? If she married Micah, won him over, gifted her brother with a truce and promised her children would never again harm him? There'd be no bloodshed. They'd become one big, happy family. Micah could maintain his kingdom here, and Kaysar could preserve his position at the palace. All could be well. For real.

"I went to check on the oracle earlier because she pushed an image into my head." Elena traced a finger around the rim of Micah's abandoned goblet. "Do you want to know what I saw?"

"Your tone tells me I don't, so I'll go with no," she replied, as if she hadn't a care. But inside she trembled. "That's my final answer."

The blonde ran her tongue over her straight white teeth. "I'll tell you, anyway. I saw you stab Micah in the gut using the dagger currently sheathed at your waist."

What! "How dare you suggest such a falsehood!" She would *never*. Not for any reason. Unless he hurt someone she loved. Which he wouldn't do. He couldn't! Kaysar was too strong, and her children wouldn't dare vacate the swamp without permission.

The little orphan's words chose that moment to replay. Belua *always hunt him*.

No. No, no, no. Krunk would stop the others from venturing to the camp, putting themselves directly in Micah's crosshairs.

Wouldn't he?

Hand shaking, she drained her goblet. The liquid settled like lead in her stomach. What if her children did venture here... and what if Micah did harm them?

No! She would act. Put safeguards in place. Something!

"I dare because it's true," Elena intoned.

The spinning cranked up, no longer fun. "Micah won't believe you." *And if he does?*

Safeguards...

Her thoughts returned to a possible wedding, a single question plaguing her. Why not?

CHAPTER ELEVEN

Frustrated, Micah transferred to the common tent. He'd been gone for hours, but he'd found no oracle, no former mistress and no evidence to point to traitors willing to risk life and limb to save them.

Now, he only wished to be with Red. *She* liked him. At least somewhat. She would pick him in a lineup. Him. The female who hissed at others but curled against him, clinging all night long. She enjoyed his touch—without payment. Conversing with her satisfied him more than a night spent with a mistress ever had. Plus, he'd gotten used to having her underfoot.

He thought he might be coming to care for her…and fear her loss.

Materializing behind the royal table, he discovered the celebration in full swing. The music boomed, the crowd rowdier. Red—wasn't where he'd left her, he realized. He tensed, scanning, searching…

There. His jaw dropped. He could not be seeing what he thought he was seeing. Could not be witnessing a former hallucination come to life, as hoped.

Thunderstruck, he stared. Smiling wide, she danced in a cir-

cle of three. Or two and a half. A little girl and a doll acted as
her partners. Orphaned children encircled them, clapping and
cheering as a centaur observed a few feet away with waning
disapproval.

Strain fled from him, wonder rushing in. And hunger...

She spotted him and squealed with excitement. And it seemed
genuine. "Micah!" After kissing her dance partner's cheek—and
the doll's—she glided over to throw herself against him.

He clasped her by the waist, astonished, and held her steady.
The feel of her...soft and lush. Pliant. Willing. Utterly unaffected by the skin-peeling sensation. He cut off a groan.

"Guess what?" she exclaimed, clutching his tunic as if they
were a couple. As if she favored him.

Was this fantasy-come-true actually happening? The sweet
wine she'd imbibed before his departure—as well as after it apparently—was offered only during a feast like this one. The
potent liquid stripped a mind of any fear, helping the drinker
see their deepest desires. Did this female envision a future with
him? Truly?

"What?" he croaked.

"You're not going to harm my children, and I'm not going
to stab you." More earnest than she'd ever been, she told him,
"All will be well. It's settled."

Something hot stung Micah's chest. "You have children?"
The family members she'd mentioned before? They must be
young; she had yet to age past her immortality. "Who is the
father? Where is he? Do you love him?" The questions spilled
from his tongue. Had he stolen her from a devoted husband?

The male dies today!

Calm. What if she hadn't birthed the children? Perhaps they
were other prisoners of *belua*, and she'd assumed the role of
mother, feeling responsible for their well-being. A supposition
that made Micah admire her so much more.

He blinked as a final thought smacked him. "You considered stabbing me?"

She gave him a little shake. "Weren't you listening to me? I don't want to *ever* harm you, so I won't be stabbing you. It's been decided. I'm going to keep you instead. Best you get on board. As for the children, they've never had a father. Are you volunteering?"

No father. Ever. They *must* be prisoners. And *keep him*? He gulped. She peered up with something akin to affection, her guard obliterated.

His heartbeat sped up. "I will help you care for the children, always and forever. But just to be clear, you aren't in love with another male?"

"I mean, I once thought I loved Laken, but he betrayed me. He died before he ever had a chance to meet any of my darlings."

Someone had this creature and failed to see to her care? "He was a fool. I will *never* betray you." Not now, not ever. If she belonged to him, he would forever cherish her. "Tell me where the children are, and I will fetch them."

"You meant what you said? You will protect them? Always? You promise?"

"I promise." The roughness of his voice might've embarrassed him in another situation. Here, shock kept him in flux, his emotions swinging from pleasure to caution, tenderness to disbelief. *She might care for me.*

"I'll introduce you soon. Right now, they're safe from everyone but Kaysar." She rested her cheek against his chest to nuzzle him. "I'm so glad I dreamed of you while I slept."

"No member of your family needs to fear Kaysar." Wait. "You dreamed of me?" Reveries like the hallucinations he'd experienced? What did that mean? They were meant to be? Drawn together by Fate itself?

Made for each other.

"Mmm-hmm. I sure did. Maybe we're fated." She fiddled

with his tunic. "And good news! I've changed the plan. We're getting married. Congratulations!"

Plan? *Married?* She issued the world-changing statements without hesitation or teasing, and his entire body jolted once, twice, thrice.

"Married?" He gave another clipped shake of his head, hoping to empty his mind of any misunderstandings. Already, longing lurched. For once, there was no tempering it with the usual reminders: people betrayed him, women feared him and, as a chimera, he was destined to die alone. "You must be jesting." Mustn't she? What if the children despised him on sight?

I can win them over. I must.

Pouting a little, she met his gaze. "I can learn manners probably."

He gaped at her. She feared the problem was *her*? And a lack of manners?

"Do you doubt me?" she asked, worrying her bottom lip with her teeth.

"Not at all. I…" Honestly, he had no words. Was out of his element.

"Oh, I see," she said, losing some of her merriment. Her irises glazed with embarrassment. "You long for a queen who will read to the orphans, smile sweetly at your people no matter the situation and obey your every command. You don't want the evil seductress. And that's fine. Really. Because you were right. I was only jesting about marriage." She forced a brittle laugh as she released him, drawing away. "A union is foolish."

No, she hadn't been jesting. He *felt* her hurt, and it did strange things to his insides.

"You are not an evil seductress." Seductive, yes. But evil? No. He tightened his clasp, letting her go nowhere. "I want you, Red. My desire isn't the question." He *yearned* for this woman. Badly. He could barely think at night as he pretended to doze; again and again, she rolled closer until she ultimately draped her body over his. A dream and a nightmare. "But there are problems," he reminded her.

"You want me?" Melting, winding her arms around him, she challenged, "Name one problem. If you can."

Hold your silence. Take what she offers.

Do what's right. Shoving the words past his tongue, he told her, "We don't know each other. Not really. We have no idea what glamara the other wields." No, not true. She'd admitted to unearthing secrets. Could she withstand the stigma of being wed to a chimera? And she had yet to see his scars. What if his body repulsed her, the way it had anyone who'd ever glimpsed it? The way it repulsed *him.*

What's more, he was soon to be at war with the most feared being in all Astaria. If he had miscalculated his plans in the slightest way, he could lose as his oracle had threatened—and Vee would become Kaysar's primary target, worthy of double the wrath. That was how the Unhinged One worked.

"Let's solve this here and now." She toyed with his hair, and a short, choppy moan burst from him. "What two glamaras do you wield?"

"That isn't something I'll discuss." Not here, not now. Perhaps not ever. His motive hadn't changed. The less others knew about his abilities, the less likely someone learned his weakness. But...if she were his wife...maybe. One day.

"Are your abilities dangerous?" she asked.

To her? "No."

"Then I see no obstacle. Especially not today." Pure carnality, she leveled a coy smile on him. "Isn't that right?"

She uses the celebration against me. He had only himself to blame. "What of your glamara? How do you unearth secrets?"

"Oh. That." She deflated a little. "I should refuse to say, like you. But, because you feel so nice pressed against me, I'll tell you a tidbit. You see, I...commune with nature. Yes. That's true."

Communing with nature. The reason she powered the trees?

It made sense. What if she could oversee a garden for his—their—people?

Fated…

"Well?" She chewed on her bottom lip, pure feminine charm, and peered up at him through the fan of her lashes. "What do you say?"

His fingers flexed on her. His thoughts spun, merged and twisted. Marriage. Red…his wife. In his arms every night. Draped over him every morning. The fulfillment of deep, hidden fantasies he'd never dared to entertain, now manifested and his to touch.

"Micah," Elena said, stepping from thin air to reach his side. Concern radiated from her. "Tell me you aren't considering this."

How long had she stood nearby, listening, hidden by her glamara? A muscle jumped in his jaw.

Vee released him to rub her temples. "Where'd you come from? Hmm, maybe I should forgo the wine. No, that's pure silliness. I should probably have more."

The spy continued, "You need to know what Fayette showed me. Soon, this girl will—"

"Fayette is a traitor," he interjected. "You know as well as I that the oracle is well able to manipulate the futures she projects." Through her, he'd learned that anything someone perceived as their fate, whether accurate or not, they actively pursued, whether wittingly or unwittingly. The mind chased what it considered fact, whether those facts were true or false. "What's more, a predicted future is never guaranteed."

Protests left Elena.

"No," he barked, ending her tirade. Change your thoughts, and you changed your words. Change your words, and you changed your actions. Change your actions, and you changed your habits. Change your habits, and you changed your character. Change your character, and you changed your destiny.

He kept his gaze on Red. As usual, she kept her gaze on him, too, utterly unafraid.

Her. She's my destiny. My fate. I will change the world—my world—to have her.

As if she heard his thoughts, she returned her fingers to his tunic and allowed a new smile to lift the corners of her plump, cherry lips. A sweeter one than before. Playful and beyond tempting.

His muscles tensed one after the other. His temperature rose. To have this creature forever and always...

Leaving one hand on her waist, he lightly pinched her chin with the other. This perfect female liked him enough to hold his gaze and welcome his touch. If ever she betrayed him...

"Marriage is permanent. You are sure you wish to do this?" *Sure you desire me the way I desire you?*

"Let me answer your question with one of my own." Eyes full of mirth, she glided her hands to his shoulders, then lifted to her tiptoes and kissed his lips. An innocent brush of her mouth against his, yet his body reacted as if set on fire. "Will you do everything I demand?"

He barked a laugh, the sound rusty, foreign to his ears. Many of his people stopped what they were doing to gawk at him. Some even grinned, a rare occurrence.

He kept his attention on Red, reservations frayed. "There's a good chance I will." Here, now, he longed only to indulge her every whim.

"Then there's a good chance I'm sure."

The way she purred those words... He had no other defenses to shore up against her. "Very well. Let's wed." He would be a father to her children. They would become a family. A unit. He would lay the Dusklands at her feet.

"You mean it?" A higher-pitched squeal escaped her, and *he* smiled. "Do it, then." Palms flat, she traced her fingers up his pectorals and around his neck. "Make the declaration."

Despite her isolation with the trees, she knew how weddings worked. Knew his word was law and he needed only to declare a merger to make it so.

A small whisper in the back of his mind rose. *Rushing this?* "I will do this...tomorrow, after the wine has worn off," he forced himself to add. *Wait to claim her? Fool!* Despite the protests being screamed inside his head, he did not negate the words. Instead, he pressed on. "Take the night. Consider the ramifications. If you still desire to do this in the morning—" *still desire me* "—I will take the steps to wed us."

She pouted again, and he had to lock muscles onto bone to stop himself from fully claiming those lush lips in front of everyone. "I *always* have to wait for everything." The pout migrated to her voice, and he thought it might be the most adorable thing about her. "I had to wait for my parents to recover, but they didn't. I had to wait for my brother to return, but he never came back. I had to wait for a friend I never found. I don't want to wait anymore. Please don't make me. You'll be good to me, and I'll be good to you. Yes? Does anything else matter?"

Her parents. A brother. A lack of friends. This was the most information she'd ever shared about herself. Because she didn't merely seek him as a husband—she sought *him* as a friend. Miracle of miracles, his feral beauty had decided to trust him. An amazing development. How could he deny her *anything*? Especially this. What's more, the wine never lied. This precious female wouldn't be changing her mind about him.

Micah swiped the tip of his tongue over dry lips and nodded. Fear should never dictate his actions. "I will wed you today. Tonight. Now."

Grinning, Red jumped up and clapped. "You won't be sorry, Micah."

"Stop and think this through," Elena pleaded. The spy was still here?

He nodded to the musicians who played flutes and drums in

the far corner. The music ceased abruptly. Around him, conversations died as well. Quiet reigned, not a whisper to be heard.

He returned his focus to Vee. His little Red. His dream come true. His future—for better or worse. "I claim you as my wife, Vee…my Red." He didn't even know her last name or moniker. Yet he was still going to do this. "I pronounce you queen of my people." As she melted against him, her expression luminous—soul changing—his heart clanged against his ribs. He scanned the crowd, linked his fingers with his bride's and lifted their arms, presenting her to their people. "Now and forever."

Gasps erupted. Jaws dropped. Elena groaned as if she'd been punted in the guts. Norok, whose arrival Micah had missed, paled, and bellowed a vile curse.

Lowering their arms, he faced her once more. "Do you accept my claim, Red?"

"I do. Very much so." She peered at him with something akin to adoration, almost shy, confirming the rightness of his decision to do this. "So we are truly wed now? Irrevocably tied?" Joy filled her words.

Tenderness proved stronger than any malice he'd ever experienced, razing what he'd once considered the best parts of him. No longer. "We are." It was done. Spoken, accepted and sealed. Red was his wife. His partner. A royal sovereign.

Pride infused his spine and puffed his chest as he faced the onlookers yet again. "Come. Greet your new queen." *She is mine. Forever.*

One by one, the people bowed. All but Norok, Elena and Lavina. Micah glared at each. Lavina was the first to break. She executed a shaky bow before fleeing the tent. Elena finally nodded her head in acknowledgment. The most she would do. After minutes of silence and stillness, Norok worked his jaw and gave a nod of his own.

Micah didn't press for more…yet. He would give the siblings time.

"Oh, I like this," Red said, gaze sweeping over the masses. "I like this indeed."

Satisfaction inundated him, nigh overflowing. "This is only the beginning." He'd meant what he'd contemplated; he intended to give her the world.

To his bafflement, the people around him began to relax. Some even beamed genuine smiles at him.

"To the marriage bed," someone called, and laughs followed.

The throng urged him and his bride out of the common area, then escorted them to his tent. A task performed for all newlyweds and not something he'd ever thought to enjoy himself.

Along the way, fae called out well-wishes and advice. "Never go to bed angry. Stay up all night and fight!"

"Never forget one person is always right, and the other person is the husband."

"Always remember the husband is the head of the house, but the wife is the neck. She turns him wherever she pleases!"

At his side, Red twirled and danced and chuckled. A vision of joy. And his.

Sweat beaded on his brow, desires he'd fought for so long flowing to the surface. Finally, they stood inside his—their—tent, the crowd dispersed. His heart clanged harder. Streams of sunlight illuminated the twirling dust motes. Other scents washed away, the fragrance of citrus and flowers teasing his nose. An aroma he longed to explore in great detail...

"Alone at last," he rasped, hooking a lock of hair behind her ear.

Her breath hitched, a hint of nervousness invading her features. She kicked off her shoes. "Are we going to get naked now?"

"You are." The rough tenor of his voice shocked him. Had he ever sounded less civilized?

"But not you?" she asked, unable to mask her disappointment. Her hand strayed to his chest.

When she saw what lay hidden beneath his clothing... No, best to give her time to get used to him. He clasped her wrists and moved her palms to his shoulders. "My tunic stays on this time."

"But why—"

"You won't even notice," he interjected, refusing to answer. Though he hated the need for this. His actions with his wife should differ from what he'd done with his mistresses, with whom he'd merely unfastened his leathers. Still, he ended that line of conversation when he lowered his grip, cupping her backside and spreading his fingers wide. Such lush, giving flesh. "We have time. We'll get there." Perhaps one day.

"Oh, all right," she said, toying with the ends of his hair. He loved when she did that.

Moving his grip to her face, he cupped her soft, silken cheeks. "You are my every fantasy come to life."

Her expression glowed with a feminine power he wished to see each day for the rest of his life.

"If I do anything you do not like tonight," he told her, "you have only to tell me and I will stop. We will go as slowly as you wish." No matter the strain it put on his body.

Mine to protect from any *threat.*

"What if I don't want to go slowly?" she asked, shocking him to the bone. "What if I want to go fast and hard?"

Questions he'd never thought to hear directed at him. Muscles flexed and toughened in response. "Then I will oblige you— the second time." Happily.

He bent his head, and she rose to her tiptoes once again. They met in the middle, their lips pressing together. A heated collision with staggering results. His cells burst into flame. His senses deepened. The taste of her—the purest temptation. The scent of her—intoxicating. The feel of her—electric. The wisp of her breath—a caress inside his ears. The beauty consumed him.

A groan rumbled in Micah's chest, up his throat, liberated as she opened for him. Tongues rolled together. Only his second kiss in the whole of his life, but oh, the difference! He'd taken his former mistress's mouth like this only once. The first female to ever show interest in the act. But she had pulled away soon after he'd started, and he'd never tried again.

He licked at Vee's tongue. Savoring. He *refused* to speed up. Why would he want to hurry to the end? He *loved* this. The twining. The mingling of breaths. Clutching hands. Gasps and mewls. Rasping breaths. More fire, burning hotter and hotter.

Who cared that his body ached? He'd never known desire like this. Such ferocity!

He felt Red in each racing beat of his heart, as if desire alone powered the organ. He...couldn't think anymore. Thoughts fragmented, each one revolving around a single objective: *more*. Kissing. Hands roaming further.

She wrenched her face from his. Between rasping breaths, she told him, "I want to see your body. Show it to me. Please! Don't make me wait for this, either."

His blood flashed cold; his cheeks heated. Should he oblige her in this? Shouldn't he?

If he waited and she despised the sight of him, regretted wedding him and avoided his bed—*after* he'd tasted her feminine bounty? A travesty not to be born! But...wouldn't it be better to know her reaction now?

Acid seared the back of his throat. Was she soon to be disappointed? "I must warn you. I am heavily scarred."

"You have more than one? Really?" Almost giddy, she traced her fingers to the hem of his tunic. "Show me, show me, show me right now. As queen, I insist."

He reached for the edge of his tunic as well. Gulped. Was he truly going to do this?

As he began to lift the material, a bell tolled in the distance. An alarm bell. Once again, his blood flashed cold. A threat approached.

When the bell tolled a series of three short clangs followed by a long one, he knew. *Belua*. They'd come for him.

"What's happening?" she asked.

"Invaders." He gripped Red's chin, peered deep into her eyes and pressed a swift kiss to her lips, then issued a single command. "Stay here. Guards will be stationed at the door in less than a minute."

"But—"

"No." He would hear no protest. After giving her another swift kiss, he told her, "You are the most important part of my life now. There is no line I won't cross to keep you safe. Even if I must leave you behind and angry. The farther you are from me for this, the better." *Belua* tended to focus the bulk of their malice on him and those closest to him.

The color faded from her cheeks. She opened her mouth to respond, but the bell tolled again. He kissed her once more and flittered to the common tent and utter pandemonium.

Panic had consumed the once-festive crowd. Only those who'd trained with him on the battlefield exuded calm. Several of the retired soldiers had even taken the initiative. Alston and Oren shouted commands to the people to ensure a safe evacuation.

People tripped this way and that in search of safety. Children cried out. His presence only seemed to amplify their distress where only moments ago they'd teased him. He spotted the headmistress who oversaw the care and feeding of the camp's orphans, herding her charges out of the tent. The young child was crying, pointing at the doll now being trampled by frightened fae.

"Halt," he called.

Only his command broke through the terror of his people. He stooped and scooped up a fallen doll from the packed earth, then handed it to the owner, the little girl he'd seen dancing with Red.

Despite the pained uneasiness in her gaze, she hugged him. "Are we going to die?"

"No." He gave her a curt nod, followed by a wink only she could see. "Follow the orders of Alston and Oren. They'll lead you to safety." Micah moved on, pointing to the strongest soldiers in the area. "You, you, you and you. Go to my tent. One on each side. Guard your queen with your lives. Not one scratch is to mar her skin."

"Yes, Majesty," they called in unison. They were gone a second later.

Norok and Elena flittered to him. Whatever reservations they'd entertained regarding his marriage had vanished in the face of danger. In battle, they fought as an unbreakable unit.

"To the death," he snarled. *Belua* had dared approach his wife. Today they died without mercy.

CHAPTER TWELVE

The wine was messing with Viori's head, her spinning mind racing from one wild thought to the next. Oh yes, it was absolutely the wine, and not the cataclysmic kiss she and Micah had just shared. A shocking merger of strength and weakness, of serenity and madness, with pure need at the helm, directing her every action, rendering her unable to think.

But he was gone, and she could think now. *So do it. Think.* She paced through the tent, just as she'd done her first day in camp. Oh, how much had changed since then. From a captive to a queen. Married to Kaysar's enemy. A male she had practically begged to strip naked before he'd departed from her. Ruler of a people she didn't like. Well, mostly didn't like. Cakara and Nema were nice. Wonderful, actually. The other orphans, too. Plus, after the wedding Micah's people had grown kinder toward her. And to him, for that matter.

Strange indeed. So many well-wishes for a happy, long life, and healthy children. A lump formed in her throat. A baby made of flesh and blood. With Micah. Who wished to reunite her with the children she already had. To be a family…with his enemies. He just didn't know it.

Worry seized her, tremors invading her limbs. What was going on out there? Bells had tolled, and Micah had reacted as if the world were about to end. Had her children come? Had Kaysar returned to break the truce? Either way, she should be out there. But what would she do? Who would she side with?

Figure it out when you learn what's going on. So guards blocked both exits—the door and the vulnerability in the canvas, as evidenced by their shifting shadows. So what? As a royal, her word was law as much as Micah's. If she wished to leave, she should leave. And she could, *without* detection.

Viori clutched a tiny pebble in her hand. Before she'd lost her wits during that fiery kiss, she'd stolen the thing from Micah's pocket.

Guilt tightened her chest. If she did this… Would Micah consider it a betrayal? If she returned before he did, would he even know she'd left? And if he did know she'd left but she saved his life or the life of his—their—people? Could he really find fault with her then?

Viori fortified her resolve…and did it. Still clad in her fancy garment—her wedding gown—she flittered into the darkness, several feet from the tent. Her eyes widened as she took in the scene. And she'd thought there'd been chaos before. Fae sprinted in every direction, trapped in a panicked haze as they fought to return to their homes.

Foreboding pricked her nape. Whoever or whatever had arrived, Micah's people—her people—were terrified. She should help them. A sudden sense of duty and protectiveness outshone every other emotion, demanding attention. What belonged to her, she safeguarded. Always.

Units of soldiers sprinted north, south, east and west. Did they encircle the camp? How much danger was Micah to combat today? A bride shouldn't have to fear losing her husband or her children or her brother on her wedding night.

How to proceed? Viori checked her glamara. Excellent! Since

her arrival here, she'd been recharging nicely. Faster than usual, in fact. She could, possibly, create and animate multiple small creatures without weakening too much or creating a doorway between worlds. A task she hadn't performed in forever, preferring to save her strength for her giants. But small creatures had the ability to guard Micah in secret, shielding him as necessary.

Yes. She liked this plan.

Sticking to the shadows, she followed a group of torch-bearing soldiers. They stopped several yards from the cluster of mud huts, joining the well-lit circle around the camp's perimeter.

Her heart thudded. Where was Micah?

She scanned the sea of faces. Incoming soldiers without torches raced to a cart, each male grabbing a thick wooden club from a pile. Norok stood atop that cart, issuing orders.

Spotting him, Viori darted out of his line of sight and crouched. Micah must be nearby. The two warriors were never far apart. They were bonded in some way, as evidenced by the way White Beard had leaned against Micah at the banquet—and Micah had let him. She only hoped Norok proved more loyal to his king than he had to his wife.

An unexpected wrench of envy startled her. Once, she and Kaysar had enjoyed such a bond. Until she'd done the unthinkable and murdered their parents, of course, ruining his future.

Blinking back a sudden well of tears, she looked left, right, then left again. No one paid her any attention. So why did she feel like someone watched her intently?

Viori shoved the sensation aside. *Another worry for later.* This was an occasion for action. With her mind set, she stretched out her hands—and sang. The soft melody crackled with power, masked by the cries of a stampeding people desperate to return to their homes.

A gust of wind swept in, lifting and swirling grains of dirt together. Drawing them closer and closer...

She increased her volume, pouring bits of herself into the

words. As a child she'd learned there were two songs necessary for this. One for creating, and one for sparking life. It was best if she didn't combine them, rushing the process as she'd done with Fifibelle and Drendall. But sometimes exceptions must be made.

Viori could kick herself for not sneaking away from Micah each night to create and hide shells of potential children throughout the camp. Instead, she'd opted to savor the time she spent in his arms.

When the dirt began to compact, two distinct shapes became clear, both feline in nature. Sweat beaded on her brow. The tremors worsened in her limbs. The song tapered to silence when the little darlings stretched and rubbed against her, eager to please.

Love flooded her. Love *always* flooded her when she gave life. Talk about a bond. Unbreakable in every way that mattered. As she peered at them, allowing herself a moment to bask in their adorableness, their names were etched into her heart. Sprinkles and Muffin. Pure sweetness.

"Hold!" Micah called from somewhere behind her. "I see them." Fury dripped from his voice, sending shudders raining over her spine.

The intruders, whoever they were, had made a grave mistake today. "Go, my darlings," she commanded. "Stay close to King Micah." These young babies should recognize him through scent and their connection to her. "Guard him. Reveal yourself only if someone attacks him. Or seems to be a threat to him. Then strike to kill."

Off they flew, weaving through the masses, eager to please. No, not the masses anymore. Only small groups of fae remained.

As Viori adjusted her position, the ground shook. Gasping, wobbling, she peeked around the tent that shielded her from the coming battle. Most of the soldiers held a club—a torch. The ends blazed with fire, embers crackling.

"I understand now, the truth so clear. You are their maker," a familiar voice growled behind her. "Small and big. You are the reason so many good warriors have died throughout the centuries."

She whipped around, coming face-to-face with Elena. Vibrating with rage, the blonde drew back her elbow and threw a vicious punch.

The blow landed. Bones broke on impact, and she crashed to her backside. Pain registered only as she healed. The urge to jump up and launch a counterattack threatened to overwhelm her, but she resisted.

Splayed, she smiled up at the blonde. "You shouldn't have done that." When she'd told Micah she knew how to fight, she'd meant it. Now, she would prove it. "By the way. As queen, I'm enacting a new law, effective immediately," she purred. "Harm me and experience an agonizing death. No exceptions."

"You're the only one dying tonight." With a snarl, Elena dived at her.

She anticipated the action and kicked, nailing the underside of Blue Dress's chin. As the female toppled, spitting blood, Viori attacked, getting downright nasty.

What will I be forced to contend with today?

The stonemen? Trees? Something made of dirt, brambles or cloth? Micah had dealt with each creature at some point.

At last, his newest challengers stepped from a thick white fog, forming a line of aggression roughly a hundred feet away. He frowned. Trees. The very trees that had once guarded Vee—he recognized those menacing expressions. They clearly wanted her back.

Vee had only assumed she'd killed them, as suspected.

There were eighteen in total, each blooming with a veritable feast of delicacies. Fruits and nuts he hadn't sampled since finding his sleeping beauty.

Whispers of shock and awe rose from his men. Most had never seen so much goodness in one place, there for the plucking.

"Norok," he called, sheathing his sword, and holding out an empty hand.

His second didn't have to guess at his meaning. An axe whooshed through her air, and Micah caught its hilt.

A rough, gravelly voice rang out. "Give. Mother. Back. *Now.*"

Oh yes. They'd come for Viori. Though the speaker clearly didn't know the meaning of the word *mother.* Unless... No. No! But when had the trees learned to speak? None had done so the last time they faced off. Nor had any of the other *belua* he'd battled in the centuries since.

"Why don't you try to take her from me?" he challenged with relish.

Fury electrified the atmosphere a split second before a tree swung a thick branch in his direction. The movement was so swift, Micah almost couldn't track it. Almost. Fruit flew across the distance, and he ducked. Except, the missiles weren't aimed at him but at his men. Apples, pears, plums and lemons slammed into soldiers like cannonballs, exploding upon contact. Victims dropped amid grunts of shock and groans of pain.

Other trees wasted no time, launching fruit as well. Nuts joined the mix, the hard shells splintering, slicing through flesh and muscle as easily as butter. But again, the missiles circumvented Micah entirely. But why avoid hurting him when he presented the only true threat?

The ground quaked harder and harder. Soldiers wobbled, struggling to stay upright. Even Micah fought to maintain his balance. Cracks spread through the dirt, the earth seeming to split apart... Sharp roots shot from the openings. Cries rang out as his men toppled, releasing their torches. Flames spread over the ground but failed to stop the invasion.

These *belua* had new tricks, too. Noted.

Growls brewed in Micah's chest. He was no longer a fifteen-

year-old boy without resources or hope. Waste time exchanging more threats? Show the trees the same mercy they displayed
toward him? No. He flittered as he swung the axe, landing directly in front of the speaker. The blade whistled as it descended;
the torch in his other hand wasn't far behind.

The tree had quicker-than-expected reflexes and blocked.
Metal sliced through bark, removing a branch, nothing more.
Flames jumped from the torch to the foliage, swiftly spreading,
but only charred the outer shell. The fight tolled on.

Micah attacked with more vigor, but no matter what he did,
no trees struck at him. Why? Whenever he approached, they
reared back, pulling their blows. None of this made sense. No
matter. He had no such problem making contact.

A blur of motion at his left caught his attention. He spun,
ready to block the coming attack, expecting another branch.
The threat did not aim for him, and it didn't come from a tree.
Two cats positioned themselves before Micah, hissing and swiping at the trees. And the trees backed up.

Wait. These weren't cats. They appeared to be made of sand.

A horrifying realization struck him. More *belua*!

He geared to attack when a soldier tripped and fell at his feet;
the sandcats launched into action, clawing the fae's face. "No,"
Micah bellowed, and the cats ceased, prowling backward.

What...? Why...? He didn't understand.

As a tree swung a branch at the fallen warrior, Micah returned
his attention to the battle and blocked the blow with the axe,
saving the male's life. And what a battle it was.

The enemy continued to strike. His army did an excellent
job of hacking, blocking, dodging and torching, using their
greatest strength to their advantage—the vastness of their numbers. And yet, the trees refused to depart. With their fruit gone,
they fought with unending savagery, seemingly mindless as they
brandished those razored branches. Scraping. Slicing. Stabbing.

Killing. It wasn't long before the fae numbers began to dwindle. Limbs flew. Heads, too.

Micah launched into action, sprinting for a specific foe, losing sight of the sandcats. Along the way, he dropped his torch and picked up another fallen axe. Leaping...

He hacked through bark so swiftly, the tree couldn't heal fast enough. Could only scream in pain, fueling his aggression. He fought harder, moved at a speedier clip, a familiar haze overtaking him. The thrill of breaking his opponents before ending them. *Yes, yes. Destroy the threat. Prove you are master here. Unconquerable.*

Protect your mate.

Instincts collided, waging a war of their own, stripping him of civility. His own ferocious savagery sprang loose. He slammed his axes into a trunk, again and again, never pausing. Bits of bark flew in every direction. A crack widened. Lengthened. Wham, wham, wham. More cracks formed. More and more. His biceps pulled and eased, pulled and eased, as if stuck in a loop. Then a tree fell over, dead.

His instinct pinged, alerting him to a problem. He felt as if he were hurting...his mate. As if he were breaking some kind of vow.

No, no. *I protect her. The* belua *hope to enslave her.* He split the dead tree in two, just in case. *Revive from that.*

A grin spread. One opponent felled. Seventeen others to go. Never had anything felt so right. Or so wrong. Other *belua* arrived on the scene, exiting the shadows. Multiple stonemen and a beast Micah couldn't begin to identify. These creatures attempted to avoid him as well. He wasn't so merciful. They were right to fear him.

In a constant state of motion, he tore through his enemies, wreaking absolute havoc. After the second, third and fourth death, his grin faded. This felt...wrong. Far more wrong than right.

"No!" Red shrieked. "Micah! Do not hurt them! Please!"

Another hallucination. She occupied their tent, as ordered. She was safe. Because there was no way the real queen commanded him to spare the lives of her former captors. Creatures who had used her. Drained her of energy, forcing her to sleep. Not unless…

No. No, she had not lied to him.

He hacked and hacked and hacked. More trees fell. Down went the stonemen. The mystery creature. *This is right. Surely only right.* Yet he felt as if he were yanked in two directions.

"Noooo! Stop!" Red's voice hit his awareness again. Terror and pain saturated her tone.

He frowned as he felled another enemy. She'd sounded closer to him. Hack, hack, hack. Another tree ceased moving. No others? He puffed with…disappointment? But shouldn't he feel satisfaction? His mate was now out of danger.

He blinked rapidly, the world coming into view once more. The camp loomed in the distance. Smoke billowed across the battlefield. Red raced toward him, scarlet hair streaming behind her, cheeks wet with tears.

He opened his arms to catch her, to hold and soothe her. Everything would be all right now.

A sharp sting registered, and he frowned again. Looked at the source of the pain. His bride had…stabbed him?

CHAPTER THIRTEEN

My babies!

The trees had finally budded again, only to…to… Devastating emotions deluged Viori. She stood before Micah, her dagger shoved into his gut, his hand shackling her wrist as warm blood dripped over them both.

He gaped at her, confused. "Vee?"

Hot tears streaked her cheeks, her emotions surging. First came shock. Then rage and grief. Finally, agony. Each built upon the backs of the others. She struggled to make sense of what had happened.

No, not true. She knew what had happened. *I've lost them.* But, but… Not Patrick and Nala. Not Rocklord, Linda, and Prickles. Please, not James Thaddeus Puddingstone III, too. Not her precious Krunk. Beings who'd been with her since her earliest days in the forest. Her beloved children. Her oldest friends and fiercest protectors. Dead. All dead. Lost, like the children she'd created in the mortal world. Her dear, sweet Mothan, Nessa and Harry.

Nothing but bits and pieces around her. Only John and Snowy were missing from the rubble, and only because they relied on their habitats for survival. Her knees shook, threatening to buckle.

She longed to flitter to a world far, far away. One she'd never visited. To lose herself in new oddities and feel out of place yet again. To scream and sob. To forget what she knew. But she'd dropped her pebble as she'd sprinted toward her husband—her greatest enemy. The male responsible for the slaughter of her family.

They'd fought so valiantly. Even without receiving her instructions, they had ignored Micah, the very king who had hacked and torched them one by one. The only reason they'd lost. All the while, his people had watched, cheering him on.

Praises still rang out. "All hail Micah the Unwilling!"

The Unwilling. The title clanged in her ears. A title belonging to the one who'd killed more of her family members than Kaysar.

Micah is the Unwilling. Sickness churned in her stomach. She should have known, should have guessed. Now, it was too late. Her precious ones were dead and gone, never to be seen or heard from again.

Horror washed over her with increasingly intense waves. "No!" The denial burst from her at last. There must be a way to fix this. To bring them back. A song had always worked in the past—a new song! Yes!

"Why did you attack me?" Micah demanded. Despite the hardness of his tone, he gently caressed her cheek with his free hand. "I've saved you. They'll never again hold you prisoner."

Then. That moment. She let the rage overtake her. Rage directed at him and yes, even herself. Would he have stayed his hand if she had opened up to him?

No, probably not. His hatred for her children ran deep. Perhaps deeper than his hatred for Kaysar.

She'd been a fool to wed Micah. They were never going to make a marriage work. They'd been fools to try. Something else to blame him for. Had he not blinded her with talk of an obstacle-free life…

There was no such thing as an obstacle-free life.

Her eyes narrowed, her gaze leveling on her new husband. The cause of her pain. *Kill Micah. Gather the remains of the children. Create.*

Excellent plan. None better. With a sharp battle cry, she twisted the dagger.

He grunted and squeezed her wrist, bruising. "What are you doing, wife?" Their gazes held, *his* rage amplifying by the second. "Answer me."

"I'm fixing what you destroyed!" Here he was, her brand-new husband. The warrior who had slaughtered her loved ones right before her eyes while she could only scream herself hoarse, begging him to stop. "Consider our kingdom officially divided."

His nostrils flared. "What I destroyed? You mean your jailers?"

"I mean my family."

"Family," he echoed with a hollow tone. "You love them. You lied to me." He thrust her backward, out of her blade's range. "We aren't fated. You used me. Why?"

She stumbled but righted quickly, tightening her grip on the bloody dagger, preparing for another strike.

They faced off, two foes with nothing else to lose. Viori *dared* him to act against her. Never mind the hurt and confusion that molded his features.

"I did betray you," she spit. "From the very beginning."

"Tell me why," he reiterated, the flow of blood going from a river to a trickle, to nothing as he healed.

Unfair! He had suffered so little, while her pain was eating her alive. "For centuries you have killed my children," she snarled. "You must pay."

"*Belua* are your children?" He waved his arms to encompass

the slaughter. "The beings who have plagued my territories for generations did not hold you prisoner?"

Guilt attempted to flare anew, but she stamped it out. He made it sound as if her brood had gotten bored and decided to play stomp-stomp and stab-stab with new toys. No. Absolutely not. That wasn't what had happened at all. "They are—were—creatures with high defenses, and they targeted perceived threats for extermination." Because they were extensions of her, driven by *her* defenses.

Warriors closed around them, forming a wall of strength, clearly eager for a command to strike, their suspicions in full force despite their earlier cheer. Muffin and Sprinkles prowled circles around Viori and her despised spouse, hissing at anyone who dared step too close.

"I brought them to life with my glamara," she continued, pushed past her limit. "They were—are—my everything." Wanting to lash out at him, to hurt him, she forced one corner of her mouth to curl into an icy smile. "They were also your stepchildren. You *did* agree to see to their care. A lie, obviously."

Even as she spoke, questions surged. Why had the trees broken her command and come here? Worry alone? Or something more? Why had they budded again? Why now? Micah must be responsible since they'd only ever done so when she neared him. But how? Why, why, why?

"You...you made them." He reared back, shock and agony playing over his features, both as staggering as hers. Grief followed. "They truly are your children."

Then. That moment. She watched as *his* rage overtook him. He all but spewed malice at her.

The surrounding soldiers leaped back, as if afraid to get too close to him.

"I understand your plot now," he continued. "You came here to seduce the beast tamer. To punish the one who has destroyed so many of your abominations. You are as evil as the monsters you form. Toying with innocents, treating them as your prey."

"I see no innocents here," she countered. "Soon, I'll see no one at all."

"You think to make more." He gasped the words. Without removing his gaze from her, he barked a command to his men. "Gather the ash. Scatter every speck. Blight the *belua* from the realm."

How *dare* he? Without the ash, she couldn't re-create her children. Start from scratch, yes. But re-create? No. Exactly what Micah hoped to prevent. Fury and hurt morphed into pure, undiluted hatred.

"Do. Not. Move," she shouted, dropping and clawing at the ground, drawing mounds of ash nearer. "That is an order from your very powerful queen."

The men didn't so much as twitch.

Kaysar was right. This Dusklands royal should be eliminated posthaste. Something she could handle on her own. No truce stopped her. She might not have the strength to create a new army, but she could combine the elements of each creature, constructing a new being entirely.

Arrows, spears and swords were pointed in her direction as the fae alternated their glances between her and Micah.

"She is not to be harmed," he grated.

His mistake—one that would cost him dearly. *No mercy!* Viori spread her arms, lifted her chin and tilted back her head to sing. The first notes left her, her voice crackling at the edges. The soldiers conveyed confusion, then a growing horror. Gradually, the notes of her song solidified. Her volume grew louder and louder, sweeping across the land. Pained groans rose from Micah's soldiers.

Too bad. She planned to hit Micah and his forces with everything she had all at once. And she would.

There would be no survivors.

Viori sang even louder, a thick fog seeping from the ground, rising to form a wall around the army. A torrent of winds kicked up. Locks of hair whipped before her face. Shouts replaced the groans.

"Can't see!" someone cried as mutilated bark, crumbled rocks and leaves whirled together, collecting, adhering…becoming something beyond beautiful.

Her finest creation. His name was Gravemaker. Graves for short.

"Whatever you are attempting to do, don't," Micah bellowed. Blood leaked from his ears. "I order you to stop this!"

She did not stop this. Not even as she weakened. That weakness started as a lapping wave in her heart, spreading through her. If she continued singing much longer, Graves would come to life, but deep sleep would be forced upon Viori—his creation was draining more energy than she'd expected. More energy than she'd ever expended for one being. But if she stopped, Graves would be fully formed yet lifeless. Defenseless. Micah could carry out his plan to destroy her newest handiwork. Conversely, if she slept, *she* would be defenseless.

Or would she? *Thump, thump, thump.* Her heartbeat slowed, the sleep approaching.

There's still time to stop…

But she didn't stop. Not yet. *Think!* What was the better bet for victory here? She would be imprisoned at best and Graves would be destroyed, as feared. And what if Micah chained her up and gave her whatever pain toxin he'd used on the oracle and his former mistress? How much worse would the *queen* be punished for a betrayal?

Soldiers collapsed, writhing and thrashing on the ground. Micah labored over each of his inhalations, his muscles bulging from strain. Blood no longer leaked from his ears but poured. But fall? No.

If only he would topple. Graves could carry her away from

the camp, wreaking destruction on the way out. They could return when she awoke. Creating a single giant should require only a short rest. A few days. Perhaps a week. A time frame she could work around. Maybe. Possibly.

And if Micah didn't fall? Graves would have to fight his way out while protecting her. Could he succeed?

"Vee," Micah shouted. "Enough! Let us talk this out."

Talk? Talk! The time for chitchat had ended. *I'll* make *the king crash.* Viori sang louder, the wind growing fiercer. The hem of her gown flapped against her calves.

Other soldiers collapsed, but Micah locked his knees, a tower of immobility, glaring at her. "You don't have to do this," he grated between panting breaths.

Not sure how much longer I *can stay upright.* Gah! Micah was too stubborn and powerful to topple. Very well. She would do it; she would command Graves to do whatever proved necessary. As big as her little giant was, he could do anything. *Please, do this.*

For the first time, a plan struck Viori as, perhaps, possibly wrong. But that couldn't be correct. Because what other choice did she have? Without Graves, most of her children would be forever lost. What's more, she would never escape this battlefield. At the moment, Micah could flitter. Without the pebble, she could not.

What if Graves were gravely injured during a showdown?

No choice then. She must encourage Micah's determination to keep her and her child alive and unharmed.

She serenaded a command to the still-unanimated Graves. "Take me home as soon as you're able." Then she sang to Micah himself. "Never forget I am your forever queen, and you vowed to protect my children as if they are your own. If you have any honor in your being, my safety—the safety of Graves—will always be your highest priority. Isn't that right, husband?"

Graves jerked, roaring to life as a blanket of darkness swept over Viori's mind...

★ ★ ★

Betrayed! Micah huffed each breath, shackled in place by a rage and agony unlike any he'd ever known. Not Red. Anyone but her. The female he'd trusted. The one he'd prepared to show his greatest shame. But all along, she'd known her creations had demolished his lands. Killed his people. Nearly killed him.

No, not Red. Anyone but her. Whether he'd wanted to admit it or not, every dream he'd ever entertained had revolved around this female. Without her, what would he have? More loneliness? No hope for a family of his own? An eternity spent as foes?

Their actions this day had assured it. What couple could recover from such treachery?

His hands curled into fists. He should have expected this. He was a chimera, destined to be alone. He'd known better than to try to make a relationship work. Especially with a beauty like Vee. He should have suspected she had come here with an agenda. Their attraction had been too visceral, their connection too quick. But what was that agenda, exactly?

Wed him and then what? Destroy him from the inside out? As punishment for what he'd done to her creations throughout the ages? *Her children.* His rage reached new heights. She had risked her own family to conquer him and his army, and she had lost. The fault for this belonged to her, yet she blamed him. Hated him even. Good. He hated her right back. But...

Guilt proved an ever-constant thorn in his side. For a moment, he'd glimpsed her inner pain, and oh, it proved nearly unbearable. And he was responsible. He'd killed a part of her. Unknowingly, yes, but even if he'd comprehended the truth, how should his actions have differed? He must always do what was necessary to protect his people.

Now, at least, he knew the facts. She was his enemy, plain and simple. A foe he'd foolishly invited into his bed. His life. His *future.* A bellow of agony lodged in his throat.

But agony wasn't allowed, only logic. With brutal precision,

Micah ripped through each of his emotions, leaving only shreds and logic. *Think this through.* His wife's glamara was as horrifying as it was awe-inspiring. An ability that involved her voice— exactly like King Kaysar's.

Had she murdered the man's parents, hoping to destroy her competition? Or had she lied about her dealings with the Unhinged One, along with everything else?

A bitter laugh escaped Micah. Well, well. Look at that. An emotion had survived his assault. *She never wanted me. Always plotted to ruin me. To destroy my people.*

The wind died, and the fog thinned, his army appearing again. Men ceased writhing and lumbered to their feet, wiping blood from their faces. Everyone looked to him, expecting direction.

The felines wound through his legs, and they, too, seemed to expect direction. He scowled and kicked, shouting, "Get!"

A whimper sounded as the sandcats skidded across the dirt, and his guilt sharpened. He didn't care. They weren't real.

The animal—*things*—remained nearby, but kept out of striking distance. They hissed at anyone who approached, as if protecting him.

He would deal with them later. There were more important matters to attend now.

"Surround the *belua*," he bellowed. The giant would be allowed to go *nowhere.*

So far, it hadn't attempted to move. But then, Vee had told the abomination to take her home only when it was able. Because she assumed she had tied Micah's hands with her parting words. That he would choose to keep her and her abomination safe. How smug she'd been before collapsing into the new *belua*'s arms.

That smugness still pricked Micah's pride, the urge to prove her wrong nearly overwhelming him. Not that the life he intended to grant her would amount to much. She would spend the rest of her days in a dungeon, able to hurt no others. But the creature? It would be eliminated.

Soon she will discover why I'm called the Unwilling.

Once he made a decision, he never backtracked. He refused to reroute or withdraw.

His men obeyed him, hurrying to form a circle, trapping the beast from every angle. The thing was tall. The tallest and widest *belua* he'd ever faced. At least double the height and triple the width of the others, all coiled strength, bark shards and stony force. It held Vee in the crook of its arms, pressing her against its belly. Shielding the most important parts of her from any attack—because she slept again.

Ripe for the plucking.

Eyes made of jagged rock darted over the soldiers, who inched forward, closing in. More and more agitated, the monstrous amalgamation shifted from foot to foot. Soon to strike? If she were injured in the fray...

A muscle jumped beneath his eye. "Stay out of range, but maintain the circle," he commanded. There would be no battle yet. "Do it. Now!"

As they scrambled away, a plan formed. He would use his *glamara*. Prove his strength without combat and simply command the beast to release its mother. It would be compelled to obey him.

Mother. Vee's betrayal. New flames of rage erupted. *No mercy!* He didn't care about causing Vee more of that soul-crushing grief. The slightest sliver of compassion would only act as a reward for her evil. Something no king should do. Her monsters had killed hundreds of his men over the centuries. How many of *their* families had grieved, blaming Micah for the deed?

She will pay. But perhaps he shouldn't kill this beast, after all. A soft wind rattled the budding leaves. Where there were leaves there could be *fruit*. The idea stopped him cold. What if this... thing could grow fruit and seed others able to do the same? In the past, he'd had no luck transplanting the trees, but these had first sprouted in the Dusklands; they might succeed whether others had failed.

Imagine it. A new forest, and a true, valuable resource for his people. Kaysar and Cookie would no longer be the sole source of such delicacies.

Yes! "Farther back," he instructed his men. Seemed his wife's protector would be surviving this encounter, after all. "And gather the fruits and nuts but eat nothing."

The beast calmed a bit, though its strain never lessened. It watched Micah more intently than anyone else. Because it knew. They always knew. There was no threat worse than the Unwilling.

He ran his tongue over his teeth, sensing this *belua* merely waited for him to sleep or leave the area to run.

Well then. *Here I stay.* No matter what.

CHAPTER FOURTEEN

Heavy eyelids slid closed. *So tired.*

No! Micah jolted, forcing his lids to pop apart. The *belua* came into view once more. Six days he'd stood immobile. Six days since his treacherous wife had created a monster and fallen asleep in its arms. Six days of facing off with the abomination. A creature he utterly despised. From his stare to his posture, Micah dared the beast to take a single step in any direction.

All the while, the sandcats protested anyone's nearness to him.

The sun glared with passion, harsher than the day before. Which had been harsher than the day before that. Any section of exposed skin charred and healed, then charred again. Sweat rolled over his chest and back, soaking his tunic. His lips remained chapped. Fatigue ebbed and flowed, but Micah dared not reveal a weakness.

The moment he slept or exited the creature's line of sight, it would bolt. He sensed this. Because, in the chaotic tangle of his thoughts, he believed he'd been interpreting the crackle of the beast's radiating emotions since day two. *Terror. Love. Fury. Hate. Hope.*

No, Micah must be mistaken. Hopeful? What *belua* would ever experience such an emotion with a chimera nearby?

What he knew beyond a doubt: if he attacked, the men surrounding him would attack as well, and the strange creature would fight to the death to defend Vee. While such combat could serve a purpose, proving his strength, forcing his opponent to submit to his will, the end result would do him little good if his wife were harmed.

She deserved to hurt. *Evil.* From the very beginning, she'd sought his downfall, attempting to save her "children." Had used the war with Kaysar to burrow into Micah's life. Any excuse to stay by his side and seduce him into forgetting his purpose. He intended to punish her for it, to make her suffer as she'd made his people suffer, but not through death.

No, he would use the beast to do it. But first, he would break its spirit—with patience. Anyone could use a sword; only skilled warriors brandished unshakable persistence. A difficult weapon to employ, but far superior to battle, giving him a stronger hold of his opponent's mind. But, as proven, this strategy required more time and energy on Micah's part. Time, however, was running out. The truce with the Unhinged One ended in only three weeks. Then, his focus became divided.

Who was he kidding? His focus was already divided. The easy victory against the other king—the one he'd boasted of at the feast—now struck him as an intangible dream. Take out a depraved, bloodthirsty king and queen...while dealing with the mother of monsters. How?

A muscle jumped beneath his eye. Had Kaysar sent Vee for this very purpose? A weapon meant to destroy Micah from the inside out? Had the other king heard rumors of his rival's obsession with a green-eyed, scarlet-haired beauty, then hunted and recruited her to his cause? If so...

Muscles hardened as rage burned away the last vestiges of his

civility, leaving him raw. Vee had sought to garner his capitulation for Kaysar.

Agonized moans rose from the men around him. A soldier
clawed at his own cheeks, as if attempting to peel off his skin.
Someone toppled to his knees.

Micah floundered—*I'm responsible for this?*

The soldier on his knees crawled closer, reaching for Micah, as
if he hoped to unseat the source of his pain. The sandcats reacted
in an instant, delving beneath the ground, vanishing from view.

Foreboding electrified the air. What might happen next...?

In a blink, the felines burst forth and tore into the warrior
who'd fallen, shredding his torso in seconds. To end any threat
to Micah? Why? Why did they continue to do this?

A pained shriek rang out, the male scrambling backward.
The sandcats retreated, returning to their preferred positions
near Micah.

Oh yes. An ending. And a showing. An example had just
been made.

Their protectiveness only tossed fuel on his fury. He worked
his jaw while attempting to calm. Difficult to do, now that he
grasped how his oracle and mistress had escaped. The sandcats
must have dug their way to the underground maze to find and
free the women from their chains. A supposition he'd never entertained. Had Vee created the pair for such a purpose as this?

Forget calming. Hot coals heated the rage another hundred
degrees. More moans pierced the air. More clawing. He'd bet
the cats served as spies as well. Had they found the trolls and
alerted Kaysar?

Inhale. Exhale. "Widen the circle," he commanded. Out of
his range. "Don't stop until you calm."

The soldiers stumbled ten feet back, and yes, the skin-peeling ceased.

I'm as much a monster as this belua. *And a fool.* Chest flayed raw,
Micah castigated himself. He had played right into his enemy's

plans. Right into Vee's. She'd never sought his protection. Only his attention. A distraction. She'd never been a vulnerable female fleeing a crazed male. Kill Kaysar's parents? No. A story, nothing more.

Had she done this for payment? Were the two lovers? Family? Friends? They possessed similar abilities, which suggested they were born near each other, at the very least. Villages tended to produce a multitude of powers through the same glamara.

His hands curled into fists. The sooner he imprisoned her, the better. Nothing mattered more than her capture. Then, he could deal with the grotesque consolidation of creatures before him.

In more ways than one, this *belua* was different than any other he'd faced. When spears and swords pierced its bark, stone or foliage, it healed within seconds. He knew this because he had pierced it thrice. Not to kill it, but to learn.

A blast of a horn suddenly erupted. A short ring. The creature tensed, but not with fear. Instead, indignation and anger vibrated across the connection. The same emotions the beast projected every time the horn had sounded, signaling one of Micah's men had discovered another jewel.

The very jewels he'd given to Vee. Pieces he'd foraged from trolls, centaurs and goblins all those centuries ago. She hadn't lost or discarded the gifts, as implied. She'd stored them inside her trees, as if she'd sought to maintain a link between them. As if she'd missed him the way he'd once missed her.

More lies! He didn't know why he'd commanded his men to alert him to the finding of each piece, to store everything for him and keep nothing for themselves. No, not true. He knew. Currently, the acquisition provided his only source of satisfaction—because he hoped to use the pieces to hurt Vee in some way.

Fuming, he stepped forward, erasing some of the distance between him and his opponent. Let the creature feel the full force of his dual chimeras. The felines moved with him.

The *belua* stiffened but didn't growl yet; like the sandcats, it only made noise when one of his warriors neared or Micah issued a command to it. Warnings.

Vee wasn't the only reason Micah let the creature live. So far, only leaves had grown from its limbs. No fruit or nuts yet. But sustenance *would* come—a feast for his people. He sensed this, too.

And then?

Micah would use the first seeds to foster a garden. He had only to tame the creature.

"Open. Your. Arms." The same command he'd uttered every day.

As before, the beast had huffed and growled, doing everything in its power to resist the compulsion to obey his glamara. And failing. At least somewhat. Again and again, it had rotated its arms toward him, revealing more evidence of Vee's unconscious form. The same occurred today.

The huffing started. Then the growling. Its nostrils flared, and its chest heaved. Stone muscles shook. Bark flared, sticking out in spikes. Vines slithered over limbs and branches like snakes.

The crack between its upper arm and chest widened bit by bit, a beam of sunlight flooding Vee's motionless form. Like a man dying of thirst, Micah guzzled the sight of her. Her features were relaxed, her lips slightly parted. Golden skin glowed with health, those deceptively adorable freckles on display. A strand of scarlet hair caught and lifted in the breeze.

A familiar pang of connection erupted, stronger than what he felt with the *belua*, and he inwardly cursed. When would the link to her die?

The answer struck him as obvious: *When I kill it.* There was a way...

Satisfaction unfurled. Yes. Satisfaction, not dread. While there wasn't a way to pry Vee from the protective grip of her "child," there was now room to neutralize the wicked temptress's glamara.

"The collar," he called.

Norok stood off to the side; the warrior had refused to leave the area as well, lest Micah had need of him. The very reason the male had been awarded the position of second.

"The fortifications have been made to the metal, per your instructions." The warrior pitched Micah the collar in question. A metal band embedded with multicolored stones, each performing a singular task, negating specific abilities.

He grinned. The bright red crystal in the center of the collar ensured he could find Vee, no matter where she happened to be. If she did somehow escape him, he could hunt her without problems.

Micah weighed the collar in his grip. Light. Perfect. Bumps littered the outside, but the inside was as smooth as silk. He had insisted. The band was solid, unbreakable, yet thin, further protecting her skin. As long as Vee wore this—and wear it she would—she would be as powerless as a human. Unable to create her beasts or flitter. All in all, she would be unable to escape the wrath of her captor.

His satisfaction deepened. But so did guilt and his own protective instincts. *Must handle with care.* No. No! He had handled her with care before. With patience, consideration and generosity. Look where it had gotten him. The protectiveness surged anew only because he'd been foolish enough to wed her. Now she bore the titles of wife and queen. A mistake he couldn't undo unless he killed her—a dishonorable path.

Do no harm to the innocent. Protect what's yours. Always do what's right. Never be without a backup plan.

He'd made a mistake. Not just by wedding her but wedding her without crafting a backup plan. Now he could only forge ahead, working with the tools he had.

Gaze locked on the beast, Micah stepped forward again and again, approaching... The time had come to end the standoff.

Viori lay in the comforting embrace of her family, the sting of her sorrow easing. Through Graves each of her darlings lived on. She felt their love for her, radiating from her newest creation. That love provided a protective bubble of inner peace. And yet, despite that bubble, turbulent dreams plagued her...

In the latest dream, she watched as the stubborn Micah neared the vulnerable Graves, who seemed rooted in place.

Run! she screamed internally. But her baby did not run. He didn't even walk or hop. Still, he stayed put, surrounded by countless armored men, as if Micah wielded a strange power over him. Maybe he did. He'd called himself the beast tamer. Was he?

Closer and closer the two came, soon to touch... A cry of upset left her. Micah had killed her children once, and he could do it again.

Only a dream, she reminded herself. *Only a dream*. But it wasn't, was it? Her stomach twisted. Once, she'd thought she'd dreamed the little boy with the jewels. Then she'd awoken to find him nearby. Somehow, she had seen him then—and she was seeing him now. In real time?

Helplessness filled her as Micah ascended Graves, scaling up, up. Limbs shook. Oh yes. Real time. And she could do nothing about it. Why wasn't Graves pounding Micah's bones into powder?

Multiple weapons were now anchored to her murderous husband. The axes he'd used in battle. Swords. Spears. Daggers. A bow and quiver of arrows. Things Norok had tossed him throughout the standoff. How many of those did he hope to use against her child while she could do nothing but watch? Or did he plan to murder her before attacking the newborn? Something he could absolutely do. The crack between Graves's arm and torso left her vulnerable. Slip a sword through, and he could slice her open from nose to navel.

Must wake. Kill him before he kills us!

Although, he'd had plenty of opportunities to destroy them. All the dead-king-walking had to do was torch the giant, cooking her inside his palm. But he hadn't. So far, Micah had speared Graves a couple of times, seeming curious rather than malicious.

Graves heaved his breaths, strain emanating from him and enveloping her. With all of her might, Viori fought to rise.

Micah reached out with the collar in his hands. A slave band? Or something more? What would the piece do to her?

Fighting so hard… Argh! Why didn't Graves shake him off and stomp him while he had the chance? Then, he could simply walk her out of the camp. The encompassing army would do *nothing* as long as Graves held their queen.

But her darling didn't act, and she never awoke. With careful contorting, Micah anchored the collar around Viori's neck. Cold metal. A jolt of power slammed into her, and she gasped, her eyelids popping open.

Graves jolted, too, at last flinging Micah to the ground. She scrambled to her knees as the king smacked into his soldiers, their armor clinking as they fell. Leaning over the top of her child's arm, she attempted to flitter them both as far as possible. Just in case Micah had dropped a special pebble nearby, allowing the action… Alas. Frustration scraped at her calm facade.

Bright sunlight burned her eyes. As she struggled to remove the collar, she kept her attention from Micah. He sprang to his feet and withdrew his axes, gripping the hilts so tightly his knuckles bleached of color. He looked terrible. The sun had burned his pale skin, leaving red, blistered patches. Good! No one deserved to suffer more.

Members of the army righted and readied their spears, pointing the tips in her direction.

"We really must stop meeting like this," she called.

"Trust me," he responded with equal nonchalance. "That is the plan."

A threat. "Kill him, Graves," she commanded, glaring at the male she despised with the whole of her being.

Micah glared right back, even while issuing a command to his men. "Hold until my signal."

Graves's strain intensified, but he didn't move. "Mother. Father. Not fight." The stilted accent was more mist than substance, but each word packed a formidable punch.

He'd found his voice so soon? As only Drendall had done? But how was that even possible? And what did he mean, *father*?

When Viori had referred to Micah as the boy's stepfather, she'd meant to taunt the king, nothing more. "He's not—" she began.

At the same time Micah belted out, "I'm not—"

Going quiet, they glowered at each other. Then he raised his axes, as if ready to chop her baby to pieces. Would Graves fight back? With his confusion about the king's role in his life... He might not.

Not knowing what else to do, she announced, "Let Graves go, and I'll stay." A promise she would keep—until her child was safe. Then... Viori smiled. Then she'd let the acid in her heart spill out, pouring over Micah and his land. For her children. For Kaysar.

For herself.

Micah smirked up at her. "Wife, you'll stay, anyway. This, I promise you."

Was that so? "Do you hear this?" she demanded of Graves. "He threatens me. Do as you're told and kill him."

"No," her darling spit, reminding her of a petulant child. He shook his head no, proving his will was somehow stronger than hers.

That her own creation had dared to naysay her—what did it mean? This was only the second time in Viori's life that a created being had refused to obey her slightest whim. First Fifi-belle, now Graves.

Her mouth floundered open and closed. This boy could *not* be an extension of her. What was she even supposed to do right now? "You listen to me right now, young man. I told you to attack—"

"I. Said. No!" Graves drew back an arm and tossed her. Her! He flung her across the entire campground and then some.

Weightlessness. Wind. Realization. Viori was slicing through the air, screaming with indignation and fury, flailing and flipping end over end. Despite clearing the campground, she couldn't flitter to protect herself from a crash landing.

Micah shouted a denial— Impact came faster than she expected. A heavy thud registered. Thoughts fragmented. Things inside her smashed together. Other things cracked. Blood and dirt coated her tongue. Another thud. Then another and another until she caught the rhythm and rolled to the edge of Grimm Forest.

When she stopped, she held her position, panting. Blinking. Trying to think and see past the cloud of dirt. She coughed and spit, her indignation only magnifying. Why, that little *brat*!

The air cleared and her dizziness faded. With her brain no longer rattling against her skull, she rallied the good sense to climb to her knees. Sharp pains accompanied each movement. The pain only elevated as broken bones snapped into place and joints knitted back together. Her stomach protested, threatening to empty. Deep breath in. Out.

Angry shouts sounded in the distance. Wait. The shaking. Worse by the second. Coming from…the ground?

Understanding dawned, sure and bright. Graves had tossed her, removing her from danger as quickly as possible, then sprinted in the same direction, giving chase. But he'd tossed her amid a temper tantrum, his strength causing her countless injuries at a crucial moment in her marriage.

Well. Why waste the lad's efforts? Later, though, she'd be giving him a stern lecture. And a spanking!

With a huff, she dashed ahead, plunging deeper into the forest. Graves would catch up. What's more, Micah wouldn't injure him or allow his men to strike. There at the end, she'd sensed the change in him. Her children were secure—for now.

Graves arrived, long legs allowing him to bypass her entirely. "I said no," he told her with a snotty tone, humphing as he left her in his dust.

Are you kidding me? He dared to *pout?*

Speeding after him, she— Argh! She screeched and halted abruptly. Her new collar. The metal had heated, burning white-hot. No, not just heating but pulling. Hard. Attempting to yank her back to Micah? She did her best to press on, but felt as if she were walking through a pool of molasses. Each step required staggering amounts of strength. Her thighs soon trembled. Once again, she tried to flitter and failed. Also the collar's fault? Outside the camp, the ability should work.

"The king hacked and burned you, for goodness' sake," she called, puffing her breaths. "He isn't your father. He's your murderer!"

Once she got Graves under control and safely tucked away, she would find someone to remove the collar. Then, she would return and finish the original plan—overseeing Micah's sabotage, earning Kaysar's forgiveness.

Never should have deviated. Lesson learned.

CHAPTER FIFTEEN

Micah rushed through his tent, preparing for the hunt. He scrubbed from head to toe, hoping to energize as much as clean up. He dressed in a clean tunic, leathers, fresh boots and the cloak, then loaded himself with weapons.

Every so often, he rubbed his thumb over the red stone anchored in the center of his wrist cuff. The newest addition to his accessory. An eternastone. The reason Vee could never escape him. Cut one of the rocks in half, and the two pieces forever called to each other, desperate to reunite, no matter the distance between them.

Some lovers wore the stones as a sign of their unwillingness to part. Never had Micah desired to do so. Until now. He doubted he would ever part with the thing.

The sandcats followed him through the enclosure. He allowed it, too busy to deal with their presence right now. They wanted to protect him? Very well. Let them. It wouldn't save them when the time came. He had plans...

As he stuffed anything he thought he might need into a satchel, the felines inspected everything, pushed maps from the table, clawed at the cloth walls and got comfortable in the pallet of furs.

The cuff burned and tugged him in the direction Vee had flown. His thoughts whirled all the while. *Do no harm to the innocent.* Vee wasn't innocent. *Protect what's yours.* The creature she'd named Graves belonged to Micah now. Payment for the devastation her other "children" had visited upon his people throughout the centuries. Vee herself would spend her days in his dungeon.

Always do what's right. Neutralizing her was for the good of all.

Never be without a backup plan. To stop her from creating more monsters, he must chain her or kill her. No other paths lay before him.

His tiny guards hissed when Norok stalked into the tent, pale hair damp with sweat. "I have readied Cavalry."

Cavalry, Micah's personal centaur. A cantankerous, difficult male with the bloodline of the ancients—the biggest, strongest and fiercest among the species. "I won't be requiring a mount for this expedition." He preferred to do this alone. "Fetch Elena and Sabot."

"Very well." Norok wrinkled his nose in distaste when he spotted the felines and reached for a dagger. "Shall I dispose of these little beasties before I go?"

The sandcats lunged at Norok, and the warrior reared back, yelping like a small child.

At any other time, Micah might have laughed. "Leave them be." When the time came, he would be using them against Vee. Another reason he wasn't taking a mount. Cavalry would stomp the two into powder at the first opportunity.

"As you wish." Norok vanished, but reappeared a few minutes later. "The two you requested are on their way."

A sullen Elena stalked into the tent. This was the first time Micah had seen her since the invasion of *belua*. From what he'd been told, she'd battled Vee and lost—epically—and only recently recovered. Sabot followed on her heels. Unlike other former viceroys, Sabot had never displayed a beat of resentment. He performed any task he was assigned promptly and without complaint. He always treated others with respect, no matter their station, earning Micah's admiration.

"Micah," Elena immediately rushed out. "I'm so sorry I allowed the—" she cringed "—queen to escape. So sorry I wasn't able to warn you of her ability to—"

"We all made mistakes that night." Time to issue orders and go. "Norok, you're in charge during my absence. Be on watch for any new *belua*. Trap those who dare approach. I'll deal with them upon my return." Any able to grow fruit would be spared. All others would die.

His friend bowed his head. "It shall be done."

"Elena—" Micah turned to her "—you'll return to the palace to listen to Kaysar and Cookie. Sabot will accompany you, making himself known only if you have need of him." Not even an oracle would notice her.

Sabot nodded, his gaze darting to the blonde and lingering. Heating? "No harm will come to her—you have my word."

Excellent. "I shouldn't be gone more than a few hours. No more than a day at most."

"Are you sure you can imprison your queen, when the time comes?" Norok asked, as hopeful as he was curious.

Micah flinched at the title he had oh, so foolishly bestowed upon a treacherous female he could never fully sever from his life without heaping great dishonor upon his name. "I am *very* sure." What other choice did he have?

Churlish, he stalked from the tent. The cloak's hem whipped against his calves. As expected, the sandcats followed. They even shot ahead of him to take the lead. He could have flittered to the edge of Grimm Forest, but he didn't want to risk losing his new shadows. Not yet. Not until they'd served their purpose.

As he stomped forward, his people scurried out of his path.

Micah picked up the pace, jogging, running into Grimm Forest, where huge footprints offered a perfect trail. Straight ahead. The pull on his cuff continued to increase, his stone ready to be rejoined with hers.

Soon. He was no more than fifteen minutes behind Vee. When he got his hands on her...

Inside him, fires died. His rage turned icy, freezing his veins. *No mercy.* But though he never veered off course, he never came across her. Not the first hour. Not the third, fifth or seventh, either.

A flame of worry sparked, melting a portion of his rage. How did she hide from him, resisting the constant pull of the stones?

Finally, he stopped. The sandcats halted, too, their tails vibrating. Micah took stock as his companions rushed here and there, scenting everything. The sun was due to set, the heat of the day cooling. Insects buzzed and chirped. Gnarled trees towered in every direction, the ground nothing but a sea of raised roots and dirt. An assortment of aromas coated the air, citrus among them.

His muscles turned to stone, preparing for battle. She *must* be nearby.

The fur—grains—on the backs of the sandcats stood up. A second later, a crackle of energy prickled his nape. He palmed two daggers. He knew what that crackle meant—Cookie had opened a doorway nearby.

He stiffened. His ears twitched. A sound caught his notice. Familiar. Vee mumbling? His heart thudded as he sprinted forward...

Vee. There! Her red tresses acted as a magnet for his gaze. Micah braced for impact and flittered to her, grabbing—nothing. He spun, confused. His arms were empty, and there was no longer any sign of her. But his ears continued to twitch. The noise. Her voice ebbed and flowed.

The cats stalked the area, sniffing. She reappeared for a moment, then vanished again. Then reappeared. Vanished. Her image continued to flash in and out, never actually solidifying.

He scowled as his confusion magnified. What was happening? Her head was bowed, her face streaked with dirt, and her hair tangled. She was limping and yes, mumbling under her breath.

He didn't understand. Why was she flittering again and again, despite the collar? One of the stones negated her abilities.

A stronger electric pulse brushed his neck, signaling another doorway. Cursing, he jumped in front of Vee and scanned...

The doorway. Twenty feet ahead, a tear spread through the air, growing longer and wider in equal measure. Leaves unfurled around the edges, creating a window into another landscape. A paradise of plush foliage, blooming flowers and lapping water—*his* paradise. Once Kaysar and Cookie were dealt with, his people could return and thrive as never before.

He tightened his grip on the hilts of the daggers. Queen Cookie stood in the middle of it all, wearing a pair of formfitting blue pants and tunic with the words This Princess Saved the Prince etched across the center.

The sand-spawn hissed at her and batted their paws.

Long brown locks streaked with gold formed a crown on her head. Big silver eyes glittered with excitement as the royal feline sat at her feet. A true feline. A sleek black cat named Sugars. Everyone in the Dusklands knew to avoid the animal. By Cookie's royal decree, to harm him meant you would feel her vines slowly creep and crawl through your veins for centuries to come.

She looked nothing like the sovereign who had threatened to toy with him only days ago. But then, her appearance changed with her clothing—and her personality. Of which there were legion. You never knew which of her incarnations you would be forced to face. Micah only knew he despised them.

Only the truce stayed his hand. Had he not given his word, this female would be bleeding to death. But breaking his vow to destroy his fiercest enemy came with consequences he couldn't afford to pay. Namely, the loss of his self-respect and the trust of his people.

"Hello, Micah," Cookie said with a wicked grin she never lost, no matter which version of herself she happened to be. "Is now a good time to chat?" She motioned to Vee's image, still flashing in. "Pretty neat trick, huh? I'm learning how far I can push my powers. Stack a series of doors today, make a specific someone's new wife the only key, and voilà, she walks in circles for the rest of eternity. Or until she notices she's walking in circles and ends the loop. Whichever comes first. No harm, no foul. No broken truce."

Cookie had trapped Vee in a looping gallery of doors? He gnashed his molars.

He wasn't surprised by the queen's knowledge of his wedding. Word traveled fast when you worked with a dishonorable oracle, planted spies in your enemy's camp and commanded said spies to wed their hosts.

"You will free her of your own volition. Now!" He lowered his chin. Perhaps there were ways around a truce. "Or I will *make* you."

"Hardly. I worked on this. Plus—" She whipped her attention to the left and snarled, "I thought I told you to shut it, Pearl Jean, and make me a sammich. A gamer girl's gotta game. No, not another word from you, either, Jareth. Trust me, I know the hubs is gonna be ticked. Yes, I'm doing this, anyway. No! No more out of you two. Go away and let me offer Mike his final lifeline."

Pearl Jean and King Jareth must be standing near her, but out of the doorway's range. Enemies! To reach them, Micah had only to dive through the opening. Which he could do. He had never vowed not to harm the old crone and the errant king.

Cookie's attention swung back to him, her scowl easing into the wicked smile once again. "Where was I? Oh yes. Your desperation to free your brand-new wife." Her gaze dropped to

the still-hissing cats, and her eyes narrowed. "Call off your...
whatever those things are."

An obscenity boiled at the end of his tongue. "I. Will. Have.
Her. Back. Now!" He would lock her up as planned and be
done with her!

"Dude. Chill," Cookie interjected and rolled her eyes. "She's
fine, promise. I haven't approached and given her my hard sell
yet. That'll come in a bit if you continue to prove unreasonable.
I wanted to offer you a onetime, too-good-to-pass-up deal first.
Are you ready? Here it is. I'll concede to nothing, and you'll
concede to everything, and the war stops before it starts."

Concede? "I would rather die." He kept his gaze on both
queens. Vee still winked in and out of view.

"Look," Cookie continued with a sigh. "You're a family man
now. You and the old ball and chain might dream of popping
out a couple of brats. Or enjoying a decade of Naked Tuesdays
first. My point is, you'll be busy. You won't wanna be preoc-
cupied, trying but failing to fend off my brilliant attacks. And I
get it. So stop being selfish and concede already. You aren't the
only one ready to enjoy wedded bliss, you know."

Realization dawned, shining light on a well of hope. His
own smile bloomed. "You fear you'll lose." A prediction of her
oracle or spy? Or both?

Muffled voices seeped from the doorway.

She stomped her foot, then drew in a deep breath and pinched
the bridge of her nose. A soft breeze brushed a lock of fallen hair
over her face. "Shut it, Pearl Jean! You do *not* tell Amber she got
this one right. Agreed?" Another stomp of her foot. Cookie lowered her arm and glared at Micah. "As for you. You've made your
choice. It was the wrong one. And, like, superdumb. Enjoy your
time-out. Or not. I plan to make you as miserable as possible."

In a snap, the foundation beneath his feet vanished, a doorway opening beneath him. He shot through the air, landing on
an icy mountain, and rolling over carpets of sharp ice. Stings

registered, a freezing burn following. Numbing cold seeped deep into his bones.

Thunder boomed as he caught himself and crouched, taking stock. A storm raged in a lightning-lit night sky. Wind billowed, sharp crystals pelting him. No trees. A cave over there.

Micah's wrist cuff vibrated, forcibly extending his arm in the direction of the Dusklands because Cookie had portaled him into the farthest reaches of the Winterlands. He geared to flitter back. Had the queen forgotten he possessed the ability? She had wasted a good doorway.

Then a roar Micah recognized sounded in the distance. His chin snapped up, his ears twitching. Rage stormed once again, far colder than the ice. The snow beast. His guardian's killer.

Vee's child. Another roar, this one shriller. The ground shook.

Micah growled low in his chest. He had a choice. Return to the Dusklands and find Vee before Cookie did, or slay the abomination?

Viori trudged through Grimm Forest, exhausted, thirsty, furious, overheated and dragging her tired, aching feet. She had been alone for hours and hours. Truly alone for the first time in forever. Reminded her of the morning she'd awoken in an Earth forest, no children around her, men with torches and pitchforks bearing down on her, shouting, "Witch!"

Once she'd found safety, regrouped and recharged, she'd hunted *the men*—and she'd left destruction in her wake. Exactly what she would do to Micah.

She swiped her claws at air, willing to attack any available target. Even her husband's name provoked her fury.

Where was Graves? Despite his incredible size, there was no sign of him. Did he not care that she required a companion? That she was too weak to create someone else? Why punish her this way? Especially while she was in the middle of a separation from the male who was soooo not his father.

Had her child abandoned her like everyone else?

She kicked at a mound of sand and kept moving forward. The collar anchored to her throat burned and tugged and chafed.

With a quaking hand, she swiped at the sudden moisture in her eyes—just as the collar tugged harder, yanking her from the path. She tripped to the side as if she'd exited the other side of the realm. Wait? Had she? Were those interworld doorways closing before her?

"*Pst*. Over here."

Viori righted and dug in her heels, fighting the pull, knowing it would lead her straight to Micah. Her heart thumped as she came face-to-face with the speaker. A woman. Kaysar's queen. Cookie. A black cat perched at her feet.

Stomach turning inside out, Viori dragged in a breath. *Ignore your inner clench. And the urge to lash out. And the desire to pet the tiny animal.*

"Before you freak," the other woman said, her hands lifted in a gesture of innocence, "don't. I'm not here to hurt you. Technically, I can't. You're married to Micah, so you're considered an extension of him. His truce is your truce, amirite?" she ended with a forced laugh.

Conflicting emotions bombarded Viori. Run away. Race to the girl. Hug her. Shake her. Threaten to flay the flesh from her bones.

Kaysar probably loved this woman. Definitely considered her family. All well and good, but was this Cookie worthy of his affection?

Was anyone? Not even Micah had proved to be honorable.

Viori's insides compressed, making her feel hollow. Did Cookie know Kaysar had a sibling? The one who coldly, callously murdered her husband's beloved parents?

The queen puffed up her chest and snapped, "Look. I'm newly married, too, so I get it. You want to spend your days in bed with your hubby, not on the battlefield. Well, good news. I'm here to make your dreams come true. Tell me where Micah stores his trolls, and I won't display his head above my mantel when the truce ends." Her tone hardened, every word as heavy as stone.

The trolls. Yes! Viori should find the trolls. Rip the army from Micah's control, and he had no weapon to use against Kaysar. Tremors invaded her limbs. "You are newly married to Kay— *King* Kaysar?" Saying his name still hurt.

"I am." A wicked smile curved the other woman's mouth. "Some call me the Uncrumbled. Though for some reason more people refer to me as the *Really* Unhinged One."

That smile... *Threat!* Viori lifted her chin, gearing to unleash a horrifying song.

Cookie must have sensed the rise of aggression. Vines coiled over her arms, black thorns extending from her fingers. Leaves stood at attention, the tips as sharp as blades. Even the cat's fur stood up.

When seconds passed without incident, hostilities muted. They straightened, one after the other.

Cookie cleared her throat. "As I was saying." Her eyes dipped to Vee's new collar. "I see you like to play dress-up, too. Except, I prefer to make my husband wear the collar."

Did the other woman refer to...? Viori almost gagged. She didn't need to hear about her brother's bedroom adventures. "Have no fear. I'll find the trolls." Did Kaysar dread the unleashing of Micah's army? Had he sent his wife to negotiate a deal?

How did Micah force even a single troll to serve him, much less an incalculable number, anyway? And he *must* force them. Trolls were notoriously malicious to...everyone and everything. Basically, they thrived in destruction and chaos.

"You'll tell me where they are?" Cookie asked. "If you do, I'll grow you a paradise like mine. For the record, yours will be smaller."

She glanced over the (other) queen's shoulder and struggled to hide her awe. Had she ever beheld such a beautiful land? Flowers and water for miles. A field overflowing with fruit and nut trees.

"I might." Guilt singed her. If she betrayed him, she betrayed his people. The orphans. What would become of them? "But I might not." She could handle the trolls on her own and earn the paradise another way.

A place to raise her children. At some point, she and Kaysar would reunite. Maybe they'd even grow to be friends.

"Vee!" Micah's voice boomed through the forest.

Her guilt burned hotter, along with the collar, but they were no match for her rage. He'd found her.

Cookie winced. "Guess break time is over since Big Dog has returned from his minivaycay." The doorway slowly closed around her. "I'll let you two lovebirds resume your honeymoon. But I'll touch base real soon, and we'll finish our chat. Maybe you'll be wiser by then. If not...well, it's your funeral."

CHAPTER SIXTEEN

Micah sprinted through Grimm Forest, ice crystals sloughing from his skin and garments, warmth returning to his extremities. Bark sliced him, tearing his clothes, his flesh. Blood trickled and ceased as wounds opened and healed, leaving thin white lines in his skin.

A wildfire stormed through his veins. The scent of citrus filled his nose, acting as a combustible fuel to his every thought. *So close to Vee.* The cuff around his wrist heated with increasing intensity as he drew nearer, his eternastone desperate to be reunited with hers.

Minutes ago, he'd returned to the Dusklands to discover Vee was no longer caught in the loop of invisible doorways. Or even in the area. Had Cookie visited her to give the "hard sell?" Maybe. Probably. But there'd been no sign of the queen, either.

A growl vibrated in his chest. The sandcats were long gone, too. And he didn't miss them. Not even the tiniest bit. Good riddance! He only wished he'd had the chance to use them against their creator, as planned.

He quickened his pace. The cuff continued to heat, nearly blistering him. *Closer...*

A limb snapped up ahead, and his ears twitched. Toward the left. He adjusted his route and pumped his arms. His legs gobbled the distance. Eyes scanning...

There! Sunlight streamed through a canopy of tangled branches, illuminating tendrils of red. A hot blaze of satisfaction overtook every inch of him.

Vee sprinted as fast as her feet would carry her, but he gained ground fast, closing in.

Sensing him, his treacherous wife cast a panicked glance over her shoulder and yelped.

Almost there... Micah sheathed his daggers, freeing his hands, and dived. Boom! They collided and hurled toward the ground. Midair, the sides of his cloak enveloped them, creating a world of their own for one brief moment. Warm softness registered, instantly dulling the worst of his rage. Finally! He had her.

At the last second, he acted without conscious thought, twisting to take the brunt of impact, saving her from bruises, scrapes and broken bones. Even still, air erupted from her lips. Then they were rolling over dirt and rocks and slamming into a huge tree.

She recovered quickly. All claws and teeth, she fought the shackles of his arms. As he healed, she popped to a stand.

As she turned, preparing to dash off—shoeless, he realized— he lunged from his supine position and clasped her ankle, yanking her off balance. She fell, and this time he wasn't there to soften the landing. Another burst of air from her. Did this slow her? No. She attempted to scramble away. This time, he held firm.

Dousing all guilt, Micah flittered to a stand and hauled her to her feet. He wasn't gentle about it.

"Do not run," he snapped—and let her go.

Miracle of miracles, she obeyed, spinning to face him. "Why are you as cold as ice?" Glaring at him, puffing for breath, she snarled, "Never mind. I don't care. Take this collar off me, you Neanderthal!"

Neanderthal? He raised his chin a notch. "The collar stays. And I'm cold because I took a forced trip to the Winterlands— where I found your precious ice beast." The final words dripped with relish. "The one who savaged my guardian. The only parent I ever had."

Pain contorted her features. "You murdered another of my children?" With a screech, she launched her body at him, clawing anywhere she could reach. "I'll destroy everything you've ever loved and leave you with nothing but pain and misery. Only after you've suffered decades of agony will I sing your spine to life and command it to slither out of your body."

The tears in his tunic spread, blood trickling from new wounds. Micah reeled as he struggled to subdue her. Had he ever seen a more shocking display of agony and outrage? Emotions she had no right to feel! *She* allowed her creations to murder his guardian and many of his citizens. *She* used his desire against him from the start, overseeing his destruction. *She* betrayed his trust.

Eventually, he pinned her against him, pressing her back to his chest. Arms wrapped around her middle, he held her hands together.

Panting and squirming, she refused to admit defeat. "I'll remove your genitals and roast them on a spit! I'll—"

"Enough. I didn't kill your vicious abomination," he grated against her ear. The reminder of his madness infuriated him— and every bit of that fury was directed at himself.

Why had he walked away without removing his longest foe's head? He'd hunted it, planning to do precisely that. He'd even cornered the monster within its own cave. Finally, after centuries, he'd found Erwen's killer. At long last, Micah had glimpsed a chance to eradicate a beast who had scarred him inside and out, like the trees.

"I don't believe you," Vee grated. "Why would you leave him alive?"

"He's merely a vase. I'd rather destroy the clay responsible for it."

She flinched as if he'd struck her, and guilt sparked. Guilt he shouldn't feel.

At the time, he'd told himself he couldn't waste a minute, that he must return to Grimm Forest as quickly as possible. But that was a lie, wasn't it? He could have easily slain the *belua* and returned after.

"Go ahead and do it. Beat and kill me," she demanded. Though she trembled, she sounded much calmer. "Or do I need to beg for each strike? You've tortured me with your presence long enough."

So they'd reverted to commands for beatings. "Oh, little wife. You won't be escaping my wrath so easily, I promise you." Though he yearned to shake her, to kiss her, to slay her, he focused on the conversation—for the moment. "You see our marriage as an assurance of your survival, but you will learn better. Some things are worse than death and living inside a coffin might be one of them. Soon, you'll know firsthand. I have a special room in my dungeon. When I designed it, I didn't know who I would be cruel enough to leave there. Now, I do."

The threat only softened her demeanor. She rubbed against him, purring, "Admit it. You don't want to be without me."

He gritted his teeth, tolerating the carnal contact, pretending he remained unaffected. When he could stand it no longer, he moved her hands behind her back, shackling them with a hard grip before putting a little distance between their bodies.

She chuckled. "A little slow to stop me, eh, beast tamer?"

Fuming, he bent down without compromising his hold and ripped strips of material from the hem of her wedding dress. As he straightened, she twisted as fast as lightning and tried to bite his ear.

He forced a chuckle of his own and bound her wrists with the cloth. "A little inept, eh, beast maker?"

She hissed at him. "I'm going to beat *you* for this!"

"Shall I gag you, too? Be quiet."

Her struggles intensified, the newly shortened skirt inching up her legs. "I'll stake you to Graves and allow his brothers and sisters to cut you open and feast on your organs."

"Most of his siblings are dead now, yes? Do as you're told and be quiet."

She flinched, but did, finally, obey him. *Ignore the spark of guilt. Ignore the feel of her.* He needed a moment to think. If possible. Glimpses of her smooth, flawless calves were making his fingers itch to linger. To savor the heat and softness while he had the chance. To draw goose bumps to the surface of her skin before traveling higher... To make her beg for what he would never give her.

A fever heated him. With sizzling desire, yes, but also more self-directed fury. This was what he was reduced to now? Hungering for another peek of a traitor's leg?

He would flitter Vee back to camp, as planned. He would lock her up and...what? Visit her in her new chains? Never see her again? Never speak to her? Constantly return to her cell, unable to stay away? All to wait for Graves and the sandcats to come for her, putting his people in harm's way?

The questions stopped him cold.

No, he wouldn't flitter her to camp. Not yet. He *shouldn't*. Instead, he would journey with her on foot, using the time to regain control of his body and center his mind. Added bonus: he could use his prisoner as bait, luring Graves and the sandcats within reach. He could end the trio without ever endangering his people.

Once he had Vee locked away, he could return to the Winterlands and deal with the ice beast.

Yes. He liked this plan. Very much. So his chest was tightening. So what? There would be no touching Vee along the way.

No looking at her. No scenting her and craving what he should not desire. Only developing his resistance to her appeal.

Micah gave her a little push in the direction he wished to go. "Walk."

"I hate you," she snapped, but again, she obeyed him, tripping forward.

"I'm devastated." More tightening. Another small push. "Go faster."

"*Die* faster!" she retorted. But she did lapse into silence. Well, her version of silence. She huffed and puffed and mumbled under her breath.

He led her through the forest, continuing to covertly flitter her farther and farther away from the campground, assuring they had more ground to cover to reach home. The more fatigued she was when they arrived at their destination, the better.

"Did you command your iceman to kill my guardian?" he asked. "Or has the beast racked up so many victims, you can't keep track?"

Some of the steam oozed from her. "I didn't command it. Not outright. I hate you, but I *am* sorry for your loss. Trust me, I'm keenly aware of how awful a loved one's death feels. Okay?"

He almost believed she meant it. Almost. But there was no better pretender than Vee. "Not okay. His name was Erwen. We hunted the creature for weeks. A violent snowstorm waylaid us, ruining everything of value we owned. Our maps, compass and weapons. Your *child* appeared out of nowhere and ripped into Erwen. I fought back, barely emerging with my life." He would have hunted the culprit once he'd healed, but he'd somehow stumbled through an invisible doorway, appearing in Grimm Forest…soon to discover a sleeping beauty.

"Well, I null and void my apology. Of course Snowy attacked you! You planned to *kill* him. What did you expect? For him to let you do it and not protect himself?"

Snowy? A sweet name for a killer. "Not another word," he snapped, "unless you want that gag."

The journey persisted in terse silence. For hours. She acquired new layers of dirt with each mile, but he gained no satisfaction from it.

"Well?" she demanded, opting to risk the gag. "What happened to your parents? Why were you under the care of a guardian? Why didn't you know your parents? Did they die?"

Admit the truth? That he was unwanted by all, even those who were supposed to love him most. Hardly. "That isn't your business."

He expected more questions about the pair. Instead, she asked, "Do you truly intend to lock me up, Majesty? Or am I marching to my execution?"

He waggled his jaw. "Oh, I will indeed be locking you up. Have no doubts on that score." But as far as they were now, her incarceration wouldn't happen for days to come. By then, he should have completed each of his missions. Controlling his body's needs. Calming his mind. Ending Graves and the cats.

Vee cast a brittle smile over her shoulder. "Will I be receiving the pain toxin like your oracle and mistress?"

"You deserve it. There's no question of that," he remarked with a flat tone. "You released Fayette and Diane. You should replace them and share their suffering."

"Don't put that on me. I'm not the one who released them."

"No more lies, and no more chatter. The gag isn't a threat but a promise."

"Go stab yourself." Contorting, she shot out her leg and tripped him. As he stumbled, she wrenched free of his hold and broke to the left, only to turn sharply and sprint right when he followed, racing away from him.

Micah flittered to her, letting the wrist cuff guide his landing. He materialized in front of her, and she slammed into his body, stumbling backward.

He flittered again, snagging her from behind before she hit the ground. "You cannot escape me," he told her, setting her on her feet and giving her a little push. "Start walking and stop trying to escape. From now on, I'll punish you when I catch you. And Vee? I will always catch you. Nothing can keep me from you."

"Are you sure? Because I've traveled to the mortal world on multiple occasions. I seriously doubt you can follow me there."

The mortal world? Truly? "You are able to open doorways?"

"I am."

His stomach knotted. Dare he believe? "Do it then. Open a doorway." He wished to see this for himself—and somehow stop her from ever doing it again. If she were to escape him... His whole being cringed.

She sputtered for a moment. "I'm not a dancing monkey who performs on command!"

So she couldn't open doorways at will. A handy piece of intel to have. "Your odd speech patterns make sense at least."

As they navigated the forest, she lapsed into silence at last. Not that he was granted a reprieve. His stubborn feral turned her efforts to escape, bolting again and again and again. Her mulishness staggered him.

What was he supposed to do with a female like this? He couldn't bring himself to whip her; he refused to mar her lovely skin. Was he supposed to deny her food? An even worse idea!

Despite her antics, they covered mile after mile, surrounded only by hot, dry air and bare, twisted trees, each of which served to darken his mood. There was nothing to source out here. No delicious fruit. No hearty nuts. No refreshing bodies of water. Just thought after thought after thought after thought.

The way her body moved...

He bit the inside of his cheek, tasting blood. Why was his lust growing instead of shriveling? The callous beauty was nothing but destruction to him. He should have saved himself a host of trouble and killed her when he'd struck at her trees.

Instinct pinged in the far recesses of his mind—*protect!*—reminding him of the battle. No, not a battle but a slaughter. The trees hadn't resisted or retaliated. But they'd hurt his men, so they'd deserved what they'd gotten. And yet...

I might regret.

Biting harder...more blood. This female had tangled him up, making him long for the days when he'd had only a kingdom to consider.

Before Vee, he'd been resigned to his lonely fate. No wife. No family. No affection. No touching or kissing. No holding his wife all through the night. No dreaming of a better future. Before Vee, he hadn't known the heights he could reach. But he knew now, and she was to blame.

"I'm thirsty, and I'm starved," she lamented. "Give me water and feed me. I deserve a reward. I haven't run away for three whole minutes."

"Suffer. I don't care." But he did care. And not because he wished to quench her thirst and ease her hunger. No. He was done seeking her comfort over his own. Done providing for her. Looked like he would be denying her food, after all.

Maybe.

Probably.

But probably not.

"What happened to you?" she asked, as if disappointed in him. "You used to be such a caring, generous boy, bringing your unconscious hostess gifts."

"That boy got savaged by your darling children and nearly died. Or rather, he did die. A stronger man grew from his ashes."

"You invaded our home, Micah." How reasonable she sounded. "What did you expect?"

Always the invader, never part of the family. And he despised her more for it. Loathed her dry tone and her dismissal of his trials. But most of all, he detested the reminder. She had a family, even if the members were monsters; he did not, and he never would.

"By the way. I found the jewels," he said. "You'd hidden them inside your trees."

"Those trinkets are mine!" she shouted, only to calm seconds later. "Why are you complaining about the past, anyway?" Hiking up a shoulder and lowering her head, she scratched her cheek. "That quote-unquote stronger man got to marry his favorite fantasy."

His lips pulled back from his teeth. Of course, his malicious little kitten had gone there. "That man desired you. This one does not." Because yes, he'd died yet again. A brute had replaced the king with aspirations of more.

"Ohhhh. What does this one long for then? Do tell. I can hardly stand not knowing."

Her dry tone irritated him. He craved loyalty. Honesty. Smiles. Genuine affection. Sizzling passion. Nothing he could have.

In the end, he sighed, weary to the bone, and told her, "I seek someone worthy."

She sputtered again, then lapsed into terse silence. A silence that continued on and on, until he hated that, too. When the sun began to set, he spotted the glint of light against water and foliage. But that was impossible. Nothing grew here, and anything liquid quickly evaporated. But even still, Micah thought he smelled a floral bouquet on every cool, damp breeze.

He spun Vee around and ducked, pressing his shoulder into her stomach and lifting her off her feet. Carrying her like a sack of *cibus* bulbs, he quickened his step. Rather than fight, she let her body drape his, bouncing against him. Tormenting him. Reminding him of the feast. Their wedding.

The wedding night they'd skipped.

Micah bit his tongue. This might have been a huge mistake. He didn't think he would ever get used to the feel of her. To having those lush breasts smashing into his shoulder blades.

Lest she sniff out his enjoyment, he grated, "For someone

who despises me as much as I despise her, you seem awfully comfortable in my arms."

"Please! I'm tired and using you for your muscles," she said, then yawned. "Don't go thinking I've forgiven you or anything like that. Our truce will end once I'm rested."

He wasn't charmed by that. Not excited or anticipatory.

Spotting something odd up ahead, he slowed. Stopped. Gaped. Was that...?

Yes, it most certainly was. An oasis. Trees and bushes capped by colorful leaves abounded. Pink, violet and green. Yellow, purple and blue. Bark that appeared as soft as velvet. Flowers and fruit in every direction. Moss-covered stones circled a small, bubbling spring that trickled into a crystal clear lake, where more of the blue flowers floated over the surface.

He flittered closer, frowning when he noticed a scroll nailed to a tree. After setting his captive on her feet, he ensured she remained pressed against him, unable to strike as he read the parchment.

Yo, Micah.

Consider this a honeymoon suite as well as a taste of the possibilities. The kind of benefits package I offer each of my citizens. So go ahead. Stay awhile with my compliments. Enjoy your first legitimate wedding night. My seer tells me you could use the rest. And the release, if you know what I mean. (I'm wagging my brows at you.) I hear your new wife is going to keep you up for the coming nights, you lucky dog you. You're welcome, by the way. You'll find clean clothes and refreshments in a picnic basket near the water. No poison, I swear. As soon as you wise up and relinquish your crown, ceasing to divide my lands, I'll make the Dusklands the most prosperous kingdom in all Astaria, the people the most joyous. Or kill you. The choice is yours.

Queen Cookie the Uncrumbled

He ripped the page from the trunk and shredded the words. Enjoy his first legitimate wedding night. *She taunts me now.*

His next inhalation felt like razors. What Cookie had offered masqueraded as the perfect outcome for everyone but Micah. Provision for all. A fact he could live with. But her offer wasn't perfect anywhere but on the surface. Even the most bountiful of kingdoms couldn't be enjoyed under the rule of a tyrant.

"What did the letter say?" Vee asked. "I, um, didn't get a chance to read it."

He popped his jaw. "Kaysar's wife fears I'll win our war. She seeks to make me desire you again, hoping to use you against me a second time." Whether Vee was witting or unwitting. He wasn't sure about her allegiance anymore. Her vehemence struck him as genuine. Though she'd tricked him before. "It won't do the queen any good."

"Are you sure?" Scarlet hair lifted in a soft, sweet breeze, curling in front of Vee's smug face as she pressed herself against him. "Or is that a dagger hilt in your pants?"

Even though his cheeks heated, he met her gaze without hesitation and smiled coldly. "It's a dagger hilt."

"Show me," she countered, far from intimidated or upset. She nipped his bottom lip. "If you dare…"

CHAPTER SEVENTEEN

Viori fumed as Micah rummaged through the picnic basket. *Without* showing her that supposed dagger hilt.

Would nothing go right for her?

She perched on the ground with her arms tied behind her back, uncomfortable thanks to him. As stealthily as possible, she sawed the binding over the sharp edge of a rock. Muscles she hadn't known she possessed strained and ached. Perspiration beaded on her brow.

The sun had lowered significantly, casting muted rays of lavender and amber over the land. Those rays bathed her companion's mighty frame. For the first time in their acquaintance, she experienced a little of that soul flaying Elena had mentioned. Ferocious power emanated from him. Sharp and stinging. Every cell in her body screamed, *Danger!* And yet, she believed she might kind of…like it.

What was *wrong* with her? She despised this male. But still she drank in the sight of him. Sweat-dampened hair clung to his brow. Several locks adhered to his cheeks. A thick shadow covered his strong jaw. His pale skin glistened, as if dusted with diamond powder. And good gracious, was he smuggling rocks under his clothing? *The strength he wields…*

Thankfully, she wasn't alone in this unwanted attraction. No matter what he claimed, he absolutely, positively enjoyed the sight of her as well. Anytime he glanced her way, his attention immediately dipped to her lips. Or the pulse in her throat. Her breasts. Each location left him flustered and Viori delighted.

Not want me anymore, husband? Unworthy? Try again. He might despise her with the same fervency she displayed toward him, but not an ounce of his desire had faded or cooled. On the contrary. It had grown and heated, soon to boil over. But how was she to use this information to her advantage? And she *would* use it to her advantage.

Forget his past crimes. Not that she could. But. This brutal king planned to imprison her for eternity and destroy her children. For that, he must die. Her plan hadn't changed: escape, find a way to remove the collar, hunt the trolls, destroy Micah, present herself to Kaysar.

Her nerves vibrated and her stomach churned; she shook off the malaise. For better or worse, she intended to charge ahead. But how best to escape? Nothing she'd attempted had gotten her far. If she failed in this, she lost everything, falling victim to Micah's plan: carting her into his camp, sealing her in some dank, dark prison and surrounding her with his troll army.

And that wasn't even the biggest problem she faced! Viori had found no trace of Graves, Sprinkles or Muffin. She knew they were fine. Healthy. But…they were avoiding her. Which she didn't understand!

And why hadn't Micah killed Snowy when he'd had the chance? Her third creation, made soon after Drendall, often proved a wee bit more temperamental than most. The son she'd sung to life when Winterland soldiers had captured her. A simple creature made of ice, fear and fury. He tended to lash out at anyone who dared approach him. Even Viori. But oh, she loved him dearly. During her first year without Kaysar, Snowy had saved her countless times.

The fact that Micah had allowed him to live... Perhaps the king wasn't as terrible as she believed?

What are you doing, veering off course? No, no, no! She knew better. What was it her husband said? Oh yes. *He's merely a vase. I'd rather destroy the clay responsible for it.*

She glowered at him while working harder at her bindings. Perhaps he was worse than she'd ever suspected.

When the tie frayed, freeing her hands, Viori decided to try a new path. Rather than running away as usual, she opted to test her companion. She drew her arms forward gradually, waiting for his protest. Her shoulders both protested and rejoiced.

Micah stiffened, noticing her new freedom right away. But then, he noticed everything always. For once, he didn't rush over to tackle and retie her. A courtesy she refused to appreciate.

But honestly, why bolt right now? She was tired, starved and weakened. To facilitate a successful getaway, she'd have to swallow her pride, douse his anger, charm him and convince him to lower his guard enough to feed her, then let her rest and recharge.

"Nothing to say to me?" she asked with a casual tone.

"I have plenty to say. Be grateful I'm willing to keep the words to myself. I'd appreciate the same courtesy."

"Fine. You seek silence. I'll give you silence. I have better things to do, anyway." Determined, she stood and tore off her dirty wedding gown, dropping the material at her feet.

Had Micah sucked in his breath? Without glancing her way, he intoned, "What are you doing, Vee?"

"I'd tell you, but I'm too busy being silent, remember? Besides, you aren't attracted to me anymore, so my nakedness shouldn't matter to you. And really, I'm eager to enjoy what's left of my life before someone I know and hate locks me up forever."

A growl left him...but still he didn't protest. Head high, naked but for the hated collar, she strolled ankle-deep into the cool water.

"Do you even know how to swim?" he asked.

"Kind of."

Another growl. "What do you mean, kind of?"

"I lived near a lake once. I taught myself to mostly stay afloat." With the waterline at her knees, Viori eased down and stretched out. She submerged herself in the soothing liquid, letting it engulf everything but her eyes and nose. Locks of hair soon floated around her face. Oh, this felt nice. Cool and refreshing. Forget any kind of plan for a moment. She needed this.

Her lids turned heavy and sank as she soaked. Had she ever enjoyed anything more than this luxurious, weightless sensation?

Well. Yes. She had. *Micah's kiss…*

Great! There went her relaxation.

A shadow fell over her, and she blinked open her eyes. The beast tamer towered on the shore, minus his cloak. He peered at her. No, he *glared* at her. He clutched a thin length of rope in one hand, and she tensed.

"You are clean enough," he barked. "Out. Now."

Ugh. What had soured his mood? "No. I'm dirtier than ever," she purred. "Ask me what I was thinking about before I stripped, and I'll prove it."

"I will not. You will get out because I commanded it."

Double ugh. Rather than protest, she sat up. Droplets dripped from her nipples. Oh, oh, oh. What was *this*? He'd definitely sucked in a breath this time.

Heart fluttering, she asked, "How about this? I'm sure you have questions for me, starting with my original scheme to snare you. I vow to answer each query honestly, but only while I'm in the water. Deal?" She could enjoy the water and torment him with her responses at the same time. Win-win.

He opened his mouth. Snapped it closed. Opened. Closed. Then he barked, "As if I can trust anything you say."

"No, you cannot." She grinned slowly, coldly. "But you'll agree to my terms, anyway. Be honest. You like watching me." A statement, not a question. "Perhaps as much as I like being watched by you."

"Now I know you're lying."

"Am I? What if I told you I like watching *you* even more? Surely you've felt my gaze upon you. Specifically, on a certain *overlarge* location..."

For a long moment, he white-knuckled the rope. His nostrils flared with each inhalation. Then he gave a stiff nod. "Very well. I accept your terms." He tossed the rope. "You may bathe. I will question. Because I'm curious. No other reason."

"Of course." She followed the tether with her gaze, overjoyed by its distance. When she noticed the array of toiletries provided by Cookie, she nearly whimpered. Micah had lined up the necessities near a waterfall. Cleaners for her hair. Scented oils for her skin. Items she'd craved very badly as a child. Things her parents had been unable to afford. Items she *still* craved very badly. More than ever before.

Viori barely stopped herself from leaping from the water and rushing over to gather everything close. *Mine!* "You didn't let me finish," she said, licking her lips. "As long as I'm in the water *and* using those gifts from Queen Cookie, I'll answer your questions."

"You didn't let *me* finish," he countered without missing a beat. "I accept your terms—as long as your hands are tied."

Gah! "Why did you toss the rope? And how am I to use my toiletries?"

"You won't. I will. And I'll show you."

Anger sparked—until she realized the implications of his demand. And caught a whiff of his satisfaction. Well, well, well. Seemed her husband had a diabolical plan of his own, and it involved putting his hands on her.

Why does this excite me? "If you wanted to rub soap all over my body," she rasped, "you should have said so. I would've agreed to your terms ages ago." She extended both arms toward him. "Hurry. I'm eager to begin."

A muscle jumped beneath his eye. From the shore, he clasped her hands and slowly glided her through the clear liquid, toward the waterfall. The deep end of the lake. Her heart fluttered as the rocky bottom disappeared, forcing her to rely on Micah to stay above water. But she wasn't afraid. He had a look in his eye every time he glanced at her over his shoulder...

As she paddled her legs and rested her elbows on a moss-covered shore, he sat between her and the array of toiletries, then collected the rope. After re-tying her wrists together, he relaxed—and smoldered.

Naughty Micah. He'd planned this. Set her up. And she wasn't sorry about it.

He removed his boots, rolled the hem of his pants up, then dipped his feet and calves into the water and lifted a small opaque bottle. He was going to do it. He was going to bathe her, facilitating his own doom. Because he *wanted* to. He wanted *her*.

Feminine power flooded her, heady and delicious. Had anything ever tasted so sweet? Viori settled more weight on her elbows, raising her upper body above the water. With her breasts framed by her biceps, she created maximum cleavage.

"Where would you like to start?" she asked, batting her lashes at him.

He jutted his chin, his stubbornness on full display, and met her gaze. At first. His attention dipped. A quick peek at her chest before snapping up. He gulped, his Adam's apple bobbing. His irises blazing. A dead giveaway. How desperately this male craved her...

Mmm. This power wasn't heady, after all; it was *beyond* heady. And distracting... Tempting her to enjoy herself while working her wiles and charming him. But why not? After the day she'd had, she deserved a little pleasure. Didn't she?

With a teasing tone, she asked, "Forget the conversation. Why won't you remove your clothes and join me, husband? Or are your muscles fake, as I suspect? Are rocks strapped beneath your tunic? They are, aren't they?"

His eyes slitted. "I told you. I'm scarred, thanks to you and your trees. Fae tend to sicken when they behold my ruined flesh."

Her small smile faded. How many injuries had he sustained as a young lad? How severe had the cuts and gashes been?

Guilt flared deep, deep inside her. "You startled me, and I screamed, spurring my protectors into action." But it wasn't terror she'd felt as her eyes had locked with young Micah's. No, he'd sparked a desperate yearning to throw herself into his arms. She'd thought, *At last! All is truly well.* In that moment, terror had come. Trust another fae? How could she?

And yes, an innocent boy had suffered for it. Still suffered. "They love me and react to my slightest emotion," she added. The guilt continued to burrow, but she finally headed it off. Mostly. *Hold on to your hate. Prepare the way for your escape.*

"Is that supposed to make me feel better?"

"Can *anything* make you feel better? I merely explained the situation." To mask a tremor, she ducked under the water. As she surfaced, he turned her, putting her back to him. Without eye contact, she was able to douse the sudden spike of tension. She rested her elbows on his thighs, saying, "I keep hearing about these so-called scars. I'm afraid the time has come to prove it, husband. Rip off your tunic quick or pull it off slow. Majesty's choice, of course, but either way, get to stripping," she said, trying for a teasing tone again. "This girl is ready for the show to start."

"Do you think your opinion means anything to me?" He lathered her hair with jerky motions, only to slow and gentle his touch of his own volition. Soon he was massaging her scalp, and Viori was moaning in astonished delight. Once he rinsed out all the bubbles, he tenderly applied a softening cream to the locks. He took his time, combing his fingers through the strands, and she could do nothing but let him, leaning against him for support, trying to remember to breathe. Doing everything in her power to resist the potency of his scent. She could enjoy this, but she shouldn't love it. For her, love had always equaled pain.

Viori roused from her semiblissful state. *Focus.* He'd said something, and she needed to respond. Besides, while his ministrations did strange things to her insides, he was still her enemy. Best she remembered that.

Tease him, but do not soften. "If you didn't care about my opinion, we wouldn't be having this conversation, now would we? You'd be baring all to your cherished wife, as commanded." Oh...no. The knowledge threatened to crack her calm facade. This big, strong beast tamer had a weakness, a vulnerability—her.

"Where is Graves?" he asked as he rinsed the smoothing cream from her hair.

Mmm. "That, I don't know. He left me. On purpose! He huffed at me like a silly child and marched away, leaving me in his dust, never glancing over his shoulder to ensure himself of my well-being. Can you believe the nerve of him, insisting his former killer is his current father?"

Micah's fingers flexed on her scalp. "It's something *you* suggested."

"Yes, but I was merely taunting you."

A soft growl left him—a common occurrence now, apparently. "Tell me your original intentions with me. That was our deal, yes?"

Was the truth painful to him? Well, too bad. He was about to get another dose. "They are exactly as you feared. To stop your war with Kaysar before it started."

"It had *already* started. The final battle was simply delayed by a year." He filled his palms with liquid soap and spread the bubbles over her throat. Her shoulders. Her breasts. His palms grazed her nipples. Slowly. Again.

Air hitched in Viori's throat, hidden parts of her awakening from slumber as if for the first time. His touch remained gentle. Soothing. Mesmerizing.

Seriously. Focus! She was allowing a killer to touch her, and she was indeed loving every second of it. That was unacceptable.

"Is King Kaysar really so bad?" she asked, utilizing her snottiest tone again. "Or are you really so stubborn?"

"Both." Did Micah sound less angry now, despite the seriousness of the topic? "How long have you aided the Unhinged One?"

Careful. "I knew him as a child. We were friends once." Deep breath in. Out. "We grew up in the same village, but haven't spoken since..." A lump grew in her throat. "Not since I m–murdered his parents."

She'd admitted as much before, yet the statement seemed to shock him. His fingers flexed on her again.

"Now," she finished, "I owe him a debt."

"And you decided to make me the key to its payment," Micah concluded.

The truth, and yet the implication turned every word into a lie. Her only response? "Mmm-hmm. You are."

"You realize you sacrificed your children for the sake of a past you cannot change and a male who will never thank you, yes?" His voice hardened. "And do you know what it will get you in the end? Grief."

Chills rained through her, and all she wanted to do was curl into a ball. "You don't understand. I've tried to shed the guilt born from my actions for centuries," she admitted softly. "I *need* to shed it. This is the only way."

His fingers flexed yet again. Finally, though, he softened, as if he did, in fact, comprehend the weight of her clinging guilt. With an almost tender graze against her throat, he told her, "You were a child then. You are a woman fully grown now, yet you are making a far worse mistake."

"Perhaps. But I can't let that stop me. I *must* do this, whatever the cost."

"Easy to say, difficult to live with after." He wrapped a hand around her neck, anchoring his thumb beneath her chin and spreading his fingers to cover as much ground as possible. Applying pressure, he tilted her head to an uncomfortable angle to force her to meet his gaze.

Though he appeared upside down, he was no less intimidating. Actually, he was more than intimidating. He was more everything. Aggressive. Angry. Gentle. Tender. Contradictory in every way.

"How often have you visited the mortal world?" he asked.

"Ten times or so." But rarely in chronological order. Her doorways cut through time as much as space.

"Why go? What's there?"

Chaos. Cruelty. Danger. Pain. Padded cells. "I have children there, too," she replied softly. One day, she hoped to bring them to the fae world.

She and Micah stared at each other for a long while, everything wrong but somehow right, and it was maddening. She didn't know what to think or feel anymore. The story of her life.

"I would have been good to you," he said, using that flat tone, "if you had only let me."

Sadness washed over her, thicker than the water. Colder, too. Before she could stop it, more truth spilled from her lips. "You might have tried to be good for a time, but in the end, you would have failed. Nothing lasts forever, Micah. Nothing."

CHAPTER EIGHTEEN

Micah glared at the female who had become a fever in his veins. He wanted her more than ever. Ached for her so badly, he could barely think of anything else. Daydreamed of enjoying the fate she'd taken from him.

Remember her crimes against you.

Remembering wasn't the problem. He now struggled to make those crimes matter. His resistance to her? Deteriorating fast and soon to shatter. Inside him, pressure mounted. *Scraped raw.*

As they continued to stare at each other, her sadness receded. Awareness crackled in the air between them. His breath turned shallow. Hers did, too.

Did she fake this? She must. Except, her pulse raced beneath his palm.

Perhaps she suffered with the same problem he did, craving what she shouldn't. Perhaps he could have what she'd almost given him before, even though they were at war. It didn't have to mean anything. They could help each other. Scratch an itch that tormented them both. Momentary satisfaction, easily forgotten...followed by deeper discontent?

No, he knew better than to travel this road. What he wanted

was never what he needed. As his life had proved time and time again.

Fuel drizzled over the fires of his fury, snapping and popping. Steam enveloped his mind. Suddenly, he wasn't struggling to make her crimes matter. Those crimes mattered *greatly*. She had given him hope for a bright future. Made him long for what he'd never had, resurrecting old dreams that refused to die a second time. He hated her for it. And yet...*the view...*

She is exquisite. For now, she is mine. And he was falling right back under her spell of enchantment. But he didn't think he cared. No female should be this lovely. All that golden skin flushed and sunlit, glistening with water droplets, as otherworldly as the first time he'd spied it, all but beckoning his fingers. *Touch...*

Her mane of wet hair appeared black, the change in color highlighting the delicacy of her features. Her air of vulnerability. In her eyes, enlarged pupils overshadowed jade and swirled with lust. Red lips parted, as if pleading for a kiss. The rise of her breasts every time she inhaled, those puckered crests sometimes bobbing over the surface of the pond. The sight of her bound wrists, floating in front of her...

"Maybe I'll keep you chained to my bed for the rest of eternity," he rasped, tracing his thumb along her jugular.

With a throaty voice, she replied, "Maybe I'll enjoy it."

"Now I know you lie." *Do I? The way she's looking at me...* He narrowed his eyes and tightened his grip on her, loving how her throat quivered as she swallowed. "There's a lone reason you would dare to taunt me so while I hold your very life in my hand."

"Oh? Please, do tell."

"You hope to distract me and run again."

"Give the king a prize. I *will* run. When the time is right." She didn't appear the least bit abashed by her admission. "But

I promise you'll enjoy yourself in the meantime... The question is, will I?"

In that moment, he recognized the truth. She fully understood her power over him—and how to wield it well. He fought to resist her allure. Fought with every ounce of his strength. Resistance was the correct path. He recognized this truth, too. Anything else would lead to his destruction. But he smelled her each time he inhaled, all the sweet florals and citrus, and his thoughts fragmented, one after the other. Desire prowled through his veins, a hungry beast desperate for sustenance. Nothing else mattered.

"Know that I will catch you when you run, wherever you go," he growled. Even if he must find a way into the mortal world.

Micah swooped down and claimed her mouth in a searing kiss. The last time they'd done this, he'd striven to learn, savor and coax a response from her. Today, he took, *demanding* more. Demanding everything. For once, he didn't attempt to filter the ferocity of his desires. Let her feel what she did to him. If she frightened—

His feral kitten? Frightened? No. She met him thrust for thrust, *feasting* on him.

Inside him, pressure mounted, expanding. Muscles bunched with tension. Soon, his clothes were pulled taut and restrictive. Far too tight. A thousand times, he nearly ripped the garments from his body. A thousand times, he resisted.

When their positions prevented him from deepening the kiss, he wrenched up his head and hauled her out of the water, splaying her over the shore. He meant to stretch out directly beside her, but the sight of her nakedness arrested him. Water sheened her and pooled in select places while dripping from others. Had he ever beheld such lush curves? So many scintillating dips and hollows?

A banquet of femininity, mine for the taking...

Holding her gaze, hating her, ravenous, he reached between

them and unwound the tie around her wrists, leaving her in the collar alone. Wholly vulnerable. Gloriously so. Part of him expected her to run again. Instead, she wrapped her arms around him, drawing him closer.

Surprise uncoiled, as lethal to his discipline as everything else. He bent his head, swooping down to resume the kiss. As their tongues rolled together, she tightened her grip on him. More and more of his control slipped...

She clings to me? The knowledge affected him, his need for this fantasy female amplifying to a maddening degree. The pressure inside him doubled. Pride threatened to shatter. He hovered over her, sharing breaths, exchanging kiss for kiss. Passion for passion. Micah knew he had a choice. Stop now or regret later.

He should stop. Absolutely. Starting this had been foolish. Or not. No risk of conceiving a child with the mother of monsters. Not with his wrist cuff in place. And the picnic basket *did* contain everything needed for a seduction. From the sexiest gown he'd ever wished to see a female wear, to the toiletries, a bottle of wine and a book of erotic sketches. There'd been a canteen of water as well, plus clothes for him, a plethora of foods and a blanket. In other words, a bed. Why not take advantage?

No, no. He should stop. Yet he let one of his hands wander...

She mewled; he groaned. Yes, he would stop. Any minute now.

I can halt this at any time...

Kneading...

I'll cease the second I'm ready...

Stroking lower...

Vee sank her nails between his shoulder blades, ripping his tunic, and Micah sucked air between his teeth. The sting didn't bother him. On the contrary. He liked it. Her uninhibited response thrilled him. *Finish this. Regret later.*

He cupped, kneaded and stroked her with more force, as if he were conquering village after village, claiming the territories as his own. *The way she moves...* The slightest graze of his fingertips left her writhing. Firm pressure induced pleading and thrashing.

The sounds she makes... Breathy groans, deep moans and insistent cries. Sometimes she even issued commands.

"More! Harder! Micah," she gasped out between panting breaths. She gripped his wrist with one hand and used the other to move his fingers where she desired them most. Her spine arched, her breasts thrusting up. Another cry parted her lips. "I'm so close. So close. I need...need so badly...need you...need."

The things she says... The way she takes what she wants...

Will give her anything. *Everything.*

He ripped at the buttons on his leathers and experienced an easing, but only for the briefest reprieve. His control frayed further.

Moaning, she gripped his length and Micah nearly humiliated himself then and there. The sudden, searing skin-to-skin contact wrenched a roar straight out of his deepest depths. A sound he'd never made.

A sound he shouldn't be making now. Not with her. His greatest betrayer.

He froze. Her eyelids popped open as she gasped. They stared at each other, silent and searching. Hot desire radiated from her—at first. The more she panted, the calmer she became.

Did she think he intended to force her to continue?

Micah released her as if she were toxic and shot to his feet. She scrambled to hers, and they faced off again, minus the contact. Her panic thinned and faded, anger taking its place. The urge to snatch her back bombarded him. But he knew better. He'd been a fool to touch her in the first place.

He tried to calm his breathing, inwardly commanding his brain function to return to normal. Common sense hesitated but ultimately obeyed, Vee's plan so much clearer—and far more diabolical than he'd realized. She'd intended to work him up, leave him frustrated and keep him distracted. And he'd let it happen. At least she'd gotten lost in pleasure, too. They could regret it together.

"Well? Why'd you stop?" she demanded.

Wait. What? He raked his gaze over her naked form; there was no stopping the action. Her hair was lightening and curling as it dried, the strands returning to a rich scarlet. Plump breasts with gorgeous crests. More scarlet at the apex of her thighs…

He licked his lips, ravenous.

Disgusted with himself, needing to put an end to this attraction, he ripped off his tunic and yanked at his pants, stripping fully. Revealing the maze of scars from his collar bones to his calves he'd sometimes attempted to hide with tattoos. But tattoos never lasted more than a few days for chimeras. Now, jagged pink lines connected one after the other, every mark a shame he must eternally bear. Reminders that he'd failed his guardian, that he had nothing and no one of his own, forever isolated from those around him. That even at birth he'd been unwanted. Singular. Set apart. Cursed.

"Go ahead. Have a good look at what your precious children did to me." He spread his arms, puffed his chest in a mimic of pride and stepped toward her, as unabashed as she was. A single step, no more, but she stumbled back as if he'd rushed at her. "I spent weeks caring for you. Not once did I harm you. Yet you drove your *belua* to attack me."

He turned away from her then and dived in the water. If she ran, she ran. He would catch her as promised, then flitter them both home. No, not home, but the campground. He would imprison her as planned and end this. Prolonging it had done him no favors.

Motions jerky, he scrubbed himself from head to toe, keeping his prisoner—the traitor—in his periphery. Yes, he would get rid of Vee as soon as he finished here. But why hadn't she bolted for the woods? Why was she standing so still, gaping at him?

He shot his gaze at her—and his jaw went slack. She...she was toying with the ends of her hair and she...she *leered* at him.

There are muscles, and then there is strength. Micah had both, and Viori couldn't tear her gaze away from him. How utterly delicious he was. More than she'd ever dreamed possible. The pain he had overcome. The evidence stamped into his flesh, there for all to see. And see she did. A visual buffet.

She licked her lips and traced the metal collar locked around her neck as she imagined tracing every raised mark on his body with her tongue. Had there *ever* been a more perfect male? Oh, to get her hands all over *that*... She should have done it while she'd had the chance!

Why, why, why had she allowed fear to swamp her, ending the sublime pleasure before they reached the end? She'd allowed him to leave her aching and wanting and needing and—

No. Nope. Not needing. And what was she even doing right now? She shouldn't admire him. Not in any way, shape or very sculpted form. He plotted to destroy her and everyone she held dear. She wasn't foolish enough to truly enjoy herself with him. Pretend to do so, yes. But do so, no.

Viori raised her chin and marched to the picnic basket, where she found a clean dress. A sheer, iridescent creation that molded to her curves, revealing more than it concealed. Better than nothing, she supposed.

Deciding to eat and regain her strength before her next escape attempt, she spread a blanket and displayed the perfect meal. Though her stomach now twisted with hunger, she didn't eat. No, like a good captive, she waited for her host to join her. Because she was too tired to argue with him. Most definitely not because she missed the meals they had shared in his tent, when he had selected the choices pieces for her, and she tasted contentment for a little while. A dream of something better than she'd suspected possible.

As she waited, her eyelids grew heavy. A yawn cracked her jaw. See? Far too tired to argue. Or escape. Yes, she should probably postpone her next attempt until tomorrow. A good rest was often the difference between victory and defeat.

So, it was decided. A meal and a rest. All-out war tomorrow.

A shadow fell over her, and she jolted, concentrating on the present. Micah stood on the other side of the blanket, fully dressed, his scars hidden once again. How disappointing. Or appropriate. Yes. A far better description.

He looked over the feast and frowned. "You waited for me."

Her cheeks heated. "It was an accident and means nothing. No need to discuss it. Let's begin. I'm famished."

A stiff nod preceded jerky motions, and yet his expression softened. He sat and filled a plate with the best morsels. Viori extended her hands to accept the offering—but he dug into the dishes himself.

Her mouth floundered open and closed. He hadn't selected anything for her. Hadn't watched to ensure she considered the first bite pleasing. She…she…hardly cared, that was what. She didn't need his help. She never had, never would.

Trembling, she filled a plate and nibbled on this and that. Nothing settled right. When she could stand the quiet no longer, she asked, "Are you truly going to imprison your queen and destroy her—your—family?" She tried for a conversational tone, and she thought she succeeded. Kind of. Mostly. "We're all you've got, I'm thinking."

To whom are you speaking? Micah? Or yourself? No. No! She had the kids. Her brother.

"You aren't my family. I have my people. And yes," her husband said simply. "As Kaysar's wife has taught me, it's better to have no queen than a feral beauty you cannot trust."

He wasn't wrong, yet his words still hurt. With a humph, she brushed her hair from one shoulder. "I knew you thought me beautiful. And I suppose I *am* feral. I've been alone since the age of five." The information spilled from her, and she didn't think she was sorry to share a bit of her history with him. A hidden part of her wanted him to understand. To know who she was. *Why* she was.

He continued eating without a care, not even sparing her a glance. "Please, go on. I've been expecting a sob story meant to earn your way back into my good graces since your capture. Please, do continue. Tell me why I should go easy on you."

Viori's hurt sharpened. She yanked her gaze from him and concentrated on her meal, pretending her hand wasn't shaking. This was for the best, anyway. Micah didn't deserve her truth. The agony of months spent alone with her memories and re-grets, suspicious of everyone who approached her. Certain they plotted her downfall, as the centaurs had. Then the Winterland soldiers. So desperate for companionship, she'd felt like a bot-tomless void, needing, always needing. Willing to risk waking up in a strange world just to create a friend. A link with some-one, anyone.

The reason she had created baby Krunk. A sapling when she'd fallen asleep, and fully mature when she next opened her eyes. He had guarded her well upon her return to the fae realm, en-suring her safety. Thus had begun the cycle of her life. Create. Rest. Strengthen. Create more. Rest harder. Strengthen slower.

"Nothing else to say?" Micah grated.

Her chest compressed, air seeping from her lungs. "There's no need for me to go on," she replied as airily as possible. "I don't wish to be a queen. Not if *you* are the king." How she ever convinced herself otherwise, she didn't know. They'd al-ways been headed for a royal split. Too many obstacles stood between them, each insurmountable. If not Kaysar, the war. If not the war, their past. If not their past, Micah's expectations.

As she'd feared the day of their wedding, he preferred a fe-male able to enchant his people and read. A skill most fae de-veloped at a young age. But Viori's schooling had ceased when her parents had died. Impossible to learn letters while you scurried from village to village, scrounging for food.

Her shoulders rolled. Back then, Kaysar had asked only one thing of her. That she speak to him. But she hadn't. She'd shut him out, the fear of harming him too visceral. If only she could go back and do one good thing for him. Just one. Maybe then the burden of guilt would lessen.

She sniffled, blinking rapidly, and the next thing she knew, Micah was gently removing the piece of fruit pinched between her fingers, poised halfway to her mouth, forgotten as she'd delved the depths of her mind.

For some insane reason, he gathered her close, and she let him. She just... She didn't have any defenses left. She'd only recently grieved the loss of her family and re-created a new one with Graves. She'd run for her life, made shaky bargains with an irate husband and nearly climaxed in her future warden's arms.

As he reclined them both and spooned her on the blanket, she realized he had already tidied up. She'd skipped a meal, and her stomach didn't care? Wow.

He petted her hair, saying, "You once asked about my glamaras. With one ability, I raze the control of others, sending them into a frenzy. With the other, I subdue them."

She didn't know how to respond. Why trust her with the information now when she could use the information against him? "The subduing. That's how you control the trolls?"

"Yes."

A yawn stretched her jaw. "Don't take this the wrong way, but that's kind of disappointing. You're so secretive, I expected something dangerous." To subdue *Kaysar*, Micah must wield the stronger glamara. Before, he'd told her one ability battled the other without a winner at the helm. Put the two together, and he had no chance of defeating her brother. And that was good. Great. Wonderful.

Wasn't it?

"Such as?" he asked.

"I don't know. Making a body explode from the inside out. Causing flesh to melt from bone with a glance." Another yawn. "Making someone else invisible, forcing them to remain alone for the rest of eternity." She shuddered. No future sounded worse.

He continued running his fingers through her hair. "Sleep," he whispered.

"Yes." Helpless to do otherwise, she closed her eyes and drifted off...

CHAPTER NINETEEN

Micah held the slumbering Vee tight against his body, his turbulent thoughts refusing to settle.

She had cried. A little. The barest glint, really, but tears *had* gathered in her eyes. And they'd been genuine. Her chin had trembled. She had sniffled. A sound he never wished to hear again.

This luscious female with such highly developed defenses had revealed her weaknesses. Had displayed vulnerability. To him. The husband she regretted wedding. Her former, present and future captor. He didn't… He couldn't… He…

A curse blasted through his mind, filling even the narrowest of corridors. She was affecting him. Changing him. Again.

He pinched the bridge of his nose, at a loss. Raw emotions jumbled together, as sharp as razors and coated in salt. A toxic mix of fury, desire, hurt, devastation, grief, guilt, shame, regret and more desire. All topped by a need for justice. And even more desire.

Had she raised herself since the age of five? He desperately yearned to know. Why had he opened his foolish mouth and stopped her from admitting more? *Why?*

Fool *is too good a description for me.*

For the first time, he thought he might be seeing this beauty for who she really was—and the truth about himself. He had harmed an innocent and failed to protect what belonged to him. He'd made the wrong choice at every turn, without a backup plan.

Remorse intensified, overshadowing everything else. Muscles tensed, gripping his bones. He imagined young Vee on her own, with no hope or safeguards, and he cringed. No wonder she feared being alone for the rest of eternity as much as exploding from the inside out. She had created a family with the only means available to her. Wouldn't he have done the same, if ever he'd possessed the ability?

Honestly, he *had* done the same. Or tried to. He'd built his kingdom and lived for his people...and never known real happiness until this female had entered the picture.

Perhaps we can find a way to be together.

Perhaps Vee can be won.

He waited, expecting to recoil at the idea. But as she lay in the crook of his arms, as he breathed in her sweet citrus-and-floral scent, he experienced only anticipation. Bone deep. Undeniable.

To battle for her heart... How he longed for more time with her. To have her by his side, overjoyed to be part of his life.

To have his wife in his bed. Every night. Every morning.

Desire seared him, branding him with a sense of possession. Could he do this—could he win her and make her forget her debt to Kaysar? Should he even try?

A growl bubbled up, and Micah tightened his hold. *Yes. I should and I can.* She might hate him, but she loved sleeping in his arms. And she had already softened toward him. Proof: the feral kitten had waited for him to eat. A first. A miracle.

He could have this contentment forever. He could have *her.*

I must have her.

Never had he craved another the way he craved Vee. But

what about her children? Micah couldn't harm them *and* end up victorious with his wife. But he couldn't let the beasts live, thereby endangering the people under his care.

With time and patience, he could, mayhap, gain control of *belua*, the way he'd gained control of the trolls. No. No "mayhap" about it. He would do that, too. Look at Graves. The creature had spent six days in camp without harming anyone. Micah could use the remaining *belua* to grow his garden.

Hmm. Was this more foolishness on his part? Even if Micah tamed the entire species, he couldn't count on Vee. She might be vulnerable, but she was still treacherous. A cutthroat beauty who had helped reinforce what Fayette and Diane taught him—never put your confidence in the unworthy. A mistake he couldn't afford to repeat. Besides, he had no more trust to give. And yet...

How he despised that word. *Yet.* But there it was. A big part of him had never ceased itching for the opportunity to win his wife...who had done more than soften toward him, he realized. She had melted. She must have. Not only had she saved food for him, but she had *leered* at him. How could he forget *that*? The woman found him nigh irresistible. She'd been unfazed by his chimera status. She'd made no mention of it, in fact. None of the usual derogatory remarks.

He's a good man—for a chimera.

As he recalled the sear of Vee's gaze, the insult disintegrated. This female desired him, whether she wanted to admit it or not. Whether she wanted to do so or not. Yes, oh yes. The more he considered it, the more certain he became. Soon a slow, almost-calculated smile bloomed. As he had pinned her to the soft carpet of grass, touching and kissing her, she had faked nothing. How wet she'd grown...

Even if she'd planned to leave him frustrated all along, she had suffered the consequences as well. An arousing thought.

He could do this; he could live his dream. Win her over and keep her in his bed. Prove a future with her husband mattered more than a childhood debt. Of course, Kaysar might cease to matter, anyway, as soon as the truce ended. Once the male died, Vee's loyalties would be divided no longer. Until then, Micah had only to ensure she avoided the royal and his bride.

She would protest. Might feel cornered. But she would get over it. In this, he wouldn't budge.

Looked like they would be walking back to camp, after all. Thankfully, she seemed to have accepted her lot. She'd ceased attempting to escape him.

When a low groan escaped her, concern filled him. "Vee?"

Another groan as she jerked, as if she were recoiling from an attack. An unseen enemy? Micah untangled from her and jolted upright, a dagger in hand. His gaze darted, but he found no one waiting nearby.

More groaning and jerking from Vee, until she was thrashing over the pallet. He frowned. A nightmare?

"No," she gasped out. "No, no. Don't! Stop! Let me go!"

Acid poured through him, suspicions arising. Was this a bad dream, or a bad memory, raised to the surface of her mind, thanks to their conversation?

Trembling, Micah eased down and gathered her close. He held her against him, petting her and cooing assurances into her ear. "I'm here. You're safe. I'll allow no harm to befall you."

Calm overtook her gradually, until she curled against him trustingly, willingly, and slipped into a deep, peaceful sleep. Relieved and perhaps a bit prideful, he kissed her temple.

For the rest of the night, he held her close, alternating between the most magnificent wonder and painful agony over what horrors she might have endured throughout her life. He slept not at all.

As sunlight brightened the sky, he cupped her shoulder and shook her gently. "Time to wake, Red." Though he hated to disturb her, he required a moment to collect himself.

She blinked open her eyes and stretched lazily. "Mmm. Five more minutes. Not ready."

As he averted his eyes—*too beautiful!*—his hands balled into fists. Her hair had dried, returning to its natural shade of auburn. The ethereal gown provided by Cookie should be burned. Or granted the title of hero. The material cinched at Vee's waist, two silken scarves stretching over her breasts, secured at her nape. The flowing skirt had far too many slits, revealing a tantalizing amount of thigh.

"We have many miles to cover today," he said, considering his options as he detangled from her. How did one start to win back his wife? "Be ready to go in ten minutes."

"Aw." She offered him a smirking smile. "Is someone tired and grumpy because he didn't trust a certain someone else to stay put during the night? Did he toss and turn while I enjoyed my beauty rest?"

He definitely shouldn't start with a spanking. Should he? "Nine minutes." After gathering the essentials from the picnic basket, he stalked to the lake, cleaned his teeth, and kept his gaze on— "Vee!" She was gone. Nowhere in the vicinity.

The little temptress had bolted again.

Should have started with the spanking. Muttering curses, he flittered to the blanket, scanned the area around it…there. A set of small footprints. He gave chase. Scanning again…

A twig snapped to the right. There. She raced ahead, weaving through a thick stretch of trees. Red hair streamed behind her.

Flitter. Snag. He captured her by the waist, stopping her in her tracks and yanking her against him. With his mouth poised above one of her pointed ears, he snarled, "You won't get away from me. I *told* you this."

A throaty chuckle left her, razing his control. "Your reflexes need work, don't you think?"

He stomped back to camp, gathered their belongings and resumed their journey to the campground.

The stubborn beauty put him to the test for hours. No matter how many times or ways he secured her wrists, she always found a way to free herself. Again and again, he was forced to dart into action, pursue and tackle her. He lived in a torturous state, escalating hunger at war with iron determination. *Kiss. Resist. Kiss! Resist!*

KISS!

"I think you *want* me to escape," she said, laughing up at him as he pinned her to the ground once more.

"You think wrong." *Move away. End this.* But he didn't end this. He clung. His blistering lust never had a chance to cool.

"If that's true, you'll keep a better watch on me next time."

"There won't be a next time." Muscle jumping beneath his eye, he hauled them both to their feet and finally severed contact at last.

Less than five minutes later, he attempted to stop her from scaling a tree. "Enough, Vee." The words echoed through the forest, birds taking flight from a vast number of branches. "You come down this instant."

Laughing, she straddled a branch. "You come get me."

"Just come down," he grated, holding up his arms and waving his fingers.

"Why?" She maneuvered to a stand on the too-thin limb, lifting the hem of her dress to reveal her bare feet. "Is the big bad wolf afraid of heights?"

Micah popped his jaw. "All right. You brought this on yourself." He flittered to the perch—but she had already leaped.

The limb snapped in half under his heavier weight. He toppled, landing in a heap at her feet, losing his breath.

Rather than dart off, she peered down at him, her hands on her hips. "I should bring this on myself more often."

Digging his knuckles into his eye sockets, he muttered, "Let there be a truce between us." He stood, flittered behind her, and shackled her body against his. "Give me one hour of peace,

Red." His lips hovered directly over her ear. "Sixty minutes. Please."

She reached back to cup his elbows, thrusting out her breasts. Leaning her head upon his shoulder, she smiled, the embodiment of seduction. "What will I get in return?"

Do not lose your train of thought. Focus. "What do you want?"

Voice pure silk, she told him, "Remove your cloak and shirt. And keep them off."

Putting his scars on constant display while trying to win her? A horror and a delight rolled into one. He didn't know whether to howl with satisfaction or crumple with defeat. "Very well." If he was correct and she relished looking at him as much as he relished having her gaze upon him, the delight would win. Only one way to find out... "The shirt goes, and you adhere yourself to my side. Deal?"

"For one hour?"

"One hour." Could he trust her to hold up her end of the bargain? Probably not. Let this be a test of sorts.

"Then yes. Deal," she purred. He loosened his hold, and she spun, facing him, gliding her palms up his arms. "But only because you jumped into the water before I inspected your body thoroughly. And Micah, darling? It should go without saying that you can't complain when I take myself a little feel of you now and again. I mean, really. You shouldn't grow your muscles like that if you don't want my hands all over them."

He cleared his throat, his heart thudding. The things this female said. "What is *like that* exactly?"

"So big and scarred."

"You cannot admire the marks." Could she? That leer...

"Why not? They reveal the trials you've survived. A show of your strength."

He...didn't know what to say. But he knew what he yearned to do right this second...

Her breath caught as if she'd read his thoughts.

Would she let him put *his* hands all over *her*?

Fighting a slight tremor, he reached out and palmed her backside through a slit in her gown. The softness!

Careful, careful.

"What do you think you're doing, husband?" she rasped, not the least bit upset.

"Taking a little feel of my own before we restart our journey." *Acting on desire rather than reason.*

"In that case, carry on."

Be smart about this. Taking everything before he'd settled things? Foolish. Though it cost him parts of his sanity, Micah released her gradually and eased back, half expecting her to bolt again. But she kept her word, merely arching her brow at him in expectation.

"Well?" she demanded. "Do your part."

Her eagerness went straight to his head. Micah held her gaze as he undressed—slowly—revealing his upper body in the bright light of day, up close and personal. His heart thudded faster as she looked him over. Her lids dropped, her eyes slanting with desire.

She flicked her tongue over an incisor. "Maybe I'll keep you chained to *my* bed."

And like that, he throbbed. Needing a moment, he busied himself, gathering their satchel—the blanket—his discarded clothing and their supplies. Things he'd scattered over the ground as he'd chased his wife through the forest. Vee held a post nearby as promised, but without a hint of remorse.

As he led her through the oasis, his thoughts refused to settle. At any other occasion, the lush, dewy foliage and wealth of flowers would have mesmerized him. A dream come true. Now he could think of nothing but his companion.

Make her surrender soon.

When they exited the paradise, they entered a stretch of land that offered mile after mile of sandy ground and bare, gnarled tree limbs. He hardly noticed because he still scented his wife.

"You left Norok in charge of our people, didn't you?" she asked with a disgusted tone, sidling up to him to keep pace.

"My people," he corrected without heat. For now. "And yes."

"For the record, your queen advises against this always. He isn't loyal or reliable."

"And you are?" Irritation spiked. She sought to drive a wedge of dissension between him and one of only three people he *could* trust. "Norok has his faults. Many faults. Since the day he swore his fealty to me, he's been nothing but steadfast. But you?" He planned to win her, yes. He would not pretend they had no issues. The very reason they were trapped in this mess. "You, I cannot trust."

"That's true. I'll betray you at the earliest opportunity." She dabbed a bead of perspiration from her brow before patting his cheek. "I'm not trying to hide it. That doesn't mean I won't help you out upon occasion."

"And Norok *is* trying to hide it?" Micah shoved a branch out of their way then changed the direction of the conversation. Gentling his tone, he asked, "Why didn't you seek out a fae family when you were a child?"

"Oh, you care about my past now?" She snorted. "You think I didn't try? I assure you, I did. Soon after I killed… Kaysar's parents—" her voice caught "—I was forced to escape two hungry centaurs. Their brethren chased me through the Forest of Many Names for weeks. Then I came upon a group of oh, so unhelpful Winterland soldiers. Little did I know they were in the Summerlands to hunt child slaves for their king."

He stiffened and missed his next step. "Were you hurt?" He'd only recently learned of the atrocious crimes perpetrated by Winterland royals. Collecting the young to use and abuse in the worst ways. Something King Kaysar had apparently experienced firsthand. Not that his horrifying past excused his present-day actions.

"Yes and no," she admitted softly.

"Tell me all of it." He moved the next branch with a little less force. He needed the information like water. "Please."

Up went her defenses. He felt it happen, the very air around them thickening with challenge. "Why should I share my sob story with you?" she snipped.

Deserve that. She wished to make another bargain? Very well. They would make another bargain. "Tell me, and I'll give you back the jewels."

She perked up, allowing him to help her over a fallen log. "All of them? Nothing missing, nothing broken?"

"Nothing missing, nothing broken," he agreed.

"Okay. Yes. But I'll tell you when I'm ready, and not a moment before."

Rather than press for more, he nodded. "Deal."

They cleared the tangled limbs as the sun descended, darkness just beginning to paint the land. He spotted the entrance to a cavern in a lone beam of light and drew to a halt. Other than the oasis Queen Cookie had cultivated in only a matter of days, he knew every inch of the Dusklands, inside out and underground. This deep, shadowed opening did not belong here.

Another change made by the Unhinged One's queen? Did she hope to encourage more "honeymoon"? Make Micah long for a permanent truce so he could concentrate fully on his wife?

A terrible, brilliant plan. Micah glared at Vee, blaming her for his weakness. "Keep your word. Stay put while I search the area for threats."

"Whatever." She shrugged, offering no assurances.

He huffed and flittered deeper into the cave. Deeper still. Hmm. No hidden surprises. Merely a cavern and cenote. Ebony crystals covered the entire ceiling. Pinpricks of light danced inside them, making each resemble a swirling star.

He returned to Vee, gathered her close and flittered her to the cenote. "We'll spend the night here."

When he released her, she remained pressed against him,

peering up. "Why are we taking the scenic route to camp, huh? Why don't you flitter me back?"

"Reveal my schemes to a foe? Do you know nothing about your husband or the art of war? Tsk-tsk."

She maintained a pensive expression as they splashed water on their faces. Even as they ate the last of their food on their blanket. Without prompting, she cuddled up beside him the second he stretched out. Yet another shock. He held her close, unwilling to let go.

With her cheek resting on one of his pectorals and her palm flat on the other, she said, "I believe I owe you a childhood tale."

"If you aren't ready—"

"I'm ready, okay. Jeez. Anyway. When we left off, I had been captured by a unit of Winterland soldiers. They carted me to Frost Mountains. I created Snowy, and he took care of the problem for me, killing the guards. The other prisoners feared him and ran. Maybe they died due to freezing temperatures, maybe they escaped. I don't know. I slept for a time, then awoke in a place called Scotland. There, I created Lochnessa—Nessa—and fell asleep yet again. When I woke up, I was with Snowy, and we were alone." She paused. "I really am sorry about Erwen. Tell me about him."

His heart stuttered. She remembered his name. "He was the best. No one better. Loyal. Honorable. Kind. Brilliant. He found me as an infant and raised me as his own. He owed me nothing, yet he gave me everything."

"That's wonderful," she said, even as she grew waxen. "I could have used someone like him as I made my way through a realm I no longer recognized, sticking to the edge of civilization, watching, learning, creating protectors as needed."

He could imagine they'd learned the same lessons in the shadows. A kind smile often hid a heart filled with hate. Selfishness and greed abounded in all species. Trust no one but yourself.

He pressed his tongue to the roof of his mouth. "What else?"

"Eventually I came across a nice family. One of my least favorite memories. I don't like to think about them, much less talk about them, so I'll just skip ahead—"

"Tell me. Now." He *must* have this information.

Sighing, she glided her nails lightly over his chest, almost absently. "All right, so. I finally came across a nice family. A loving couple with a little girl. She had this doll, you see. The most beautiful in all the land, according to her. But I knew better. I'd seen my doll, Drendall. We argued but decided to become friends, anyway. I visited her for weeks before she convinced me to meet her parents. They must have felt sorry for me. They fed, clothed and sheltered me for months."

He tensed, sensing the encroaching dread. "And then?"

"And then centaurs raided their village. Said they smelled something special. That they were soon to attend a banquet and were ready to select the main course and side dishes. When they settled on the girl's parents, the mother offered me in exchange for the safety of her family." Her shoulders rose and fell. "The thing is, I understood her choice. Protect yourself and those you love, whatever the cost. That's when I created my first six trees. I stayed awake long enough to witness the destruction of every threat. The centaurs…the villagers." Her voice wobbled. "After that, I was rarely in a trusting mood."

He didn't want to ask. He shouldn't. But he did. "Where did you awaken? With the trees?"

"Nope. I ended up in West Virginia, where I created a magnificent creature made of smoke. His name is Mothan. I didn't return to the trees for three decades." Affection dripped from her tone. "They were so happy to see me."

He traced his fingertips along her spine, asking softly, "What of the male you loved?"

She sighed, her breath a warm rasp against his skin. "He was a human in the mortal world. A healer. He found me injured in an alleyway and patched me up. For months, he provided me with food, shelter and clothing. He worked hard to earn my trust. Once I offered it, I noticed things. He never stayed the night with me. Someone phoned him constantly. A phone is a device— Oh, never mind. It doesn't matter. The point is, I followed him one night and discovered he was married. That he merely used me as a receptacle."

As righteous fury sparked, Micah curved his arm, conforming it to the shape of her hips. For the human to shatter the fragile bonds of trust with both Vee and his wife, the one he was born to protect... It was unconscionable.

Are you any better?

He didn't know, and the uncertainty caused guilt to unfurl. Micah had watched his second betray his wife again and again and again, and he'd said nothing. How many broken hearts had Norok left in his wake? Hearts that belonged to his people. Those looking to Micah for safeguarding. On the other hand, how could he blame Norok for his actions when Micah himself treated his wife no better than a prisoner?

His blood flashed cold. "How did you punish the fool for his betrayal?"

"I made an example of him," she said with all kinds of satisfaction.

Just as she will make an example of me? The moisture in his mouth dried. "What you did to Kaysar's parents was not the same, Vee. It was accidental. You owe the Unhinged One nothing." And that was the truth.

She went still for a long while, then extracted from him and glided to her feet. Heading for the cenote, hips swaying, she rasped, "All right. I'm done sharing. I'm taking a bath." She dropped her gown and stepped into the warm bubbling water, wearing only the collar. "Try to resist. If you can."

The sight of her soft, lush curves—*mine for the taking*—nearly proved to be his undoing. But he gripped the blanket and stared up at the glittering ceiling above him. Anywhere but Vee, bathing in the pool. Naked.

Deep breath in, out. The first and only rule of taming: never be the first to break.

Micah would prove the depths of his strength or he would die trying.

CHAPTER TWENTY

Oh! Husbands were beyond frustrating. And sexy. Very, very, very sexy. Annoyingly so!

After sharing intimate parts of her life, Viori expected Micah to share intimate parts of his. An equal exchange. Instead, he went quiet and hands-off. For three days! Had she ruined everything, as always?

They spent the time traveling through Grimm Forest on foot and camping, seemingly the sole survivors of some cataclysmic, realm-destroying event. Well, that and stare at each other, all while the most intoxicating heat simmered between them.

The guy hungered for her; she had zero doubts about that. Or maybe one doubt. Possibly ten. No more than thirty. It was just, he never touched her anymore. Never kissed her or embraced her through the too-long nights. Never did more than grunt at her.

Pride said, *You mustn't be the one to initiate contact. He must.* But more and more she suspected pride was a buffoon. She wanted what she wanted—him—and she wanted it now.

She did everything in her power to tempt him. Ask for help

dressing and undressing. "Accidentally" bump into him. Complain about aching muscles.

He never wavered in his resolve. He *always* resisted.

Today, he'd clearly planned to take her torment to the next level, and Viori could only swallow her whimpers. She sat nearby, her wrists bound behind her—because yes, she continued to try to escape, just to provoke a response from him— watching as he chopped wood. Shirtless. Amid a beam of golden sunlight, he placed the logs on the stump, one after the other, then picked up his axe and swung. *Chop.*

Her breath caught. The way his muscles strained and flexed…

He swung again, and her heart leaped. *Chop.* She shifted, too agitated to be still. *Chop.*

She licked her lips as sweat glistened on his scars. Who knew the simple act of slicing through tree bark could be so utterly… delicious? She might demand he cut wood every minute of every day for the rest of his life and even after he died, only stopping to throw her to the ground and ravish her senseless at least once an hour.

As if he sensed her growing arousal, he glanced her way. The smolder in his amber eyes nearly proved to be her undoing.

Time to make him stop this illicit act. "We have enough wood for an army, Micah. Why continue?" *Put me out of my misery!*

"This isn't for us," he groused, "but the family trekking behind us." Well, well. He'd done more than grunt.

Wait. A family trekked behind them? And she hadn't sensed it? What was wrong with her? "Do you know this family?"

"No." He stacked the pieces into a pile.

"Then why aid them? They won't thank you for it."

"I told you. I don't need thanks, but they do need aid." He gathered their gear and hoisted her to her feet. "Let's go." He gripped the rope between her wrists and dragged her through the woods once again.

She stumbled behind him, too flabbergasted to respond. He'd

spent hours doing manual labor to help total strangers? Something no one had ever done for the de Aoibheall siblings after their parents had died. Or before. Something they had desperately needed at times.

Argh! How dare Micah confuse her like this, continuing to display genuine goodness. "At least you didn't leave them our dinner," she grumbled. "They'd follow us to the ends of the realm then."

"I did leave them our dinner."

What? Not their food! Anything but their food. "Here's a riddle for you. How can you be so nice to strangers while being so cruel to your wife?"

He stopped abruptly, removed the tie around her hands and launched back into motion. "There. Am I sufficiently nice to my wife now?" he asked, a vein pulsing along the side of his neck.

"No!"

They lapsed into silence, panting, breathing each other's breaths before continuing their trek through the Dusklands. Viori's thoughts whirled. Why had he freed her from the bond? Was he willing to trust her again? He must be. There was no way he would've removed the tie otherwise. And really, despite their harsh words today, she had to admit animosity no longer crackled between them. Maybe because she had possibly, perhaps, forgiven him?

No, no. Impossible. She forgave no one ever. Holding on to your hate protected you from future hurts. Yes?

Perhaps the lack of animosity stemmed from Micah's newfound understanding of her. A prospect that made her doubly curious about him. What kind of life had *he* lived?

Though she hadn't forgiven him—really, truly, she hadn't—she was no longer certain she needed to kill him for his crimes against her. Or even make an example of him, as she'd done to Laken. She and her children had hurt Micah first, and he had retaliated. Tit for tat. If the situation had been reversed, she would've done something similar. Why destroy him for it? And really, there were other ways to neutralize Micah, distracting him from the coming war...

Shivers rocked her. She'd issued the taunt about chaining him to her bed. An idea she liked more and more.

His glare smoldered at her as he helped her jump over a fallen log. Heart racing, she nibbled on her bottom lip. The fun they could have...until he discovered her familial tie to Kaysar.

Ugh. Would Micah think to use her against her brother? Her life for *Kaysar*? Or did Micah think to sway her loyalty? Something he could never do. Right?

They marched on. "Are we there yet?" she demanded.

"You are that eager to enter a cell?"

"Ha! You won't imprison me." At least, despite everything she had serious doubts. She traced her gaze over his sculpted backside and licked her dry lips. "So thirsty," she said with a moan. "I want to drink and drink and drink and—" A gasp escaped her as he pivoted, already holding their canteen to her lips.

Viori swallowed the crisp, fresh water, the delicious liquid soothing her dry throat and parched tongue. No matter how much she drank, the container always refilled. She figured Cookie had offered the precious gift as a constant reminder of the plan: learn where Micah held his army of trolls and win an oasis.

As he pulled away, Viori wiped her mouth with the palm of her hand. Their eyes met, connected. The smolder. The simmer. They never faded, only increased. An electric charge filled the space between them.

Most times, he'd have looked away and moved on at this point. But here and now... He backed her against a tree. Her heart raced faster, like a mortal-land car zooming around a curvy road. Tree bark bit into her shoulders, but she loved the sting as Micah kept coming. He positioned himself flush against her, hardness to softness, and he never dropped his stare.

Her hands shot to his chest, not to push him away, but to draw him in place. She sank the tips of her nails into his scarred pectorals. "What do you think you are doing, Micah?" Thinking to push her to release her debt to Kaysar with promises of pleasure?

His gaze searched hers. With a silky tone, he said, "I've given you time to see me as a provider rather than a killer. Now, I want you to see me as a husband again. What would you give me if I vowed not to imprison you or harm your children again?"

He'd *what*? "I'd give anything." The words left her without thought, and she scowled. No, no. "Almost anything." *Think. Maintain focus.* He'd opened the door to negotiation over a highly important situation. An arrangement skewing in her favor, perhaps. He just, well, he felt so good he scrambled her brain, ensuring intelligence was beyond her. Maybe if she moved a little…? No! Bad. Big mistake.

"I see schemes in your eyes, Red. You seek to make me your willing slave, no more. Admit it." He didn't sound upset by this. No, she detected intrigue. And a lot of it.

Her pulse leaped. "Silly, Micah." The sweetest aches overtook her; soon, staying still wouldn't be an option. Not for her. Muscles bunched, preparing to grind against him. "You are already my willing slave. You simply haven't realized it yet."

His lashes fused together. "Is that so?"

"Mmm-hmm. Want me to prove it?"

"Yes," he hissed at her. "Prove it to me."

Viori undulated her hips. Softness brushed against hardness, only two swaths of material separating their bodies: her dress and his leathers. He sucked in a breath—but he didn't start tearing at her clothes as she hoped. No matter. She wasn't done.

"Give me what I long for, Micah," she rasped, whipping her hips with more and more force. "And I'll keep doing this."

"Keep doing that." Leaning into her, letting his lips hover over hers, he snarled softly, "What do you long for?"

"You." Again, the admission left without permission from

her mind. Pleasure mounted when he whipped his hips in turn. Heated breath sawed between them. His air, her air. Their air. Their everything.

Still, they held each other's stare. Rocking together. It was… it was…*so good*. Too good. Too intense. Viori couldn't make herself care as she plucked her nails free and roamed her hands over the perfection of his chest. Muscles, muscles, everywhere. Scars that teased her palms.

He was so incredibly beautiful, his features sculpted in pleasure and strain. His pupils had exploded over his irises, only a ring of amber visible.

He quickened his pace, rocking, rocking. She quickened hers. Then again. He growled. His gaze dipped to her lips. She gasped again. The next thing she knew, their lips were crashing together in a tangled rush.

They devoured each other. Kissing and rocking and clutching. Kissing harder, rocking faster and clutching desperately. Over and over, again and again. Pleasure rocketed higher. Higher.

"Is this what you want from me?" he growled against her lips.

"Yes. No. Yes. Want more."

"Then take it." His low tone dared her to obey. He rubbed the perfect spot, earning a gasp from her. "Take what you need."

The command shoved her near the edge, setting off an explosion of heat. Sharp pleasure. Nearing bliss…an avalanche rolling through her, growing stronger. Stronger still. Viori cried out as she ground against him, seeking the culmination.

Losing my mind. "Micah!"

He ground against her, too. Hard. Harder. Yes, yes, yes! There! Crying out, she broke apart inside. Clutching at him, she soared, overwhelmed, and overcome…but finally right.

When the haze thinned, she was panting and holding him tighter than ever before. Viori peered at him, wide-eyed. *Never want to let him go. Want to keep him always…* The instinct surged to the surface, demanding her complete attention.

He lowered his chin and met her gaze again. He panted, too, his color high. Something odd happened to her then. Various streams of warmth spread through her, as if multiple dams had broken and now flooded her.

Was that...*feelings*? Oh yes. So many feelings. Glorious tides of affection, admiration and wonder. The deepest yearnings. They were awful and wonderful and terrible and intolerable and *dangerous*.

She gulped. *This male can hurt me worse than anyone else ever has.*

What did he feel for her? Something? Anything other than sexual desire?

"Remember this," he stated, withdrawing from her clutches before claiming his own release. Her legs shook, weakened as her skirt settled around her ankles. "When you crave more, you must pledge your fealty to me to get it."

Oh! He hadn't wanted her too much—he'd wanted to win their battle of wills, and he'd tried another tactic. How *dare* he use her own plan against her. "I pledge nothing but your downfall!"

"Consider your pledge fulfilled." He sounded deadened inside. "I fell the first moment I saw you." He walked away from her then, setting up camp, acting as if she wasn't there. Meanwhile, she couldn't put a single thought together.

He had already fallen? For her? He... She... Argh! What did this mean?

Viori leaned against the tree for balance, reeling and fuming and reeling some more. By the time he placed their evening meal on the blanket, a sense of vulnerability overtook her. He was crashing through her defenses, one by one. Now she was supposed to dine with him?

"Come," he said, waving her over. "Eat."

Swallowing a whimper, she plodded over and plopped beside him. She'd grown to hate this part of their day *so* much.

He reached out, elevating a loaf of sweet bread he'd foraged from an abandoned caravan. Would he offer her the crusty end or the soft middle? In other words, the worst or the best? Wait. What was that noise? Her ears twitched.

Micah must have heard the rustle of leaves and branches, too, because he palmed two daggers as he flittered upright.

"I'm sure whoever it is will go away," Viori cried, desperate to know the truth. *Had* he fallen for her?

"On your feet. Be ready to run."

Viori rose, as ordered. Run? Yes. She wore her husband's stupid collar, making her as helpless as a newborn. Relying on someone else—anyone else—had never ended happily for her. But she stayed put. Like a fool!

Elena and Sabot materialized a short distance away, both riding a centaur at top speed. Viori didn't mean to, didn't realize she'd even done it until too late, but she inched closer to Micah. The male who had collared and chased her. Pleasured and abandoned her. Who might still plan to imprison her and hurt her children.

The newcomers drew up short, stopping only a few feet away before she decided how to proceed.

Micah sheathed his weapons and snagged an arm around her waist, keeping her nearby.

Well. She might as well make the best of this terrible situation. Relaxing against him, she examined their uninvited guests. Elena wore a tunic and leather pants, her pale hair hanging in a braid over each shoulder. Sabot was shirtless, like Micah, his leathers streaked with dirt.

The centaurs were both male, beautiful and big. The largest Viori had ever seen, with wide shoulders, barrel chests and muscular bodies covered in spotted fur. Tattoos covered their torsos.

She bristled on instinct, gearing to launch an attack. Micah reached out and cupped her shoulder. A gesture of comfort and assurance.

"The centaurs won't touch you." The simple statement packed weight. Both the creatures and their riders paled.

Viori cleared her throat and smoothed her dress with trembling hands. "As if I didn't know that."

Elena and Sabot dismounted. The rides bowed to Micah and trotted off to the side, where they settled and helped each other unpack supplies.

"Micah," Elena began. Her gaze fell to his bare chest, and her eyes nearly bugged out, as if she couldn't believe what she was seeing. "You are... You..."

Micah raised his chin, radiating defiance.

Viori's irritation surged anew. Had the female never seen Micah without his shirt? Well, too bad for her. The blonde wasn't allowed to ogle him now. *Mine.* She rested her head on his shoulder and petted a tangle of his scars in a blatant claim of ownership.

"You are interrupting your king and queen, so of course you are scheduled for immediate execution," she announced with her snottiest tone. "We were minutes away from retiring to bed. Together. Isn't that right, darling?" She angled her face toward her husband's and nipped at his earlobe. For his hearing alone, she whispered, "Perhaps we should stay in bed *forever*. There, our fight ends, and our pleasure begins, eh?"

He jolted, his fingers flexing on her waist. "Bed. Together."

Elena looked between them, becoming pallid. Good!

"I'm waiting," he told the intruders. "Why are you here?"

"Tell them," Sabot commanded the blonde, his disgust clear.

"I returned from the palace this morning," Elena began with a defiant jut of her chin, "and I have much to share about Pearl Jean. Among other things."

Cookie had mentioned this Pearl Jean before. A fae who desired the king for her very own. But how did *he* feel about his admirer? "Who is this Pearl Jean person to you?" Viori demanded.

"No one. An old crone. A hag of the highest order." He arched a brow. "Why do you care?"

She pressed her tongue to the roof of her mouth. "Why do you care why I care?"

Did amusement spark in his eyes?

"Shall I tell you the rest?" Elena inserted, not masking her irritation.

Micah stiffened before giving a single shake of his head. "I'll hear your report in a bit." A command to keep the details secret from Viori.

A twinge of hurt toughened her spine, too. Obviously, their truce was over. Though, yes, she understood the need for concealment. She wasn't *that* self-deluded.

"Why are you here?" he demanded of the blonde.

More chin jutting. "Norok suggested I patrol the campgrounds and alert him of your return. I opted to find you, and Sabot refused to relinquish his duty as my guard."

"So you disobeyed a direct command from a superior." A leader never issued a suggestion. Micah crossed his arms over his chest. "Whatever your reasons, you will face the consequences of your actions. You know this, yes?"

A nod without reservation or apology. "I do."

Yet she'd done it, anyway. Well. Viori kind of hated how much she admired the girl right now. But Elena still ogled Micah's chest, as if she had every right to do so, and Viori longed to address the matter with the fight of the century.

Micah moved toward his people, abandoning her yet again, snapping at her over his shoulder, "Stay there and behave."

He... She... Oh! She wrapped her arms around her middle, fighting a sudden sense of rejection. So she was alone. So what? No other fae nearby, no problems. *Nothing to see here.*

She didn't care that Micah, Elena and Sabot whispered heatedly to each other on the opposite side of the glen. Nope. Not even a little. Because she was too busy eating the bread Micah had foolishly abandoned. Bread he didn't deserve. But he would certainly miss it when it was gone, wouldn't he?

Defiant, she swallowed every crumb, not the slightest bit upset when the pieces settled like lead balls in her stomach.

Not. Even. A. Little.

It wasn't long before Elena broke from the males and stomped over to settle beside her. Viori prepared to bestow a stinging rebuke, but pressed her lips together when the beauty winked in and out of view, as if flittering in place.

"You're staring," Elena snapped.

"Ah. It's only rude when I do it." Her snotty tenor revived. "Noted."

A flush bloomed in the other woman's cheeks. "Please also note the fact that I have no desire to be near you right now, but I've been ordered to guard you. As my punishment."

Well. The time to find the trolls and reopen negotiations with Cookie had come. Waiting had been a mistake.

"By the way," Viori said, all sugary sweetness. "I'll pluck out your eyes again, if ever you examine my husband like he's yours."

The angry flush deepened. "He's your husband now, is he?"

She smiled with sinister delight. "I'll take your tongue again, too."

Elena pursed her lips, as if she'd sucked on something sour. "You are the worst, you really are."

"Yes," Viori replied. "But I'm an excellent fighter."

The other woman thought for a moment, then breathed deep, deflating as she exhaled. "You're right about your skill…and my behavior. I do owe you an apology. So. I'm sorry, Majesty. I should not have eyed another woman's mate."

Wait. What? Viori froze in astonishment. Had her nemesis referred to her as Majesty? A willing admission of her authority?

"You consider me queen now." Perhaps she should stick around a little longer, after all.

Elena froze too. "I do not," she huffed. "It was a mere slip of the tongue. An error I'll never make again."

"You *do* consider me queen." And the knowledge was oh, so heady indeed. If Viori could win over this hater, she could win over *anyone*. Including Micah. Why give up now?

"Maybe," the other woman said, grumbling now, "you are good for him. At times."

Curiosity got the better of her. "Well? What times?"

"All times, okay? Happy now?"

Well. She flipped her hair over her shoulder. Someone had finally gained some good sense.

Someone…but not Micah.

I seek someone worthy. The memory of his insult lashed like a whip inside her brain, and she flinched. *Oh, yeah. Gonna find those trolls.*

CHAPTER TWENTY-ONE

Micah led Vee and the two-soldier search party through the Swamplands. Muted sunlight filtered through a large canopy of dark leaves, reflecting from muddy pools of water. Cypress trees—without faces—waved twisted branches in an astonishingly cool breeze. Damp air smelled like his wife. Flowers with a hint of citrus.

With every step he took, he moved farther away from Grimm Forest and the campground. Micah knew he should turn around. He should have returned to his people a thousand times over. Why continue? He'd made no progress with his wife. In fact, she was steadily reverting to her most feral state, his cause quickly losing ground. Win her? Hardly.

Was he supposed to revert to his original plan and imprison Vee? No. He couldn't. Wouldn't. Not yet. Maybe not ever. He wanted his wife in his life. So, why not keep her collared and chained in his tent—neutralized—as he'd once threatened? Because why not? Shouldn't he go down swinging rather than throwing his hands up in defeat? At least he'd still have a chance with her. Except, the idea of stealing her freedom didn't settle right.

His mind a war zone, he continued trudging forward. He wasn't sure he had the strength to stop. For the second time in his life, an invisible force pulled him toward a specific destination. Before, he'd found the trees and Vee, forever altering the course of his life. What would he find this time?

A year ago, he'd encountered a swamp beast here. A *belua*—her child—whose attack had allowed a foe to escape a much-needed beheading. Had little Red been sleeping nearby?

So close, yet so far. He should be on high alert for threats. Would the beast come for her? Challenge Micah for rights to her future? How would he react if so? Hurting the thing would only drive Vee further away from him. But allowing his own defeat wasn't—and would never be—an option.

Torn. Always torn.

"Remove my collar at once." Vee trudged behind, kicking sprays of dirty water over him.

Elena and Sabot trailed her, always listening to husband and wife with unabashed curiosity while navigating their mounts on foot. Thrice Micah had ordered the pair back to camp, but his favorite spy had refused, so his dedicated soldier had refused as well. And it was beyond galling! He couldn't even control two of his most dedicated soldiers. No one did what he wanted anymore.

Elena, it seemed, remained determined to convince him to flitter Vee to the dungeon without delay while Sabot spent an abundance of his time admiring the blonde.

"The more I hate it," Vee added, "the more I hate you."

"I'll try to find a way to survive," Micah replied with a dry tone, doing his best to mask his spike of misgiving, guilt and regret. How dearly he missed his cuddly kitten.

Your fault she's gone. You know this.

No. No! This was *not* his fault. It was hers. Her stubbornness and unwillingness to bend. Besides, the collar protected her as much as everyone else. No glamara meant no need for further punishment.

"Well. I hope you're happy," she snipped at him. "Another piece of my heart just turned to stone."

Happy? Far from it. "Surrender to me, and we'll go home." He held a tree limb out of her way, allowing her to take the lead for a moment. Home? The campground? Never. They belonged at the palace. *Soon.*

"How adorable. The king has jokes," she retorted as he strode ahead.

His irritation soared to new heights. But so did his admiration. Vee's sense of survival was strong. Something he admired about her. So why was he attempting to break her?

Elena and Sabot held their silence and even that was irritating. Micah was tempted to *insist* they return to camp. Very tempted. There were ways to make them *eager* to obey. But he owed his spy.

She'd learned Kaysar and Cookie were keeping a secret from Pearl Jean and King Jareth, their allies, who were keeping a secret of their own. What those secrets were, Micah didn't yet know. But petty arguments constantly broke out among the foursome. A point in his favor. Loyalties could be tested and broken.

What's more, Elena had stolen an artifact from the Unhinged Ones. A powerful stone able to generate an impenetrable dome around a small area. She'd hidden it in camp before coming to find Micah, and he wanted the thing always guarded. But he wanted Vee guarded more, so he contained his insistence.

As he passed a particularly eye-catching tree, the trunk snagged his attention. Words, carved in the center. Three words to be exact. He read them and barked out an unexpected laugh.

The laugh surprised his companions. Elena and Sabot palmed weapons, scanning for hazards.

Vee gaped at him. "Really, Micah. Must you act so undignified in front of my lowly subjects?"

Elena garbled out a choked response. "*Your* subjects?"

He proceeded without thought, ignoring the spy and slinging an arm around his wife's waist to pull her to his side. With his free hand, he pointed to the words. "Graves left us a message."

"He did? He's okay then?" Relief coated her tone. "Wait. He can read and write? But...that's impossible! Isn't it? I mean, he shouldn't know more than—my other children." For some reason, hot color darkened her cheeks. "Well? What does it say? As you can see, his handwriting is deplorable."

No, it wasn't. And why was she so embarrassed? Unless...

Ahhhh. She couldn't read, could she? But then, when would she have had a chance to learn?

Sympathy superseded his buffet of other emotions, directing him to kiss her cheek. "Graves says no. That's the entire missive."

"What does that even mean?" Elena piped up.

Both Micah and Vee ignored her.

"Why, that little *brat*," his wife huffed.

Micah nearly barked a second laugh, another baffling turn. To find amusement in anything concerning a *belua*? The horror. And yet, much of his tension drained.

He kept his arm around his wife as he led her forward, saying, "Now you know how I feel."

"He takes after you, and I'll hear no arguments about it. I am *so* angry," Vee fumed, stomping at his side. "With you. With Graves. Especially with Graves. But mostly with you. I give and I give and I give, and this is the thanks I get?"

"So you know how I feel."

"I... You... Oh! When is our next meal?" she snapped. "I'm starving."

At least her appetite had reignited. He reached into the satchel he carried, searching for the piece of sweetcake he'd saved. He'd found a small satchel along the way, filled with a multitude of delicacies. Left by Graves or Cookie, Micah didn't know.

Elena beat him to it, slapping a sweetcake *she* had saved into Vee's hand and grumbling, "Do you ever stop eating?"

"Next time bow when you serve your cherished queen," Vee told the spy with a snotty tone—while chewing on her second bite. Crumbs sprayed from the corners of her mouth.

Females. He might never understand them. Though the rancor between the pair had died, they continued to snip at each other.

He looked back to catch Sabot's eye and share a moment of understanding. Or tried to. As Elena sputtered with indignation, Sabot stared at her, his lips curved into a smile.

Was anyone sane anymore?

The sloshy pathway steered him to a patch of dry land surrounded by massive stones. Dry land intermixed with wet, one ringed by the other, with a stone altar in the center. One of Vee's beds?

The familiar sight arrested Micah, the procession stopping behind him. The pulling he'd endured for days suddenly faded, a hated and beloved memory surging to the fore. He would never forget the first look at his sleeping beauty, bathed in lightning, splattered in raindrops. Or the way different desires had singed him. Desires he'd never shed. Buried, yes. For a short while. But permanently cast off? No. With each of his mistresses—all redheads—he'd attempted to replace her. A truth so obvious now.

His hands fisted at his sides. Would he *ever* cease craving this woman?

He scanned the area. No sign of Graves or the swamp creature. "We'll rest here." He jumped from dry ring to dry ring until he reached the bed, where he dropped the satchel.

Thinking to remove his soaked boots, he perched at the edge of the stone. Lifted a foot. An image shoved its way inside his mind, and he shot to his feet, a harsh denial choking him.

The image remained. He saw Vee, wearing her collar and blood-soaked rags. A troll held her unconscious body. Not just any troll, but their king, Ragdar. A male Micah had nearly died defeating. But the result had been worth the injuries. Ragdar had become clay in his hands, fully moldable. With strength of will alone, Micah still held the powerful male immobile in the underground tunnels, as helpless as his people, forced to remember the pain he'd caused so many others.

His companions reacted to his sudden aggression, a chorus of questions ringing out.

Elena: "What is it?"

Sabot: "Majesty?"

Vee: "Remove this collar this instant!"

He shook his head hard, the mental picture dissipating. His tension lingered, a snarl rising from him. The oracle had done this. Someone had given Fayette the pain antidote, and she'd pushed the grim future into Micah's head. But had he seen a glimpse of the truth or a manipulation of it?

There was only one reason Fayette would reveal something like that to Micah. She had learned his weakness, his greatest vulnerability; she knew the slightest amount of fear severed his control over his opponents, giving the creatures control over *him*. She hoped to make him afraid, thereby freeing the trolls of their immobility and dividing his focus, aiding Kaysar. Putting Vee in danger.

"Freeing the oracle might cost you your life," he snapped at her. "I hope *you're* happy."

She made a crude hand gesture. "I told you. I didn't free her."

Truth or lie? If not her, then who had betrayed him?

Foreboding sparked, but he maintained his calm with a reminder. Trolls couldn't flitter. Even if they escaped the shackles of his control, they would be stuck in their doorless prison. Unless a traitor provided transportation. But only he and Norok knew their exact location, and Norok would *never* turn on Micah. No matter what Vee believed about the male.

Another possibility was Elena. She'd visited the dungeon often. Except, she'd never entered the chambers with trolls.

Not to his knowledge, anyway. As a spy well able to hide herself...

No. No! The Adelina siblings wouldn't work against him. They just wouldn't. In the entire realm, they were the two he trusted above all others. Vee *must* be wrong about them. And aid Warren's killer? No. Not for any price.

The image punched its way into his mind a second time, and a tattered moan parted Micah's lips. Ragdar. A bloody Vee. Trepidation swelled as he tugged at hanks of his hair. If his wife died...

"Micah?" she asked softly, agitated and apprehensive rather than defensive.

Concerned? For him? Did a part of her care? He thought maybe...yes. His feral kitten had saved him food. She hadn't run off after the expiration of their bargain. Constantly leered at him.

To lose her...

Losing his grip on his composure, he focused his thoughts on her. On their future. *I can have a life with her. Taste joy and satisfaction daily.* He had only to let go of the past and grab hold of her, *despite* the obstacles between them.

Shouldn't he try? He was miserable without her. *Not guaranteed a tomorrow. Should go down fighting, all right—for better.* His family. Vee, Micah and their terror of children. Somehow, they could make it work; the alternative was intolerable.

Instincts and desires converged, and defenses crumbled. Lingering fears doused, making his new—and final—plan crystal clear. Claim her. Today. Tomorrow. Always and forever. Mark her so completely all others would know: *she belongs to Micah the Unwilling.* From the beginning, he'd been drawn to Red. An eternastone to its mate, always pulled in her direction.

Fated. No way around it, over it or under it. Only through it.

For so long, he'd held on to his kingdom with little payoff.

He had fought, sacrificed, protected, expanded, but he had never enjoyed the fruits of his labors. He'd never had something all his own. Until Red. She was his, their connection undeniable, and he was keeping her. Whatever the cost. That was that.

The war in his head ended between one heartbeat and the next, the picture of her demise dissipating once again. For the first time in…ever, he felt settled. Right.

Trembling like a lad, he studied his wife's lovely features. She studied his right back. No longer did he see hatred in her eyes. No, he saw concern. But that could change in a blink, and he could lose her for good. *Without* the troll king's help. Micah had only to leave her collared, keeping her vulnerable and incapable of flittering. Proof she shouldn't trust him to have her best interests at heart. And if she could not trust him, she would not stay with him willingly. But no bonds, no Red.

Panic flared, expanding and contracting. Lose her before he'd done everything in his power to win her?

Determination turned his bones to steel, and he jolted. If he did the right thing, regardless of the expected outcome, she would learn to trust him—or she would leave.

Everything or nothing.

"Micah," she demanded. "Snap out of it, man. You're frightening the peasants. Tell us what's going on with you."

He yanked his gaze to Elena and Sabot, who clawed at their own cheeks. Trickles of crimson poured down their faces. Their fault for disobeying his orders.

Struggling to rein in his aggression, Micah locked his sights on Red. Her jaw dropped, and she stumbled back a step. He lashed out an arm, snagged her by the nape and yanked her closer. Hardness to soft, lush curves.

He sniffed the length of her neck, an action he couldn't stop. She gasped. With a throaty rasp, he told her, "You aren't the only one who hungers."

"Is that so?" Slowly, she went liquid, molding her body to

his. Her eyelids hooded as she flattened her palms over his pectorals. "What does His Majesty crave?"

"I'd like to start with a taste of your apples." The scent of citrus thickened around them. His heart raced. The feel of her... "Your scent drives me wild."

"My scent? No, darling. This is *your* scent."

Was it? "Perhaps it's our scent together."

"P-perhaps." Her warm breath seared a sensitive path across his bare chest. He tightened his grip, desperate for her mouth to follow each exhalation. "Are you attempting to seduce me?"

"No. I'm succeeding." He craned his head, pinning his spy in place with a glare. "Within the next thirty seconds, you *will* return to camp, and you *will* inform your brother of my return tomorrow." He won or lost his wife tonight. "And do not think you can refuse me again. You *will* return to camp. There is no *or else*. No other option exists for you."

Red quivered against him. Keeping her gaze on him, she snapped, "Elena, consider the king's command an order from your much scarier queen, and do it. *Now.*"

The blonde huffed, and the clawing ended. The wounds healed. "Fine! I'll go. But only because I'm no longer afraid for your life. The beast is helpless."

"How *dare* you!" Red burst out, surging forward. She would have tackled the other woman if Micah hadn't held fast. "I am *far* from helpless. My vengeance has only begun."

"Of course, you're not helpless," Elena shouted back. "As if I was talking about you."

"Oh. Well." His wife humphed and settled. "There was no need to state the painfully obvious. *Micah* is the weak one, and everyone knows it."

Yes, he was the weak one. But with Red, he thought he might enjoy it.

Elena mounted her centaur and vanished. Sabot quickly followed suit, leaving Micah and Red alone. He wasted no time, flittering her to the altar. With his hands on her hips, he lifted her and sat her atop the flat, upper stone, directly in front of him.

She gulped. As he returned his grip to her nape, he could only imagine the intensity of aggression he exuded. An intensity that only sharpened as locks of her silken hair wedged between his fingers.

Applying pressure, he tilted her head backward, baring her throat to him. "Do you want all of me, Red? If there were no obstacles between us, would you wish to be my cherished wife?"

Her eyes widened, and she gulped with more force. "Cherished?"

He gave a single dip of his head. "I cannot hide how much I yearn for you, and I do not wish to try anymore."

She gulped and offered a similar dip. "Yearn?"

"You are it for me. I've done you many wrongs. If you'll give me a chance, I will do right. I know you don't trust me now, but you will. I'll prove it. Tell me the obstacles between us." A command from her husband and king.

Relaxing into his hold, she licked her lips. "There are four."

"Let's hear the first."

"Well." Gulp. "I killed Kaysar's parents, as you know, so I owe him a debt I *must* repay."

A statement he'd expected. "I understand." He didn't like it, but he understood nonetheless.

"Do you really?" A deep, shaky breath before she admitted, "Because I'm determined to oversee his victory against his greatest enemy…you."

He drew in a deep, shaky breath, too. Deeper. Shakier. A thousand thoughts swirled, thinning one by one until a response became clear. "Kaysar is an obstacle no longer. Your husband has decided to help you pay your debt. He is agreeing to a truce." What had once held him back no longer seemed important. A building? "It is the right move. No war, no trolls necessary."

A gasp parted her lips. Her eyes rounded. "You'd give up your palace for me?"

He'd constructed one. He could construct another—to his wife's tastes. "Kaysar can keep his kingdom, and I will keep mine. The people will be free to choose the king and queen they wish to serve."

That said, Micah separated the two pieces of the collar and tossed the metal aside. He plucked the eternastone from his wrist cuff and tossed it to the ground, allowing the two stones to draw together, like magnets pulled one to another.

He remembered the vision. In the troll king's arms, she'd worn the collar. She was safer without it; nothing mattered more than her protection.

Her breath caught, but doubts swirled in her irises. "What of the other obstacles? My glamara and my children."

"They no longer apply. You are free to create whatever you wish, how often you wish. Know that your children are my children. Graves demands this. I ask only that our children are not allowed to attack our people."

"Th-that is doable, but what about the fourth obstacle?" Her gaze darted. "A secret I'm keeping from you?"

What other secrets could she possibly have? Why not tell him now, during this fresh start? But he already knew the answer. He hadn't yet earned her trust. "I would tell you to keep your secret, if you feel you must. Which makes this a nonissue, yes?"

She floundered, panted. "What if I'm never worthy to be queen? Some obstacles you can't make go away so easily, Micah. Your people mistrust me. With good reason! How could they not? Plus, I'm unrefined, and I don't like shoes." Tears gathered, and her chin trembled. "I don't even know how to read."

His chest clenched at the truth, and he hated that he had ever made her doubt herself. With a soft smile, he tenderly cupped her cheeks. "As of this moment, shoes are outlawed in our kingdom. Offenders will be punished severely. And Red? We are royals, and we decide what is refined or not. As for reading, you can learn. No obstacle there."

"Well, yes. But—"

"No buts. You are the strongest, most courageous and wily creature I've ever battled. Your ability to recover and rebound astounds me. Those you love, you protect. They have your wholehearted loyalty. My people—our people—will come to see that and grow to love you. How could they not?" he asked, using her own question against her. "There are few beings who are worthy of *you*."

The tears spilled over, her irises turbulent pools. "You have no idea how wrong you are. I *ruin* things, Micah."

"That can't be true. You've made everything better for me," he rasped. "I will do anything to have you, Red."

Her lids dipped, her lashes dropping, attention fixing on his lips. She tapped the tips of her nails against his shoulders and throatily asked, "You want to keep me so much?"

"I've never wanted something more," he admitted without hesitation.

A suspended pause. Then she glided her fingers into his hair and fisted the short strands, urging him closer. His lips hovered over hers. They breathed for each other. "Take me, husband. Tonight, I choose you. I'm yours."

CHAPTER TWENTY-TWO

Viori moaned as Micah claimed her lips in a wild kiss, then moaned again when he tore at the straps of her dress. To her delight, the material shredded easily, baring her chest. Cool, damp air sizzled against her overheated skin, setting off a new tidal wave of arousal. A stronger wave that brought others. One by one, they crashed over her, drowning her, taking her to deeper depths.

Was she really going to do this? Forgive Micah and try marriage again? She didn't know. But she knew she yearned for him, too. And he was *trying*. He'd granted her freedom. He hadn't teased her about her inability to read. He'd agreed to a truce with her brother. A miracle! So, yes. Here, now, she would have him. Later, she would consider the risks with a clear head. Until then, she... He... Mmm, he nipped her bottom lip, then nibbled across her jaw. He drew her earlobe between his teeth, and she shivered.

"You are my delight," he breathed against her flesh, the words as thrilling as his touch. "My prize. I'm happiest when I have you in my arms."

She was? He was? "You are my... Micah!" she cried. He

licked her throat, sucked on her hammering pulse. Something
he couldn't do with the collar, but she was free now. And sensitive. Oh! Goose bumps spread like wildfire.

"That's right. I'm your Micah. Don't ever forget." He kneaded
her breasts, kissing and licking and sucking from one to the
other. "I'll always be yours."

"Mine." A broken groan left her, and she arched in offering,
clutching his broad shoulders for purchase. Beneath her hands,
his muscles bunched and strained. "Don't stop. Never stop."

"Never," he agreed. He scooted her to the edge of the stone
and pushed her legs open with a hand on each of her knees. He
stepped between her thighs. Leaning in, his weight settling into
his hands, he imprisoned her gaze. "I'm going to do things to
you, Red."

Her breath caught.

"You want me to do these things, don't you?" A statement,
not a question.

Voice wobbling, she told him, "Yes. Do the things. All the
things." She might die if he didn't. Then a thought hit, and she
gasped. "What about birth control?"

"Taken care of, wife." He tapped a stone in his wrist cuff.

A slow smile broke free. "Well. Aren't you the resourceful
royal."

A wicked gleam lit his irises. "I'm going to love this." He
lowered to one knee, then the other, in a purposeful procession.

Tremors invaded, a siege she couldn't regret. He never broke
eye contact or freed her from his iron grip. No, he left her utterly open to him. Pinned and vulnerable. And she liked it.
Ached to be exposed and defenseless before her husband. Just
as he laid himself bare before her.

As he peered up at her from a position of surrender, pride
squared her shoulders. For the first time, she felt like a queen
without equal. This besotted war king had won her hand in

marriage and reignited the fires of hope in her heart. He might be hers, now and always.

He leaned closer to where she ached. But he did nothing else. Her nerves buzzed with eagerness and anticipation. She licked her lips.

"I'll always be yours," he repeated. "You'll always be mine." Leaning...

She held her breath...

Contact! "Yes!" She gasped as pleasure seized her. Threading her fingers through his hair, Viori undulated against his tongue. "Yes, Micah, yes! Harder. Faster. Slower. Faster." The words tumbled free, without first being filtered through her mind.

Tension coiled, drawing tight. Moans and broken cries escaped. His name. His title—*husband*. Oh, the things this magnificent male made her feel. The way he attended to her need, fully engaged in her reactions, as lost as she was.

She imagined how they must look right now, wild in the moonlight. A warrior and his female, adrift in the throes.

"I like, I like, I like." Her cries spurred him on.

He didn't stop until she shattered with a scream. As her body shook and her heart soared, he leaped to his feet, already ripping off the remainder of his clothing. Viori basked in the beauty of him. The powerful body, sculpted with the most amazing muscle. Exquisite pale skin littered with those tantalizing scars. Barely banked ferocity.

He stepped between her legs once more. She clasped the hard globes of his backside and flipped her gaze to his face. Moonlight framed him. His chin was lifted, his gaze downcast, locked on her, and glittering. Relentless. His chest rose and fell with his breaths, the air between them thicker by the second. He was brutal yet controlled.

"Do you want more from me, wife?" Pride stamped every line of his being. Dark hair unkempt, irises darker than usual yet set ablaze. He was the culmination of a myriad secret fantasies she'd feared to entertain.

"I want…" She leaned into him to kiss one of his scars, then ran her tongue over another.

His exhalations grew ravaged, broken. "Vee. Red," he growled.

"Viori," she whispered, the admission slipping out. Her defenses were cracking and falling. "My name is Viori." Would he peg her as the sister of his most hated foe? End this before it began?

"Viori." He kissed the corner of her eye, not missing a beat. No, he hadn't pegged her, and she exhaled a breath. Born from relief or regret, she didn't know. "Sweet Viori." He kissed the tip of her nose. "My Viori." He traced the tip of his tongue along the seam of her lips. "You still haven't answered me."

A response rose from her deepest of depths, where pleasure still raged. "Yes," she rasped. "I want more from you."

"Be very sure you mean those words." He reached up, combing his fingers through her hair before closing them around a fistful of strands, tilting her head to a new angle. "When I take you, I keep you. That is nonnegotiable."

To belong… "I am—" she squeezed his backside before stroking his erection "—very sure."

Air hissed between his teeth. Then he was lunging at her, kissing her, driving her against the stone bed. His delicious weight pinned her to the surface. His scent—their scent—intoxicated her senses, leaving her dizzy.

He positioned his length at her entrance.

"Do it," she pleaded.

With a groan, he pushed his way in, slowly filling and stretching her. Consuming. Possessing. Owning. When he thrust the rest of the way, she cried out for more.

He thrust again. And again. Plunging. Their ragged moans blended, creating the sweetest music. But all too soon, madness set in, and she could no longer think beyond her need for him. For more. More. *More!*

"Yes, Micah. Yes." Viori wrapped her legs around him, meeting each plunge with a whip of her hips, taking him deep. Deeper. Kissing him again. The most intimate exchange of her life.

Crying out, he wrenched his mouth free from hers. As he slowed his pace, he gripped her nape and pressed their brows together. They exchanged breaths. "I want to be in you, exactly like this, every day for the rest of eternity," he rasped. "There's nothing as good as you."

"Micah. Want. Eternity. Yes!" Pressure was building inside her. Too much, not enough. She didn't mean to, but she clawed at him, leaving bloody furrows. "Good. It's so good. So, so, so good. Give me more. More!"

She clung to him, needing, and scratching, and biting. Panting and moaning and begging. Still, he maintained that slow pace. Agonizingly slow, as if he savored each increasingly forceful glide. Forceful yet languid, making the madness so much worse. And better. Yes, yes, yes. So much better.

Soon, she lost her ability to think beyond fragments. *Need to think.* This was…wasn't…but she…this…he…argh! Something was happening inside her. Something more than the shaking and quaking and falling of defenses. His stare was everything. Holding her captive in a way the collar had failed to do. Making silent demands for…what? *What?*

The pressure expanded further. Pleasure mounted, threatening to overtake her and change her forever. Beads of sweat glistened on his pale skin. One trickled from his temple to his chin. She watched it, desperate to escape the intensity of his gaze. The strength of their connection. When the droplet hit the top of a scar, she whimpered. There was no male more perfect than Micah.

Her focus returned to him of its own accord, drawn by an

irresistible, invisible force. It was then, that moment, when she
knew exactly what he'd been demanding from her all along.
Not just forever, but her loyalty. He was willing to give up his
war for her. Now, he expected her to relinquish the war she
waged with *herself*. To trust him with her everything; the thing
that frightened her most.

He asked her for too much. More than she had the power to
grant. But she couldn't...she... Yes!

Pressure and pleasure collided, and Viori broke, coming apart
at the seams. Arching her spine, she screamed into the night.

As if her bliss fueled his own, he roared, shuddering against
her. Through it all, neither of them looked away from the other.

Micah held a dozing Vee—*Viori*—close. They lay atop the
stone bed. Well, they lay on half of the blanket Cookie had provided, with the other half draped over their naked bodies. An
hour had passed since he'd experienced the greatest pleasure of
his life, yet his heartbeat had yet to slow. What they'd done...
It was nothing like the tame, polite trysts he used to share with
his mistresses.

Spread your legs for me.

This far, Majesty, or farther?

He bit his tongue—

Am I hurting you?

I don't mind, Majesty. You may do whatever you wish to me.

—tasting blood.

Viori had told him what she hungered for and demanded more
as her due. He reeled from the high of it. The total satisfaction.

He toyed with her wavy mane, running the strands through
his fingers. If he'd been obsessed with her before, he was utterly
gone for her now. When he'd offered her a chance at forever,
he'd meant it. He would try this one more time, putting everything on the line. Trusting her with his body. If she took care of
it, he would offer more. But either way, they had started afresh

today, the slate clean. On his end, at least. In time, he hoped she would grow comfortable enough to reveal whatever secret she shielded. He could *teach* her to believe in him.

"What are you thinking about?" she asked sleepily.

"Forging a future together," he replied. "I want to. Do you?"

"I… Yes? Maybe." She squirmed against him. "I think."

"You think?" he roared. "The time for thought is over! We agreed. I keep you."

Such a tone would have sent anyone else running for cover. She settled down and kissed the hollow of his neck. "I meant, I'd like to take it one day at a time. Just until I share my secret. Okay, Micah? Please?"

Please. Her first true request. How could he deny her this? "Very well," he said, though foreboding struck. That secret… What could it be? "One day at a time." He would use the time to prove himself. "But we stay together."

"Thank you." The remaining tension drained from her, a teasing light entering her eyes. "Now, let's discuss the next order of business. Namely, Elena."

"Elena? Oh, I see." He fought a smile. "You think to use my compromised mental capacity to your advantage and wring concessions from me."

"Obviously." She petted his chest, as if pleased with him.

"You wish to see her punished more severely for disobeying Norok?"

"The opposite. She is my personal lady's maid. Therefore, any disciplinary action should occur at my sole discretion, and I'm inclined to give her a reward."

Not a topic he'd expected to address today. He'd known Viori and Elena had ceased hating each other, but he hadn't realized his Red had become so fond of the blonde. And she must be fond of the other woman. Otherwise, she would request a harsher penalty.

"She is a soldier in my army," he explained, "and she disobeyed a direct order from a person of higher rank."

"I disobey you all the time, yet *I* get rewarded. As I always say, what's good for a royal is good for the people."

"Oh, you *always* say this?" He grinned. "The problem is, I'm particularly motivated to show you leniency. You and no other."

"Is it because I look so good naked?" she asked, wiggling against him. "It's because I look so good naked, isn't it?"

"That is a reason, yes." He traced his fingertips along the ridges of her spine, then cupped her backside and groaned. Never in a thousand lifetimes would he get enough of this soft, curvy body. The outrageous things she said. How she challenged him.

"Well? How many other reasons are there?"

"Many."

"Like how amazing it feels to be inside me?"

"Without question. Nothing compares to you." Already he wanted her again. He kissed her temple. "Before we explore this topic further—and we *will* explore it further—I have a query for you."

She went still, evincing dread. "All right. Ask."

He gave her temple another kiss, an offer of reassurance. "Why do your trees sometimes bear fruit?"

"Oh. That. I don't actually know," she admitted. "Though I kind of suspect you have something to do with it."

"Me?"

"Well, it's happened only twice. But both times you were nearby...and I was kind of...happy."

Micah made her happy? He almost couldn't process the idea. "All of my life, I've dreamed of providing a paradise for my people. Fruit for the taking. Flowers in bloom. And now I can do it, if only I make my queen smile often?" Hope spread through him.

She squirmed again. "I mean, it isn't impossible. But, um, what happens next? Between us."

"What do you want to happen next?"

A moment passed in silence before she maneuvered to her stomach and propped her hands on his pectorals, directly over his heart. She peered at him through the fan of her lashes while worrying her bottom lip.

"I think I want to tell you my secret, but I don't think I should. It might be a betrayal to someone else. So I think I'll find my children instead and—"

"Our children," he interjected. What belonged to her belonged to him, and what belonged to him belonged to her. That was how things would be from now on.

She flushed. "Yes. Well. We can all return to your camp and—"

"Our camp."

She gulped and nodded. "We'll give this marriage a try. See how things go. Rule over your—our—people. Enjoy the truce with Kaysar and Cookie."

A try was all he needed. "Let's hear—" His mind went blank, flashing black before displaying a new, horrifying reality. Another glimpse of the future, courtesy of Fayette.

He jolted as the image of a bloody Viori and the troll king filled his awareness. Only this time, Micah saw what happened before and after her death. Ragdar, beating her with his meaty fists. Her slight form unable to withstand the abuse. When she had no fight left in her, he ripped at her skirt—

"No!" Micah roared, springing upright to attack the male—but he swiped at air, only air. He was panting, in the swamp, on the stone bed, with his wife at his side.

"Micah?" Pallid, Viori went to her knees, crouching beside him. "What's wrong?"

"Nothing. Everything. I'm sorry," he said, scrubbing a hand over his face. "I didn't mean to frighten you." Should he inform her of the truth or not? Would leaving her in the dark place her in more or less danger? Would she worry when she shouldn't? What was truth and what was twisted lie?

He slid his hand to his nape and massaged the bunched-up muscles. The right thing? Giving her the truth. "The oracle. Fayette. She keeps pushing an image into my head. It is…not pretty. I'm sorry," he repeated lamely. No, he shouldn't tell her what he'd seen. Right now, there was no reason to do so. The oracle *must* have twisted the image, showing him a false future, nothing more. Micah would never allow Ragdar to gain freedom. Would never allow the troll to near the queen. Would never fear…

Except, the image hit him again and again and again. Relentless. Ruthless. Until he couldn't distinguish fantasy from reality. Viori, beaten. Broken. Dead. His heart raced faster. Sweat trickled from his temples, and it had nothing to do with spent passions.

Beaten. Broken. Dead.

Beaten, broken, dead.

Beatenbrokendead.

A series of vicious roars cut through the forest, birds taking flight. The awful image vanished in an instant, and Micah snapped into sudden focus.

Viori gasped. "Trolls!"

Cursing inside his head, he flittered to his feet and tossed Viori a tunic. He donned his pants, then palmed a set of daggers. All the while, his mind whirled, cataloguing details. Six distinct roars meant at least six trolls. Ragdar among them?

Had the group wandered the forest and caught Micah's scent? Unlikely, considering he'd been all over this area for days and found no sign of them.

His fear freed them from stasis? If so…

He worked his jaw. Someone had indeed flittered them from the underground maze. Someone who'd known Micah's whereabouts.

Only two people had. Elena and Sabot.

No. No! She would not betray him, as Fayette and Diane had done. And Sabot's sense of honor would not allow it. The male had a core of nobility; Micah sensed this. There must be another explanation, and he would figure it out. Later. Right now, nothing mattered more than killing trolls and protecting Viori.

Fantasy would not become reality again.

"Get dressed and hide behind the bed." He flittered to the edge of the farthest ring, putting the swamp water at his back. "Do not move until they're dead." *Or I am.*

CHAPTER TWENTY-THREE

Wearing only an overlarge tunic, Viori obeyed Micah and rushed behind the bed. Not to hide from the coming battle. She wasn't afraid of the seven-foot-tall beasts with bulging, corded muscles and razor-sharp claws who'd once hunted their victims without cease. Beings who enjoyed eating fae.

They didn't need immortality, like centaurs. No, they considered the organs of their victims a delicacy, often dining straight out of a split-open torso while the heart still beat. From capture to table. Allow Micah to fight a group of these brutes by himself? Hardly. She intended to help.

How *dare* these trolls interrupt cuddle time with her husband? The personal exchange she'd missed so badly. The shocking intimacy she hadn't known she craved. The incomparable connection she thought she would forever seek. All found within the arms of the sexiest male in existence.

The trolls shall pay dearly.

Where had the beasts even come from? She'd seen no sign of them anywhere she and Micah had traversed.

The ground shook, signaling the enemy's nearness. Emotion check—under control. Viori gathered her strength. Easier than ever to do. Power she'd stored up while wearing the collar suddenly deluged her veins. Good! And bad. The goal wasn't to use so much power she slept and opened a doorway. The goal wasn't even to create and awaken a new protector. No, she sought to control the elements only for a limited time.

Careful. Bones vibrating, she spread her arms and released the first note of a new song. A soft melody drifted through the air. Ripples disturbed the murky surface of the pond. An excellent start.

More shaking. Behind her, splashing and grunts sounded. She threw a glance over the stone and gasped. The trolls had arrived, and there were more than expected. Nine in total. They converged on Micah, going straight for the kill. Beefy arms swung this way and that, claws flared to inflict maximum damage.

Fury mixed with fear, her song cracking at the edges. *Careful!* If she were to accidentally hurt Micah…

With a squelching gurgle, watery arms shot from the pond, snagging three trolls by their ankles and yanking them into the depths. The trio disappeared, water churning—until it didn't. The cresting turmoil ebbed to nothing.

Six trolls to go. A much more manageable number.

Confidence restored, Viori sang louder. Stronger power flowed through her. Out of her. A troll stumbled from Micah, doing his best to remove the axe in his sternum; another watery arm shot out to snag him. He screamed as he disappeared beneath the violent maelstrom.

Goodbye, troll. Five to go.

Her husband stepped into her line of vision, and her jaw slackened, her song ending abruptly. *As much a monster as the ones he fights.* He was a tower of cold vengeance. Vicious and unstoppable. He was beautiful. Even more so than usual.

"Viori?" he shouted.

She caught a note of apprehension. Not so cold, after all.

"I'm good," she called, a new round of shaking registering. A fresh contingent of trolls on their way?

Yep. Five others stormed the clearing, swarming the king. She erupted into another song. Wait. Only four swarmed Micah. The fifth locked his gaze on her, bounded over the bed, and landed in front of her. Though her voice wobbled, she launched into another song.

He smiled, his horns flaring. She backed up a step, spotted the creature sneaking up on him and stopped, returning the smile. The poor fool. He had no idea death had come for him.

Graves stabbed a sharp, three-pronged branch into the troll. His throat, his heart and his guts. The ends of the prongs came out the other side, dripping with blood and heavy with tissue.

"Nice of you to join us," she said.

Graves lifted the troll off his feet. An offering to the pond. Those water arms shot out, coiling around the dying foe's wrists and ankles and yanking. Limbs ripped from his body. Blood gushed and rained.

John, her swamp baby, rushed into the clearing and joined the fray, tearing into other trolls. After Graves assured himself of Viori's good health, he joined the melee. The two darlings worked with Micah, cutting through the opposition. When she noticed her sandcats nipping at the heels of the trolls, her heart swelled. They were a family, working together for a common goal. *Her* family. A dream she'd never realized she'd entertained, finally coming true.

Viori cheered encouragements. "Gut him! Off with his head! Shove his heart down his throat!"

Soon, a measly three trolls survived. Blood splattered Micah, Graves and John as they each faced off with a single opponent. Gashes littered her husband's chest. Several of Graves's branches hung by the barest sliver of bark. John had lost an arm.

Forget encouragements. She initiated a new song. A healing melody that burned through her power. Worth it. Micah's wounds wove together. Graves jolted with renewed strength, and John regrew his missing limb.

Gratification stirred within her. *I'm helping!*

Micah won his match first, his opponent falling, motionless, a dagger hilt protruding from his throat. Her king glanced from Graves's battle to John's, no doubt deciding who needed help most, when a surprise fourth troll dived out of nowhere, one arm drawn back, a fiery spear clutched in a tight grip.

Her song morphed into a scream of horror. Micah's head whipped up. He followed her sight line. But not soon enough. For Viori, time slowed. She watched, helpless, as the troll launched a killer shot at her husband. The missile flew at dizzying speed. As Graves spun in front of Micah, Micah flittered in front of him, and the flame-drenched spear sliced through his heart.

No! No, no, no. She flittered to him, catching him when his body collapsed. They fell together as she batted at the flames. Blisters popped up all over her hands; some of her flesh melted. Searing pain consumed her, but she didn't stop until she extinguished the last flame.

So badly she wished to sing another healing song. More than anything! But her emotions had just taken a wrong turn. A song might assure his death. *Momma and Papa all over again.*

Graves skewered the troll with a branch, while John finished him off. The sandcats ran circles around her and Micah, howling their distress.

Her gaze never veered from her husband. "You fool! Why did you do that?"

Blood leaked from the corner of his mouth. "Protect... what's...ours."

"Fool," she repeated, hot tears cascading over her cheeks. "I can't sing you better."

"Hurt you once...not ever again."

A sob parted her lips. Panic rising, she lifted her gaze. "Help me. Graves. John. Please!"

John rushed over to yank the branch from Micah's chest.

"Not like that," she screamed as a tide of crimson gushed from the open wound. Warm blood welled between her fingers when she tried to block the flow with her hands. Desperation pierced her.

Micah grunted, then coughed up sprays of blood.

The tears fell faster, her chin trembling. Words spilled from her lips. "What do I do? How do I help him?" She'd never doctored a fae other than herself before.

Could Micah even survive this? Could anyone? Most fae were swift healers—superswift compared to humans—but they were not invulnerable. And what of Micah, who scarred?

He's survived worse. Yes?

"Brace yourself. I'm doing this." She ripped off her tunic, uncaring about her sudden nakedness, and pressed the material into his wound to stop the exit of blood.

His eyelids drifted shut.

"Stay awake, baby." She pressed harder. With all her strength. "Tell me something. Anything. I am your queen. Obey me!"

He pried those heavy lids apart, his glassy eyes finding hers as he continued to gurgle up blood. "Thank...you. For today."

"No!" A new cascade of tears streaked her cheeks, burning. "Don't you dare thank me. You get better. Do you understand?" This male—this good, good male with his honorable heart— had saved Graves. He shouldn't die for it. *Please, don't die for it.*

"I'm taking him to get help. I'll come back for you when I can," she told her children. Wasting no time, she flashed Micah to their oasis, next to the waterfall. Something she could do now that he'd removed the collar and they were outside of his camp.

"Cookie!" she screamed when Micah's eyelids slid closed. His head lolled to the side. The movements of his chest slowed.

Soon to stop altogether? "Queen Cookie! Cookie! Kaysar! Pearl Jean!" Anyone!

"Ugh. Please, monitor your tone. I'm here because my oracle said you'd need me or whatever, so let's get on with this. What's the problem, what do you expect me to do and what will you pay me to do it?"

Viori whipped around. Not too far away, Cookie stood inside one of her mystical doorways, vibrant leaves framing the edges. The royal wore a strange tunic of her own with the words Property of Sugars Bardot underneath a knitted sweater, tight black leggings and fluffy white slippers. Her dark hair was piled into a mess on the crown of her head, with errant locks spilling over. Puffy eyes and sunken cheeks spoke of a recent sickness.

"Oh. Wait. Your clothes. Amber mentioned you would need fresh duds." Cookie tossed her a new garment—a silken blue robe Viori caught and donned hastily, shoving her arms through the proper holes. "Now that my corneas aren't scorched from your hotness—serious props, girl—let's get on with this, please. But why are you covered with blood?"

"Fix him," she commanded, motioning to Micah. "Fix him right now or rue the day you were born!"

"Oh. That's the big emergency, is it? Ha ha, very funny, Amber," she called over her shoulder. "Like I'm really going to save my enemy. Especially when his wife is *threatening my precious life*."

"He is your enemy no longer. Rather, he is your ally. He has agreed to accept your truce, with certain tweaks." *If* he'd meant his words. And he had. Viori truly believed he had. Except, he didn't know the full truth yet. He didn't know the identity of her brother, that he'd really never stood a chance of winning her to his side and that a marriage to her meant forging a familial bond with a (once) hated foe. He might be a bit reluctant to trust Viori and her motives a third time. Might regret the accord and seek to nullify it.

No, no. Surely not. He'd jumped in front of Graves, saving their child. Theirs. He'd insisted. He would not turn away from his family.

Would he?

She needed to tell him everything, and she would. As soon as he healed. "Well?" she demanded. "Fix him."

Cookie winced. "Sorry, baby doll, but that agreement is now off the table. Why would I agree to a compromise with a dying man? If I let him pass on to the other side, my problem kind of solves itself."

"Save him," Viori snarled. If she mentioned her connection to Kaysar, Cookie might be more amenable...or less so. "Refuse, and I will awaken every cell in your body to attack you from the inside—"

"Oh, my gosh, shut up already. Your voice is giving me a headache. And a stomachache!" The queen shut her eyes and rubbed her temples. "Fine!" Her eyelids popped open. "I'll do it. But only because I'm so benevolent. Just give me a second to breathe, and I'll make sure he lives or whatever."

His next breath... Viori heard a death rattle. Desperation sharpened into despair. "Do it now. He might not have a second!"

"Girl, please. He has plenty of seconds. Amber assures me he's going to be fine, so stop worrying already."

"You will help him now or I will... I..."

"Okay, okay. I'll get to work." Her brother's wife sighed and motored forward, only to stop when someone caught her wrist.

She followed a tanned arm to a stunning face that belonged to a female with a short cap of blond hair. Big curls framed delicate features. Big blue eyes. Heart-shaped red lips. She perched atop a small metal horse known as a...scooter, maybe.

"Let go, Pearl Jean. If this is a trap, I'll kill everyone and that will be that. No harm, no foul—for me. But you *know* Amber also assured me this is necessary."

That *is Pearl Jean?* The old crone? *The hag of the highest order?*

The blonde looked Viori over, challenge crackling in her eyes, and humphed, but she also released the queen. "If she makes one move in your direction, I'll run her over with my scooter. See if I don't."

Forget the woman's beauty. Her concern for Micah proved all-consuming. He *must* live. She couldn't lose him. She wouldn't.

Cookie huffed and approached them, utterly unafraid. "Here." She extended her hand, revealing a dark, coin-size disk resting in her palm. "Feed him this and he'll power up lickety-split."

She accepted the disk, snatching it with lightning-fast speed before the other woman changed her mind. "What is this?" What if it hurt Micah? Would he be able to eat it?

"That," Cookie said, "is elderseed."

Her eyes widened. Elderseed? Truly? Well. Micah would be eating that disk if she had to shove it down his throat. Talk about a treasure beyond value. Produced by enchanted trees, far before Viori's time. Used as the most potent of medicines, as well as a temporary supercharge of a fae's glamara. But wars had been won and lost over the few shards of elderseed left, and several courts joined forces to eliminate the trees themselves. How had Cookie gotten this? And why part with it...unless she hid a stockpile?

"You should use only the barest sliver to heal him," the queen explained, as if they discussed how to bake a common sweet bread. "Too much of a boost too fast and he's likely to jump out of his skin. Besides, you can save the rest for his next cat-astrophic set of injuries or, I don't know, start your garden or something. Enchanted trees grow under any conditions. Totally up to you. But one day, I'm told our kingdoms are gonna join forces to defeat a big bad unlike anything we've ever known."

Start a garden in the campgrounds, Micah's dream? Perhaps create her own army of enchanted tree children to protect their campground from intruders? *Yes, please.* "If you are lying, and you've given me poison... I don't care who you are, I'll do as promised and sing your cells into my own personal army to de-stroy you from the inside out."

Cookie rolled her eyes again.

After breaking off what she hoped was "the barest sliver," she crumbled the piece into Micah's open mouth, then massaged his throat, forcing him to swallow. Seconds passed. She waited with bated breath, hopeful, afraid, dying inside second by second until...

He sucked in air, filling his lungs, his entire body jolting. Bone, muscle and flesh wove together at a fast clip, color returning to his pale skin. His chest rose and fell, choppy at first, but quickly smoothing out.

Relief poured through her, potent beyond imagining. He would live.

"Told you," Cookie said, smug. "Maybe next time don't threaten the gal aiding you. She might decide to drive a vine through your spinal cord. Or choke you out and pop off your head. That's a particular favorite of mine. Or we could go with my husband's favorite and cut out your tongue. Nah. I think I'll go with mine."

As she spoke, a vine sprouted from the ground, slithering up, up Viori's legs, pinning her in place. That vine continued to grow, soon enwrapping her throat and applying pressure. Not enough to incite damage, but plenty to prove a point.

Cookie smiled with sinister delight. "Sometimes we like to do both."

Viori smiled, too—then hummed a little tune. The vine slowly uncoiled from her neck, blinking open a pair of pretty green eyes and nuzzling her along the way. Another temporary animation. "Show Queen Cookie who you obey," she whispered to her newest creation.

The living vine retracted from her, focusing on the now frowning queen with narrowing lids.

"Are you *looking* at me?" Cookie demanded of the vine. To the female's obvious shock and horror, the stalk slithered over and wound around *her* body. Nothing she did stopped it.

Before the vine could tighten, healthy green became ashy black and drifted away on a soft breeze.

Viori balled her hands into fists, and Cookie backed up, re-entering the doorway. Neither of them relinquished the other's gaze. Challenge arced between them.

One scowled, then the other.

"The truce stands," Cookie grated.

Good. They understood each other. Viori wasn't powerless. She nodded confirmation, even as she petted Micah's hair. "The truce stands."

For some reason, the queen hesitated to leave.

Why not take advantage and ask the questions she'd longed to ask? "How did you and Kaysar meet?"

Cookie smiled again, as if dreaming her favorite dream. "I received the heart of a fae princess. The wife of King Jareth Frostline. Kaysar planned to impregnate me and put his child on Jareth's throne. They had a centuries-long beef. Anyway, I won Kaysar's eternal love with a grand gesture."

A grand gesture. Hmm. Something Viori needed to do for Micah? "What did you do?"

"I killed his greatest enemy." The queen wrinkled her nose. "How do you not know any of this stuff? We've been the subject of realm-wide gossip for nearly a year." Gasping, she glanced over her shoulder. "Never mind. I gotta go." She vanished as the door closed around her.

What had happened? Oh, no matter. Viori had other things to deal with. She returned her attention to Micah, who'd begun to blink open his eyes. "Husband?" she whispered, hopeful, caressing his cheek.

He jerked upright, panting, his focus darting. When his gaze landed on her, she waited, expecting to be snatched by his arms, yanked against the hard line of his body, and hugged oh, so close. Why not spend the rest of the day celebrating his recovery and their fresh start? But he never snatched her, and disappointment set in.

He scrubbed a hand over his face instead, then asked, "You are well?" His voice emerged rougher.

"I am, I promise."

"What of Graves? And the swamp...thing?"

The fact that Micah hadn't used the term *belua* spoke volumes. "His name is John, and both are fine. How do you feel?" Better to admit what she'd done now. "You weren't healing, so I fed you a piece of elderseed that I acquired from Cookie when I authorized the truce. Is that acceptable?"

As silence stretched, she searched his grim-set features for an indication of rising anger or deep-seated regret.

Finally, he gave a stiff nod, his expression solemn. He flittered to his feet. "Stay here. I'll return after I check the perimeter for threats."

Wait. What? Viori popped to her feet, spinning, heart pounding. "You're leaving? Seeking another battle?" When he'd only healed a handful of minutes ago? "We're safe here."

"We aren't safe *anywhere*," he barked, making her flinch. No need to search for his anger anymore; she'd found it in the valley of his devastation. "I have been betrayed once again. Only Norok knew the location of the trolls, and only Elena and Sabot knew ours. They could be working with Fayette, using her against me."

His pain wrecked *her*. "Maybe someone sought to incriminate them. Fayette herself? Kaysar and Cookie, before we accepted the truce? Or someone else? An unknown?" She reached for him. "Micah—"

"Do not leave this spot," he snapped and vanished. But not before she spied the frothing anger spilling across his irises.

She wrapped her arms around her middle. Had he lost all faith in his fellow fae, Viori included? Did he have plans to return as promised, or had almost dying quickened his mind to the truth? She ruined things, and she wasn't worth the trouble he'd suffered on her behalf.

CHAPTER TWENTY-FOUR

Incredible power buzzed inside Micah as he materialized in the swamp. More power than he'd ever wielded before, thanks to the elderseed. No sign of Graves, John or the sandcats. No sign of trolls. The only evidence of battle? A pool of blood congealing on the stony ground.

He flittered to the outer edge of the oasis and explored the boundary. No trolls congregated here, either. When he inhaled a waft of Viori's citrus-and-florals fragrance, he nearly returned to her. *Not yet, not yet.* She was safe from danger, and he needed time to process what had transpired—and what he must do next.

Eager to burn off some of this energy, he ran…sprinted…flew over the terrain. Arms pumping, legs gobbling up the distance. He covered the entire circumference of the green paradise, uncaring when branches sliced him. The sharp stings served as fuel, driving his aggression higher.

The exercise didn't help. Because it wasn't what he truly required. No, he required a showdown. A conference with Norok and Elena. A face-to-face to demand answers. To hear an explanation. Surely his most trusted advisers had not done this terrible thing.

With a roar, Micah punched a tree as he passed it. The strength of the blow snapped the trunk in half. If the siblings, his oldest friends, had deceived him… He wasn't sure what he would do.

How much perfidy could one male withstand in his lifetime before he shattered?

Micah felled another tree. Bones cracked; flesh tore and bled. The wounds healed in a heartbeat, leaving no scars behind. Why not initiate a meeting *now*?

He seized upon the idea and switched direction, racing for the campground. Breath sawed in and out as he entered the wastelands, then the flatlands, and blazed over hills. A golden sun rose on the horizon, lighting the way. The elderseed ensured he never tired.

This wasn't the first time he'd ingested the stuff. Long ago, he'd found a brick in a village he'd conquered. He'd planted that brick in a secret location, and waited, hoping to cultivate an enchanted tree, thereby spawning others to at last produce the paradise of his dreams. Instead, months had passed, not a single sprout ever clearing the surface. When he'd finally given up and decided to consume the brick as needed, it was gone. He wondered now if Kaysar had unearthed it.

Sunrays intensified, glaring at him, but he didn't break a sweat. His heart rate didn't increase until he stopped in the shadows near the mighty wall of soldiers that surrounded the edge of camp. His camp. His kingdom. Fae after fae, standing shoulder to shoulder, either extending spears or holding bows already notched with arrows.

They await my arrival.

The truth cut as surely as a knife, pain ripping through him, spurring a flood of devastation. Norok and Elena had indeed betrayed him. Had freed the oracle and now worked to oversee Micah's ruination.

The two people he'd trusted most. Counted on as friends. Saw as family. *My enemies.*

Another roar brewed, but he held it back. His breath heated, searing his nostrils, his lungs. He opened and closed his hands. Acid churned in his stomach. How could they do this? Why did this happen to him, always and without fail? Why could he not have what so many others took for granted? Why did he give honesty and loyalty and receive lies and betrayal?

I still have Red. She has accepted me, just as I am.

But will she turn on me a second time?

That secret... The acid churned faster.

"I know you're out there, Micah," Norok called. Two warriors stepped apart, and the white-haired traitor emerged. Shining silver armor covered everything but his face. The hilts of two short swords rose above his broad shoulders. "Come and talk with me. I'm sure you're confused."

How reasonable the betrayer sounded. Fury joined the barrage of shock and hurt raining inside Micah. Talk? Yes. They would talk. "Where is Elena? Shouldn't she join us?"

"No need. I speak for her. Besides, this is between you and I."

Very well. Shirtless, scars on display for his people for the first time, he lifted his head and stalked from the shadows, entering the sunlight. He was exposed and vulnerable to ambush, but he didn't care. When he halted, he assumed a battle stance: shoulders back, hands fisted, legs braced apart.

Tension radiated from the onlookers, but none sheathed their weapons. Another blow of betrayal. He had worked himself to the bone providing for these people. Now they turned their back on him, serving Norok. Did anyone feel *any* loyalty to Micah? They would soon find out.

Three words shoved their way past his tongue. "Tell me why."

Norok raised his chin. "You must be more specific. Why did I hide the oracle from you? Why did I encourage Fayette to spark your greatest fear, freeing multiple trolls from your control? Why did I flitter those trolls to your location, hoping you and your monster-maker die? Because the oracle showed me the truth, the night I captured her." He presented the information without artifice, revealing the depths of his hatred for the first time. "You will accept a truce with Kaysar and Cookie."

Every word hit like a blow.

"I have accepted the truce already," he announced, murmurs of outrage rising among the masses. "It's a done deal, the war over. No more must die. All may partake of Queen Cookie's bounty." A development he had yet to consider. He had planned to accept the armistice for Red's benefit. Planned to start fresh with her. Now that it had happened, he didn't know how to feel or proceed. But he couldn't regret it. *Viori is mine now. My one ray of light.* As fragile as that light was.

The blond brute recoiled, as if struck by an invisible fist. "You ally with them, *after* they killed a contingent of your men and murdered Warren?" He shouted the question, spittle spraying from the corners of his mouth.

"I do. How many men did we slay when we invaded villages? We struck at each other because we were enemies. Afterward, we took them in, soon becoming a unit."

Norok scowled. "If that is how you feel, you are *my* enemy. I will avenge Warren, one way or another. Whatever the cost. And I know you don't understand this. You can't. You've never had family."

He flinched internally. "You think I did not love Warren? That I do not mourn him? That I do not mourn the others? That I do not regret my hesitation to strike at Kaysar and Cookie the moment they arrived?" Instead, he'd allowed his supposition— Kaysar, a possible chimera—to cloud his judgment. "I did. But I cannot deny the royals have been honorable enemies, who keep their word and admitted to their deeds. They didn't lie. They didn't slink in the background, cutting their loved ones from behind."

"How dare—"

"I'm not finished," he snarled, treading forward. The frontline soldiers sucked in breaths and braced. Even Norok retreated a step. "Should I deprive other parents of the choice to serve Kaysar and Cookie and sample the fruits of their pastures? Do you think I'm unaware of my inability to provide the same? That I missed the whispers and murmurs and complaints? Do you truly believe you'll be able to provide better? You, who constantly deceive your king as well as your wife?"

Viori was right. Never trust a cheater.

Norok bowed up. "What comes next? A plea for those who wish to follow either you or Kaysar to leave with you?" A maniacal laugh boomed from him. "Unfortunately for you, Fayette has spent the past few days showing everyone what happens if a truce between you and Kaysar is allowed to stand."

The warrior returned to his leadership post, lifted his hand and waved his fingers. The soldiers behind him parted, Fayette striding past them. She stopped at Norok's side, defiant as she met Micah's gaze. But then, she had lost both of her sons the day Kaysar and Cookie invaded the Forgotten Court.

"You'll want to see this," Norok told him, almost smug. "It involves your little Red."

An image overtook his mind, and he couldn't stop it. In it, Kaysar and Viori held hands. Both were splattered in blood, their heads thrown back as they sang. Utter carnage surrounded them, Micah's dead body among the victims. *Belua* tore the camp apart while Micah's soldiers writhed on the ground, screaming in agony.

No! He refused—absolutely refused!—to consider this falsehood.

"She betrays you," Fayette called before she laughed and laughed and laughed. "They all betray you."

As his head swam with possibilities, he displayed zero emotion. A struggle for him, but one he fought to the bitter end. Red would choose him over the childhood friend she had hurt and had now repaid in full; she would not turn on Micah and

the people he would protect with his dying breath—no matter
how they felt about him.

Would she?

"Your glamara allows you to twist what you project," he stated
flatly. "I will believe *nothing* you show me."

"Now, we both know that isn't true." Norok sounded like
a parent scolding a child. "Fayette showed you what the troll
king does to your traitorous wife, and you believed her, or the
battalion of trolls never would have gotten free. As you should.
I will send more visions. More trolls will gain their freedom.
They will kill her. I will kill Kaysar and Cookie. I will kill you,
too, if you get in my way."

"And if I unleash trolls upon *you*?" Would he? Should he? So
many others would die.

"You'd have to find the armies to issue a command." Now,
his former second sounded smug.

Norok had moved the legions? How? When?

"Once, you crowned yourself King of the Forgotten Court,"
the male continued. "You overpowered your opposition. Now,
I have outwitted you. A traitor counted among my enemies. If
you force my hand, I—the new king—will command Fayette
to send you more visions, unleashing more trolls. If you near
my camp again, you will be killed on sight." He raised an arm,
calling, "Because we were once friends, I'll give you a chance
to depart today. Fire on my count. Three."

Tension thickened the air.

"Two," Norok spit. "One."

At first, nothing happened. Then a single arrow sailed through
the air, landing near Micah's feet. Other arrows followed. He
didn't move, his shock making his feet heavy as boulders. Was
this truly happening?

One barb sliced into his shoulder. As the sting registered, he
flashed to the tunnels. Specifically, the largest room with the

biggest number of trolls. Empty. Another room. Empty. Another. Also empty.

Betrayed. Again.

Always?

Viori was a mess by the time Micah returned. Her nerves were frayed and her instincts on edge, keeping her jumpy. She was reminded of her early years, when she'd first wandered in the forest alone, her parents dead and her brother gone. If something had happened to her husband...

The second he materialized, she rushed over and hurled herself at him. "What happened? Where did you go?" She didn't catch sight of the arrow in his shoulder until it was too late—until she beat at those shoulders to protest his earlier disappearance. "How dare you leave me—" She gasped. "How dare you get injured!" A far worse crime! She yanked the missile free.

Blood trickled from the wound but swiftly stopped as his flesh wove back together, leaving a small, puckered circle. He said nothing, merely stared at her with bleak amber eyes.

Had something worse happened?

"Micah?" Viori threw herself into his arms once again. "Talk to me. Please." For endless hours, she'd filled the time worrying and fretting and pacing. Did he regret his decision to be with her? Had he learned the truth about her connection to Kaysar and now wished to sever his tie to her? "What happened? What are you thinking? Who hurt you? Talk to me. Please!"

Moving as fast as lightning, he locked his arms around her, holding her tight. Incredibly tight. Uncomfortably tight. Seconds passed in silence, his breaths coming hard and heavy. She didn't dare complain.

"Micah?" she repeated, squirming a little. The moment he eased up, she lifted her head and cupped his cheeks. Her chest clenched as she surveyed his wrecked expression. "Tell me what's wrong, baby."

"I need to hold you." He shuddered before he bent his head, pressing his brow to hers. "You were right. The man who betrays his wife will betray his king. Norok unleashed the trolls, hoping to kill us both. He schemes to punish Kaysar and Cookie for the death of his son. He blames me, too."

She hugged him close. "Oh, Micah. I'm so sorry." Another disloyalty. How deeply this one must cut. For once, she would have loved being wrong. "More than sorry."

As she held him, a terrible thought drifted through her mind. *He will never forgive me.*

Her stomach twisted into knots. She needed to confess her secret. But how could she bombard him with such an unexpected truth at a terrible moment like this? On the other hand, how could she not? To risk him finding out another way...

No. Either she piled on the bad news, or she extended the length of his ignorance after he'd been nothing but good to her. The first was cruel, the second so much crueler. To them both!

Until he knew the truth, they had no real foundation. Without a solid foundation, they would eventually lose everything they built.

He shuddered against her, as if the dam holding back his pain had cracked, and all she wanted to do was soothe him.

Petting him, she said, "There, there, baby. We won't let Norok keep your army or our home. We'll get them back. We have strong allies now and—"

"No." He stiffened against her. "We have accepted the ceasefire with Kaysar, but we won't be associating with him. We won't ask him for help or offer to help him. Not now, not ever. Your debt is paid in full. We need never deal with him again."

"Oh." To never again speak with Kaysar. Especially now that she'd taken such large strides to earn his forgiveness. To never apologize or hug him. Something she'd yearned to do most of her life, unable to confront the reality of his pain. If she had only *listened* to him. Do not sing to Momma and Papa. What was so difficult about that? Now, to let him go forever…

With a hand on her nape and her waist, Micah captured her gaze. "Tell me you agree."

She gulped, licked her lips. The secret *must* be shared. Here. Now. Build the foundation before it was too late. If it wasn't too late already. No more teetering on sand, always expecting to fall. Better to stand on solid rock. She'd tasted of joy and security, and she only wanted more. There was a chance she would lose everything being honest, but there was a guarantee she'd lose everything remaining deceitful.

"Micah, there's something I must tell you," she croaked. Maybe, somehow, he would understand.

"Cough, cough, cough." Cookie's voice rang out.

Gasping, Viori spun. Micah stiffened.

"What do you want?" he demanded, hauling her behind his back.

She didn't stay there, but plastered herself to his side.

"I hate to interrupt such a meaningful moment or whatever, but my oracle tells me this is the perfect time to test a crazy theory I've developed based upon our last conversation." The queen stood with her arms behind her back. She wore a gown of black silk, the material clinging to an hourglass figure. "Are you ready? Because I don't know if I am."

"What are you even talking about?" Viori groused. The other woman's "perfect time" just happened to be her worst time.

"I'm here because I'm curious about your reaction to this." Cookie swung her arms forward, revealing the cutest doll in all the world.

Viori lost her breath. With tears brimming, she cried, "Drendall!"

The doll blinked. A second later, the softest, sweetest voice cried back, "Momma!"

Cookie yelped as if she'd been stabbed, dropping the wiggling doll and screaming, "Spawn of Chucky!"

On the ground, Drendall clambered to her feet, then ran to Viori, who captured the darling with open arms. "I found you, I found you, I found you!"

"Where have you been, my beauty?" she rasped, too afraid to glance at Micah. He'd stiffened further. "I missed you terribly. For decades, I searched high and low."

"I slept like you, Momma, but I was also awake," Drendall said, nuzzling her cheek. "A little girl found me and took me to the castle being built. I got stuck in the treasure room."

"You're really her," Cookie said, shell-shocked. "You're Viori."

Viori stood with Drendall cradled against her chest. "Yes." Finally, she allowed her gaze to dart to Micah. He appeared confused—and full of dread. "I am." For better or worse.

"Kaysar has searched for you for so long. I must tell him you're here. You know that, yes?"

"I need a bit more time," she pleaded, her heart thudding.

"I'm sorry, but that's out of the question. For me, he comes first, always." The doorway between locations was already closing around the queen. Within seconds, Viori and Micah were left alone. Well, as alone as you could be with a living doll in your midst, brought back to life—empowered—at the mere sound of her creator's voice. Would Kaysar come and change everything?

"Viori," Micah stated. She swung around to face him fully, and his narrowed gaze fell to Drendall, who fiddled with the lapels of Viori's robe. "Explain."

"I... I have to tell you something," she said. "What I tried to tell you before. The secret I've been keeping. It's more of a fact, really. I'm, um, more than childhood friends with Kaysar."

A blank film fell over his features. "Go on." Flat tone. Scarily flat.

Can't stop now. "I am his...sister. He is my brother. I killed our parents. They were sick, and I sang... I gave birth to my first creation, trying to help them heal, but it...it murdered them. An accident, but also not an accident. How could it be? I think Fifibelle killed them to please me. Because deep in my heart, I desired their deaths. Their peace. I haven't spoken to Kaysar since. Not for centuries. We were separated soon afterward and..."

Her husband gave no reaction. None. Zilch. Zero.

She pushed through her trepidation, telling him, "I didn't know you warred with him when I first came to your camp. I'd just awoken from a seeming eternity of sleep, after spending years in the mortal world. I was hungry and searching for food. Micah, are you hearing what I'm saying?"

"You are Kaysar's sister." Same flat tone. At his sides, his fingers lightly flexed. "You are his family."

"Yes. No. Maybe? But either way, you are my family, too. Aren't you?" *Please.* "Micah," she said, cradling Drendall with one arm and reaching for him with the other. When he stepped out of range, she let her hand flop to her side. "I'm sorry. I should have told you sooner. Maybe? What would you have done if the situation were reversed? Everything seemed wrong and right at the same time. You were my enemy, but I felt connected to you in a way I'd never felt with another. I wanted to be with you. Still do. I long for the future you promised me. Everything you—"

A bellow of fury cut through the air, seeming to come from everywhere at once. Kaysar had learned of her existence, and he was indeed coming for her.

"Micah?" she pleaded. "Do you still seek a future with *me*?"

CHAPTER TWENTY-FIVE

And the blows keep coming.

Micah stood rooted in place, silent. A warm breeze blew past. Its citrusy, flowery scent brought no comfort, only agitation. In his veins, blood froze. In his lungs, air crystallized. The betrayal he'd feared had already come to pass. Weeks ago, in fact. He just hadn't known it.

His wife had betrayed him from the beginning. Fresh start? No, they'd enjoyed no such thing. Not when she'd harbored such a costly secret. She'd tried to warn him at least.

Only a few feet away, she peered at him with vulnerable, questioning eyes.

Vulnerable? Lie!

Her lips parted, as if too many words crowded her tongue. She held a small toy like a mother with her firstborn child. Maybe she was. The thing had spoken to her. Was *still* speaking while examining him with porcelain irises.

"Who is he, Momma?"

"He's…Daddy." Viori chewed on her bottom lip. "Isn't he?"

Not knowing what to say, he remained silent. Viori hoped to smooth over the bumps created by her duplicity and continue as if nothing had changed. But *everything* had changed. How was he supposed to reconcile this new revelation with Fayette's vision?

His wife, holding hands with Kaysar, killing soldiers who'd once served under Micah's command. Micah, dead as his wife's children ravaged the campground. A real possibility now. Viori and Kaysar were siblings. Of course she would work with him.

Puzzle pieces of information locked together, forming a complete picture for Micah. More calculated than he'd realized. The timing of her arrival. Her reaction to seeing Kaysar. Her determination and ferocity to protect him from war.

Her willingness to wed Micah—and stay with him.

He understood the reason for keeping quiet about her familial connection. He did. It had been a smart move on her part. Very smart. Every foolish move had been made by Micah himself.

"He's big," Drendall remarked, pulling him from his thoughts.

"Yes, he is," Viori rasped. "But he's wonderful, too."

Wonderful. His mouth turned down. Did this female genuinely desire him? Maybe. Did she wish to be his forever? Again, maybe. But it didn't matter anymore. They had no future. How could they? The first time Micah and Kaysar disagreed—and they would—Viori would side with her brother, her real family, as she'd done from the beginning. Micah would never be the recipient of her loyalty. Never be her first choice. The scale would only ever skew in his disfavor. He would give, and she would take. He would always wonder, *Does she stay with me to stop me from turning on her sibling?* Every day he would expect the next betrayal.

Can't live that way. Yearning for a future that Fate seemed eager to deny him. Wanting what he couldn't have—what he gave. Loyalty. He was desperate for it, willing to compromise everything he held dear. So…no. No, he couldn't be with Viori and survive. Even now, hope, joy and peace were dying inside him.

Better to be on his own. Erwen had lived alone most of his

life. Had even warned him. No kingdom. No people or friends. No risk of betrayal. The downfall of every chimera.

No more leering looks. No more incomparable pleasures. No more cuddling throughout the night.

Pain seared him, and he nearly doubled over. Too bad the elderseed couldn't heal a heart destroyed.

Revealing nothing, he set his sights on escape. This wasn't a time to present a verdict about next steps. No, this was a time for battle preparation. Any moment, Kaysar would arrive; the king wouldn't welcome his brother-in-law with open arms but closed fists. Micah had no doubts of it. That enraged bellow…

"Micah?" Viori asked, a tremor in her voice. She petted the squirming doll's hair. "Talk to me. Please. Tell me you understand why I did what I did. Let's settle this before Kaysar's arrival."

"There's nothing to settle," he replied, shockingly calm. Eerily so. "I do understand."

Tides of relief and hope seemed to pour over her. She clutched the doll tighter, tears welling in her eyes. "You do? Truly?"

"I do. But my understanding only hurts your cause," he explained softly, and her expression fell. "Kaysar is your brother. He will always come first for you, as you've proved time and time again, leaving your husband to make do with leftover scraps." *Careful.* "Tell me honestly, Viori. Would you be willing to accept so little from me, if I constantly chose someone else over you?"

She gulped. "A-are you asking me to choose between you and Kaysar?"

He canted his head. "If I am? Would you do it?" *Stop! Do not push this.* But…he must. A foolish part of him still wanted to be with her, and there was no other way.

"Micah," she croaked.

An electric charge sliced through the atmosphere. A patch of air parted down the middle, the sides rolling in opposite directions, propelled by the leafy vines now growing between them.

A crack formed first, and Cookie appeared in the newly opened space, saving him from issuing a response. The crack spread.

"Incoming," the queen said, exuding all kinds of worry as she rushed into the oasis.

Micah braced. Too late to go. The next thing he knew, a scowling Kaysar stalked through the doorway. The oracle, Amber, as well as Pearl Jean and King Jareth, followed on his heels. A quick scan revealed the newcomers sported multiple weapons. The entire group appeared unaware or uncaring of Micah's presence, the bulk of their attention centered on Viori.

Her breathing shallowed, her wide eyes reminding him of two open wounds as she peered at her brother. Pupils blown. A deeper well of tears. Chin quivering, she placed the doll—Drendall—on her feet.

"Chucky!" Cookie shouted, jumping when the porcelain girl clung to Viori's calf.

Kaysar halted mere inches from Micah's wife. The king wore a black tunic and leathers, paired with his signature metal claws as the rest of the crowd formed a half circle behind him. Everyone inspected Viori from head to toe, but no one did so more intently than the king.

Brother and sister looked nothing alike. The big dark brute and the tiny flame. They stared at each other for several long minutes, steeped in terse silence. But no words were needed. In that moment, Micah glimpsed the inevitable. The truth of his suspicions. Hope radiated from Viori while Kaysar projected a combination of agony and affection. The array of emotions birthed burgeoning need, filling the space between siblings.

"My little love." With an agonized groan, Kaysar threw his arms around the girl, yanking her into the hard line of his body.

A sob left her. She sagged against him, returning his embrace and clutching him close.

The pain in Micah's chest magnified. No, this female would never put her husband first.

If he'd hated Kaysar before, he truly despised the male now. The king often killed without mercy, living by no rules but his, yet he was allowed to build a loving family? Him, but not Micah the chimera?

"You are all right, sister?" Kaysar demanded, pulling back far enough to search her face.

Red-rimmed eyes glittered with more tears. "I am."

Pearl Jean clutched the necklace strung around her throat. "I feel a case of vapors coming on. Where's my fainting couch? I want my fainting couch!"

"Do I really need to be here for this?" Jareth scratched his chin. His pale hair stuck out in spikes, and lines of fatigue rimmed his eyes. He was shirtless and heavily tattooed. Unbuttoned leathers sagged on a lean waist. No shoes adorned his feet. "I do have a kingdom to run, you know."

The oracle held up a picnic basket. "Should I set up refreshments now or after the fight?"

Kaysar kept his focus on Viori. "You spoke to me. You spoke!" He hugged her again, laughing and crying simultaneously, so joyous Micah almost looked away. He did take another step back, needing more distance between the pair. But Kaysar's triumph didn't last long.

The king peered at Viori with narrowing eyelids, fury overtaking his features once more. "What happened when I left you in the forest? Tell me everything. If anyone harmed you, I will have their names. And their heads! I'll place their organs at your feet. Whoever they are, they'll know suffering in its purest form, I swear it!"

"You don't hate me?" she asked softly. "I destroyed your life. I killed Momma and—"

"I could never hate you, love." A myriad of emotions crossed his face. Exasperation. Fondness. Anguish. He yanked her closer, enfolding her inside his strong arms. "You aren't the only one to kill while learning to use a powerful glamara."

An example of unconditional love. The first Micah had ever beheld in person. Not something he'd ever experienced on his own.

Suddenly, he couldn't hate Kaysar quite so much. Even as envy joined his deluge of emotions, choking him. He shouldn't be here for this. This was a moment between brother and sister.

"You suffered because of me," Viori said, sniffling. "I heard the rumors. You were imprisoned for a year and tortured daily. Because of me," she repeated, her chin trembling.

"No, love." Kaysar gently collected one of her tears with the tip of a claw. "I suffered because bad fae exist in this realm. Bad fae do bad things. It had nothing to do with you. Now. In a few minutes, I wish to hear what happened to you during our centuries apart. And I *will* have those names straightaway. First I must deal with another emergency."

He craned his head toward Micah, his eyelids slitting once again. "You." Kaysar flittered directly in front of him. "You wed my sister without my permission, thinking to use her against me."

"No! He didn't know who I was," Viori said, materializing beside Micah. She clasped his hand. Though part of him longed to cling, he did not clasp hers in return. "He found out when you did."

"And that makes it okay? No." Kaysar circled Micah. "I heard what you did to your wife. Collared her. Chased her. Donned her in rags and left her homeless."

"Don't forget that he killed her child-creations, too," a dark beauty spoke up. Amber the oracle. "Remember? I told you all about her the other day. How she sings monsters to life and considers the results her babies. What?" she asked when Cookie, Jareth and Pearl Jean glowered at her. "Better he gets everything out of his system. Otherwise, he'll remember later, and we'll have to deal with—"

"How dare you!" Kaysar boomed.

"That," Amber finished lamely.

"You murdered my nieces and nephews, breaking our former truce," the king continued, rage brewing in his voice. "Therefore, the new truce cannot stand. We fight to the death *now*."

Micah expected Kaysar's punch. He didn't block, but let it happen, taking a steel-hard fist to the stomach. Viori screeched protests as he flew into the water. Kaysar showed up in the pond without delay, throwing another punch. This time, Micah's wife didn't stand within range; he blocked, catching the fist, and squeezed.

As multiple bones broke beneath his grip, he smiled coldly at the opponent who was, technically, his brother-in-law. "To the death? Very well."

Viori readied to flitter after the men, but Cookie caught her arm, staying her.

"Don't," the queen said, unconcerned as Kaysar and Micah continued throwing vicious punches, slashing at each other. As the water turned red with blood and the two combatants fought their way to shore. As the savagery of their strikes increased. "Let them work it out among themselves."

"But they're fighting over me."

Cookie shook her head. "Wrong. You're the excuse. What you're seeing is the culmination of a yearlong beef."

Viori tried to break from the other woman's grasp, but the queen held fast. "They'll kill each other." They'd just threatened to do so, and neither male was the type to go back on his word.

Again, Cookie shook her head. "Amber assures me—"

"Ugh! Find a new phrase already," Pearl Jean interjected. "I'm tired of hearing those three words. Seriously, you say them more than you've ever said *I love you* to the hubs. Or me!"

"Anyway," Cookie continued with a roll of her eyes. "Neither dumbo will bestow a fatal blow. Otherwise, I would've buried Micah in vines long ago. After I popped his head off his body, of course."

Fury burned through Viori in an instant. She drew her hands into fists, getting free no longer a problem. No threats against her husband would be tolerated. Not even by her sister-in-law. "Do *you* want to die?"

"Please. We're family," Cookie said with an easy tone. "We don't have to like each other, but we don't get to kill each other, no matter the provocation. It sucks, but what can you do? Rules are rules." She motioned to the beautiful black woman holding the picnic basket. "Viori, meet Amber the oracle. Pearl Jean the royal pain and King Jareth Frostline of the Winter Court. The nuisance I can't shake."

"So lovely to meet you in person instead of in my head. Sit, sit." Amber placed the basket on a patch of grass and withdrew a satchel filled with bread and cheeses. "The battle should endure the rest of the day, overnight and into the morning. By the way, Viori. You've been hidden from my inner sight for so long. Care to share why?" A second later, she laughed with delight. "Never mind. I'm brilliant, and I've already deduced the answer. With your children, you were everywhere at once. Both in the fae realm, and the mortal one."

"Let's get comfortable." Cookie extended her arms toward a clearing. Five vines sprang from the earth in quick succession. Other vines branched from those, each grouping creating a chair. Thrones, really. Chin up, the queen eased into hers—the biggest of the bunch. "So. You traveled to my world?"

"A handful of times, yes," Viori admitted.

"What'd you think?"

Pearl Jean and King Jareth strode over and plopped beside Queen Cookie. Even Amber claimed a seat while holding a loaf of bread—a loaf Viori snatched straight from her hands.

"A horrid place with predators on every corner," she said, snatching the satchel and the rest of the food as well. Micah might be hungry after the fight.

As the group peered at her, she curbed the urge to hiss. Her attention returned to the fighters. Both males were graceful, masterful and brutal beyond imagining, hurling insults along with their punches.

When she grew tired of standing, she sank onto the free chair and tucked the food into her side. Let someone try to take something. They'd see what happened.

Drendall climbed into her lap, holding a string of diamonds that Pearl Jean was no longer wearing. "Look what I found for us, Momma."

"Chucky!" Cookie burst out, flattening a hand over her heart.

"That's mine, you little—" Pearl Jean pursed her lips before mumbling, "My children will have better manners. That's all I'm saying."

For some reason, King Jareth recoiled. "Your children?"

"Don't worry. It's not like you'll be involved when the time comes."

He scowled at her.

Viori did the same. "Let's talk about this crush you have on Micah."

"Oh. That. There's no need. I'm over it. I'm currently using a temporary meat stick to meet my needs." The hag wagged her sculpted brows. "I'm using him often."

"Meat stick?" Jareth bellowed. He was a handsome man. Tall and muscular, with thick blond hair and dark blue eyes.

"Don't remind me." Cookie scowled. "The flashbacks and soundtracks make me nauseous."

He pointed at her. "Cease your lying. You love it. Consider it inspiration."

This foursome was *beyond* bizarre.

"Mom-ma! Did you even notice my necklace?" Drendall whined.

"I did." Viori kissed her cheek and secured the necklace around her throat. "Wonderful job, darling." With a shake of her head, she refused the oracle's offer of a misshapen cookie withdrawn from a pocket. Her stomach was in knots. "May I ask you a question?"

"You wonder if Micah will forgive you for misleading him about your connection to Kaysar." Amber nibbled on the cookie. "The answer is, I'm not sure. I've seen differing paths, each leading to an altered future. One where you are together. Another where you are apart. Others where either of you is dead. Each outcome depends on the decisions you make in the coming days."

Viori swallowed a whimper. Anything could happen. The good, the bad and the ugly. "With responses like that," she grumbled, "I'm not sure how wars are won and lost with the word of an oracle."

"Exactly what I say," Cookie retorted.

"Son of a troll," Kaysar shouted, in the water once again. The battle raged on.

Amber laughed as if her king was an utter delight and passed around cups of tea she produced from a second satchel Viori had missed. "Do you love Micah?"

Love. Did she? She knew she felt safe with him. Knew she adored the way he sometimes looked at her, as if she were his reason for being. Knew she wanted him more than she'd ever wanted another. Knew he was a good man. Special. Rare. Knew she yearned for what he'd offered. Knew she craved his intensity and enjoyed the care he took with her. Admired his strength. His stubbornness. When he set out to acquire something, he refused to give up.

"I think I might," she whispered. "I also think he...won't forgive me." He'd come close to asking her to choose. He still might. And what would she tell him then, hmm?

He took a nasty blow to the groin, but he didn't slow. No, he broke Kaysar's jaw with a single strike. A tooth went flying, and Viori winced. There'd been a whole lot of rage behind that particular strike.

No, he might not forgive her in the slightest.

Her shoulders rolled in. Until they didn't. What was she doing? Fearing the worst? She didn't have to accept unforgiveness. She could fight to win him back. And she would! She was Queen Viori of the Forgotten Court, Mother of *Belua*. The one Micah had chosen for himself. She could do anything. Couldn't she?

Pearl Jean dug a small bottle of whiskey from her pocket and poured half the contents into her tea. She offered the bottle to Cookie, only to draw back before the other woman had a chance to respond. "No. Not you. But would anyone else enjoy a top-off?" She drained her glass without awaiting a response. Rather than pour herself more tea, she poured herself more whiskey, then drained that, too.

"Why not, Queen Cookie?" Viori asked, declining the offer with a shake of her head.

"She's pregnant with twins," Amber announced, buttering a toast point. Where had *that* come from? "That's the real reason she and Kaysar sought to solidify a truce with Micah. They also plan to find and slaughter every troll in existence before the babies are born, so that the species will never be used as a threat again. What?" she demanded as her friends gaped at her once again. "In the future, Viori already knows this information. So why not tell her here and now?"

"Because she didn't know until you told her?" Pearl Jean said, clearly exasperated.

Kaysar, a father. Viori, an aunt. Her heart raced. The fight tolled on.

I want a family with Micah, and I will have one!

No, she would not be giving him up.

CHAPTER TWENTY-SIX

Afternoon sunlight glared at Micah as he swung. Muscles quivered from exertion. Sweat soaked his chest and back. He'd burned through any lingering elderseed long ago, ensuring he healed at a slower clip. But then, Kaysar had begun to heal at a slower clip, too, his energy depleting.

The male had removed his shirt. Or rather, Micah had shredded the material. No scars marred his skin. Meaning, the other king was not a chimera. Meaning, a year ago, when Kaysar first returned to the Dusklands with Cookie, Micah had spared him for nothing, as suspected.

"What are your intentions toward my sister?" Kaysar demanded between labored breaths. Punch.

Duck. "You'll know after I do." Punch.

"How can you not know?" his opponent demanded. "What are you hiding?"

"Yes, let me divulge my secrets to you." They circled each other. "The king I've envisioned killing for a year."

Swipe. "If you do not value your prize, you do not get to keep it."

Slash. "Save your sage wisdom for someone else. Your words matter as much as your opinion."

The spectators perched in their vine chairs. Most of them had slept through the night, growing bored with the battle. Not Viori. She'd sat in place, stiff as a board, utterly still with the doll napping in her lap. Her gaze drank in Micah's every action. Micah's, not her brother's. Her ears had twitched at every word he'd uttered. Not that anything more than insults and threats of dismemberment had been said. He thought she might have flinched at the announcement of his lack of intentions, and his chest clenched. What did any of it mean?

Don't think, don't feel. Fight.

He and Kaysar swung at each other with more and more determination, coming out of their stupors and going for vulnerable spots. Eyes, nose, throat, vital organs and groin. Until an image shot through his head, stopping him cold.

Micah clutched at his temples. He shut his eyes, but he couldn't block the sight consuming his mind. Trolls, invading the oasis from every direction, surrounding the area. Too many to count, all focused on Viori. Though he fought with all his might, he couldn't get to her in time and—

Air exploded from his lungs as Kaysar's fist connected with his gut. "What are you doing?" the king hissed. "Battle me."

Fear overcame Micah for one, suspended moment. Long enough to change the entire course of his life.

The oracle cried, "Trolls!"

Each of the spectators jumped to their feet, awake and alert. The battle ended, both Kaysar and Micah rushing to their women as Pearl Jean and Jareth drew together. Viori set the doll on her feet and hastened over, meeting him halfway.

Fatigue instantly forgotten, he palmed two daggers; the fact that his wife had aimed for him rather than her brother left him reeling. What's more, her sibling had chosen Cookie and Amber, as if trusting Micah to care for Viori.

"To the palace," Kaysar shouted. "It's the safest place to be right now."

Micah flung his arm around Viori and flittered—nowhere. He frowned and glanced at his wrist cuff. The *amplio* stone was gone. Courtesy of Elena?

Bewildered cries rang out. "I can't flitter!"

"Why can't I flitter?"

"Something's wrong."

"At some point during the sparing match, Norok must have dumped *tollo* dirt in the tunnels beneath us," he grated. "Without an *amplio* stone, we'll be unable to flitter anywhere until we're out of range."

"How much time do we have?" Kaysar demanded of Amber.

The oracle closed her eyes, looking inward, and breathed deep. "Minutes. Maybe seconds. They're closing in fast. If Cookie opens a door, she won't be able to close it in time. Trolls will follow us through."

"Chantel goes alone, and we guard the doorway until it closes," Kaysar shouted. "Go now, love. Don't argue."

Chantel. A name only the male used for his queen.

"Screw that. I'll build us a wall of protection," Cookie said, spreading her arms. The ground shook, slithering vines ripping through the soil roughly fifty feet away, shooting up and out. New vines branched off the old ones, quickly establishing a border around the trees.

Nowhere out but underground now. But they couldn't risk delving underground. No telling how many traps Norok had prepared.

"Jareth, you know what to do," Cookie called.

"On it." The Winterlander angled his hands toward the developing vines. Ice sprayed from his fingertips, glazing the foliage and filling in any cracks.

"Chantel, remember your promise to me." Kaysar snapped the words. The harshest tone he'd ever used with the female.

"Protect the babies, no matter what. Take yourself home. Please, love."

Babies? The queen was pregnant? Micah reeled harder.

"I stay and fight," she insisted. "I remember my promise to protect you as much as the twins. I won't go one-on-one with a troll unless necessary. So, I'll stay and vine myself, watching the battle through the foliage in case I'm needed. Pearl Jean's healing abilities might be needed. Amber's foresight might be needed, too. They stay. Viori gets a one-way ticket home, though."

"I *knew* leaving the palace was a mistake," Pearl Jean lamented.

Viori pressed closer to Micah. "I stay. I can help."

Kaysar huffed an irritated breath. "Very well," he told his wife. "Vine the other females. Especially my sister. Viori, dear, be sure to touch nothing and all will be well." His shoulders rolled in. "This time, I swear it."

Micah had tangled with Cookie's poisonvines before. They paralyzed upon contact.

"You might need me on the battlefield—" Viori went quiet as vines grew around her feet, despite her protest, forcing Micah to sever contact with her. Those vines spread fast, soon to create a cocoon that would separate her from the rest of the world.

"I'll let nothing happen to you," Micah vowed as the doll dived into her arms. His gaze fastened on hers until the last second, when foliage blocked those luminous eyes filled with concern.

"Let nothing happen to *you*," she countered from within.

A cocoon grew around the oracle and Pearl Jean as well, leaving only the three kings.

As the wall of bark and ice completed, at least fifty trolls scrambled over the top, entering the clearing—now the arena.

"Oh! I should probably warn everyone," Amber exclaimed from her cocoon. "When Viori starts singing, cover your ears. Nothing has ever been more important in your life."

"Do not sing," Micah commanded his wife. Put herself into

a prolonged sleep? Risk a return to the mortal world? No! Even if they were apart, he wanted her protected.

As Micah, Kaysar and Jareth launched into battle, Kaysar erupted into a song of his own. His voice...the pain of it...the horrific tenor. Micah ignored the excruciating agony, doing his best to resist the madness clawing through his mind. Hot blood poured from his ears and nose. What he wouldn't give for *surdi* root. Anything to deaden the sound. But the trolls bled, too, some collapsing and thrashing, out of commission. Others fought on.

As if they sensed Viori alone, the entire enemy horde converged on her cocoon. Micah slashed, clawed, punched and kicked. A troll with massive horns slammed into him, shoving him to the ground, its sharp teeth aimed at his throat. But ice spread over the creature's face, thanks to Jareth, allowing Micah to roll free and disembowel the fiend.

The winter king hacked so many trolls with his shards of ice, a new wall formed, one made of body parts. Kaysar used metal claws to turn his opponents into confetti. Black, tarry blood sprayed in continuous arcs, a foul stench coating the air.

As soon as enemy numbers dwindled, the battle nearly won, other brutes scaled the original wall. They, too, headed for Viori.

Rage boiled in Micah's veins, much of it self-directed. *My fault.* He should've killed the beings when he'd had the chance. They weren't a backup plan; they were a fool's mistake.

Then more trolls arrived and attacked. He killed with savage abandon, taking no prisoners. Death-spray coated his hands, leaving blisters. Horns and talons grazed him. Fangs ripped through various muscles. Did he stop? Never.

Kaysar's song tolled on. Still trolls poured in. The largest contingent yet. With the biggest brutes. Veins bulged from corded muscle. Fangs wider than some tusks. Spikes protruded from each vertebra. Each warrior frothed aggression.

"Not sure how much longer I can go on," Jareth admitted

between panting breaths. Using a sword of ice, he decapitated two trolls at once.

"You'll do this as long as needed," Kaysar snapped, ripping out one troll's throat while stomping on the face of another.

Still more trolls arrived.

Never had Micah thought he would one day fight beside his greatest enemy. Or who he thought was his greatest enemy. Or that his greatest enemy would become his ally against his closest friend, his new greatest enemy.

His ears twitched, and he frowned. Was that…? His eyes narrowed. It was. Ignoring his orders, Viori sang inside her cocoon. Until the stems of her cocoon opened with a jolt, revealing a poisonvine beast with two arms and two legs—a soldier at attention behind his maker.

Roaring, the newborn *belua* launched into action, attacking with brutal force. Swipes of his powerful vines sent trolls flying over the ice wall. Other trolls were stunned upon contact before being torn into pieces.

Though the creature reduced the number of opponents, the battle raged on, trolls continually pouring in, each group more determined than the last. Wind picked up, gusting around Viori, lifting locks of her scarlet hair. The hem of her robe danced at her ankles, revealing a fearless Drendall sitting at her feet, weaving blades of grass together. Then, as fire crackled in her eyes, Viori altered the tone of her song.

The enemy army stopped in its tracks and dropped. They writhed, screamed and thrashed as— Micah's eyes widened. Their bones. Bones sliced through their flesh to reveal faces.

Belua. Made from bones.

His own bones began to vibrate, as if about to come to life. Remembering Amber's warning, he dropped his weapons and plugged his ears. To drown out the horror of his wife's voice, he hummed to himself.

Only when the last troll drew its final breath did she quiet.

As the last note faded, the bones toppled like their former owners, eyes closing for good.

Micah lowered his hands and took in the scene. Utter carnage littered the area. The bloodiest battlefield he'd ever beheld. Her power...he'd had no idea. She'd tried to warn him, but he hadn't believed. Unleash rage? Oh yes.

Kaysar pressed a hand to his chest, radiating pride. "My little love. I've never been so proud of you."

Blood poured over the grass, a great ebony river. No more trolls climbed the wall.

The cocoons around Cookie, Amber and Pearl Jean receded, revealing pale, worried fae who rushed to their males. Well, one pale, worried fae rushed. Pearl Jean finished off the last drops in her canteen before strolling to Jareth as if she hadn't a care.

Tremors rocked Viori. Chewing on her bottom lip, she peered at Micah. She looked ready to catapult to him, but was also unsure of her reception.

In the end, he couldn't stay away from her. They hadn't worked out their problems, but he allowed his long stride to eat up the distance, anyway. If he'd lost her today...

She stumbled toward him at last. The moment she entered his reach, he hauled her into his arms.

Though he was soaked in sweat and blood, she clung to him. "Are you hurt?" she asked, pulling back to study him. She cupped his cheek. "The smallest scratch, and I swear I'll sing the trolls back to life and kill them all again."

"I'll heal," he replied, gruffer than he'd intended. "Are *you* hurt?" Tremors shook her against him.

"Expended a bit of energy, is all. Are you hungry? I saved food for you." She pulled back enough to slide a satchel full of crumbled biscuits from her pocket.

He...did not know what to say. An emotion clogged his throat, but he wasn't sure which one. He didn't know anything anymore.

"Let's go home, love." Kaysar kissed Cookie's temple. "Open a doorway. Viori, you're coming with us, of course."

She met Micah's gaze, and he gave her a stiff nod.

"Go with them," he told her. She needed a chance to reconnect with her brother. That, he knew.

"You're coming with me, right?" she asked, pressing her nails against his collarbone, holding on to her prey.

He almost couldn't look at her. The weakening of her glamara had stripped her of defenses, leaving her vulnerable.

That vulnerability... It had always served as his ultimate weakness, hadn't it? For a moment, he almost believed they could forge a joyous future together. That he could trust her with his life. That the siblings wouldn't join forces and sing him to death on a battlefield, making him a fool for the final time. Yes, he almost believed it.

He said nothing as Cookie spread her arms, vines curling from her fingertips and converging. The leaves cut through the air, forcing two layers of atmosphere to part.

Pearl Jean and Amber hurried through, Jareth on their heels. Drendall skipped. Kaysar moved to stand between the two locations, half of him in the oasis, the other half in a sunlit courtyard teeming with colorful flowers. Having watched the queen create other doorways, Micah knew she must be the last to enter it. As soon as she did, it would close.

"Come, Viori," the king commanded with a royal wave of his fingers.

Her gaze probed Micah's, searching. "You're coming, too, right?"

"Go." He kissed her brow. "Be with your brother. You've dreamed of this moment for ages, have you not?" To reunite and discuss the dynamics of their renewed relationship without the interference of a former foe.

"Yes, but—"

"No buts. There are things I must figure out."

Her brow wrinkled. "Things? What things?"

He gave her a little push toward the doorway. "Go on now."

"Micah, what things?" she demanded, stumbling in a bid to return to him. "I'll stay with you. We can figure out the things together."

No, he must find this answer on his own. Whether to seek an eternity alone or forever with the wife who couldn't help but betray him over and over again. Whatever he decided…he must be ruthless. Execute his chosen future without remorse.

"Let him go, if that's what he wishes." Kaysar clasped her wrist, drawing her farther away. "I can always fetch him for you later."

"Micah," she cried, and he nearly stomped after her, dying a thousand deaths as her brother dragged her along.

Fight for what's right, no matter the cost, or you'll be forced to live with the wrong.

But which path was right? Which was wrong? He didn't know anymore.

She refused to give up, and it ripped his insides apart. "I declare this day a Feast of Remembering. I'm a queen, so I can do that. That means there are no obstacles between us."

"I'll be spending this feast alone." He forced himself to turn. To march away. She shouted his name, and he cringed. This was for the best.

Wasn't it? All he sought was a little time. A few days to think.

Dead bodies crunched beneath his boots as he approached the icy wall of vine. As he neared, leaves dried to ash and fell, piling on the ground or floating away in a cool, crisp breeze. He strode to the waterfall and dived into the cool liquid without pause, hoping to douse the flames of uncertainty blazing in his chest.

After washing up by rote, he swam in place. Tired muscles revived, but his thoughts roiled on. He concentrated on those involving Norok.

The troll attacks wouldn't stop until the male was dead.

Which meant Viori wouldn't be safe until Norok was dead—which meant Norok had to die. The best way to accomplish such a goal? Neutralize him the same way Micah once neutralized the troll hordes. Stride into camp, slaughter everyone in his path and force all others to bend to his will.

Elena and Fayette must be neutralized, too. So, they would partake in the same death as their king. On the offensive rather than the defensive, with a clear goal boiling in his heart, the Unwilling could not be stopped.

Once he'd unchained the people from the oracle's twisted vision of the future, he would hang up his crown, ending his service to the citizens of the Forgotten Court. They could swear fealty to Kaysar and Cookie or not. Crown a new king or not. Micah could start over. Build a home for himself. Or himself and his...family?

Everything circled back to her. The feral female with divided loyalties paired with the magnet for betrayal. A recipe for delights and disasters. And there would be other disasters. How could there not be?

Would he survive the next?

Did it matter? Could he enjoy anything without her?

Could he enjoy anything *at all*? He thought he might be broken now. Wrong.

No "thought" about it. He *was* broken, and there was no way to repair himself. And yet...a part of him still longed to be with her. The fool inside him, he supposed. A poor travesty of a man willing to endure the worst for a mere sip of the best.

The best. Two words, packed with countless memories. In the few weeks Micah had spent with Red, he'd experienced his lowest lows, yes, but also his highest highs. More joy than he'd ever thought possible. The way she looked at him. Teased and played with him. Clung to him. Sought him. Run to him. Shared herself with him.

He could have more of those highs. He had only to accept more lows—and his doom. But wasn't he doomed, anyway?

He slammed a fist into the water and droplets flung in every direction. This back and forth was driving him insane.

To empty his head, he swam laps. A failed endeavor. His mind veered on the most dangerous road yet. Today's Feast of Remembering, enacted by his queen.

If he removed the obstacles and re-asked each of his questions, his answers would change. And there was no denying it. Her. He wanted her more than he'd ever wanted anything. He might not have the ability to trust her or anyone anymore, but they could make *something* work. If she would accept him.

His blood iced. Would she push him away now? How much had he hurt her, abandoning her after she'd pursued him? Him, not her brother.

Realization stabbed him, bleeding hope. She'd raced to Micah after the battle, yet he'd turned her away. Turned away the girl who'd spent centuries alone.

Desperation struck. He needed to find her. He needed to find her *now*. Leaving things so open-ended had been his biggest mistake to date.

Flittering to the shore, he discovered a picnic basket. As before, necessities filled it, including an *amplio* stone and clean clothing. If the strange black pants with yellow stripes that fit his legs as if painted on could be considered clothing. Two stretchy bands attached to the waist, stretching over his torso vertically and hooking around his shoulders.

A note from Cookie accompanied the garment.

Enjoy the wildfires you're sure to spark in your wife's loins...

Whatever that meant. He dressed at record speed and flittered to the palace, eager to find Viori.

CHAPTER TWENTY-SEVEN

He left me.

Viori barely listened as Kaysar and Cookie led her through a massive stone palace with erotic statues, elaborate chandeliers, gold furnishings and stained-glass windows—everything fit for royals. Objects she'd never imagined seeing up close and personal. But here she was. *A queen without her king, mingling with another king and queen.*

The happy couple chattered about everything and nothing. Drendall ran here and there, giggling. Meanwhile, Viori wanted Micah. He'd made her count on him. Had gotten her used to spending her days and nights with him. To sleeping in the comfort of his arms. To thrilling over his every touch. Being the recipient of his intensity and the object of his desire. Now he might not want to be with her? He needed to do *things*?

Kaysar and Cookie showed Viori to a spacious, private suite with decorations fit for a young, spoiled princess.

"I kept this room for you," Kaysar told her proudly. "Just in case."

She scanned her surroundings. A ruffled pink comforter draped a canopied bed. Gilt-framed portraits of dresses hung on the walls. An assortment of porcelain dolls perched upon a mahogany dresser.

Kaysar moved in front of her. He cupped her cheeks gently, those metal claws covered in dried blood and other things as he forced her gaze to meet his. Tears welled. He looked so much like Papa, before the plague had come. Dark and strong and perfect. Capable.

"I want to know you again, sister," he told her, using the softest tone. "I want to learn what happened to you, all those centuries ago. Where you've been, what you've done. But not today. Today, you require rest. And what you require, I shall provide." Gently, he swiped his thumbs under her eyes, collecting any escaped tears. "Do not cry. I don't think I can bear it."

"Rest. Yes," she croaked. "I'll rest." She eased from him as a sob bubbled up inside her. Not wanting anyone to see her like this, she pushed the couple out of the room and shut the door in their confused faces, sealing herself inside. Alone, but for her guilt. The way she longed to be.

She spun and pressed against the door, flattening her hands on her stomach to ward off the ache. Before Micah had left her to do those "things," he'd looked so sad. Utterly destroyed. She'd yearned to have him in her arms. But he'd refused. He needed time to decide his—their—future, she supposed. Time she owed to him.

In the beginning, he'd given her everything she needed. In the end, he'd given her a choice. It was only fair that she do the same for him, no matter how much she frothed to fight *for* him.

More tears escaped, falling without her brother's interference. *Come back to me, husband. Please.*

She hurried through a shower and dressed in a new robe. A lovely pink silk garment she found hanging in the closet, alongside a note she couldn't read. Then she paced, her mind whirling. Give him time? Yes. That was decided. But he shouldn't make his ultimate decision about their relationship until she'd made her grand gesture. And there was only one "grand" thing she could do. Butcher the trolls. Then, Norok couldn't use them against Micah.

"There are some obstacles I cannot shake, wife, but I yearn for you, anyway."

Gasping, Viori spun around. Micah! He stood near the window, framed in golden light. His dark head hung, his chin seeming to rest on his sternum. His narrowed gaze pinned her, wet hair dripping from his forehead. He was shirtless save for a strap of material over each shoulder, his scars on stark exhibition. Though his gashes had healed, bruises remained. Black pants with yellow stripes molded to his powerful thighs. He was barefoot.

Her heart skipped a beat. He'd come back for her. And he looked both weary and hungry. The hunger could be stoked.

Though she wished to jump into his arms, she resisted the urge. Better not to spook him. Striving for a teasing tone, she said, "My charm must be slipping. You came after me in less than twenty minutes, though I expected you in ten. But that's okay. I forgive myself."

The barest smile made a momentary appearance. "You are happy to see me?"

"Of course I am. You're my favorite person, Micah."

He blinked. Uh-oh. Had she admitted too much too fast?

She wrung her fingers. "How did you find me?"

"I knew there were only a few rooms Kaysar would put you."

All right, she could stand it no longer. "I'm so sorry I hurt you, Micah." The words burst from her. "So sorry I withheld my secrets from you. I want to be with you more than anything."

A muscle jumped beneath his eye. "I want to be with you as well, so we will do this. We'll stay married."

"But?" she rasped, wrapping her arms around her middle.

"But. My ability to trust is damaged. I'll give you everything I can. Except that."

Damaged. *I fractured him the way Laken fractured me.* No. No! Laken had pretended not to know her when she confronted him about his misdeeds. She would fight to the death to make things right with Micah. "I can prove myself to you. I will."

"Not after Norok and Elena, Diane and Fayette, and everyone before them. Not after...us." He compressed his lips into a grim line, then shook his head. "You must take what I can give you."

"No," she repeated, raising her chin. "I'm as unwilling as you are. I won't give up."

"Viori—"

"No. You came back to me. Now deal with the consequences." Heart thundering, she glided closer. He watched, and though he might not mean to be, he was rapt. Once she stood within range, she snaked her arms around him and rose to her tiptoes. Her gaze held his as she slowly leaned in...and claimed his lips with her own. A soft peck. Another. She licked the seam.

At first he offered no response. Then...

A ragged moan escaped him. He opened up and kissed her back, hard, tangling a hand in her hair and cupping her backside. His grip remained tight, as if he feared she might slip away.

Desire ruled her. The sumptuous scent of him. The sweetness of his taste. The rasp of his breaths. The warmth of his skin. The knowledge that he couldn't walk away. He might not trust her—yet—but he craved a future with her. That was something.

She could work with something.

Viori clung to him, returning his kiss with wild abandon. Waves of love flooded her, one crash after another. Filling her. Drowning her.

Reviving her.

Another moan escaped him, and he lifted his head. He stared, panting, his lids hooded. "What are you doing to me?"

"Showing you how much you mean to me." She stared up at him, letting her emotions glimmer in her eyes. "You are everything to me, Micah. Let me prove it."

He jerked, as if she'd shocked him. In his irises she thought she detected a flame of hope sparking to life, and she thrilled.

"Do not say things like that," he growled. Bunching a section of her robe in his fist, he edged her to the wall.

Stone behind her, aggressive male before her. He kicked her legs apart.

"You're right." For balance, she gripped his shoulders. "I should have admitted more. I covet your years and your months and your weeks and your days, and each moment in between. I won't be satisfied until I have your mind and your body, your thoughts *and* your trust. I covet everything. Because that's what I'm giving you."

His breath hitched. "Stop it, Red. You'll change your mind about me at some point, just like everyone else. You won't be able to help yourself. I won't be able to handle the fallout."

In that moment, her heart broke for him. For the rejections he'd faced time and time again. But reveal her inner turmoil? No. With a soft smile, she asked, "Do you know me at all, baby? There's no one more stubborn."

The flames of hope brightened, but he said, "Let's stick to pleasure right now." He dragged his knuckles between the lapels of her robe, parting the material. Slowly, he bared her body to his view. Her breasts, her belly, the apex of her thighs. He leaned back the slightest bit. Enough to run his gaze over her before meeting her eyes. The flames *spread.* "Lots and lots of pleasure. I swear there's nothing more perfect than you."

A flush tracked his gaze, burning her inside and out. The way he looked at her...with a hunger like no other. The power went straight to her head. Her nipples tightened, and the ache between her legs intensified. Between them, the air thickened.

"I disagree," she purred, arching against him. She traced a fingertip along several of his scars. "I believe you are equally perfect. One of the reasons I fell so deeply in love with you."

His eyes widened. His pupils flared. "Don't say—"

"I love you." Holding his gaze, she slid the suspenders from his shoulders and gripped the waist of his pants. With a simple tug, the material split down the sides, leaving him magnificently naked.

He hissed when she stroked him. "You…you love me?"

"I do." She smiled up at him, letting her adoration for him shine in her irises. "Every magnificent inch of you." Slowly, she sank to her knees…

His jaw went slack. "You are going to…?"

"Oh yes. I'm going to." She'd never performed the act, but she'd stumbled upon others in the middle of it throughout the years, when she'd visited villages for food. The males had appeared lost in the throes. The way she wanted Micah.

This beautiful brute had given her everything she'd never known she needed.

He moaned when she started, groaned as she worked him over and over and over again, then roared at the end. But he recovered only seconds later, yanking her up off her feet and swinging her into his arms. He carried her to the bed and lowered her to the mattress as if she were the most precious treasure in all the realm.

Delicious male. Excitement and arousal kept her at a razor's edge of pleasure-pain. Naked, he climbed up her body.

She spread her legs, creating a cradle for him. His weight pinned her. "I need you," she breathed into his ear.

"You can have me." He reached between them, placed his length at her opening and surged deep inside her. Filling and stretching her. Pumping slowly. Then faster. Faster. Harder. The bed rocked. "You can have me *always.*"

"Always. Yes. I demand nothing less." Every roll of his hips incited a roll of her own. She kneaded and scratched his shoulder, chasing a release. The pressure mounted. So good, so good, so good. "Yes, yes, yes. Micah…"

The next thing she knew, he was flat on his back, and she

was poised over him, straddling his waist and balancing on her knees. He plunged into her, letting her control the depths and the speed. Yes! At this angle, he hit deeper than before. And he had unlimited access to the heart of her need, which he stroked with the pad of his thumb...

Yes, yes! The pleasure...incomparable...too much, too much... Pressure broke inside her, a storm of bliss bursting forth. Viori released a ragged moan as her insides splintered, coming and coming and coming.

Micah gripped her hips and thrust his own with more force, sections of his lower body lifting from the mattress. He thrust again. And again. Harder. Faster. A roar ripped from him, her name buried within it.

As he sagged on the blankets, she collapsed atop him. He coiled his arms around her. One around her head and the other draped across her backside. A protective, possessive hold, and possibly her new favorite thing in the world. With her ear pressed against his pectoral, she heard his racing heart. A tempo matched by her pulse.

Contentment settled over her. In her. What a wonderful turn her life had taken. Micah, her husband forever. Kaysar, her brother again. Drendall, in her care once more. Graves and the others, alive and well. Incredible sex with a male she adored, whose body drove her wild. And yet, Norok and those trolls threatened everything.

Voice low and deep, Micah said, "I like you this way. Soft and satisfied."

"I think you like me, period," she teased.

"I do." He kissed her brow, almost smiling. Then he grew serious again, if not a little, well, bashful. "Is the like mutual, Red? I know you said you loved me, but that was probably—"

"I do love you. That isn't a phrase I use lightly. And the like is definitely mutual." She lifted her head to give him a lazy smile. "I'm keeping you forever."

The almost smile returned. "Are you now?"

"The children insist."

He offered her a full-blown smile, only to frown seconds later. "I won't serve your brother."

"Why would you? You are a king, too. And I'm your queen."

Some of his tension faded. He smoothed a lock of her hair from her cheek. "There are things we must figure out about our future."

Not a declaration of love but progress all the same. "All we need to figure out is whether or not we wish to be together. Everything else is icing. So do you?"

Again, he pursed his lips. "I do." At least he hadn't needed to think about it. "And you?"

"Yes!" More than anything. "We can live our dream, Micah. You, me, and our fruit growing trees, ruling our people in the paradise you've always longed for."

He clutched her even tighter. "You deserve a palace. This palace. I built it for you—I wasn't willing to admit it at the time."

She kissed his biggest scar. "This palace is wonderful and all, but I'd rather we build a new one. The children won't be comfortable here. The ceilings are far too low for our boys."

"And here, Norok will only ever haunt my memories." Pain drenched his voice, sharper than any dagger. "I must kill him."

Viori winced. "Maybe there's another way. We can imprison him and Fayette. If we eradicate the trolls, Norok will have no armies to control." If it was the last thing she did, she would be getting his—their—people back. She had ideas for the orphanage. A new friend and protector for every child! "The camp is ours. We can build there."

"Norok wishes to kill you." His voice hardened. "He doesn't get to breathe."

Beyond sweet. But also rash? In time, would Micah come to resent her for the loss?

A hard double rap sounded at the door. "Family meeting in

the war room, Viori. Five minutes," Amber called. "There's been a new development. Oh, and your presence is required as well, Micah."

"Will I never get to keep you to myself?" he grumbled as they climbed from the bed.

"What do you think happened?

"Nothing good," he said, dressing quickly.

She shoved her arms through the proper holes in the robe. "Ugh. The robe is nice and all, but not for a family meeting."

"You wish for a gown, I will acquire a gown." He planted a swift kiss on her lips, then vanished, reappearing seconds later with a gorgeous ensemble in hand. The most beautiful thing she'd ever seen, with mesh and leather around the vital organs. A gown, but also armor.

"Where did you get this?" she asked, awed by it—and him.

"I have a secret room here. Several secret rooms Kaysar and Cookie haven't yet found. One of them is filled with everything I collected for my wife."

"A treasure room. Just for me?" Viori threw herself into his arms, peppering his face with kisses. "I accept every trinket as my due!"

He was chuckling as he kissed her back. This time, his good humor lingered, and she took heart. She *was* making progress with him.

"Oh! Before we go," she said. "What does this say?" She fetched the note left with the robe.

Micah read it and ran his tongue over his teeth. "It's a note to you from Amber. It says,

This robe will work until your husband grabs something from his secret treasure room he thinks I know nothing about. But he shouldn't worry. I haven't touched anything more than twice."

Sighing, he tossed the note into the hearth.

"I don't know why, but I like Amber," Viori admitted. "And Cookie. And maybe even Pearl Jean."

"I don't know why you do, either. Ready?" he asked. When she nodded, he flittered them both to the war room, something Viori had never even heard of. And oh, wow, what a space. She gazed about, her eyes widening.

Potted plant after potted plant—all enchanted trees. Some had already sprouted elderseed. A long table was scattered with maps upon maps upon maps. Maps decorated the walls as well. Kaysar, Cookie and Amber were already there, and each had changed clothes. Her brother wore the same kind of outfit as before, but Cookie had decked herself in an array of leather, like Viori. She'd changed the color of her hair, too. The black strands were plaited and twisted all over her head in a weird design. Amber wore a sunny yellow frock and passed out scones with a smile.

Micah and Kaysar glared at each other, her brother clearly worked into a temper.

"Did he crawl back properly," Kaysar asked her, "or shall I remove his feet and ensure it gets done? Does he know he made you cry? Or that I won't aid him with his foes unless he begs for your forgiveness?"

"I am the one in need of forgiveness," she said.

"I do not want or require your aid," Micah snapped at her brother. "I'll be handling this alone."

Viori leaned her head upon her husband's shoulder, showing her support. Wait. She jolted. "Alone?"

"The family feud can wait." Cookie pointed to multiple places on a map. "Before our battle, groups of trolls were spotted coming up from underground tunnels here, here and here. The ones we fought, I'm guessing. They raided several homes on the way to us, slaughtering most of the occupants. We know only because of the survivors. While you two have been screaming with pleasure, sending Kaysar into fits of minirage, I've been questioning the witnesses."

Viori's cheeks heated, and she looked anywhere but at her brother.

"The trolls are underground then." Micah swerved from confusion to sadness to determination. "The vastness of those tunnels... Norok could've moved the prisoners anywhere." The determination intensified. "I'll extract the information from him before I kill him. Fayette dies, too. I'll do the deeds tonight, ensuring no more trolls escape."

Viori envisioned the fallout from such a path and winced. "There *has* to be another way."

At the other end of the table, a familiar blonde flickered into view. Elena, with puffy, red-rimmed eyes. "Trust me. There isn't."

Everyone braced. Micah clutched two daggers. Kaysar flared his claws. Cookie released vines, the foliage coiling around her neck, wrists and ankles, capturing the spy.

Elena didn't fight. But then, she couldn't. The queen had used poisonvine, paralyzing the other woman and momentarily negating her glamara. To the best of her ability, she croaked, "Norok intends to unleash more trolls. Which he can do as soon as Micah is dead. Kaysar will be his next target. And don't think you can find the trolls before their escape. My brother lied. He has a glamara. An ability to hide *anything*. Or anyone."

"Why should we believe you?" Viori demanded, aggression all but sparking off her husband's shoulders.

"You shouldn't believe me. But I'm telling the truth. He murdered Sabot," the blonde croaked. "As soon as we returned to camp, my brother imprisoned us. He threatened to kill Sabot if I declined from sharing your location. So, I did it. I shared, and he killed Sabot, anyway."

"Listen, all. Heed my words," Amber announced, her gaze far away. "If Micah goes alone, he will die, but so will Norok.

If Micah goes with Kaysar and Cookie, Micah, Kaysar and Cookie will die, but so will Fayette. Norok will live. If Micah goes with Kaysar, Cookie and Viori, he wins and both Norok and Fayette die…but so does Viori. If Viori goes alone, both Norok and Fayette die, but so does Viori."

Her head spun as she tried to fit the oracle's puzzle pieces together. Micah and Kaysar must have reached the same conclusion at the same time. "Viori stays here," they burst out in unison.

Micah…dead. No. No! Viori would allow no such outcome. And she didn't want Cookie and Kaysar risking their lives, either.

"I'm sorry, but there's no other path to victory." Amber blinked into focus, her shoulders dropping. "And you must achieve victory. If Norok and Fayette aren't stopped, the trolls win and take over the entire realm."

So. To save her loved ones and the realm itself, all Viori had to do was die? When she'd only now begun to live?

"I'll do it. I'll save the day," she announced, only to gasp. An image flashed through her mind. Then another and another. She cried out, clutching her temples and pulling her hair. Every image featured someone she loved dead or dying. Micah. Kaysar. Cookie. Even Amber. Graves. John. Drendall. Oh, look. There was Jareth and Pearl Jean. The orphan girl. Her parents. The images flashed again and again. "Make it stop. Make it stop, make it stop!" So much pain. So much blood. So much death.

Micah's warmth enveloped her. "I'm here, Red. I'm here. Breathe with me. I think Fayette is pushing images into your mind. But they aren't real. Believe nothing you see. Know that she cannot sustain this type of projection for long. It's painful for her, and she'll eventually drain. This will stop soon."

"She can twist the truth, yes," Viori cried, "but that doesn't mean she's doing any twisting right now."

"Make this cease *now*!" Kaysar demanded. "Viori, calm yourself. Sleep."

But she didn't sleep. She heard the compulsion in his voice, felt the incredible power of his glamara, but she experienced no urge to obey.

"Viori," Micah said, gentler with her than usual. "You told me to trust you. Very well. I will trust you if you will do the same for me. Believe me rather than a treacherous oracle."

He kind of—definitely—had a point. But the images kept coming and coming and coming. Pain. Blood. Death. So much death. Emotions followed, and she couldn't halt the deluge. Fear turned to panic, and panic turned to hysteria.

"Viori," Micah repeated, and this time he used the harshest, coldest voice she'd ever heard.

"I trust you," she rasped. Hearing the words helped. She did. She trusted him. He had always helped her, never hurt her. Never lied to her. Calm infiltrated the panic, which downgraded to fear. The fear faded...

"Good. Now sleep, Red," he commanded, and something inside her stood to attention. "Sleep for me."

Yes. A short rest might do her a world of good. A cloud of black descended over her mind, and she knew nothing more.

CHAPTER TWENTY-EIGHT

Micah caught Viori as she sagged in his arms and hefted her slight weight against his chest. All the while, shock bubbled in his heart and fury boiled in his veins. She had chosen him. Kaysar had failed to calm her, but Micah had succeeded. She might have meant what she'd said; she might love him. While she'd given him the words, a part of him hadn't dared to believe. Before, he'd considered himself an idiot. A coward. A lovesick fool. But...

If she loved him as much as he loved her—he sucked air between his teeth. He did. He loved her. He loved her, and Fayette and Norok dared to attack her. Micah's fury overtook his shock. The warrior and oracle did not deserve death. Only eons of pain and suffering. But in the end, death was what they'd get. That, he wouldn't compromise on. No backup plans. No alternative path. He needed to put an end to this, and he would settle for nothing less.

Kaysar looked from Viori's calm, even features to Micah's ironhard expression, then hissed, "Norok and the oracle die."

"Yes," he agreed, earning a look of grudging respect. "I will stop at nothing to get this done." Their war was with him, not with his wife. Why attack her here and now? To provoke an attack as soon as possible? Wish granted. "They die today."

Do no harm to the innocent. Protect what's yours. Always do what's right. Never be without a backup plan.

Rules he'd lived with all his life took center stage in his mind. Norok and Fayette were not innocent. They were not right, and they were not his. They'd allowed their hatred and bitterness to order their steps and direct their paths. Something Micah had been dangerously close to doing himself before Red had entered his world, saving him in a thousand ways.

"How do we prevent Amber's visions from coming to pass?" Cookie asked, nuzzling into her husband's side.

Micah didn't know the answer. The image of his broken, beaten body flickered in his mind. He wanted to live. Demanded the life his wife had promised with her vow of love. Determination infused every muscle, every bone. Nothing less than a true marriage would satisfy him. So die? Now? No!

A new image hit him like a physical blow. A repeat of the first one he'd seen. Viori, held in Ragdar's arms, limp and splattered with blood. Every muscle in Micah's body tensed.

"Fayette has turned her sights to me," he grated.

"Let's see if I can distract the hag while you guys figure something out." Wearing an eager smile, Amber popped her knuckles and rotated her head from side to side. "I've been practicing."

As her gaze slipped far away, Micah's mind began to clear. "It's working," he announced.

Kaysar vanished without a word. However, he returned only a few seconds later with a sleeping Drendall clutched in one arm and a cot anchored by the other. He placed the cot in the rear of the chamber, against a line of enchanted trees.

"Place my little love here," the king instructed, patting the cot.

"You treat her like she's still a child," Micah grumbled. Though he hated to be without her, he obeyed, easing his bundle upon the taut fabric. Then he took the doll—their…child—and tucked her into Viori's side and caressed her cheek.

"I'll have you know I treat her as if she is precious because she is. Best you watch your tongue before I snatch it," Kaysar groused as he led the vacant-eyed Amber to sit next to the cot, his touch surprisingly gentle.

Cookie secured Elena to a chair on the other side of the room.

"Norok expects you to strike tonight. He wants you to do so," Elena piped up, imploring Micah with her gaze. "And if you don't reach the camp by a certain time, he plans to bring the battle to you here. Why do you think he took out your beloved queen? He fears her monsters. He has scouts searching for the living *belua* even now, with orders to kill on sight."

"As if we hadn't deduced all of that on our own." Cookie rolled her eyes. "Stating the obvious to earn our trust. It's an adorable move that will gain you nothing but my wrath." She waved in the other woman's direction, and a poisonous vine grew from the one wrapped around Elena's neck—straight into her mouth, silencing her.

The spy's blue gaze pleaded with him. *Believe me.*

He did, and he didn't. He needed to think. His heart had yet to slow as he, Kaysar and Cookie approached the table covered with maps.

Micah shuffled many of the maps out of his way, searching for a drawing of his camp. There. "Here, here, here and here you'll find entrances to a series of underground tunnels and rooms. Before any battle, a contingent of soldiers usually wait in this one. The people are usually stored in this one. This is an escape route that leads to the wastelands. This is a trap rigged to collapse."

"You're telling us this because you'd like us to make the rooms collapse like the trap and crush your soldiers and people to death?" Cookie wobbled her head from side to side as if balancing a scale. "It's cruel, but quick and effective. I like it. Though, honestly, there's no reason to go to so much time and trouble when I can simply collect everyone with vines and pop off their heads.''

And she is my ally. The lesser of two evils. "The people aren't to be harmed," he grated. "If possible." They sided with Norok and placed themselves in Micah's crosshairs, so he couldn't be blamed for a violent end. "Norok probably expects me to lead you to any of the rooms but the trap. Which means all the rooms will be traps, rigged with unknowns, making the trap I know about a viable option. As for your vines, there are traps set here, here and here. At the first sign of your glamara, you will be snared. And your voice won't work," he told Kaysar. "The entire army has already drunk *surdi* root tea, I'm sure, making themselves deaf."

Kaysar rolled his eyes. "As if a beverage can thwart me."

"You are not as indestructible as you think." Norok and Micah had fought against one another for centuries. They knew each other's strengths, weaknesses and preferences. To win, Micah would need to fight as he'd never fought before. A feat he was certain he had already achieved. Working with a former enemy. Intent on the death of his foes rather than subduing. A willingness to knock over anyone in his path. No mercy!

"How do you wish to play this then?" Kaysar asked him. "Because my sister seems to...hold you in some regard, I am willing to listen to your ideas."

"She loves me," he boasted, his chest all but swelling with pride. "And I love her." With all his heart. Which meant he and Kaysar were stuck with each other. Forever.

His gaze strayed to Red, still on the cot, locks of scarlet hair spilled around her. His pride morphed into resolve, his muscles tightening. Really, there was only one way to play this. Go in alone. The oracle had said he would die if he did it. But so would Norok. And that would have to be enough.

Fayette would live, but so would Viori, Kaysar and Cookie, the two people able to protect his wife for the rest of her days.

A small price to pay, really. Kaysar and Cookie could take out Fayette later.

So. Yes. He would do it. "I go alone," Micah announced.

Viori clawed her way through the darkness. Something was wrong.

Voices whispered through her mind. Her husband's. Her brother's. And Cookie's. Yes. They uttered plans and schemes against Norok and his treacherous oracle.

Thoughts came at her, one after the other. *Wake. Hurry. Time is running out.* Something about Micah going alone…

Concern hit her, a shock to her system. She hadn't forgotten Amber's warning. If Micah went in alone, he died.

No, no and no. *Can't lose him. Won't.* Viori must do something to stop him. But what?

If she could wake, she could leave in secret, then take care of the problem before the others finished planning. Micah would be spared. What else mattered?

No one had ever put him first. That ended today. Nothing and no one had ever been so important to her.

I can save him, so I will. Fayette possessed enough power to take out one opponent. Only one. Which meant she'd chosen Viori for a reason. The enemy must fear her voice. Which meant her voice could hold the key to victory.

Come on, come on. Wake or lose your husband!

Her eyelids popped open. Miracle of miracles, she drew no one's notice as she slitted her lids and turned her head the most minute amount. Her family members stood around the table, casually discussing Micah's plans for the people, once he and Norok were dead.

He thinks to die for me. Her heart thudded, her stomach tied in a thousand knots. Permit her husband to sacrifice himself on her behalf? No! He was a good man. The best. That rare species the fae realm needed more than anything. Honest. Loyal. Genuinely kind. A protector to the bone. He must be protected at all costs.

Deep down, Viori relished this opportunity to save him. The girl who had killed her parents now had the chance to defend her husband as well as her brother, his wife, their twins and their world. And all she had to do was die?

She drew in a breath. The loss of her life was big. Huge. Something she'd created monsters to avoid. But...

So be it. For her loved ones, she did this gladly.

Being with Micah had changed her, and there was no going back. For so long, she'd chosen loneliness and exile, eschewing friendship and a helping hand, her heart as barren as the Dusklands. Now, with a brimming heart, there was no room for sorrow or punishment. Only blessing. Proof: her children had begun to bloom again.

For once, she would leave something better than she'd found it.

"Shh." In a blink, Elena appeared before her, crouched and flickering in and out of view, but somehow always transparent. Her features were contorted in pain, and Viori nearly gasped, giving herself away. "Listen closely. You're seeing and hearing a projection of my consciousness. One of the reasons I'm such a good spy." Her voice was hollow, as if coming from a long tunnel. Or through a stalk of poisonvine. "I know what you're planning. Free me, and I'll help you eliminate Norok and Fayette. Amber said nothing about you dying if we go together. So unleash me, Majesty. Let me act as your rage. Please."

This was real? Not a figment of her imagination?

"I brought two *amplio* stones. One for each of us, so we can flitter. You have only to remove one from my pocket. Please remove it. Norok is going to destroy this world and everyone in it if he frees more trolls," the blonde continued. "He must be stopped. But I can't flitter, even with my stone, while bound with this poisonvine. If you create a distraction, I think I can cut myself loose. I'll meet you at the swamp. But make your decision quick. Time is running out."

The projection disappeared then and did not appear again. Viori's heart thudded faster as she cast her gaze to the still-bound Elena, who peered at her with a beseeching gaze.

Her thoughts whirled. Trust Elena, Norok's sister, who might lead her straight into a trap. Risking everything, going for the happiest ending of all: living with her husband and family for the rest of eternity. *Winning* everything.

She remembered the other woman's pain when she mentioned Sabot's death. Truth or lie?

Deep breath in. Hold. Out. Viori didn't think that kind of pain could be faked. So. She would do it. She would take the risk for a chance to have forever with Micah.

To free and join Elena, she need only create a distraction and confiscate a stone. Very well. Under her breath, she hummed a little note, awakening Drendall from her sleep. The little doll blinked open her eyes and stretched, then smiled at her with pure adoration.

If we are truly connected, she will understand me without words.

Mother and daughter peered at each other, sharing a moment of silent communion. Drendall's smile grew before she nodded, wiggled closer to Elena, snatched a stone, then passed it to Viori and climbed from the cot. She toddled over and hurled herself at Cookie, biting her leg.

"Chucky!" The queen screamed, kicking for freedom.

Drendall scrabbled over the table, evading the strike. Laughing, she shoved all the maps to the floor.

Guilt pricked Viori as utter chaos erupted, and she almost cried out, alerting her husband to her plan. Would Micah consider this another betrayal? Would he hate her for the rest of eternity?

Did it matter? He would live, and she would gain an opportunity to win him.

With everyone focused on the pandemonium, Elena sliced through a vine with a dagger, no one the wiser. Then the spy vanished. Viori leaped into motion, stone in hand. She plucked a small brick of elderseed from the nearest limb and flittered after her...partner in crime, appearing in the designated location.

Well. Graves had already plunged a limb through each of Elena's shoulders—both branches hung heavy with delicious produce. The sandcats bit the blonde's calves and John pulled back his elbow, preparing to deliver a single swipe to remove her head. Defensive to the end, like their mother.

"No," Viori called, and Graves immediately retracted his branches. The cats stilled. A pale, panting Elena collapsed to her knees as Viori stuffed her pebble in her pocket and pointed an accusing finger at her children. "No more striking first. We pause and we think. If the person is innocent, we send them on their way, no worse for the wear."

Graves and John appeared chagrined. The cats settled and licked their hindquarters.

"Thanks for the concern," Elena grumbled as she clambered to her feet. She swayed as her wounds healed, the process visible through the fabric of her tunic. "And thank you for believing in me. I won't let you down. But how am I supposed to fight and defeat Norok now?"

Viori broke the elderseed in half. A bite for each of them. "Eat this, and your strength will return. Your glamara will charge, and you'll be stronger than ever. For a few hours, at least. After that, you'll weaken considerably. And, if you let me down, that's when I'll strike at you."

"An acceptable bargain." Elena accepted the piece with a shaky hand, then popped the elderseed into her mouth and swallowed. Seconds passed, and she frowned. "Nothing's happening."

"Just wait. But we can't stay here. Guaranteed everyone knows we're gone now. They'll be looking for us." And she didn't want

Micah searching for her at the camp while Norok and Fayette still lived.

"I'll go to— Oh!" Elena gasped, her eyes widening. She rolled her shoulders. "You were right. I like this very much." Lifting her chin, she squared her shoulders. "Are you ready for battle?" she asked, aglow with sorrow for the harsh necessities to come. "Because warring when oracles are involved is difficult. We must assume Fayette can foresee anything we plan."

"Then we go in without planning. And if you hear me singing—"

"Cover my ears. Trust me, I will never not cover my ears when you sing. I saw what you did to the trolls."

The dry tone made Viori laugh. She thrust a hand against her mouth, horrified that she'd displayed amusement at a time like this. If the situation were reversed and she must hunt and kill her brother for the greater good... "My apologies."

"Don't be sorry." Elena threw her arms around Viori, giving her a spontaneous hug. "I'll take all the levity I can get."

Viori hugged her back, albeit awkwardly.

The other woman cleared her throat as she drew back, as if embarrassed by the display of affection.

"If—when—we succeed, I'll promote you to the exalted position of my lady's maid."

Now Elena laughed, a high-pitched bark there and gone. Serious again, she said, "We follow our instincts from here on out." Swooping down, she picked up the collar Micah had removed from Viori's neck. "See you on the other side, Your Majesty."

They shared a half smile before the spy vanished.

Viori's first instinct? To see to her family's protection. She told her babies, "Hide near the camp. If you see Micah, stop him from entering the fray. Kaysar and Cookie, too—without harming them. Guard them." She hugged each one. "I love you, and I hope to see you on the other side of the war."

With tears gathering, she popped the elderseed into her

mouth, swallowed and nodded a goodbye to her children. She flittered to a section of forest near the camp and cloaked herself with a tangle of branches.

Through gaps in the limbs, she saw guards surrounded the perimeter, each holding a spear. And oh, wow, the elderseed hit and hit hard. Power flooded her, filling her, every crevice. Her blood heated—her *throat* heated, as if she'd swallowed fiery coal. Hopefully, the extra power would keep her from sleeping and creating a doorway to the mortal world.

Wasting no time, Viori gave in to the urge to create and released a song of conception. The melody carried on a soft breeze, tendrils of her power draining. A wind kicked up. Branches clapped as one. Twigs, stones and dirt drew together, forming five…ten…twenty…bodies, but none came to life. Not yet. These beings would not awaken until she discharged the final note.

The last time she'd birthed this many at once, she'd slept for centuries. This time, she might die afterward. Or *would* die, according to Amber. Or perhaps not. Perhaps Elena was right. They didn't know what would happen now that they were working together. But if she died, she would be taking Fayette or Norok with her, leaving Micah with protectors and, hopefully, the means of creating his paradise, so…

Worth it. But she wouldn't sing the last note unless things got critical. First, she would…what?

Don't think. Do.

Without warning, screams and shouts pierced the air, ringing out from the camp. Hope collided with dread. Had Elena already succeeded in ending Norok? Or had Micah and Kaysar attacked?

With a gasp, Viori sprang from the line of trees. Shock overtook her when she spotted the campground now. Trolls had invaded, swarming the entire camp, trampling everything in their wake. Soldiers ran this way and that, chased by groups of the ravaging brutes.

Had Norok lost control of his hidden armies? Or had he done this on purpose? Willing to sacrifice his own men for revenge? Had he and the oracle abandoned the place, or did they hide within his glamara?

If Viori sang now, awakening their bones, she would kill the soldiers as well as the trolls.

Either way, she couldn't allow these trolls to go free. Should she gamble and awaken her newest creations? Was that how she died? Falling asleep, thereby unable to protect herself from attack?

If she slept and traveled, she slept and traveled. If she died, she died. She'd lived a good life. The best. She'd known love, whether Micah had admitted it or not. She'd given it, too. And she'd meant what she'd said. These were her people. She would fight for them until her dying breath.

Except, she caught a glimpse of a running Fayette, weaving in and out between tents, escaping the action. All right. The song could wait. Remove the heads of the snake before dealing with the body.

Viori gave chase...

CHAPTER TWENTY-NINE

Micah rushed into the midst of utter chaos, brandishing a pair of short swords. He thought he'd seen Graves and John in the forest, but he wasn't sure. He'd been moving too quickly. Aggression teemed inside him, making him feel double his usual size. Muscles flexed and hardened. As he swung his weapons, his blood converted to liquid power. A troll head flew across the camp. Then another. And another. There went a clawed hand. An organ. He cut through opponent after opponent.

No mercy.

Dead bodies soon littered the ground. Trolls and soldiers alike. More soldiers than trolls. He inwardly cursed. The trolls were winning, tearing through tents as well as the army, unleashing centuries of stored-up rage. Pained screams pierced the air in a constant ebb and flow.

He wasn't yet sure how so many trolls had gotten free of his compulsion. He felt no fear. And he'd never felt enough fear to free this many at once. Unless... What if this horde had never been under his compulsion? What if Norok had hidden his *own* army all along? His own backup plan.

That would mean he hadn't betrayed Micah because of Warren's death. Not fully. But also because the underhanded warrior sought power.

Where was Ragdar? Where was Viori? Micah *must* find her. Allow her to perish out here? No. If he had to die so that she could live, so be it.

Kaysar bounded to his side, catching a troll by the wrist before the brute was able to strike Micah from behind. A slash of the king's free hand, and the creature's guts spilled out. The troll dropped and writhed. Micah kicked him in the face, and Kaysar removed his head with those infamous metal claws.

"Leave," Micah commanded as he slayed his next two targets. "You remember Amber's warning as well as I do. If we're together, we'll die. Red will need you when this is over."

"If my sister wants you, she gets you," Kaysar snapped, killing another troll. "No matter how terrible I consider her taste. We will save her, and we will survive. No other outcome is acceptable to me."

For minutes—hours? an eternity?—they fought side by side. He caught sight of Graves and John again. They attacked their opponents with relish.

When Kaysar launched into a song and grabbed Micah's hand to steer him toward a certain horde, he realized this was the vision Fayette had shown him. And yes, she had twisted what she had revealed. Rather than Kaysar and Viori fighting side by side against Micah, the two kings worked together. True allies. For the first time, he enjoyed the male's voice.

They cut through the horde with vicious precision. Any soldiers they came across joined their ranks, fighting alongside them. At the moment, they didn't see Kaysar as an enemy but a friend. Someone they needed. It helped that they couldn't hear him.

As their group marched forward, working as a unit, they left carnage in their wake. It wasn't long before they started winning. The number of trolls depleted, allowing Micah to see farther and wider. Still no sign of Viori. He clung to his cold detachment, needing it. Until—

"Die already!" The precious voice rose through the chorus of grunts and groans. He and Kaysar straightened with a snap. Red.

Unable to flitter, they sprinted across the distance and found her at the far edge of camp. Viori and Fayette were midbattle, fighting each other with savage intensity. Dirt streaked them both. Their clothes were torn and soaked with crimson, evidence of massive injuries received and healed.

The oracle swiped a dagger while Viori clawed and bit. Micah's feral kitten delivered more blows than she received. Pride and relief swelled his chest. Nearby, Lavina was sprawled across the ground, blood soaked and unmoving, with Ragdar dead beside her.

Lavina all along. Another twisted vision. Fayette had known Lavina would die by the troll king's hands. Most likely Norok had known, too. And they'd let it happen, perhaps even arranged it, simply to frighten Micah.

Norok was now engaged in a similar battle with Elena, the two wielding daggers.

Intending to kill the warrior and oracle, one after the other, Micah sprang forward—and hit an invisible wall, bouncing back. He didn't understand. He sprang forward again, his brain rattling against his skull upon impact. Next, he stabbed at the invisible block, but his sword bent. Graves and John joined him, but even they proved unsuccessful.

Realization set in, and panic hit. Norok had the stones Elena had stolen from Kaysar and Cookie. The traitor had created the dome, protecting himself from the trolls as much as Micah's wrath.

Viori caught sight of him and missed her next punch, allowing Fayette to tackle her, taking her to the dirt. As the pair rolled together in a tangle of fury, Micah and company fought against the dome with all their might.

"How do we overcome this?" Micah demanded.

"I do not know," Kaysar responded, "but we had better find a way."

The soldiers helped them, wielding swords, arrows and fists, but nothing proved successful.

The two sets of combatants, trapped inside the dome, proved equally matched, no one able to overcome the other.

Norok dodged one of Elena's charges. "Sister, join me."

"Why did you have to kill Sabot?" she cried, slashing at him.

The warrior blocked and launched a slash of his own. "He came from the Spring Court to infiltrate our land. They think to take it from us. He couldn't be allowed to report his findings. I'm sorry, sister. I am. But I won't allow you to stop this. I will rule the Dusklands, and my trolls will round up everyone who has sworn fealty to Kaysar and Cookie and kill them all."

"You are not Micah," Elena spit, striking at him. "You cannot control the trolls."

Another block, followed by a strike of his own. "I don't need to control them with force," he spit back.

Norok was shirtless and littered with gashes. A metal collar circled his throat, preventing him from flittering away. That was Viori's collar. Given to him courtesy of his sister? Had Elena returned to the swamp to collect it? Shock inundated him. Had she turned on her own flesh and blood for Micah's sake? For his people?

Norok swiped a trail of blood from his lip, saying, "They serve me willingly. They love me. They'll love you, too. If you'll let them."

"You mean they fear you because of the lies Fayette has projected." Again, Elena spit the words at him.

"It's more than that. I'm the one who has cared for them in their frozen state all these centuries, promising them a life beyond their wildest dreams. A few have been freed from Micah's compulsion throughout their imprisonment, and I had only to breed a new army. Since the arrival of his little Red, more and more have gained freedom and joined me."

Micah heard the confession, but he didn't care. He only wanted Viori safe. He fought the dome with all his considerable strength.

"Keep my sister alive, whatever you must do," Kaysar commanded before he ran from the battle. Retreating? Now? No, he most likely went for help. Cookie?

Micah's children took posts at his back, guarding him as he continued working on the dome, trusting him to protect their mother. When Fayette lost her grip on the dagger, Red swooped in and— he blinked. Unleash rage? Oh yes. That and more. His perfect little wife seized the upper hand, ripping out the oracle's throat with her teeth. Before the other woman had a chance to heal, Red swiped up the fallen dagger and struck, stabbing her opponent in the heart.

Relief flared and died inside Micah as Viori rolled to her back rather than stand. She peered up at the sky, panting as Elena and Norok continued to viciously slash at each other.

"Viori!" Micah shouted, banging on the dome. Was she hurt? Fatigued because of the elderseed?

She sat up gingerly and scanned the area. Finding him in the fray, she smiled, revealing blood-coated teeth. The most beautiful female in existence. But her attention stretched past him, horror contorting her expression.

He whipped around to see a nearby tunnel entrance had opened in the ground, and additional trolls were pouring onto the battlefield. Another horde. No, more than one tunnel had opened, and several hordes converged in the campground.

Soldiers shot into action once again. Individual battles erupted, the dome forgotten by everyone but Micah. He had no need to turn, with Graves and John looking out for him; he kept his attention on the battle inside the dome. If Norok won, Viori would be forced to face him.

Micah threw himself at the mysterious force to no avail.

Viori's attention swung to the combatants as well, then returned to the trolls. The combatants, the trolls. Then she peered at Micah and projected all kinds of sadness. "I love you, husband," she called. "With all my heart."

In that moment, he knew her plan. To sing and create, letting herself sink into another sleep, if necessary, to stop the trolls. Weakening herself when she needed to be her strongest. Dying, as Amber had predicted.

No! Can't lose her. Won't *lose her.* Micah hit the invisible wall with more force, knocking his shoulder out of joint. Another hard hit put it back in place. He didn't stop there. He hit the dome again and again and again.

Still, Viori clambered to her feet, tilted back her head and released a note of music with a tone unlike any Micah had ever heard. So beautiful it brought tears to his eyes. Trolls ceased fighting first. Then soldiers, who shouldn't have been able to hear after ingesting *surdi* root. And yet, hear they did, as if she used a frequency *nothing* could mask.

Even Norok and Elena went still. Somehow, Micah knew his wife released the sound of life itself, and nothing could stop its power. No one moved as she sang her song.

Then she went quiet. Her eyelids slid shut and her knees collapsed. She fell into a bed of lush green grass. Not dirt. It had sprung up as she'd sung, he realized. Now, in a circle around her, the grass was blurring, as if a doorway to the mortal world was beginning to open.

Coming out of his stupor, Micah banged against the unseen divider. "Viori!" *She's only sleeping. Hasn't traveled yet.* There was still time. He could save her.

The ground shook harder and harder, *belua* bursting onto the battlefield. Monstrous trees like Micah had faced so long ago. Graves, John and the sandcats approached the fray from behind the newcomers. Viori's children—*his* children. Elena and Norok battled on.

For once, the creatures didn't kill without thought or qualm. No, they shielded soldiers and struck at the trolls.

"You aren't going to win," Elena said between panting breaths, drawing Micah's attention back to them. "Surrender. Live. You do not have to die today."

"No, I do not. But you do." Norok tripped her. As she stumbled, he took full advantage, thrusting his dagger into her heart and cruelly twisting the blade.

Her eyes widened, and her lips parted on a shocked, pained gasp. Because she knew. This was a killing blow; she'd reached the end.

And Norok wasn't done. "I'm sorry. It didn't have to end this way. You had only to heed me," he said, swinging his free hand. A second dagger cut through her throat.

As she gurgled for breath, blood streaming from the corners of her mouth, her legs gave out and she collapsed.

"Elena!" Micah roared, banging the dome with great force. "Norok!"

As his sister's blood dripped from his hands, the traitor faced him. "Her death is your fault, chimera." His chest rose and fell in quick succession, remorse etched into each of his features. "I suppose it always had to come to this. You and I. The only two brave enough to take on *belua*."

Electricity crackled in the air beside him. Two layers peeled apart, Kaysar rushing out and killing everyone nearby.

Cookie stood in the opening. "Where?" she asked her husband, scanning the battlefield.

"Straight ahead, as close to Viori as possible," Kaysar replied.

Understanding came. Relieved and frantic, Micah helped him protect the doorway as the queen extended her arms. Vines uncoiled, slithering to the dome and opening a second doorway past it.

He zoomed through, entering the dome while Kaysar, Graves and John protected Cookie and both entrances.

Norok dragged the sleeping Viori from the growing doorway beneath her, and pressed a dagger against her chest.

Panic rose to new heights, but Micah beat it back. He breathed in deeply. Exhaled. Protective instincts surged. That female loved him. Micah loved her back. Loved her with all his heart, every fiber of his being, today, tomorrow and forever. There was no way he would allow anyone to harm her while he still had breath in his lungs.

An ember sparked in his chest, his glamaras battling each other more intently than ever before. That heat intensified, spilling through the rest of him. Organs sizzled. Muscles seemed to turn to stone and bone to steel. The instinct to protect sharpened, reaching the core of his being. Then. That moment.

The glamaras stopped working against each other and clicked, working together. Power flooded him. Wave after wave of it.

Kill!

Norok had become a beast—and Micah could control beasts. For once, he had no reason to prove himself stronger first. He simply was, his two glamaras in total agreement.

The other male offered a sad smile. "Now you'll know the pain of losing the one you love and adore most. You, who praise loyalty, have betrayed me in the worst way."

"No. This has nothing to do with Warren." His voice had deepened, power an undercurrent in every word. A tone far more brutal than any he'd ever used before. Maybe Norok heard him as he'd heard Viori's song, maybe he didn't. But he could read Micah's lips—and sense his intentions. The change in the very fabric of his very being. "You worked against me long before his death."

"The trolls were my contingency plan, same as they were yours. I learned from the best, after all." Norok lifted the blade with both hands wrapped around the hilt. A swift up and swifter down.

"Stop!" Micah bellowed, and the warrior froze abruptly, the blade halted an inch above Viori's heart.

Norok blinked at him, his jaw slack. Everyone surrounding the dome had frozen as well, not one person daring to move. Perhaps they *couldn't* move, Micah's command too powerful to ignore.

"Lift the dagger. Now." No bellowing this time. He spoke only to Norok, allowing a stronger dose of power to saturate the command.

The warrior's hands shook as he fought the compulsion. A vein bulged in the center of his forehead. Sweat trickled from his temple. The dagger began to lift, more and more space between the tip and Viori's chest.

Outside, Kaysar freed himself from the compulsion, a beast of equal strength. He rolled his shoulders, picked up two swords and twirled the hilts in his grip, smiling with relish. "Let the troll massacre begin." He shot into motion, decapitating his foes with much glee.

"Stab yourself," Micah told Norok, prowling closer. "Stab yourself everywhere you can reach, and do not stop until you cannot move."

Norok sucked in a breath. "Micah," he rasped. His hands shook, his biceps flexing. "Don't do this. Please."

"You know as well as I that I only control monsters. If you have any integrity left, use it. Resist my commands. If not... Do it. Stab yourself. Go on."

The male's hands shook with more force. He was panting with increasing intensity. Finally, with a shout of defeat, he swung his arms, stabbing himself in the stomach. A pause filled with a grunt of pain and gurgles of blood. Then he yanked out the dagger and stabbed himself again, in the leg. Then the groin. The shoulder. The chest. The throat. The face. He stabbed his body until he died, expelling his last breath with a shocked, watery gaze locked on Micah.

Picking up Elena's fallen sword, Micah removed Norok's head, ending the threat of him forever. The heat in him cooled. His limbs shook. He dropped the weapon and sank to his knees, checking Viori's vitals. Her pulse beat steadily, and relief inundated him.

"She lives," he called as Graves and John rushed inside the dome. Nothing else mattered. "Wake up, Red." He gently caressed her chin. "Wake up for your husband."

But she didn't. Her eyes remained shut, her body lax. She slept again, but for how long? Did it matter? He would wait as long as necessary.

"I love you, too," he told her, kissing her temple. "I want you to know that. I'm going to build you the palace of your dreams, one with high-enough walls for our children. When you wake, we will have our life together."

The cats raced in, their sand-fur soaked with blood. Kaysar and Cookie followed on their heels, the entire group settling around Micah and his wife.

"She merely sleeps," Micah assured them all. Elena, however, was gone, and his heart broke over her loss. His oldest friend—he just hadn't known it until too late. Now, he was to be parted from his *dearest* friend. The mate he adored with every fiber of his being. But for how long?

CHAPTER THIRTY

Viori drifted on a sea of dreams…

The doorway she'd inadvertently opened had closed without taking anyone to the mortal world. Micah held her as Graves, John and all their new children constructed a new stone bed for her, inside the dome, near where she'd first fallen. With so many of the kids at work—and all of them so strong—they completed the project in a matter of hours, then removed the dead bodies.

Elena's loss still hurt.

Cookie padded the stone with the softest vines while Kaysar sang the sweetest lullaby. Only then did Viori's husband relinquish his hold on her, laying her upon the bed's surface as gently as possible.

He smoothed locks of hair from her face and kissed her brow. "Most of our family members are too big for a tent, so I'll be keeping you in here. But we'll see to your safety, have no fear."

Outside, the trees took up posts around the invisible walls, ever-faithful guards.

She dreamed Kaysar and Micah occupied the circle for hours, on opposite sides of the bed, conversing like old friends.

"This has happened before, I'm assuming," her brother said, collecting and squeezing her hand.

"Many times. From what she's told me, the sleeps have varied in length…growing longer with every occurrence." He winced as he admitted the last.

"How long are we talking?"

Another wince. "Decades. Centuries."

"Centuries," Kaysar echoed with a hollow tone. He motioned toward the treemen without releasing her hand. "Do you know how many of these beings I've killed throughout my lifetime? And all along, they were part of my sister." Shame and regret coated his words. "How did I not know? How did I not sense it?"

"You think I do not suffer with the same thoughts? But somehow, she has forgiven us both."

I have. Everyone made mistakes. But they had learned and matured, becoming different people.

"That doesn't lessen the guilt." Kaysar heaved a sigh. "I'm leaving now to attend to Chantel, but I will return. Every day, I will return."

"I'll remove the *tollo*, which will allow you to flitter here at will."

"No need. I stole an *amplio*." Squeezing her hand again, Kaysar said, "I would not have picked you for my baby sister for any reason, ever—and I mean that from the bottom of my heart—but I cannot discount your defense of her. You served her well. However, if there comes a day I *can* discount it, I will do unspeakable things to you. I hope you know that."

"Kaysar, if ever I fail to defend her, I will *deserve* those unspeakable things."

Her brother blinked, as though surprised by such a response. "Yes. Well. Just so we understand each other." The king was gone a second later.

Alone, Micah lay upon the bed beside her, where he stayed all night, holding her close. By morning, when sunlight lit the sky above them, the treemen had already budded with many leaves and flowers in a variety of colors. The sight stole her breath, even in her dream. Which wasn't a dream, was it? This was real. This was happening.

This was to be her life, if only she could wake.

"I must speak with our people," he told her before kissing her temple, "and put the campground to rights. I'll do as we once discussed. Those who wish to stay and serve us, may. Those who wish to leave and serve your brother are free to go. Peace will settle over the Dusklands, starting today. You will have your palace, with ceilings high enough for the children." Another kiss, this one pressed against her lips. "I'll return this evening, love."

Her heart thudded. Peace. Her own kingdom. A glorious future with Micah.

He kept his word. He returned that evening with a trinket. A glorious tiara with two golden antler horns, one rising from each side. He placed the gift at the base of the bed. "For you," he said, kissing her brow. Her lips. "*Everything* I have is for you." Another kiss. "The first time I saw you, you lay upon a stone altar like this one, with a blanket of moss draped over you, as if you were one with nature. Grown from the forest itself. I wanted you then, and that wanting never stopped. I love you, wife, and I'm very much looking forward to the day you awaken."

Awaken. Yes. She wanted so badly to open her eyes. Viori fought with everything inside her. What she wouldn't give to hold him and touch him and kiss him back. To exchange their pledges of love in celebration rather than calamity.

As he held her in his strong arms throughout the next night and the next, she would swear that she felt his heat and scented his—their—citrus scent. Maybe she did. Together, they created paradise. Even Kaysar noted it upon his visits.

More and more leaves and flowers bloomed from the treemen. Soon they created a canopy of greenery over the top of the dome. At night, they retracted their limbs, revealing a night sky scattered with stars. In the morning, they closed the canopy again, blocking out the rays of sunlight, protecting her skin.

Each morning, Micah left only to return a short time later. Many times throughout the day, in fact. Always he brought her a new trinket. Bejeweled arm cuffs coiled like snakes. A necklace dripping with pearls carved to look like thorns. A ring with a rose-shaped ruby resting inside a bed of dewy leaves.

The pattern continued for seven more days. The dome became his home—their home—his things moved here. Trunks and tables and maps and a tub—his baths were her favorite thing. King Jareth, apparently, had gifted them with massive ice blocks the hot sun had already melted into lakes and ponds. Bodies of water they owned outright! Their kingdom was already thriving.

"I can *feel* you watching me, wife." The words growled from Micah as he took today's bath. "I know you're aware of what's happening around you. Wake for me."

Trying so hard! Viori dreamed and fought, fought and dreamed. Never had she been so desperate for something. But on she slept, another day passing.

The patter continued. Again, Micah held her throughout the night, whispering sweet everythings at certain times. Visiting her throughout the day. Around her, the trees began growing fruit. More than she would have thought possible. One even grew elderseed!

What miracles the darlings were! But then, a tree's fruit depended on its roots. Now, her babies had strong, healthy roots steeped in joy and family.

Happy citizens came by at all hours to call well-wishes to her and partake of the goodness. Well, everything but the elderseed. Marvel—the name of the tree—protected her bounty, with help from the others, who shielded her from onlookers. Smart. Special power should be meant for special people. Those who would use it wisely.

Drendall dropped by often, as well. The doll sometimes chose to follow Micah, sometimes Kaysar and Cookie, who hadn't ceased referring to the little darling as Chucky for some reason.

The trees allowed no others inside the circle, however. Well, no others save the servants who brought water for the tub. The trees did help the citizens eat, lowering limbs for easier plucking. No tree produced the same thing, and no tree ever ran out of goodies. What they produced, they replenished.

More and more joy filled Viori, and more and more strength seeped into her bones. The very next morning, she made enough progress to twitch her fingers, and a greater tide of joy burst free. Somehow, she was doing it! She was pulling herself from the slumber faster than ever before.

Somehow? Ha! She knew how. Micah. Her love for him. His love for her.

Love changed everything.

"I declare today a Feast of Remembering," Micah told her as he climbed from the bed. He kissed her temple and dressed, saying, "For the first time, there truly are no obstacles. The truce between our kingdom and Kaysar's holds steady. Some of our people chose to live with him, but most stayed here. Every inch of the Dusklands now teems with life. Trolls are no more. At least, we've found no trace of others. We've begun building a new orphanage in your honor for the children, and our palace construction has also begun. King Jareth gifted us with another pond, this one outside our personal chambers. I've given Elena a warrior's send-off. One day soon you will awake, and all the Dusklands will rejoice. Drendall misses you, but she has made friends with Cakara and Nema. The threesome is more than the headmistress can handle. She misses you, too. But no one misses you more than I. According to everyone around me, I'm *very* difficult nowadays."

He kissed the tip of her nose before he left, and Viori fought harder. A feast meant a marriage line and she must, must, must be part of it! Cookie had once mentioned a grand gesture, and this was Viori's chance to perform hers.

She fought harder than she'd ever fought before, using her love for Micah like a lifeline. Climbing higher and higher until...

With a gasp, Viori jolted upright. She blinked, opened her eyes. Panting, heart thundering, she scanned her surroundings. The dome, exactly as she'd envisioned in her head.

Outside, the trees exclaimed with excitement, and she blew each one a kiss. Rising to trembling limbs, she was careful not to harm any of her magnificent gifts. When she gained her balance, she toddled to the bath, now half-surrounded by potted elderseed plants.

The tub was half-empty. Well, no matter. She— Energy crackled inside the dome, a doorway opening near the bed.

Wearing a massive ice-blue ball gown, with puffy sleeves, a cinched waist and a voluminous skirt, Cookie glided inside the circle. She smiled at Viori and waved a thin stick in her direction. "Amber told me I needed to be here at this time to dress Cinderella for her ball. So. Consider me your fairy godsister. And thank goodness you woke up! Kaysar is pouting, which means our prisoners are dwindling. Which means I have fewer practice targets. Which means my temper is budding. But I digress. I gotta remember this isn't my story right now, but yours." She rubbed her hands together. "Let's get you ready."

Cookie snapped her fingers and a line of servants marched inside the dome, each with a bucket of steaming water. The tub was filled in seconds, the toiletries left surrounding it. As quickly as the servants came, they exited. Viori watched it all in amazement.

Alone with her sister-in-law, she stripped and bathed quickly. There was no time for modesty.

"You mentioned something about a dress?" she asked. "Because I need something spectacular to wear." She wished to look her best for this.

"You'll see it when I do," Cookie said.

What did that even mean? The moment Viori finished the bath, she emerged from the water and toweled off.

"All right. Dress time. Here goes." The queen winked at her and extended her arms. Tiny vines shot from her fingers and thickened as they grew. Leaves appeared and flowers bloomed. Those vines drew together and— Viori gasped.

"A gown of leaves and flower petals." She spun this way and that, marveling.

The garment fit her every curve with a high slit in the skirt. It was magnificent, and perfect for the jewelry she planned to wear. Pieces Cookie helped her don, after styling Viori's hair in an elaborate series of twisting braids. The thorn necklace. The rose ring. And the horned crown. All gifts from her husband.

"How about a pair of glass slippers?" Cookie asked.

"No thank you." She preferred to go barefoot.

Pressing a hand over her heart, the queen said, "I am the *best* fairy godsister in the history of fairy godsisters. You are a masterpiece. Oh! Before I forget. As another gesture of my awesomeness—I mean, to celebrate our new bond, I'm going to help you travel to and from the mortal world. Micah told us you have children there. We can fetch them, one at a time."

Viori hugged her close. "Thank you for bringing Kaysar such happiness. Thank you for helping Micah and me. Thank you for everything."

Cookie cleared her throat and eased back. "Yes. Well. You're okay yourself or whatever." She wiped at misty eyes. "I'm not crying. You're crying. Or the babies are. Whatever. I'll give you and Micah a few hours to tear my exquisite creation to shreds. That's all the time I can promise you. I won't be able to distract Kaysar longer than that. Then he'll insist on seeing you. Oh! Amber wanted you to know she spoke with Micah's new oracle and arranged a marriage line to occur, like, now. But you must hurry."

With a sweep of her skirt, the queen glided through the doorway. Then, Viori stood alone.

Hurry? In this dress? She strode to the exit. The spot Micah had used to go in and out, now that he had possession of the stones controlling the thing. Tree limbs covered the area, and those limbs parted for her, allowing her to leave.

The train of her dress dragged over grass as she glided forward. *My, my, my, how things have changed.* Lush green foliage in every direction. Bushes and grass and flowers. Pools of crystal water. New—unliving—trees blooming with other kinds of fruit.

Micah had wanted a true paradise, and honestly, so had she. A place where fae helped each other, defending those weaker than themselves. What a great start!

Citizens littered the area, plucking pieces of fruit. Everyone gasped and bowed when they spotted her. Whispers rose throughout the camp. Viori saw faces she recognized and many she didn't. Soldiers were posted throughout, and she inquired of Micah's location.

"The common tent, Your Majesty," one said, bowing to her. "And may I add, we are overjoyed to see you."

"You may." She flashed a toothy smile, and for some reason, he paled.

Well. He'd get used to her. They all would. Viori flittered to the proper tent, directly at the entrance. Laughter spilled from inside, dozens of voices calling out names and suggestions. The marriage line had begun then. Perfect timing.

Head high, she swept inside. A handful of people noticed her, their laughing conversations tapering to quiet. Realization spread among the throng quickly. Every gaze swung her way.

Let's do this. "Your queen shall pick next," she announced, scanning for Micah.

A path cleared, revealing him on the other side of the tent. He was kneeling before a teary-eyed Cakara, who clung to Drendall and Nema. A sense of rightness set up camp inside her, deciding to stay a while.

His attention whipped in Viori's direction. He shot to his feet, gasping, "Red." He blinked. His gaze roved over her. His eyes widened, and his jaw dropped. When he braced to flitter to her, she stopped him with a shake of her head.

"Do not come near me, Majesty. I'm busy. As queen, I must first choose my companion for the evening."

A corner of his mouth twitched. "You are wed already, Queen Viori. You are ineligible."

"That sounds like an obstacle, darling, and today we have no obstacles. I suggest you get in line as fast as your feet will carry you."

A full-blown smile bloomed. In a blink, he stood at the end of the line. She moved deeper into the tent, fae smiling fondly at her as she passed. She didn't stop until she reached Micah, whose smile had only widened.

His chest puffed with pride. Those amber irises crackled with all kinds of hot desire.

"I choose you," she said, winding her arms around him. "I want you and only you for today, tomorrow and the rest of eternity. Say yes. Give yourself to me."

"Oh, I say yes. But I'm not sure eternity will be long enough, Red." He banded his arms around her and flittered her to their former tent, the cheers of their people echoing in the distance.

He'd added luxurious furnishings. But the only piece she cared about right now was the large bed covered in furs.

He held her gaze as he tossed her onto the mattress—where the sandcats sprang from the covers, startled, then slunk out of the tent. She giggled, and Micah smiled anew.

"There is no queen as magnificent as you," he told her.

"And no king I would rather have than you."

"You love me, Red?"

"Every inch of you. You are my family and my forever. You woke me from the dead. I'll always live for you."

He cupped her cheeks, smiling again. "You were worth waiting for, wife." He kissed her then, loving her with his mouth, with his hands. She loved him right back, her heart singing.

Whatever came next, they would overcome it. Together, they could overcome anything.

★ ★ ★ ★ ★

Read on for a peek at New York Times
bestselling author Gena Showalter's
thrilling and sexy novel,

The Immortal

the second book in her Rise of the Warlords series featuring
the son of a war god and a stubborn harpy forced to relive
the same day over and over.

CHAPTER TWO

Harpina, the harpy realm
6:00 a.m.
Day 1

"Get your lazy butt out of bed. Operation Lady O Be Good commences in thirty."

The beloved but evil voice preceded the sudden ripping away of Ophelia Falconcrest's trio of comforters, leaving her with only a sheet. Although she wore neck-to-toe flannel, frigid air enveloped her in a hurry, and she groaned. Even the most sedate temperatures affected harpymphs like Ophelia. Not that there were many harpy-nymphs in existence.

As she roused slowly but surely, she became increasingly aware of a great and terrible hangover and groaned louder. Her head throbbed, her stomach roiled, and her mouth tasted like a broken garbage disposal. *Never drinking again. Maybe. Probably.*

"Go away," she muttered. "Let me die dramatically and in peace."

"The motto you stole from *Survivor* is outwit, outplay, and outlast. Unless you've decided to go with a new one. Give up

and give in." Vivian "Vivi" Eagleshield, her best friend and favorite tormentor, clapped her hands twice and commanded with
an exaggerated Russian accent, "Up, up, Lady O! Today is big
day for you. Meaning, yes, it's big day for me. You *know* I take
my big days seriously."

"You're the best and the worst, and I love you, but I also kind
of hate you." Ophelia smacked her dry lips and whimpered. "If
you have any affection for me, you'll pretend today doesn't exist."

"Up! Up!"

"So cruel and heartless," she whined. She cracked open lids
as rough as sandpaper. Though her eyes burned, she did her
best to focus. "Come back tomorrow. Friday at the latest." Like
most single harpies, she enjoyed the luxury of sleeping on a
bed only when she was safe in her home world—and she *never*
parted with her luxuries easily. "Also, stop calling me by that
ridiculous nickname."

Although, it certainly beat her epithet. Ophelia the Flunk
Out. A title she'd earned eight years ago, at the age of eighteen.
The day she'd gifted her virginity to her boyfriend, ending her
fight to become harpy top dog: the General.

Once upon a time, virginity had been a requirement for any
General hopeful, and even the General herself. The fact that
Ophelia had willingly parted with hers for a cute smile and a
false promise of eternal love was one of her greatest regrets. Especially since she was the only sister of Nissa the Great, a previous General known for her uncompromising, unwavering
standard of excellence.

And what had Ophelia gotten out of the loss? Zero climaxes,
a bitter breakup the next day, and a derailed future. *Lady O No.*

The worst part? The soul-crushing mistake was the first of
many made throughout her life. To be honest, mistakes had
become her specialty. As her sister used to say, "If ever someone hands out an award for screwed-up priorities, bad taste in

guys, or most wrong turns, you deserve first, second, and third prize, Ophelia."

She squeezed her eyes shut and moaned. "I hate my life."

"So?" the cruel and pitiless Vivi countered. "You love me, and I'm not leaving until you get up and push me out of the room."

Ugh. There were approximately zero people more stubborn than the harpy-vampire. A combination affectionately known as "harpire" and "vampy." Either Ophelia participated in her own awakening, or her friend continued torturing her.

She rapid-blinked to clear her vision, her focal point expanding gradually. Morning sunlight streamed through the lone window in her cramped bunk room. A precious space she'd had to fight fang and claw to get, since Nissa had expected her to live at the palace.

Too bright! Her eyes stung and watered, the minimal furnishings blurring. She rapid-blinked again, finally finding Vivi. An elegant, fine-boned beauty with dark hair, darker eyes, and pale skin.

"You have two settings constantly at war. Overachiever and self-destructor." Vivi offered Ophelia a sweet grin that masked her core of iron. "Care to guess which direction you leaned this time?"

"No," she grumbled.

"That's right. Because you don't need to guess. You already know you reached rock bottom and tunneled underneath. But guess what? This is my rescue mission. You're getting up, and we're heading to the gym where you will sweat out your hangover. You aren't missing your meeting with General Taliyah."

"Don't remind me." She motioned to the empty vodka bottles on her "desk," a detachable slab of wood. "Not after I worked so hard to forget. What time is it, anyway?"

"Only 6:00 a.m."

What? Only? *What?* Ignoring her aches and pains, Ophelia eased into an upright position and stretched. The tiny, translucent wings between her shoulder blades fluttered, relieved to be free of the mattress. "The big meeting isn't until noon," she grumbled.

"I know! So we'd better start sobering you up ASAP."

Someone save me. Taliyah Skyhawk, the newest Harpy General, had demanded a sit-down with Ophelia. Her friend believed a promotion waited in her future. Maybe leading a patrol of her own or joining a higher ranked unit. Her dream. Ophelia wasn't convinced and feared the worst.

"What if she complains about me? I've served to the best of my ability, but is my best good enough?" Nissa had *always* complained.

Why didn't you throw the first punch faster, Ophelia?

Are you trying to tickle or subdue him, Ophelia?

How are we even related, Ophelia?

"So what if she does complain?" Vivi asked. "She only corrects the ones she loves. And your skill far outweighs your errors."

True. And, honestly, Ophelia *had* been an exemplary soldier lately. Mostly. Kind of. Her record shone like a freshly polished diamond. Or cubic zirconia. She'd graduated from Harpy University with high dishonors, majoring in Murder and minoring in Revenge. She'd never missed a day of class or training without an excellent excuse.

To maintain her incomparable stamina, she jogged daily upon occasion. When off the clock, she participated in countless digital combat simulations to hone her most lethal skills from the comfort of her room. She absolutely, positively *never* questioned her superiors very often. Anytime she patrolled the city, she remained almost fully alert, even when hot guys entered the picture. Even on vacations and holidays, she always sometimes avoided males as if they were a plague. Because they were!

Her first boyfriend had taught her well. Her second and final guy had served as a reminder. Romance brought nothing but heartbreak. Males desired her until they won her. As soon as they realized they couldn't satisfy her nymph side, their pride nose-dived and they bailed.

So why do I continue to yearn for someone of my very own?

As if she didn't already know the answer. She was a weak, foolish half-nymph, who sought pleasure above everything. When she got turned on, her common sense switched off.

Seriously. If allowed to run wild, nymphs became single-minded with their pursuit of passion. They wanted what they wanted, and they wanted it often. Even when a lover had nothing left to give, nymphs begged and pleaded for climax, all pride erased. No man could keep up.

Thankfully, her harpy kept her nymph buried in the back of her mind, ensuring Ophelia never again forgot her life plan—taking another shot at the Generalship. Expectations for the title had recently received an overhaul, the virginity rule axed. Any contender of consenting age could bang on the daily if she so desired.

Ophelia now had a chance to qualify for the position. And qualify she would or die trying. So. Best to avoid temptation altogether and maintain her focus. Meaning, no sex for her. With near-constant hard work and unshakable dedication, she could complete the ten requirements for General in only a handful of centuries.

Did she wish to rule the entire species, as Nissa had? Yes. But also no. The thought of so much responsibility left Ophelia shuddering. But stop her? Not for a second. She *must* prove herself. And she would. Gradually. A single step at a time.

Fingers snapped in front of her face. "—listening to me?"

Great. She'd gotten lost in her head. "No. I'm thinking about my next step. I've got to make a kill, Vee." Her cheeks flamed at the lack. Everyone in her graduating class had a substantial kill list. She should too.

"You will."

"How can you be sure?" The past few weeks, she'd fought countless phantoms—mindless, soul-sucking husks intent on draining life. Or rather, she'd tried to fight them. As soon as she had approached, they'd vanished.

"Because I know you. And I know you're afraid Taliyah will banish you from Harpina. Which is ridiculous, by the way." Vivi spread her arms wide. "I mean, maybe she does banish you, but so what? You'll fight to change her mind. And guess what? What you fight for, you win. Always. That's why I lowered myself to love you, isn't it? You waged wars for my affections."

Ophelia snorted and tossed a pillow at her favorite vampy. Whether the General found fault with her performance or not, banishment was a very real possibility.

Taliyah probably expected Ophelia to retaliate against the Astra Planeta for their part in Nissa's death.

My right. Not too long ago, nine warlords had conquered the harpy realm for reasons no one had considered Ophelia worthy of knowing. And they'd done the deed in a single day! Their power seemed limitless, their tempers more so.

Their vast armies consisted of warriors of varying species. Everything from pure-blood vampires to banshees, to shifters and gorgons. Basically anything found in myths and legends.

Ophelia had never gone head-to-head with an Astra or even a soldier under their command. Before her unit had ever reached the battlefield, the fray had ended. Harpies all over the land had fallen asleep, herself included. She'd awoken weeks later, only to learn Roc, the Astra Commander, had killed Nissa.

Nissa. Gone.

Ophelia pressed her tongue to the roof of her mouth. She had every right to declare a blood vendetta against the Commander of the Astra. Among harpies, vendettas of every kind were common. And revered. As long as the punishment fit the crime, not even the General herself had a right to obstruct Ophelia's vengeance.

Though Ophelia and Nissa had been centuries apart in age and had barely liked each other, they'd been family. The last of their line. Deep down, Ophelia had loved her sister. She still did.

She hated the Commander for what he'd done. Could she beat him in a battle, though? Not at this time, no, and there was no reason to delude herself otherwise. Did she wish to spend the rest of her life attempting to harm him while merely managing to annoy him, simply to satisfy her need for revenge? Also no. Maybe? Ophelia didn't know anything anymore.

"Chop, chop." Vivi clapped her hands with more force. "Don't just sit there, staring at nothing. Get up and get dressed."

"Okay, okay. But I'm not meeting with Taliyah." If the General had something to say, she could find Ophelia and say it.

"That's a good one. Because yes, you are. Up, up!"

Grumbling under her breath, she untangled herself from the sheet, clambered to her feet and stumbled into the bathroom. As next-door neighbors, she and Vivi shared the small space. Clean freak Vivi kept things tidy, ensuring everything stayed where it belonged, even after Hurricane O, category 5 blew through, disrupting everything. The harpire even redecorated with a new theme every month. At the moment, all things glitz and glamor surrounded Ophelia.

After double-brushing her teeth for good measure, she splashed warm water on her face. Her headache faded and her stomach calmed as she dressed in a black sports bra and too tiny, matching running shorts. The same workout clothes as all the other good little harpies. Oh, how she wished full-body coverage was the style.

With her long, dark hair secured in a tight ponytail, she rejoined Vivi. They wore the same clothing, yet they looked completely different. Tall, slender ice versus short, curvy fire.

The vampy wagged a finger in her face. "You listening? You will run on a treadmill until you sweat out the very last drop of vodka, and you will remember that I do not, under any circumstances, hang out with losers. Meaning, yes, you're a winner. So do it. Win."

Friends were the worst and the best. "Why are you so terrible and wonderful to me?" she complained, swiping a pair of bespelled earbuds she'd paid top dollar for.

"Because you're even better and worse to me." Vivi folded Ophelia in a much-needed hug, softly offering, "Everything will be all right, O."

Ophelia squeezed the amazing woman with all her strength. They'd met eleven years ago, during harpy training camp, where little girls learned to master their incredible power and hair-trigger rages. One day, Ophelia had rescued scrawny Vivi from a beating via other harpies. Of course, Vivi liked to claim she had saved *Ophelia*. Whatever had happened, they'd been inseparable ever since, their loyalty steadfast.

"Fine!" she cried when she finally eased back. "I'll meet with Taliyah."

Vivi beamed at her. "See? A winner."

They made their way from the barracks to the gym, where everything from treadmills to boxing rings and weight stations abounded. In every direction, harpies worked out at level max.

Ophelia and Vivi threw elbows and exchanged a round of threats to snag the best treadmills. Ophelia inserted the earbuds. With the soundtrack of an action movie blasting, she set her machine to the highest incline and a moderate speed. Climbing. Warming up. Sweating. Thinking of everything that could go wrong today. But the more she marched, the more doubts she shed. Vivi was right. Why would Taliyah banish Ophelia? She was, in fact, a winner.

Flunk out? No! Try beast out. Ophelia cranked the speed, gliding into a steady 100 WTFs per hour. She wasn't a disappointment or a waste of space. She would not leave a legacy of disgrace and dishonor. She had worth. Her temper was just as fierce as the next harpy's. Probably fiercer! Her stubbornness couldn't be beat. Ask anyone. If a harpy requested an assist, she provided brass-knuckle backup, guaranteed, and only ridiculed the other harpy mildly afterward.

Harpies today, harpies forever.

Outwit, outplay, outlast.

But, if General Taliyah *did* banish Ophelia, what could she do? What recourse did she have?

She slowed her pace. Where would she go? Where *could* she go? She had no blood kin, no friends outside the Harpinian army. But wherever she ended up, Vivi would follow her. That wasn't even a question. Then, at some point in the future, they would sit on matching rocking chairs and discuss retribution for their exile. The torching of Harpina. Former friends would be forced to declare a blood vendetta against *them*. On her death-bed, Ophelia would realize she'd never been the good guy in the story; she'd always been the villain. The total ruination of a once great civilization rested entirely upon her shoulders.

You ruin everything, Ophelia. Nissa's voice filled her head once again. *You lack discipline.*

Though she slowed her pace, her heart rate sped up. Her breaths turned shallow. No. No! Ophelia ruined *nothing*. She had plenty of discipline. And she would prove it. *Outwit, outplay, outlast.*

She let the soundtrack wash over her. In books and movies, superheroes faced terrible odds, but they always overcame. If anyone had reason to claim superhero status right now, it was Ophelia. Well, superhero adjacent. When she fell, she fought her way back up every time, eventually. She almost never allowed an insult to slide. And she was smart upon occasion. Those hot guys she so rarely allowed herself to approach barely gained her notice anymore. Except sometimes. Or most times. But she never failed to resist!

Mmm. Hot guys.

Arousal seared her, and she groaned again. Then she groaned.

Not a needing. Anything but a needing. A temporary but insatiable hunger without any true, lasting satisfaction, when nearly everything provoked her lusts. Not that she had ever known true, lasting satisfaction. Most nymphs didn't until they found their entwine, or other half.

During a needing, her Dumb-Dumb switch got flipped, and she forgot everything but orgasming.

Since the arrival of the Astra, she'd often felt as if she hovered at the cusp of her worst needing yet. Why, why, why did no one else seem so hot and bothered by them? Did they exude a nymph-specific vibe or something?

Whatever. Ophelia had bigger thoughts to mull. Like what did Taliyah want with her, and how did Ophelia convince the General to let her stay in Harpina and serve in the military? Harpies were in the middle of a war. Something she'd dreamed of experiencing since training camp. To get fired now? The horror! Especially when life had finally grown interesting again.

The Astra warred with a god named Erebus the Deathless. Father of General Taliyah. Biological son of the god Chaos. And creator of phantoms—vile creatures able to ghost or embody at will, raining destruction upon anyone in their path.

Every night on patrol, Ophelia yearned for another chance to strike at phantoms. Just one more. Perhaps two. If she sprinted a little faster or swung a little harder, she would totally accomplish her goal.

Movement at her right. She whipped her head— Huh. A freshly showered Vivi stood beside the treadmill, holding a thin, black cord and a squeeze bottle. No longer in workout gear, she wore the harpy uniform: a metal and mesh breastplate, a pleated leather miniskirt, arm and shin guards, and combat boots.

Her friend casually yanked the cord—the machine's plug. As the treadmill screeched to a halt, Vivi drank from the bottle.

When Ophelia regained her balance, she plucked the buds from her ears. "Seriously?"

"You've been running for five and a half hours. You now have half an hour to prepare for your meeting with Taliyah. Just enough time to shower, dress and not overthink. But you'd better hurry or you'll be late."

What? Thirty minutes to shower and change and hustle to the palace? Her wings rippled with the challenge. Ophelia rushed off.

"I guess I'm supposed to clean the machine for you?" Vivi called.

In the locker room, Ophelia cleaned up and donned a uniform, then raced from the barracks. The palace was a mere mile away, an easy sprint through wooded terrain and beautifully manicured gardens. Past a marble water fountain and up a hundred steps, the only path to open front doors.

The opulence of the royal lodgings never failed to dazzle. Priceless vases. Gold-veined marble. Plush rugs and gilt-framed portraits of past Generals. Treasures acquired throughout the ages.

Ophelia avoided Nissa's portrait, hanging just over the mantel between a set of dual staircases, and rounded a corner. The large, arched throne doors loomed ahead. Picking up speed—whoa!

She slammed into a brick wall of a male who hadn't been there a split second ago. As she bounced back, he shot out muscular arms, capturing her in a hard grip and yanking her against him.

Their gazes met, and she gasped. For a suspended moment, the rest of the world ceased to exist for Ophelia, as if eternity's time clock had just stopped. Well, why not? Her heart certainly had.

He was a brute with a faint smoked cherries and sandalwood scent—in other words, pure lust to her. His eyes were extraordinary, his brilliant gold irises circled by spinning jade and umber striations.

Hypnotic. She did her best to concentrate, her mind tossing out random particulars. An Astra. The second-in-command. Halo something. Supposedly the "kind" one. Never raised his voice and sometimes smiled. Gorgeous. Built. Sexy. *Hot*. Mmm. *Very* hot.

Generates heat like a furnace. Her entire body responded, going liquid.

Her gaze dipped to the plethora of tattoos that covered his upper body. Images she couldn't make out as they vaulted from one place to another in his skin. Wait. Information clicked. The moving tattoos weren't really tattoos but *alevala*.

When an Astra made a kill for his cause, the action stained his soul, which stained his skin. If anyone else peered at one of the images, they relived the Astra's memory of the deed in full detail.

General Taliyah had recently issued a new realm-wide rule. Never study the *alevala* without permission.

Taliyah. Meeting! Late! With a scowl, Ophelia scrambled from the warlord's embrace. "Next time watch where you flash, douchebag." Flashers—teleporters—never considered the non-flashers they impeded.

Not waiting for his response, she dashed away. *Can't be late, can't be late.* What if Taliyah had already given up and left?

Lose the opportunity to explain all the reasons Taliyah was wrong to believe whatever she believed? No!

Ophelia flew into the throne room. Scanned. Thank goodness! The General hadn't vacated her seat. The pale-haired goddess wore a gossamer ice-blue gown. A delicate creation at odds with her fiery glare. Her second, Dove, stood at her right. A harphantom with silver hair and white skin. The embodiment of an ice queen who had no softer side. A handful of harpies flittered about.

"Someone find Blythe *now*!" Taliyah bellowed. Blythe the Undoing, the General's widowed sister. The second Ophelia was spotted, the General pointed an accusing finger her way and snapped, "You're late."

Ophelia cursed the Astra. "My apologies, General." She offered a respectful incline of her head rather than excuses. "It will never happen again. You have my full assurance."

She expected a rebuke. Something. Anything. She got eerie silence instead. Wait. Her gaze darted. Everyone had frozen midaction and gone eerily quiet.

"General?" Heart thudding, Ophelia darted through the capacious room. She checked every occupant for a pulse but found none. She refused to panic, though. She could figure this out. She could.

She was Ophelia Falconcrest, and she could do anything.

Don't miss The Immortal
by New York Times *bestselling author Gena Showalter!*
Available now.